"Is It So Bad? Is It So Painful to Feel My Hand?"

She shook her head, and the movement brushed her silvery hair against his hand. He drew his breath in sharply, and she looked up at the noise. His face loomed above her, his black eyes hot and glittering in a way that made her throat constrict. His face came closer and she closed her eyes against it, and then she felt his lips against hers, smooth and soft and warm. His arms closed around her and pulled her against him, as his kiss deepened and his lips pressed into hers, caressing, consuming.

Elizabeth felt weak and helpless and strangely lightheaded. It frightened her, and yet she felt an odd elation. When at last he released her, she stumbled back. The earl looked at her, his breath coming in short rapid gasps, his black eyes aflame with desire.

The Black Earl

Sharon Stephens

A TAPESTRY BOOK
PUBLISHED BY POCKET BOOKS NEW YORK

An *Original* publication of TAPESTRY BOOKS

A Tapestry Book published by
POCKET BOOKS, a Simon & Schuster division of
GULF & WESTERN CORPORATION
1230 Avenue of the Americas, New York, N.Y. 10020

ISBN: 0-671-46194-X

First Tapestry Books printing November, 1982

10 9 8 7 6 5 4 3 2 1

Chapter One

"BALLEW'S FIELD!" THE WORDS WHISTLED ACROSS THE deceptively peaceful land, autumn ripe and golden, fleeing with the defeated men who managed to evade the vengeance of the Black Earl's sword. "William of York lies dead on Ballew's Field, and the Black Earl marches!" The tale came quickly to the Duke of Tanford, who paid well for such information. Only moments after he received word, a messenger galloped forth from Tanford Hall on a swift, sturdy horse and turned southeast toward the keep of Sir Godfrey of Beaufort.

Fenwick Keep, the seat of Sir Godfrey, stood high on a steep hillock. All trees on the slope were kept cut down to provide a clear view of any enemy who might approach the castle. No moat surrounded the keep; but the sharp rise to the residence, combined with the high, windowless walls, provided ample protection.

The lathered horse approached the keep, its huge heart providing the impetus for the climb up the narrow, rutted trail to the forbidding castle gates. Fenwick Keep towered above the ground, its smooth, sand-colored walls hardly warmed by the dying rays of the sun. No window broke the wall, and in the corner tower a sharp-eyed guard watched the rider approach, tensing to sound an alarm if he decided the visitor was unfriendly. Considering Sir Godfrey's reputation, it was likely such was the case. However, the soldier recognized the colors of the Duke of Tanford blazoned across the rider's tunic. The duke was, at least at the moment, listed among Sir Godfrey's allies.

"A man of Tanford approaches!" he called down the winding stairway behind him, and the guard at the bottom of the stairwell passed the word along.

The portcullis creaked up slowly, rising just enough to let a horse and rider through. Once the exhausted mount was past the gate, the two sweating men heaved again at the wheel to slacken the rope and drop the gate. The rider slid off wearily. "I come from the Duke of Tanford," he announced. "I bear a message for Sir Godfrey from His Grace. It is most urgent."

The soldier escorted him to the captain of the guards, who was at his dinner. The captain glared balefully at the messenger as he repeated his request, then reluctantly laid the greasy bone he had been gnawing at back on his trencher of bread. Wiping his hands on his sweat-stained tunic, he led the duke's man into the great hall of the keep. A servant halted them at the entrance to the hall and the captain growled his message. The servant nodded and preceded them into the hall, bowing servilely toward the head of the long board where the family was seated eating their evening meal.

"A messenger, milord, from His Grace, the Duke of Tanford."

The entire table stiffened into a silent tableau, every face fixed on the messenger. Sir Godfrey sat at the head of the long wooden planks laid across trestles to form a table, known as the board. Only he had the luxury of a chair with a back. He was a pale, sandy-haired man of middle age with a tight mouth and small, narrow eyes. He was dressed in a dark brown linen tunic, slightly threadbare. Though a wealthy man, he was notoriously tightfisted, and no one in his family dressed as well as did a middle-class merchant's family. On either side of him sat his sons. The oldest, Robert, was a square, heavily built fellow with the powerful shoulders of a swordsman. Across from Robert sat Geoffrey, who greatly resembled his father, and Peter, a younger mirror image of Geoffrey. Also at the table were Maud, Godfrey's wife; Elizabeth, his niece; and Stephen, his nephew.

These last two, seated in the place of least honor farthest from the head of the table, drew the messenger's eye, though he quickly jerked his attention back to Sir Godfrey. The young couple were enough to capture anyone's gaze. They were both delicate, their fine-spun hair so softly gold it was almost silver, their features small and perfect, skin a flawless ivory. Only their eyes were dissimilar. Whereas the boy's were a bright blue, Elizabeth's were as green as wet leaves. She was small and fragile, and the weight of her heavy, braided coil of hair on the nape of her neck appeared enough to snap it. Her slender fingers were devoid of ornament, as was her simple blue bliaud and full, trailing sleeves. Despite her plain clothing and low position at the table, she was obviously a lady. Her brother looked equally aristocratic, though so frail it would seem a high wind would blow him away.

"Yes?" Godfrey snapped out of his trance and barked at the man. "What is it?"

The messenger glanced at the full table and said significantly, "It is for your ears alone."

"There's naught here but my sons—and women and children," he said, dismissing them as unimportant. When the man remained stolidly silent, he waved an impatient hand at his family. "All right. Begone, all of you."

The blond lad quickly lowered his lids to mask the

gleam of interest in his eyes. "Oh, yes, let us go, Elizabeth," he exclaimed in a high, petulant voice. "The stench of horse is too much for me." He raised a delicate hand ostentatiously to his nose.

Sir Robert snorted with disgust at his statement, and Geoffrey snickered until a glance from his father cut him short. Elizabeth, her mouth tightening grimly, grasped her brother by the wrist and fairly dragged him from the room. Godfrey's sons disappeared in the direction of the kitchen, seeking a fresh joint of meat to replace that left behind on the table. Maud, Godfrey's wife, scurried toward her quarters. As soon as Maud was out of sight in her room, Elizabeth and Stephen turned from their supposed goal of Elizabeth's chamber and darted along the hall into a small gallery jutting out into the great hall below. It was an alcove where musicians could pipe for dancing or listening pleasure. When the gallery was not occupied, there was a heavy curtain drawn across it. By lifting the corner of the curtain, Elizabeth and Stephen could hear and see everything taking place in the hall. They had discovered this useful fact shortly after they became their uncle's wards five years before and were forced to move into his home.

They had missed the first part of the conversation, and Elizabeth regretted it; for whatever the messenger had related had turned her uncle as white as bleached linen. She grinned as Stephen squeezed her hand.

"Where?" Sir Godfrey choked out.

"Ballew's Field, sir."

"Are you quite certain?"

"Oh, yes, sir, he is dead. His Grace's man saw the corpse himself."

In the hidden alcove, Stephen leaned close to his sister and whispered in her ear, "Who? Do you think William of York?"

She shrugged, but her face was alive with excitement. They returned to the scene below. Her uncle rose heavily. "And what does His Grace advise?"

"Why, that you intercept him, sir. You lie closer and have more to lose."

"What?" Godfrey growled, his colorless face flushing with remembered anger. "The king has taken all the Norwen lands from me and returned them to him. I have nothing left to lose!"

The messenger raised his eyebrows, but said nothing. He supposed the knight knew as well as everyone else that if he didn't move, he'd no longer have a head. Customarily, Sir Godfrey was just complaining and struggling to digest disagreeable news.

Sir Godfrey glared at the messenger. He would have liked to smash his insolently blank face; but since the man was one of Tanford's, he didn't dare. The duke was powerful and possessive. Nothing of his was damaged without his full wrath descending on the perpetrator's head. And right now, the last thing Godfrey needed was to make an enemy of his remaining ally. "All right. You've delivered your message. Now go!" he snarled. "Get out of my sight!"

The man left quite willingly, glad to miss the ugly rage that was obviously coming. He had little respect for Sir Godfrey. His own master was a cunning man who never lost his temper. The duke was far too intelligent to let rage overcome him. Sir Godfrey, on the other hand, was well known for his lack of control. He was driven by greed, jealousy and fear, and they ruled him more than the other way around. That sort of man, the messenger thought smugly, stood little chance against the Black Earl.

Upstairs, Elizabeth and Stephen watched their uncle kick out blindly at the hounds sniffing through the rushes on the floor for a scrap of meat or bone tossed from the table. The brother and sister fled from the gallery, out of the house and through the small side door of the keep's wall. Scurrying and tumbling down the steep side slope, they arrived breathless and grinning at a small grove of trees sheltering the stream at the bottom of the hill. Scrambling through the trees, they soon reached the one they sought, a towering dead oak that had fallen long ago and was now covered densely by ivy. Long before they had discovered a small hiding hole beneath the oak. A rock had stopped the fall of the tree, so that at the far end it was raised a good four feet off the ground. Ivy had grown over it, completely covering the space. Elizabeth and Stephen had hacked out a larger area around the hole in the middle of the ivy. They knew exactly the spot to lift the thick vines like a veil and crawl beneath them, wriggling deeper until they reached their spot, where they could kneel or sit or lie down quite easily. The green leaves above were an effective cover. It was the place they ran to when their uncle was in a temper and meting out punishment to whatever hapless individual happened to get in his way.

Stephen stretched out on the ground and Elizabeth leaned against the trunk of the tree, gasping to catch their breath. Stephen was the first to regain his breath enough to speak: "What do you think it is, Bess? The Black Earl? Has he defeated William?"

"What else could it be?" Elizabeth's eyes shone with excitement. "You know Norwen vowed to kill him and regain all the land William seized when his father and grandfather were killed. And you heard Sir Godfrey say that he had had to return all the Norwen lands. They must have been talking about the Earl of Norwen."

Stephen crowed and sat up. "Then he'll come after Godfrey next, won't he? He's vowed to kill him, too, hasn't he?"

"Yes. But since King Henry returned the possessions Godfrey stole from him, perhaps he won't feel the need to."

"Oh, no," Stephen stated positively. "He's a man of honor, a very brave and great man, and he made a sacred vow to revenge his family. He swore he'd not rest until both William and Godfrey were dead!"

Elizabeth sighed. The Earl of Norwen had a reputation as a great fighting man, which earned him immediate admiration in Stephen's eyes. But she had lived too long around their treacherous uncle to have faith in any man's honor. Norwen was accounted an excellent warrior, and he had risen to great heights of fame and fortune; but Elizabeth suspected such a rise must be founded on blood and treachery. He was called the Black Earl because of his swarthy coloring, but there were those who said his soul was black as well. How else could he have gone from penniless obscurity to regaining the full glory of the Norwen name and lands?

Twenty years before the Norwen name had been one to be reckoned with. Then Sir Godfrey and William of York had destroyed the old earl and his son through sly treachery. The present earl, grandson of the old man, had escaped the destruction, fleeing with his illegitimate half brother and their aunt to Normandy. They had taken nothing with them but the clothes on their backs and had barely escaped death, the fate that had befallen the rest of their family. All their possessions had been divided between William and Sir Godfrey.

Yet, starting with nothing, Richard, the present earl, and his bastard brother had become both wealthy and popular with young Prince Henry and his mother Mathilde. They had returned in Henry's triumphant wake four years before when Henry ascended to the throne of England. Norwen was well liked by the king. He had proved himself a loyal subject, strong as well as faithful. Henry had repaid his loyalty by granting him a small keep. Later, when Sir Godfrey had been foolish enough to become involved in a plot treasonous to Henry, he had punished Godfrey and rewarded Norwen by returning the Norwen possessions that Godfrey had taken. But Elizabeth was sure that was the extent of Henry's aid. It was a certainty that the tightfisted king had not endowed Norwen with the liberal funds necessary to maintain his lands and build a mighty army.

It was said the Black Earl's wealth came from ransoms

earned in jousts and battles and from the plunder taken after sieges. He had fought in France and in the Crusades in the Holy Land, and he returned from that hot desert far richer than he had left. But there were other, darker rumors—that many of the jewels were really gifts from wives of noblemen, or that the money came from the Jewish moneylenders. Her uncle vowed that the Bastard, the earl's half brother, was in league with the devil and could by witchcraft turn common metal into gold. Of course, Elizabeth discounted anything said by her uncle because he greatly feared and hated the earl. But such power as the earl had was likely to have wickedness beneath it. After five years in her uncle's home, it was hard for Elizabeth to believe anything else.

"Well, I hope you are right," Elizabeth murmured thoughtfully. "Now you and I must put our minds to turning this opportunity to our advantage."

"Why, when the earl kills him, we shall simply throw ourselves on his mercy. We never harmed him or his brother. And our father had nothing to do with our uncle's plotting. Why, you and I hate Godfrey as much as he."

"And how is Norwen to know that?" Elizabeth pointed out. "For all he knows, we could be allies of our uncle. We are Beauforts all, however much Godfrey may be a disgrace to our name. Isn't it likely that he will wipe out the entire family, just as our uncle destroyed his?"

Stephen frowned, troubled. "I guess you're right. For a moment, I thought he might—might free us, even protect us. But I know it is foolishness. He'll assault the castle, and it's likely everyone inside will be killed, willy-nilly. Why should he believe our story? Our uncle always lies."

A smile tugged at the corners of Elizabeth's mouth. "You have to admit that we have been somewhat less than truthful these last few years."

Stephen grinned. He and his sister had been playing very exacting, careful parts the past five years and, by doing so, had managed to stay alive. Their father was Sir Godfrey's older brother and as the eldest had held the title of Lord Beaufort, as well as the vast Beaufort holdings. Upon his death, the title and lands went by law and custom to Stephen, his son. However, since Stephen was but eight at the time and therefore eight years away from his majority, he and his lands were placed in the hands of the most logical guardian, his uncle. Elizabeth, being a woman, was also made his ward, and her rich dower lands were given into his control.

Stephen and Elizabeth had learned from their father of his brother's treacherous nature. He would have done anything in his power to keep his children out of Godfrey's hands. However, he had no say in the matter. It was the king who named the guardians of minors and women, and he had given everything to Sir Godfrey. Knowing his greed, Elizabeth greatly feared Godfrey would kill Stephen before he reached his majority and could take over the control of his lands. If Stephen died, Godfrey would be the next in line.

So she had devised a plan to keep Stephen safe. Although she knew Stephen was a wiry lad who was almost never sick and was constantly into scrapes because of his daring and curiosity, his physical appearance was such that he looked frail, almost sickly. It was not difficult to convince her uncle that Stephen was likely to die at any moment. With lowered eyes, she declared that they would be lucky if some disease did not send Stephen to heaven before his time. And, if by some stroke of luck he should live to become a man, she made it clear, he would never have the strength to wield a sword or lance. Stephen pretended a great dislike for all things martial, crying out effeminately at the sight of blood, and declaring that he for one had no desire to do such silly things as ride a horse or fight in jousts or go to battle. So far their scheme had worked. Stephen was raised in a hard school. He knew that any slip in his role might mean death for him and also death, or at least pain, for his sister. He realized that he had no other choice if he was to save himself and his sister and someday regain the land from his uncle. Already, at thirteen, he was a master of self-control. With no one but his sister was he himself; never did he let his mask fall.

But he wanted more than anything to be a warrior—to be the great knight that he should be—and he was constantly torn by his frustration. Nearly always when the men practiced at their arms in the courtyard, Stephen sneaked away to a window where he could hide and watch.

Elizabeth thought about their new problem for a moment. "We shall escape before the earl comes. We'll travel to court and throw ourselves on King Henry's mercy."

"But how?" Stephen countered practically. "Perhaps we could manage to slip away from the castle, but where would we go after that? We can't steal horses and get out through the side door, but no one would let us past the front gates. And everyone knows I 'hate to ride those great, awful beasts!'" he mimicked his own false words viciously. "On foot, we'd never be able to get away from them. They'd catch us within a day, and we could do nothing to defend ourselves. Oh, God, sister," he wailed. "We've saved my life this way, but to what purpose? I don't know how to fight. I have no men, no arms, no horse, no skill. I couldn't even swing a sword. I've watched the men practicing and you have told me what knowledge you picked up from our father, but I couldn't defend you from even one trained man."

Elizabeth bit her lip. Stephen was right. It was on her mind constantly. "I know," she admitted bleakly.

"Sometimes when I cringe and whimper and cry out like a maid at the sight of blood, I wonder if I would not be better dead," Stephen continued bitterly. "I cannot bear it when he strikes you or curses you or reviles our parents. And when Geoffrey puts his filthy hands on you and I can do nothing to prevent it, I hate myself. What use am I to you?"

"And what use would you be to me dead?" Elizabeth retorted. "Oh, Stephen, I know it pains you. I hate it, too; sometimes I want to throw myself from the tower and be done with it. But we have each other. We have to live for each other." Her voice faded wistfully.

Stephen berated himself silently and took her hand. "A great help I am to you, mewling like a kitten." He might not be able to fight, but at least he could demonstrate some manhood by not voicing his fears to his sister. God knows, it had not been easy on her. She was as beautiful as the morning star, with her pale blond hair and delicately chiseled features and her great green eyes. Any man would be proud to call her his wife. Five years before she had been an heiress and much sought after, unmarried at sixteen only because her father found it hard to part with a daughter who reminded him so much of his beloved dead wife. But, because of her uncle, here she was at twenty-one, long past the marrying age, doomed to maidenhood because her uncle would not part with her dower lands, and forced to live in the daily climate of her uncle's abuse and her cousin's lechery. Stephen knew that he was all she had to live for, that the only thing that sustained her strength and spirit was the hope that Stephen would live and someday free them. "I am sorry, Elizabeth. I did not mean to sound so mournful. Don't lose heart."

She smiled at him—a dazzling smile that few ever saw. They would find a way; she had to believe that. If there was a God, they would somehow find their way out of this tangle. "I won't, I promise. I'm sure we'll think of a way to escape if we put our minds to it. And when we reach London, the king will help us, I'm sure. They say he's a just man."

Stephen frowned. "And one partial to beautiful

women. I don't like to think what price he might demand in return for his help."

"Only your loyalty," Elizabeth assured him soothingly. "I am not so great a prize. Look at me, an old maid."

"You're hardly a withered old crone. Be sensible, Bess. You're stunning, and you know it. Geoffrey isn't the only one who covets you. Why, when Tanford was here, I could see that even His Grace wanted you."

"Him?" Elizabeth's eyes widened. "Why, he's so cold and . . . I don't know, heartless."

"It wasn't his heart that prompted his looks," Stephen replied dryly.

"All right, you know you shouldn't speak of such things."

He chuckled. "No? Elizabeth, I'm no longer a little boy. I'm almost a grown man."

"Is that so?" She reached out and began to tickle his ribs. He fell into a fit of giggles, writhing and twisting in her grasp. But they both knew that nowadays he held himself back from struggling with her in such horseplay, for his strength had become too great and he feared he might hurt her. It was another reminder of his approaching manhood—and his lack of preparation for it.

Godfrey stormed through the women's quarters, where he sent maids scurrying at his thumping blows. He slapped his cowering wife a few times, but it gave him little relief. Maud, his wife, tended to grovel immediately at his feet and plead for mercy. His niece, Elizabeth, was far better, for she offered him defiance; and it was a real pleasure to bring her to her knees. To humble her was like humbling his dead brother, for she had the same look to her eyes, the same pride, the same disdain. In looks she resembled her mother; and if his hand struck her, he felt as if he had struck the face of that other woman whom he hated. But though he searched throughout the castle, he could find neither her nor her weakling brother.

After a search of the keep, his anger had abated, and he set himself to working out a scheme to defeat the earl. He knew he could not match him in arms; the earl was a strategist of great depth and a skillful warrior. Moreover, it was never Godfrey's way to meet an enemy outright. Treachery was always his best weapon, and he loved above all else to use others to achieve his goals.

Sir Godfrey was a sly, but not a strong or particularly intelligent, man. He worked best in concert with another such as he—like William of York or the Duke of Tanford. Often he lacked the initiative to carry out his treachery; he was apt to do as he had with his nephew Stephen and put off the moment of action as long as possible, all the while hoping that the course of events would aid him. He was not the coldly sinister person that the duke was. Godfrey was ridden by guilt, pushed and torn by his bitter, angry emotions—a man not so much in control of his evil as controlled by it. He had taken no action against the earl, hoping that somehow William of York would bear the brunt of the earl's anger and that he would be spared. He tended to vent his rage and fear of Norwen on those around him. But, with York dead and with Tanford pushing him, he knew he had to do something—and do it quickly. If he were lucky, Norwen's army would move slowly back to Norcastle, stopping at his various keeps to reinforce the loyalty of his newly regained castellans, and his progress would take several weeks. However, at the unluckiest, the earl would push his army immediately back to Norcastle and would be there in days. Godfrey needed to catch him by surprise, with his men tired from battle or, even better, celebrating their victory. And he had to keep him from reaching the security of Norcastle, where he could hold out for months. Therefore, Sir Godfrey had little time to act and less time to plot.

His foremost problem, of course, was King Henry. The king had little liking for Godfrey to begin with, since

Godfrey had been involved two years before in a plot to weaken the influence of the king. The king was a strong leader; he held the reins of government tightly, and there was none of the laxity that had prevailed in the days of King Stephen that had allowed Godfrey and the other nobles to roam free, engaging in chaotic, interminable feuds. Henry ruled a peaceful kingdom that he wanted firmly under his thumb. Were Godfrey to attack another noble, particularly so faithful a follower of Henry as Norwen, the king would come down harshly upon him; and likely as not he would strip him of his lands entirely or perhaps put him to death. Godfrey had to come up with a scheme by which Norwen would appear to be the aggressor or that would give Sir Godfrey an unquestionable right to attack him. He had to appear to be justified if he were to avoid the wrath of the king. But how would he do that? How did one put a loyal king's follower in the wrong?

He tried to think of Norwen's weaknesses, but the man had so few vices. He never drank to excess, never flew into mindless rages, never exhibited the perversities that Godfrey's son Robert did. Of course, all the Norwen men had always had a soft spot for women. The earl's father, Henry, a man so handsome it almost hurt one's eyes to look at him, had never been able to withstand a pretty maiden. Godfrey could remember well the dissension in the Norwen family that had been caused by the presence of James's mother, Gwendolyn, Henry's beautiful red-haired mistress. Might there not be something in that: some hostility between the two brothers—the earl, who rightfully held title to all the Norwen possessions, and James, the illegitimate brother, who held the Norwen blood, who in fact was a replica of their father, but who could never inherit legally any Norwen holdings? Surely some anger lay smoldering beneath the alliance of the half brothers that could be fanned to a burning flame. Was it not said that Richard's mother, the rightful wife of

Henry, had languished in her tower while her husband shed favor after favor upon James's lovely mother? What bastard could not be jealous of the rightful heir's entitlement—could not be pained at his own position? What son could not harbor resentment against a man whose mother had caused his own mother such pain? He liked the thought.

Godfrey could not envisage the true blood loyalty that often lies between brothers, legitimate or illegitimate. He knew only his own jealousies and resentments of his older brother, his own fear and dislike of his kin. He could not imagine any tie that would hold them together, other than the pragmatic one of their combined rise to power. If he could but split that mercenary tie with the rage of emotions that he himself felt, he could bring the earl to his knees at the hands of his own brother.

He smiled gleefully at the idea, but then stopped to think. The problem was time. He knew it took some time to split an alliance—some time to create hatred and dissension. It took spies and subtle hints and false information, and he simply did not have the time for it! God's blood, why had he not acted on this thought sooner? He had been a fool to hope that York would be able to stop the earl; nothing, it seemed, could stop the Black Earl.

Women. He began to pace thoughfully. Women. Suddenly he stopped, brought upright by his thoughts. Elizabeth. Why not use his niece to his advantage? The thought had some appeal. Not only could she be the instrument for bringing down his powerful enemy, but think of the delight it would give him to see her humbled. As his mind raced forward with this new-thought plan, he rubbed his hands together in glee. She was a proud one, just like her father. What a refined pleasure it would be to see her humiliated, brought low, and to attack Norwen for accomplishing it. She was a beautiful wench, with that fine-spun hair, so softly gold it was almost silver, and the delicate ivory skin of her mother. Norwen would want her; he was the same sort of fool as his father, according to Godfrey's sources of information. Godfrey smiled and strode into the courtyard, bellowing for Geoffrey.

Chapter Two

GEOFFREY CAME TO HIM QUICKLY, FOR HE DID NOT WISH to anger his father. He was not fond of physical fighting, as was his brother Robert; he was more like Godfrey, prone to conquer through slyness rather than outright force.

"What is it, father?" he asked; he could tell something treacherous was afoot from the look of cunning on his father's face. He wondered what the duke's messenger had told Godfrey. Did it concern the Black Earl?

"Find Elizabeth," his father said, "and bring her to me. I shall be in the great hall."

"Of course, father." Geoffrey slipped away eagerly. His cousin was a beauty and, since the first day he saw her, he had wanted her. Because he knew his punishment would be severe if he interfered in any of his father's schemes, he would never have taken her maidenhead as he wished. Sir Godfrey wanted her a virgin in case that would be useful to him. So Geoffrey had contented himself with furtive groping in the hailway and

17

the kisses he could steal from her if he caught her unawares. Godfrey would not mind that. He knew that his father's choosing him that day to find Elizabeth had been a signal that he could indulge his passion a little; no doubt his father wanted to frighten her for some reason.

He assumed she would be hiding from Godfrey's wrath, so he checked her favorite hidey-holes throughout the keep. However, she was in none of them, so he went to her room. Neither was she there. Frustrated, he left her room just as she slipped up the backstairs with Stephen. Geoffrey silently stepped back into her bedchamber. He heard her whisper a few words to her brother, then she entered her room alone, closing the door behind her. When she saw the dim figure standing there she drew up with a gasp. Geoffrey chuckled. "It is just I, dear cousin."

He reached out and yanked her to him, twisting her body so that her back was against his chest. Holding her tightly with one arm, he let his free hand roam over her body.

"Let go of me!" she hissed, struggling against his hold.

But he did not obey her. Instead, he painfully pinched her breasts and buttocks and shoved her to the floor. Pressing her down with the weight of his body, he thrust a hand under her dress and slid it between her thighs up to the place where her legs joined in the secret source of womanhood. He kissed her—a wet, long kiss—forcing his tongue into her mouth.

Elizabeth tore her mouth free. "Geoffrey, let me be. Your father would kill you if you breach my virginity, and you know it!"

He laughed and said, "He is the one who sent me to find you."

The words sent an icy chill through her. She knew her uncle would send Geoffrey only because he wanted to frighten and intimidate her. When Geoffrey brought her to Sir Godfrey, the latter would doubtless have some-thing worse in store for her. The thought made her tremble.

Geoffrey laughed lewdly. "Ah, so you tremble with desire. Do not be too impatient for me; I will have you soon. You are past the eligible age now. Soon your maidenhood will be of little use to Sir Godfrey and then, no doubt, he will turn you over to me. I shall not tire of you quickly; but when I do, never fear, I will not lock you away. I think I will give you to my men so you will not have a lack of comfort."

She winced at his words, making him laugh. Elizabeth berated herself for being a coward. She knew that any display of fear only encouraged Geoffrey to further horror. She wished his words did not fill her with such terror. Elizabeth had learned great control over the years with her uncle; but she hated the fact that her control served only to mask her fears, not to do away with them. She feared her uncle and his beatings; she feared the plans he might have for her. She dreaded her encounters with Geoffrey and was terrified at the thought that someday he might have his way with her. She hated herself for this cowardice, just as she raged inside at her powerlessness to prevent them doing with her what they wanted. If only she were braver, she told herself—if only she were not a weak woman. She knew she was a stronger soul than such poor-spirited women as her Aunt Maud, who shook and cried at her husband's every word; but she wished that she had the strength and courage of a man. She wished she could fight her uncle as she longed to and not cringe inside when she faced him. She did not realize fully the staunch courage it took to face a man she was so afraid of. Foolishly she believed that courage was having no fear.

Geoffrey stood up. No matter how delightful it was to torment her, he knew his father would not like to be kept waiting long. So he jerked her up and, holding her by the wrists, pulled her back at a rapid pace to the great hall, where Sir Godfrey was seated. At a signal from his father, Geoffrey left them alone.

"Come here, Elizabeth. Stand before me," he said.

She forced her feet to move until she stood only an arm's length away from her uncle.

"Kneel before me," he commanded.

"Never," she said.

An ugly smile crossed her uncle's face. Elizabeth's defiance always gave him pleasure. He stood up and slapped her hard, the blow sending her reeling backward. He followed her, slapped her again, and she fell to the floor. Years of experience made her curl into a little ball, protecting her head and body as much as she could from his blows.

He hit her only a few times before he said, "I have a task for you. You have heard of the Black Earl?" She made no reply, but he proceeded. "He is my enemy. I received word today that he has killed York on Ballew's Field. Now he will come against me, and I must stop him. And that is where you come in." Elizabeth froze, her mind racing. What ghastly plot was he working on now? What did he have in mind for her? She could see no way that she could be used to destroy Norwen. Sir Godfrey continued, "It is said that Richard has a taste for beautiful women. And though you are a proud, vexatious wench, none can deny that you are beautiful. I think he will be well pleased with you."

Fear rose up from Elizabeth's stomach, spreading out all over her, numbing her, suffocating her. "What do you mean?"

"Just this: The earl, on his progress home, will meet a young lady, a beautiful blond woman traveling without protection. He will assume, of course, that she is fair game, and will take her, being as fond of beauty as his father was. It will not be until the next day, when my army attacks him, that he will find out this beautiful blond lady is my niece, the sister of Lord Beaufort. . . ."

"No!" Elizabeth cried out in horror.

"What?" Her uncle's voice was dangerously smooth. "Do you not like the idea? I am only giving you the opportunity to play the whore as your mother did."

Elizabeth did not take issue with the slur upon her mother. Her uncle continuously maligned the dead Lady Beaufort. His brother had first been married to a barren woman. After she had been childless many years, Godfrey had become convinced that he was the heir to the Beaufort lands. But when Lord Beaufort's first wife died and he married Elizabeth's frail, beautiful mother, she had borne him an heir. Sir Godfrey had been enraged. From that time forward, he had hated Lady Beaufort and the children who resembled her so. He never missed an opportunity to cast aspersions upon her and to hurt her children.

Elizabeth was almost too much in shock to hear the slight, anyway. She could hardly believe that even her uncle could really mean what he was saying. Although in the time in which they lived women were regarded as possessions—mere chattel—no man of honor would allow a woman of his family to be dishonored, as it would have been a slur upon his family's name. A gentleman would fight to maintain the virtue of a lady of his house; certainly he would not plan the downfall of her virtue.

"You cannot mean it!" she cried. "You cannot intend to bring dishonor to your own name!"

Her uncle laughed loudly. "What do I care? I certainly respect my life more than the name of Beaufort. I can catch that devil this way, and the king won't do anything. I will have justice on my side."

"I will not do it!" Elizabeth exclaimed. "You cannot make me."

"Can I not?" His voice grew rich with pleasure.

She heard him unbuckle his belt and squeezed herself tighter into a ball. Again and again his belt descended heavily upon her back until at last she cried out, "Stop! Do you think he would want me with all the flesh stripped from my back?"

Sir Godfrey hesitated. There was truth in what she said; he could not leave such marks upon her that she would appear undesirable to Norwen. "Perhaps you are right. I think I must use another form of persuasion on you. I'm going to lock you in your room, and I think that in a few days you will beg me to let you play your role in my scheme." With that threat, he jerked her to her feet and hauled her to her room. Thrusting her inside, he slammed the door and shot home the heavy bolt on the other side.

Shakily Elizabeth sat down on her bed. Dear God, what was she to do! She could not agree to participate in her own dishonor. She was proud of the name of Beaufort. Her father and her brother were the Lords of Beaufort, and she would allow no shame to blot that name. No matter what her uncle did, she could not fall in with his plan; and certainly his plan would never work unless she agreed. No matter what form of force and intimidation he used, she had to keep her cowardice from getting the better of her. For Stephen's sake, she had to hold out. Stephen could not go to court and ask for the king's favor with such a stain upon the Beaufort name. She would not allow him to be put to that shame.

Her resolve did not weaken through the rest of the day and that night. No one came to her room and, even though she grew hungry, she did not give in. The next morning there was a soft tap outside her door, and she heard her brother's voice whisper, "Elizabeth?"

She ran eagerly to the door and said to him, "Stephen? I am here. I am all right."

"What has he done to you?" Her brother's voice was charged with an anger and intensity far beyond his years.

"Nothing," she hastily reassured him, afraid that he might do something foolish in his concern for her. "He hit me a little, but he dared not strike me any more, for that would spoil the scheme. I will be all right. He only means to try to make me submit by starvation. I can withstand that."

"But, Elizabeth, you mustn't starve yourself to death."

"He will not let it go that far, I can tell you. What good would I be to him then?"

"But what good are you to him alive if you do not do his will?"

"He could make me do other things to his advantage, but not this. He will realize that this far I will not go. I do not think he will kill me for it, but if he did it would be better so. Stephen, what he asks of me is impossible. He wants me to bring shame upon the Beaufort name."

"But how? What does he want you to do?"

"He thinks to defeat the Black Earl by using me as his bait. According to him, the Black Earl has a great fondness for women and he will take me to his bed."

There was a deathly silence outside the door; Elizabeth wished she could see her brother—she feared she had said too much. What if her words had pushed him past reason; what if his anger outreached his good sense? She knew he felt that as the man of his family he had to protect her and raged at his own lack of power to do so.

"Do not fear, Stephen. I will not give in, I promise you."

"But how will this scheme defeat Norwen?" Stephen asked, his voice calm.

"It will give our uncle an excuse to attack Norwen. He hopes to catch him while his army is still tired and before they reach Norcastle. And he will accomplish it without fear of reprisal from King Henry. He will appear to have justice on his side."

"I will kill him." Her brother's voice was deadly soft.

"No, do not, I beg of you. He will only murder you and then where will I be? I will have nothing left to live for then. I might as well give in to his plan if you are dead. Please, Stephen, you cannot help me that way."

Finally her brother agreed and left before their uncle or one of their cousins might find him.

Calmly Elizabeth endured the day of hunger. It was not so bad, not nearly as bad as her uncle's beatings. However, she could not stop her fear of what her uncle had in store for her. He would use some worse means of persuasion than this, she knew. In the afternoon, sud-

denly the bolt was lifted from her door and her uncle
entered, closing the door behind him. He carried in his
hand a heavy cudgel wrapped in cloth. She backed away
from him, but, like a trapped mouse, could do no more
than circle the room. There was nowhere she could go,
and soon he caught her and laid the heavy stick on her
back again and again. Pain coursed through her; but the
wrapping around the cudgel left no cuts upon her skin,
only heavy bruises that would fade. She held back her
tears until at last she could stand no more, and she burst
into racking sobs of pain and pleaded with her uncle to
stop.

"If you but say yes."

"I cannot. I cannot."

Again he began to beat her until finally she slid into
blessed unconsciousness. When she awoke she was by
herself. With a groan, she staggered to her feet. She felt
as if her body would break apart. How much of this could
she endure? For the first time she really feared that she
would give in, that her cowardice would betray her and
she would submit to the besmirching of her name. She
lay down on her stomach on her bed, her mind circling
around and around her problem. She could see no way
to circumvent her uncle. The idea of doing what her
uncle asked was horrifying. She was revolted by men's
attentions to her. Her cousin's kissing and groping made
her feel sick at her stomach, and she felt it would be
horribly repulsive to endure a man's complete invasion
of her body. The sex was bad enough, but even worse
would be the humiliation. That she could not bear. But
neither could she stand the continued beatings. She tried
to steel herself to die, but her mind would always cry
back this thought: what will Stephen do if I am not here?
How would he live? Who will help him and protect him?
Who will save him from his own anger and pride? If her
uncle killed her, she knew, Stephen would not endure.
He would blindly attack Godfrey and would be killed.

There seemed no way out, no way at all. Softly she began to cry.

Sir Godfrey sat slumped in his chair in the great hall, a tankard of ale by his side. He was not normally a man who indulged too much in drink, but that night he needed to wipe his troubles from his mind. Damn that stubborn, hardheaded niece of his! She would be the death of him—literally. She refused to help, and his plan would fail without her cooperation. He had received word that Norwen was approaching the castle of Lord Broughton, one of his vassals, but there was no way of knowing how long he'd be there. Of course, Broughton would want to feast his new lord to convince him of his loyalty, despite the years he'd accepted William of York as his overlord. But Norwen might cut the visit short and go on to another vassal's house. Sir Godfrey would have liked to attack his enemy at Broughton's, for it was notorious for its weak defenses. But the way Elizabeth was obstructing him, it would be days before he could get there—God's blood, it might be weeks.

She showed absolutely no sign of weakening. It had been four days now, and she had gone without a bite of food, taking only water. She had even withstood his beatings; and he was afraid to use any harsher treatment against her, for fear it would mar her so Norwen wouldn't want her. Godfrey cursed quietly. He couldn't allow himself to be foiled by a mere slip of a girl—thank God her brother didn't have her steel, or he would have had to commit the sin of killing his own nephew long ago.

He hardly glanced up when his second son walked in, so sunk was he in his thoughts. Geoffrey hesitated on the threshold of the room. It would not be a good time to approach his father if he was deeply in his cups. On the other hand, the scheme he had come up with would relieve his father's anxieties, and that should negate any foulness of temper the drinking induced. He smiled to himself, imagining his father's pleasure when he heard what Geoffrey had to say. He might even reward him with a keep of his own and, furthermore, Geoffrey would have the added advantage of keeping his cousin's maidenhead for his own.

"Father?"

Godfrey glared up at him. "What? What the devil do you want?"

"I have an idea I thought you might like to hear."

"I want none of your brainless schemes now. You cannot take Elizabeth. I need her!"

"It's not about that—at least, not directly. She hasn't given in to you, has she?"

Godfrey lashed out at him, but his drunken state made his aim so poor that Geoffrey dodged the blow easily. "Wait, father, hear me out. I have a plan that does not need her cooperation."

He caught his father's attention. "What?" Godfrey inquired in a surly tone, but his eyes brightened somewhat.

"I happen to know a young woman, the youngest daughter of a good family. She is blond and speaks like a lady. Although she is not noble, she has been reared well and knows all the mannerisms and speech of a lady."

"What is the purpose of all this?"

"Simply this: She can imitate a lady, could easily be passed off as one. No one would know the difference. And she is of an age with my cousin. Though not as pretty or fragile as Elizabeth, she is blond and not unattractive. Few people have seen Elizabeth in the past five years, and this woman could pass for what she might have become."

"Are you saying we could pretend she is Elizabeth?"

"Exactly."

"To what purpose?"

"The drink has muddled your brain. We can substitute her and claim that Norwen has taken her maidenhead."

"Why should this girl agree to go along with it?"

He smiled. "Because she's a licentious bawd and already heavy with child, but without a husband. Her family shipped her off to a nunnery to bear the child in secret. They plan to incarcerate her there for the rest of her life, wanting no part of her wanton ways."

"Is the babe yours?"

Geoffrey shrugged. "Could be. Or it could be one of a score of different men's. She has no more idea than we do to whom it belongs. Nor does she care. She's not one made for the bonds of marriage. She enjoys her bed life, and the last thing she wants is to be stuck in the convent. She'll be willing to swear that she is Elizabeth and Norwen is the father of her child, provided we pay her enough and release her from the prison of the convent. She has no scruples whatsoever. Believe me, she'll play the role far better than Elizabeth. I have seen her act demurely and one would swear she is an angel."

Godfrey nodded slowly, a smile touching his thin lips. "And we don't have to trust in Norwen's being attracted to her and bedding her. She has the proof in her belly already. We can simply travel to Broughton Castle and attack, taking the girl with us as proof." He laughed aloud, then sobered. "Are you sure the lass will go along with it?"

"Why not ask her yourself? She's at the abbey, not five miles from here."

Godfrey gloated, almost rubbing his hands in glee. "Good. Tomorrow morning we'll ride over. The next day we can be on our way to stop Norwen."

Elizabeth awakened with a start as the door to her bedchamber creaked open. She saw a glimpse of her aunt's worried face as she set a bowl inside the room, then slammed the door shut and relocked the bolt. Elizabeth rose and went to peer down at the bowl. It was gruel, a thin porridge that looked anything but appetizing. However, it had been so long since she had eaten that the sight of even such poor stuff started her saliva flowing in her mouth. She hesitated for a split second, wondering if this was some new trick of her uncle's to defeat her. Did the stuff contain poison or some sort of sedative? But her hunger quickly overcame her doubts and she dived in. Although it was not sweetened and was cold from the long trip to her room from the kitchens, it tasted like manna to her. When she was through, she sat down to ponder the meaning of Sir Godfrey's sudden leniency. Had she defeated him? The thought made her smile.

Maud also delivered her lunch on a tray. It was the usual fare of the castle—fish and venison served on a great hunk of manchet bread, with a tankard of beer to wash it down. Elizabeth forced herself to eat slowly so that her stomach, so long unused to food, would not revolt. Then, schooling herself to patience, she sat down to wait for what would happen. If she had defeated Sir Godfrey, why did he not let her out of the room? Was he hoping to teach her a lesson by keeping her prisoner in her bedchamber? As if being locked away from him and his obnoxious family was any punishment!

The day passed slowly. Maud brought another meal, a light supper this time, again pausing at the door only long enough to slide in the food. After eating, Elizabeth went to bed. Having had little to do, she had been unable to work off her energy, so that she had great difficulty going to sleep. Just as she was finally dozing off, a light tap at the door awakened her. She sat up, instantly knowing it was Stephen. Flinging aside the bedclothes, she hopped out, thrust her feet into slippers and ran to the door.

The faint tap sounded again. "Elizabeth?"

"Stephen! I'm here. What is happening? Sir Godfrey has started sending me food again."

"He has a new plan. He's leaving this morning at dawn—and I am going with him."

"What? Why?"

"He's worked out another scheme. It seems Geoffrey

knew a lass already with child whom they believe they can pass off as you."

"What!"

"Yes. Since you won't agree to his scheme, he's planning to attack anyway, then take this girl to the king as proof of his reason. And I am to go with them to verify that she is you."

"But, Stephen, you cannot! Think of the disgrace to our name!"

"Yes, and think of the worse-than-disgrace that will befall the Earl of Norwen. I don't know what to do, Elizabeth. He forced me to agree to go. He said he would torture you in front of me if I did not. I had to agree."

"No one would hold you to your word given under such duress. You must deny it to the king."

"If I do, he has sworn he will kill you, bit by bit, before my eyes. I know he would, Elizabeth. And I—" His boyish voice cracked. "I could not bear it."

Elizabeth figured it was more likely he would kill Stephen on the spot in his rage at being foiled. No, he could not openly defy their uncle. But she despised his shaming the good name of Beaufort. And after the pain she had suffered to keep it from happening! It was so wicked, so unjust! She could not let it come about.

"But, Elizabeth, what about the earl? He will be killed if our uncle comes upon him unawares."

"Who cares about the earl?" Elizabeth replied crossly. "No doubt he is as treacherous as all men, and I couldn't care less if he is killed."

"But, Elizabeth, I had an idea. The only way we can save ourselves and our name is by helping the Earl of Norwen. I will go with Sir Godfrey tomorrow. I must. But if you could slip away and get to Norwen to warn him, he could be prepared for battle when we arrive. If Godfrey is defeated, there will be no reason for me to go to the king to lie. And you'll be safe with Norwen."

"But, Stephen, how can I make him believe me? He

may kill me out of hand as soon as he finds out I'm a Beaufort."

"Explain our story to him. If you come to save him, how can he think you mean him harm? He'll be bound to believe you."

Her uncle had said the earl was a lecherous man. Elizabeth suspected that if she came to him with the story, even though he might believe her, he would take her to his bed, happy to humiliate a rival Beaufort. She would be entirely in his power and could depend on nothing but his good graces. Yet Stephen was right. If she could convince Norwen she told the truth, he would be prepared to face her uncle and probably would defeat him. Perhaps he would even think kindly enough of her to save Stephen. Her heart began to pound within her chest. She had no doubt that a powerful, lecherous man would bed a woman he wanted if she arrived at his castle unescorted. She would be considered fair game. Elizabeth knew, too, that she was considered lovely, that men seemed to want her. But if the earl was pleased with her, he might rescue Stephen for her. Surely that would be worth the loss of her maidenhead—even of her honor. What did a woman's honor matter anyway? Men thought nothing of a woman except how she affected them. She despised them all—most of all her uncle. She was powerless against them, but in this one instance she could defeat Godfrey. Almost anything would be worth that.

Thoughtfully, Elizabeth went on, "I'm sure I could manage to lure Maud into the room when she brings my food tomorrow, and overcome her. I'll get out of the keep somehow. But you will already have a head start. How can I reach the Black Earl before you do?"

On the other side of the door, Stephen grinned. She had accepted his plan. It was the first time he could remember doing the planning for them, and it made him feel he was truly approaching manhood. "But we'll travel very slowly. We have to take the girl with us in a litter, which will delay us, and we'll have to follow the roads. But you can cut across the fields and reach Broughton much faster."

"Is that where he is?"

"Yes. At least that's where Sir Godfrey told me we were going. Oh, Elizabeth, I know you'll succeed."

His sister had more doubts than he, but she did not express them. She wanted Stephen to leave the next day unworried. She might not be able to save him, but at least she could give him a few days' peace. "I shall do my best. Who knows, little brother? The Black Earl may decide to champion your cause and restore you to your lands."

Stephen laughed with her. Deep inside he had little more hope of it than she, but he could not help but thrill to the idea. Perhaps a miracle would happen, and the Black Earl would be a man of knightly honor and not simply another warring brute. Stephen pulled a short, slender dagger from his belt and slid it under the door. "Here. At least it will provide you with some defense."

"But, Stephen, what about you?"

"I have another. Besides, it would spoil my image."

"I love you," she whispered fiercely, her heart tearing at the thought that she might never see him again.

"And I love you. Good-bye, sister."

"Good-bye."

Chapter Three

THE EARL OF NORWEN EASED HIS LONG BODY INTO THE tub, clenching his teeth against the painful pleasure of the hot water that sought out every cut and raw spot on his skin, even as it soothed his aching muscles. Slowly the steam receded, and the man's hard face relaxed and his eyes closed. Soon he dozed as he soaked, but he woke at the touch of the maid who came in to wash him. Tired he might be; but he was a warrior, alert to the slightest noise or touch, for enemies often came upon one stealthily.

The girl scrubbed at the weeks' accumulation of dirt and dried blood. Richard's campaign had been successful, but it had left little time for bathing. He and his men had ridden hard for weeks chasing York all over his lands. They had finally run him to ground at Ballew's Field. Richard smiled, feeling again in his mind the deep satisfaction as his sword swung down and bit deeply into William's neck, nearly cleaving his head from his shoulders.

Almost—almost his father was avenged and the honor

of Norwen reclaimed. He closed his eyes, remembering that time when he was twelve years old and had been awakened in the middle of the night by the sound of battle. Running down the stairs, he had seen his Aunt Marguerite, her long hair flying behind her and clad only in her night-robe, hurrying toward him. She carried the three-year-old James in her arms and behind her trotted Gwendolyn, his father's beloved mistress, equally disheveled. "Richard, come!" Marguerite had hissed, and he had obeyed without question. She had been as much a mother to him as the dark, silent woman in the tower who was his natural mother. Grabbing his pint-sized sword— really an elongated dagger—which his uncle Philip had had made for him, he followed the others down the narrow, winding staircase.

Even now he could hear the clash of swords in the great hall of Norcastle, the rallying cry of his grandfather, the pounding of feet. "I must go to father," he had whispered to his aunt.

She had grabbed his wrist. "No! You are the heir. It is your duty to get away and preserve the name."

He hadn't understood what she meant. He had no conception of defeat then. There was no place in his world for the destruction of his powerful father and grandfather. They were important men, strong fighters, indestructible. He did not realize that a treacherous nighttime entry into the castle had his family with their backs to the wall. But he was used to obeying Marguerite. Her word was law, after his father's, and his father was not there to gainsay her. So Richard kept pace with her on the stairs and ran beside her across the strangely silent courtyard behind the castle, slipping into the stables and through them to the small, hidden door in the wall. It was a secret entrance known only to members of the family. Not even Gwendolyn or Richard's mother, Mary, knew of its existence. Nor had Richard been told of it yet.

They descended another flight of steps, steep and narrow. Richard realized they were in a hollow in the center of the high, massive wall surrounding Norcastle. They entered a passage so low even Richard had to stoop to go through it. It was then that they heard the ringing footsteps racing down the stairs after them. Marguerite shoved the others into the passage behind her, pulling a lethal dagger from her belt and turning to face the unknown assailant at her most advantageous point—the bottom of the steep stairs. Richard shoved around her and took his place beside her, his sturdy boy's legs planted firmly apart, his short sword faintly glittering in the dim light from above.

The man who burst upon them was covered with blood, and it wasn't until the last minute that they recognized him and didn't spring at him with weapons thrusting. It was Uncle Philip, Marguerite's husband. "Philip!" she cried in disbelief. "What are you doing here?"

"It's all over up there."

"Henry?" Her hand went to her throat.

Philip shook his head. "When I left him, he and his men were inching to the keep tower. Your father is already dead."

"And you left him!" She spat, her eyes shooting hatred at her husband.

"No. I tried to stay by his side and fight with him to the death, but he sent me after you. He told me of this exit and said you should be taking it with Richard. He wanted me to protect Richard. He will soon be the Earl of Norwen. I swore to guard his life, Marguerite, and help him regain Norcastle."

"Of course. I—I am sorry I doubted you." His aunt's voice turned lifeless.

Philip had hurried them through the tunnel and up more steps to a wooden door that opened upward. Covered by a small bush, it was invisible from the outside. Philip picked up James, and they took off at a lope through the night. Until three years previous, it was the last time he had seen Norcastle.

Richard shook the bitter memories from his head. After all these years he had back all of the Norwen possessions, except for the two small keeps in Tanford's hands. William of York was dead and only Sir Godfrey remained. He smiled in satisfaction. Soon that, too, would come; Godfrey, too, would lie dead at his feet.

The maid attributed his satisfaction to her ministrations and smiled to herself. She was not averse to warming his bed. He was not an unhandsome man; his tall, lean body was excitingly hard and brown. Not the match of his brother in looks, of course, for that one was the sort to make your heart stand still—but his lordship was certainly an improvement over her pudgy master. She was disappointed, therefore, when Norwen dismissed her as soon as she had dried him.

Richard threw himself down on his bed. The thought of taking the girl had crossed his mind, for he had not had a woman for weeks; but he rejected the idea in favor of a nap. No doubt James was at the very moment bedding his bather, for his brother was never too tired to tumble a maid. He smiled briefly—how like their father James was—and fell into a heavy sleep.

"What? Are you going to sleep the night away?" The light, cynical tone of his brother's voice pierced his sleep, and Richard opened his eyes to glare at him. James lounged in the doorway, his dangerous, graceful body sheathed in a blood red linen tunic, a ruby glittering on one hand.

"My, what a beauty you are," Richard mocked.

"Have you just noticed?" James smiled—a wicked, entrancing smile that reminded Richard wrenchingly of his father—and moved into the room.

"No doubt you have been wenching while I slept."

"Well, I did have the family reputation to maintain. You have been woefully short in that area lately."

"I have had a war to fight," Richard reminded him caustically.

"That's no excuse. No doubt our dear sainted father is turning over in his grave."

Richard looked at his half brother closely; but James returned his gaze blandly and Richard shook his head. James was a strange one, whom Richard never hoped to understand. He wore almost always a light, sarcastic air, as if he found the world a source of private amusement. But there were times when he sank into black, bitter moods, and his words were angry and scathing, cutting sharp like a knife. He was a born politician—ambitious, smiling, full of plots and secrets, with a lie for every occasion. James could be treacherous and he could torment one, but there was not another as loyal to the earl as he. And Richard knew that he would never have come through the court of Henry II with as much advantage if it had not been for James's sly conniving.

"Milord's vassal and his family wait for you below, most anxious to begin their meal," James continued in his mocking tone. "No doubt they feel a roasted boar will make up for the years they ignored their homage to you."

"No doubt," Norwen agreed wryly, and left his bed to dress. Norwen was a more straightforward man than his brother, and he found it difficult to smile graciously upon his vassals who had left him to rot all those years after his father's death. He was a man of honor and his ideals decried such betrayal of their oaths of homage; however, he was also a man who had been raised in the bitter realities of life, and he had fought and won in the treacherous court of King Henry II. He knew it would be folly to insult the knights who now offered their oaths to him; so he pulled on his chausses, tied his garters and threw on a clean tunic to go down to the great hall, even though he far preferred to sleep.

"Don't look so unwilling," James laughed. "I'm sure you will be quite captivated by the entertainment our host plans to provide."

"What?" Richard asked suspiciously.

"Why, his two daughters, both most dreadfully resembling Lord Broughton. One will pluck the strings of a lute, and the other will sing to accompany her—a tale they wrote themselves about your exploits as a fighter."

"Mary save us," Norwen groaned.

"No one can save you from this fate." James tossed him his scabbard and sword, and Norwen buckled himself into the sword belt. "Have you heard from our aunt?"

"Oh, yes. I forgot to tell you. A messenger came before I bathed. She congratulated us on our victory and reminded us that there was still Godfrey to be defeated."

"She's more a warrior than any of us."

"She is leaving Norcastle and traveling to meet us."

"With only my mother left at the castle?" James frowned. They both knew that Gwendolyn, while loyal, was neither as clever nor as brave as their aunt. "Or did poor Philip have to stay?"

"Are you jesting? You think he'd let Aunt Marguerite travel without his protection? They left St. John there. He's quite able to advise Gwendolyn if someone should attack. And we will be back before any siege could succeed. Aunt Marguerite is taking barely enough men to protect them, so Norcastle is well defended."

"Good. By the bye, when I heard what our entertainment was to be tonight, I let it drop that you intended to press on to Sir Robert's keep tomorrow."

"Thank God. I've become quite weary the past few years of being the prime candidate on everyone's marriage market. That was one thing which was better about being an earl without lands."

Chuckling, James followed his brother out of the room.

Elizabeth lay awake much of the night, too excited to sleep, making plans for what she would do on the morrow. By the time dawn streaked the sky and she heard the sounds of horses in the courtyard below, she was out of bed and dressed, ready to go. She had rolled a nice pair of slippers and the best bliaud she had into a tidy little roll and stuffed them into a sack. Then she lay back in bed and pulled the bedclothes around her neck to hide her clothing. When she heard the sound of the bolt rasping on her door, she groaned loudly. Maud opened the door and thrust her food inside. Elizabeth groaned again, and Maud, not an unkind person, hesitated.

Elizabeth seized the opportunity to call, "Aunt Maud? Oh, please, save me. I am dying!"

"What! What's the matter?"

"My stomach. I fear the food you brought last night was poisoned."

"Oh, no!" Maud gasped and took a step into the room. Now that her husband was gone, she was less reluctant to disobey his orders by entering his niece's room. After all, Elizabeth was merely a woman, like herself. What harm could the lass do her? "That couldn't be true." She moved forward slowly, propelled by horror. "It wouldn't benefit him."

What wifely trust Godfrey inspired, Elizabeth thought grimly. She felt bad about tricking the gentle, terrorized woman, but she reminded herself sternly that she had to save herself and Stephen. There was no room for weakness. Elizabeth groaned again and buried her face in her pillow. Maud tiptoed closer to bend over the bed in concern. Quick as a flash Elizabeth's hand snaked out and grabbed her hair, yanking Maud down on the bed beside her. Elizabeth was strong despite her fragile looks, and her surprised aunt was no match for her. Whipping out a wooden candlestick with her other hand, Elizabeth rapped the older woman smartly on the temple, and Maud collapsed on the bed. Anxiously Elizabeth bent her ear to the woman's lips. She was still breathing.

She slipped out of bed and ran to the door, grabbing up her sack and the hunks of bread and meat her aunt had brought for her breakfast. She shot the bolt home and hurried along the hall and down the stairs to her brother's room, chewing her food as she went. There she grabbed a pair of his chausses, a tunic, riding boots, and a soft cap and stuffed them into her sack. On silent feet she slid through the house, avoiding all the servants and the few men-at-arms her uncle had left to defend the keep. She didn't know what their instructions were regarding her, but she was sure that the less chance she had of being spotted, the better. Outside, she ran to the stables and chose a sturdy pony. Her father had taught her to ride, and she could have handled a faster, more mettlesome horse; but she wanted one with the endurance to last to Broughton, so she settled for the slower mount. She would have to trust that her brother was right, and that Sir Godfrey would be moving at a snail's pace because of the accompanying litter.

Quickly she bridled and saddled the horse, then led him from the stables. Striding boldly across the yard, her heart in her mouth, she approached the portcullis. The guard turned to stare at her. "Milady?"

"Open the gate!" she ordered crisply. "At once, you oaf!"

"But—but milady, I had no orders to let you out," he protested.

Elizabeth breathed a small sigh of relief. Obviously he had had no orders to keep her in, either, or he wouldn't have looked so confused. "Of course not!" she snapped. "My uncle couldn't have foreseen this emergency arising. My aunt has taken ill. I fear some of the meat at breakfast this morning was bad."

The guard visibly paled, no doubt recalling his own hearty breakfast. Had he partaken of the same meat her ladyship had?

"Open the gate, fool. I must fetch the village priest for her. She may be dead before he can bring her the last rites if you stand about with your mouth open all day!"

To die without the Church's blessing was a terrible fate,

indeed, and the guard shifted uncomfortably. Turning to the gatekeeper, he shouted, "Open! Let the Lady Elizabeth through."

Elizabeth mounted, graciously accepting his offer of help, and clattered through the portcullis as soon as it had inched up enough for her to pass. The guard watched her canter down the hill toward the village until she was out of his sight. Only then did it occur to him that it was strange for Sir Godfrey's niece, instead of a servant or soldier, to be sent to fetch a priest. Shaking his head, he resumed his post. He wasn't about to inquire about it at the house. If he had made a mistake, he wouldn't foolishly reveal it.

Once she was out of the sight of the guard, Elizabeth turned into the woods and made her way east. This way she would intersect the southern road, which was where she wished to be, but would be hidden from view of the castle by the trees. Halfway into the woods, she stopped and dismounted. Whisking off her long, tuniclike bliaud and stockings, she pulled on Stephen's chausses and tied them, then dropped his tunic over her head and belted it. With riding boots and spurs added, she looked much like the same sort of slight lad her brother was. Elizabeth piled her hair into a knot atop her head and secured it with a wooden comb, then stuck the soft velvet cap on her head to cover it. It would be safer and easier to travel alone if people believed she were a young boy, not a woman.

When she was dressed, Elizabeth dropped her feminine clothes into the sack and led her pony to a rock so she could mount. Tying the sack to the saddle, she set off again, her spirits high and bubbling. She was free for the first time in five years. She even found herself whistling and stopped, amazed. She hadn't whistled since she was ten years old. She decided it seemed a boyish thing to do and would help her maintain her role, so she cheerfully launched into it again. By afternoon, she topped a small rise and saw her uncle's men before her. Suppressing a

sharp gasp, she dropped back. Thank heavens Sir Godfrey didn't have any rear guards trailing behind, or she
would have run right into them.

She turned aside into the dense woods. She didn't like
the idea of traveling through them, for it was said robbers
lurked deep in such woods, venturing out to strike at
unwary passers-by. She certainly had no desire to run
into any of them. Also, deep in the woods, the overhang-
ing trees hid the direction of the sun, making it easy to
become lost. Tensely Elizabeth rode through the woods
at what she hoped was a line parallel to the road. After a
couple of hours she turned back toward the path and
breathed a sigh of relief when she reached it without
mishap. It was clear of her uncle's soldiers. She hoped
she was ahead of them and hadn't curled back on her
own trail in the woods and come out behind them once
more. She set off at a brisk pace, her earlier spirits
dampened by reality. It was a dangerous thing to travel
alone. Robbers abounded, especially near the woods,
and they would consider one stripling lad easy prey.
Once they seized her, they would quickly discover she
was a maid, not a boy; and then they would no doubt
rape her, as well as take her belongings. She would have
been much safer if she could have found a group of
merchants or noblemen to travel with, but she was not
secure in her disguise and hated perhaps to reveal
unwittingly her femininity. Also, they would slow her
down, and haste was of the essence here. She had to
reach Broughton long enough before her uncle did for
the earl to have time to prepare his defense. Digging her
heels into the pony's ribs, she trotted on, her hands
trembling on the reins. She was greatly relieved when by
midafternoon she had passed beyond the woods.

It was then that her second problem made itself
known. She was hungry, and she had no money with
which to buy a meal. That precluded stopping at an inn.
Inns were precarious places anyway, usually filthy and,

often, as likely a place to be robbed as the woods. Travelers generally tried to spend their nights and meal-times at a convent or monastery which offered travelers rooms and food, or sought the hospitality of one of the great houses. Strangers were nearly always fed and allowed to sleep in the courtyard or stables, or even in the men-at-arm's quarters. But, again, Elizabeth knew that the less contact she had with people, the more able she would be to keep her disguise. Her voice did not resemble a young boy's, and she would have difficulty altering it.

Her stomach growled. She could not go without food, no matter what the risks in obtaining it. She was already weakened by the fast her uncle had imposed on her. And since she thought it would be as much as a four- or five-day ride to Broughton, she knew she would faint from hunger if she attempted it without stopping for food. At nightfall, she was fortunate enough to pass through a small village where she discovered a merchant's house with unshuttered kitchen windows. The sill was lined with cooling meat pies. Although the pies burned her hands, she grabbed two, sticking one in her sack for later and gobbling the other as she rode. Afterward she stopped at a stream to drink, then set about looking for a place to sleep. Before long, she found a hay meadow where the harvesting had begun, and she snuggled deep into a hayrick to sleep, wishing she had thought to bring a cloak to wrap around herself at night.

At first, Elizabeth thought she would not sleep, lying alert and blinking at every night sound; but finally she drifted off and didn't awaken until dawn. Stiffly, she sat up, bones and muscles aching from the long ride and the night spent on the ground protected only by crushed straw. Rising, Elizabeth chased down her pony, which had strayed away, happily feasting on hay. Brushing the straw from her clothes and hair, she put on her cap and swung into the saddle, her joints protesting at the exercise. Well, she thought, she had survived one day.

Perhaps she would be able to make the others, as well. If only she was certain where she was going!

Like most women—indeed, most people—of the time, she had journeyed little, and she was not sure how to reach Broughton. But she knew it was to the south and accounted it a good four days' ride away. So, using the sun to guide herself, she kept on a southerly course, crossing meadows and streams and groves of trees, sometimes using a road, often not. She chanced upon a manor house about midday and begged a piece of cheese and bread at the kitchen door. However, she went without supper that night and slept in the crook of a tree, her pony tethered below. When she awoke, she realized it was an even more uncomfortable place to sleep and vowed to seek another hayrick that evening.

However, she was fortunate enough to chance upon a convent late in the afternoon. Weary and hungry, she decided to take the risk of lodging there. Perhaps the nuns would be less likely to detect that she was not a boy than the guards of a keep. Straightening and brushing her clothes into some semblance of respectability, she tugged at the bell of the gate. It tinkled invitingly, and moments later a white-robed nun opened the gate. They were a silent order, for which Elizabeth was thankful, and the woman directed her to a narrow sleeping cell and then to the dining hall by using hand gestures. Elizabeth followed the nuns' example and, when she did have to speak, tried to lower and roughen her voice. She slept soundly on the narrow bed that night, for once secure and relatively comfortable. When she entered the hall for breakfast the next morning, her spirits were greatly raised by the good night's sleep. Things looked better now. She had survived for three days without mishap, and soon she would be near enough to start asking directions to Broughton. She wondered where her uncle and his men were.

Her luck held through breakfast, for she was seated next to a band of traveling merchants headed for the great city of London far to the south. They were speaking of the improved conditions of travel in the area since the Earl of Norwen had returned to power. At mention of the Black Earl, Elizabeth perked up her ears. "Now that William's dead, we'll have more peace about here," a stout merchant declared. "I'll warrant he'll clear up the nest of thieves in Norwood Forest."

"Aye, and that scum along Tyndale Road."

"They say he's making a progress through his estates before going to Norcastle. His aunt and uncle are riding from the castle to meet him."

"Ah, she's a fine-looking woman, that one, for all she's near my age. Has grown sons at home, I hear."

"Where will they meet, do you think? I'd love to catch a glimpse of her."

Elizabeth almost fell off of her stool straining to hear his answer, for the man turned his head away, reaching for a ripe red apple in the center dish. "Eversleigh is halfway."

"But she'll be swift, while he's dallying, visiting his vassals."

"Him? He don't stay any one place long, I hear. Why, he's already left Broughton."

The portly merchant chuckled. "I've seen his lordship's daughters. I know why he'd make a quick exit there."

"Well, he's clear to Emsford now."

"Sir Robert?"

"Aye."

"He is a speedy one."

"Always needed to be, I'll wager."

Elizabeth swallowed her last piece of bread and faded from the room. So the Black Earl had left Broughton and was at Emsford now, wherever that was. She wondered if it was farther or closer. If only Sir Godfrey didn't learn the news also she should be able to substantially increase her lead. Leaving the convent, she kept to the main road and was soon rewarded by meeting a serf leading an oxcart full of grain. She hailed him and asked directions to Emsford.

He stared at her in confusion. "But you come from there."

"You mean it's behind me?" He nodded. "How far?"

He blinked. "I'm not sure. Never been there."

"More than a day's walk?"

"No, don't think so."

"Is Sir Robert's keep there?"

"I don't know, sir."

Elizabeth wheeled her steady, good-natured pony and trotted back the way she had come. She passed other serfs in the field but did not bother to stop and ask directions until she came to a village, where she sought out a priest. The black-robed man answered her easily. "The keep of Sir Robert? Straight ahead. Another two hours, I should say. You can't miss it."

Her veins thrumming with excitement, Elizabeth spurred her horse forward. In her heart, she had doubted she'd ever make it to find the Black Earl; but here she was, almost upon him. If her luck held, she'd see him at the evening meal, perhaps even be able to speak to him. She had ridden for an hour and a half when she saw what the priest had meant. A great, solemn gray keep rose on the next hill, dominating the land around it. A moat surrounded it and inside the moat was an almost unscalable wall. It was obviously a home built for defense. Her palms began to sweat at the ordeal in front of her.

She pulled her horse off the road and headed for a quiet grove of trees. She was rewarded by finding a stream in their midst. Dismounting, she pulled her finest dress and stockings from her sack and shook them out. She sighed over the wrinkles and hung the bliaud over a tree, hoping some of the wrinkles would fall out of it. Removing her cap and loosening her hair, she glanced around to make sure she was alone, then undressed and stepped into the stream. The bottom was covered with stones which hurt her tender feet, unused to going barefoot, but she ignored the pain and sat in the stream to wash her body and hair. The water was cool, but she had to cleanse herself. She couldn't appear before the Black Earl looking like a travel-stained boy. When she was clean, she waded out and dried herself with her older dress, then slipped into the clean linen chemise, stockings and dark green linen bliaud. She finished off the costume by tying a rope of gold silk around her waist, letting the tassles dangle down the front of her skirt. She brushed out her long golden tresses and braided them into two thick ropes of hair, covering her head with a simple, gauzy gold coverchief, or wimple, which fastened beneath her chin, framing her delicate face and making her green eyes look huge and helpless.

She appeared as respectable as she could in this situation, Elizabeth knew. Any woman who rode alone and unprotected into a keep would automatically be assumed to be a whore—free game for any man. Because she was beautiful, she hoped the Black Earl would seek her out, and that would be her chance to speak to him. But she quailed at the thought of the sly glances and humiliation she would have to endure before she could relate her story.

And after she told him? She had no idea what he would do. Beat her senseless for bringing her bad news, as her uncle would? Kill her for being a Beaufort? There was even the chance that he might not believe her tale. Then all would be lost. Or would he take her to his bed, making her his whore, his toy, and perhaps save her brother as a favor to his mistress? Elizabeth blinked back the tears. Whatever the cost, she had to endure it for Stephen's sake. This man was the only one who could save him. Her own shame would not matter. She hated to bring dishonor upon the Beaufort name, but surely it would be permissible if it saved the Beaufort heir. It was a horrible prospect, but the only one that could help her brother. She did not hope, as Stephen did, that the Black Earl would save them merely out of a sense of justice.

She eased her feet into dainty leather slippers and mounted the pony. Straightening her shoulders, she turned the horse back to the road and slowly mounted the hill to the keep.

Chapter Four

THE BRIDGE ACROSS THE WIDE MOAT WAS DOWN AND THE gate open. The keep was obviously not expecting to have to defend itself soon. From the number of soldiers milling about the courtyard with horses and arms, one could see why they felt secure. Elizabeth's pony trotted across the bridge, through the opened gates and into the dusty bailey. She was aware of every man's eyes upon her immediately. Keeping her gaze lowered, she rode to the steps of the main building. Emsford Keep was one of the original Norman motte-and-bailey keeps. Once the round tower atop the steep embankment had been painted a bright blue, a vivid warning of its power. But it had long since faded to the original gray color of the stone, and steps had been erected, so that one no longer had to climb a rope ladder to enter the second-story doorway.

Elizabeth slid off her horse nimbly. What did one do with a mount when she was no longer considered a lady, entitled to give commands? As she glanced around in confusion, a man appeared at her side. But a soldier of higher authority followed, barking, "Keep away from her. Can't you see she's not for the likes of you?" The captain of the guards turned to smile at Elizabeth, revealing several gaps and broken teeth. "I'll show you to the hall."

Elizabeth followed him, flushing at the lewd comments behind her. The round tower was three stories tall, the first level being used as a storeroom, the second for the hall and soldiers quarters, and the third for the castellan's family and honored guests. The thick wooden doors to the second floor stood open, and they passed into the great hall. It was a massive place, with rough beams arching overhead and a huge fireplace adorned by Sir Robert's arms. The dirt floors were covered by sweet-smelling rushes, and many of the cold stone walls were hung with fine tapestries. Sir Robert was obviously a man of some wealth, and his wife, a fastidious housekeeper. Elizabeth guessed him to be a vassal with inherited ownership of the keep, rather than a castellan set in charge of the castle by the earl.

Servants scurried to and fro, piling food onto the long board and the shorter table crossing it at the far end. The shorter table sat on a raised platform and here the family and people of higher rank would sit. That was where she would see the Black Earl. Elizabeth stood for a moment on the threshold of the room, scanning it for a glimpse of the man she sought; but she quickly decided he was not there. There were many fighting men standing about waiting for the meal to begin. At the head table stood a short, thick-shouldered, balding man, and beside him a plump, graying woman. Elizabeth guessed them to be Sir Robert and his wife. They were obviously waiting for someone more important than they before they sat down to eat their supper. Who else could that be but the earl?

The short man caught sight of Elizabeth and started toward her, but his wife scowled and placed a restraining hand on his arm. For several minutes they argued fiercely with one another, both growing an alarming shade of red. Elizabeth could guess at their conversation, and her humiliation deepened. The woman no doubt thought Elizabeth a loose woman since she traveled without escort, and was probably urging her husband to toss the wench out of the castle. But he, knowning the earl's reputation as a womanizer, would think it would benefit him to let his liege see the girl. Elizabeth felt, mixed with her humiliation, a sudden spurt of fear that the wife might win out.

However, the woman's face was tight-lipped when the discussion ended. The man summoned a serving girl to him. Shortly afterward, the maid came to Elizabeth and motioned to her peremptorily. "Here, follow me. The master said I was to put you at the hearth." Elizabeth gaped, unused to being addressed by a servant with anything but respect, and a hot retort rose automatically to her lips. But she reminded herself that the serving girl took her to be common. She followed without a murmur. The girl signaled her to a place on the wide stone hearth beside the fireplace, then went back to her duties.

Elizabeth sank onto the thick, cold slab of stone, hands folded in her lap, and waited, studiously ignoring the many curious glances thrown her way. She reminded herself she was doing this for her brother's very life. She had to keep from being put off by unkind stares. Besides, after that night she might be no better than they all thought, depending on what the earl decided to do.

There was the crunch of feet upon the stone stairs, and all heads swiveled to see two men emerge from the stairwell. Both were tall and had thick black hair. Their very size dwarfed all around them. The one slightly in front was dressed in blue velvet, which cast back the color of his bright blue eyes. He was lean and coldly handsome, but there was a hungry, wolfish look to him that made Elizabeth shiver. The other was not so handsome nor as finely dressed. He wore a velvet tunic, but it was a plain brown with no ornamentation save for the large buckle of his belt. He was broad chested, his slim waist circled by a wide leather belt. His face was browned and weathered by the sun and wind. His jaw was wide and set, his mouth firm. The eyes, which flickered over the room, were as black as his hair. He looked fierce and implacable.

Sir Robert hurried toward him, bowing graciously and calling him "milord." So it was he who was the earl. The other must be his bastard brother, James. Elizabeth watched the earl stride to his central place at the table, and her knees began to tremble. He could crack her like a nut between his huge, sinewed hands. The Black Earl. It suited him. Black hair, black eyes—was his soul as black? He was a successful warrior, one used to blood and pain, perhaps one who enjoyed both. It seemed quite possible to her that he was as bad as her uncle. In fact, he might even be worse. Earnestly she began to pray under her breath, "Holy Mary, Virgin Mother, protect me who has no protectors."

Norwen saw Elizabeth as soon as he stepped into the hall. He sucked in his breath sharply, and James turned to follow his gaze. James's eyes narrowed, and he glanced at his brother. The earl recovered his senses enough to turn and smile at his host, who approached, and allow the man to escort him to his seat. But Elizabeth's beauty had struck him like a blow, and after the meal began, he shifted in his chair to get a better view of her. She was perhaps the loveliest creature he had ever seen. She sat proudly and gracefully upon the rough hearth, her head high and her gaze unaverted. Her form was beautiful, slender but enticingly full breasted. Her face was a delicate oval dominated by huge, thick-lashed eyes. But her crowning glory was her hair—soft, fine, golden hair, so pale it was almost silver, bound in two thick braids down her back and covered by a gossamer-thin headdress. Her hair reminded Richard of hazy dawn sunlight, and he ached to undo her braids and slide his hands through the silken mass. The woman looked straight at him, and color touched her cheeks. She glanced back down at her hands.

Norwen entered the conversation at the table abstractedly, but he noticed that beautiful girl had no food in her hands. He signaled to a serving girl and, when she curtsied before him, he told her, "I noticed the woman by the fire has no food. Please bring her a serving."

The girl barely suppressed a grimace. It was always the wicked ones men noticed. But she knew better than to reveal her opinion of Elizabeth to him. Obediently she fetched a slab of the coarse bread fed to servants, placed a slice of goose meat on it and took it to the woman. She looked surprised at the maid's gesture, but the girl wasn't about to reveal who had ordered her to do it.

Elizabeth had been hungry, but had no idea how to go about getting food from the table where all the laughing, boisterous men sat. Servants had always placed bread on the table before her, and Stephen had carved for her. She was grateful, as well as amazed, at the servant's thoughtfulness in bringing her some food; but after she began to nibble upon the meat, she discovered she wasn't hungry after all. The Black Earl's unwinking gaze pierced through her, and she was too tense to think.

James leaned over toward his brother, his hand hiding his mouth, and whispered, "Fetching wench, isn't she?"

"Yes." Richard's voice was low, but intense.

"Do you have plans to make her acquaintance? I confess I wouldn't mind."

Richard shot him a steely glance. "You want to add her to your collection?"

James chuckled. "Only jesting, milord. Do you think I'd risk chasing the same lass you want? You were on her like a hunting dog spotting a deer as soon as we walked in."

Richard smiled. "I prefer not to speak to her in front of

this crowd. She is already subjected to too much laughter and gossip."

"Shall I bring her to your room?"

"Yes, I'd like that." He carved a piece of meat from the haunch of venison and dug into it with his strong white teeth, but he scarcely tasted what he swallowed. It seemed to him that everyone else ate at an interminably slow rate, and it was difficult for him to smile and converse with his host politely. Finally the meal wore to a close, and Richard was able to thank Sir Robert for his gracious hospitality and leave the hall.

Elizabeth, seeing him leave, almost cried aloud in frustration. He was gone without a word to her! She had counted too much on his wanting her, believing her uncle's tale of his licentious nature. Perhaps she had been too sure of her beauty. Or was it that she acted too shyly for a woman of the type he supposed her to be? Dismayed, she set her barely eaten food on the hearth beside her. One of the mastiffs roaming the hall devoured it in two gulps, but she hardly noticed him. What was she to do now? The earl had spoiled all her plans. The only thing she could think to do was try to locate his rooms; but if she was caught wandering the corridors upstairs, she would be sent straightaway back down. A possibility she hadn't thought of occurred to her now: what if, unwanted by the earl, one of the soldiers took a fancy to her and attempted to procure her services? He wouldn't be pleased if she refused him.

Lost in thought, she did not notice James's approach until he was directly in front of her. "Madam?"

She jumped at the sound of his voice. "Y—yes," she stuttered, her thoughts in wild confusion. It was the Bastard who wanted her. What use was that?

"You must be tired after your journey." His voice was low and smooth.

Elizabeth hastily pulled her wits together. After all, the man would have his brother's ear and would carry the tale to him. "Yes, I fear I am."

"His lordship noticed your weariness and bade me ask you to join him in his room, where you can sit in more comfort and enjoy a cup of mulled wine."

Elizabeth inclined her head to hide the gleam of satisfaction in her eyes. "That is most gracious of his lordship."

The dark man smiled sardonically. "Indeed, he is a most gracious man."

Elizabeth rose and followed James out of the hall and up the stairs to the earl's room, her heart racing. She was to face the Black Earl after all. She was terrified all over again, but she knew she must maintain control over herself. Stephen's future depended on her.

James opened a door, and Elizabeth stepped inside. James left, shutting the door behind him, and suddenly she was alone with the Earl of Norwen. He sat in an X-shaped chair by the fireplace, his arms folded and his long legs stretched out in front of him. The firelight played across his swarthy features, eerily sparking a flame in his black eyes.

"Milord," Elizabeth breathed and executed a shaky curtsy.

"Come. Sit with me by the fire." He indicated the X-shaped, backless chair across from him. "A cup of wine?" he asked, reaching out to the small square table beside him and pouring a cup without waiting for her answer.

Elizabeth swallowed hard and moved toward him on leaden feet. He was so large, and there was something very unyielding and assured about him. He would be much harder to fend off than her cousin Geoffrey, should he decide to take her. She sat down and sipped at the wine he offered her. It was warm and spicy, soothing to her nerves.

"What is your name, girl?"

"Elizabeth, milord."

She was even more beautiful close up. Norwen could see her eyes were a rich, dark green, the color of grass, of spring. Desire flooded his loins. He knew he would not tire of her beauty quickly. He suspected that he would take her back to Norcastle with him. Lord, but she was lovely. He wondered what such a woman was doing roaming about alone. She should be some powerful man's mistress, well protected and guarded, not traveling without even a servant to protect her.

"I trust your lordship was not wounded at Ballew's Field," Elizabeth began, to stave off any action on his part. She had seen the quick flare of lust in his face.

"No, merely a few scratches. What do you know of Ballew's Field?"

"Only what is common rumor—that you met your enemy William of York there and slew him. It is said you avenged the death of your family many years ago."

"Not quite." His eyes and voice were suddenly distant. The thick eyelids drooped to conceal his expression. "I still have one score to settle."

"I trust you do it to your satisfaction."

He smiled. "I'm confident I will. But that's enough of battles." He reached out to trail his fingers up her bare forearm where the wide sleeves fell away from the pearly skin. Her flesh was as soft as down. Elizabeth stiffened, although she forced herself not to move away. Richard frowned, puzzled. She was a mass of contradictions. The gown was not expensive, but definitely above the coin of a common whore. And she was far too lovely not to be claimed by someone. Yet she traveled without protection and came to his room freely, which proclaimed her an unattached slut. However, her skin, her hands, her voice, her grace and poise all bespoke a lady. And she was as pale and fragile as a statue Madonna.

"Nay, don't tell me I scare you," he spoke in a low, reassuring voice. "I shan't bite you, you know." He grinned, lifting the fierce lines and planes of his face. "At least, not very hard."

Elizabeth swallowed. "I—I do not fear you, milord. I do not know you."

"We'll remedy that soon enough." He leaned across the space separating them and raised her hand to his lips. His mouth was soft as velvet, warm, unsettling. His hand slipped inside the sleeve, caressing her arm. He tugged her gently to him, pulling her to her knees between his legs. His iron thighs imprisoned her. Elizabeth trembled violently. He was so huge, so overwhelming as he loomed above her. His fierce dark eyes bored into her as his hands cupped her face, then strayed down over her thick braids. "Your hair is lovely," he murmured. "Like wheat in the summer sun."

Elizabeth bent her head, no longer able to look at him. A tremor shook her. "Milord, I—"

"Yes? Why are you frightened? Am I so ill featured? Do I appear harsh or cruel?"

"No, you are a handsome man," Elizabeth temporized, not mentioning that his stern, implacable features and hard body filled her with dread.

Lightly, he touched her breast through the cloth of the dress, and she flinched. "Yet you fear me, I think. Come, little one, I promise I will not harm you. I am not a warrior in my bed. You will be safe."

His hands slid down over her slender waist and caressed her hips. He swallowed and the heat flamed in his eyes. Elizabeth knew if she did not tell him her story now, he would soon take her. "I do not fear *you*, milord. I fear what I have to tell you."

Norwen released her instantly, immediately on guard. Elizabeth stood and retreated a step or two. She knew the wrath of men, and she had no doubt he would vent his anger on her. It would not matter that she warned him. He would doubtless knock her to the ground.

"I am Lady Elizabeth of Beaufort. My uncle is Sir Godfrey."

The earl stiffened and his face became carefully blank. His voice, when he spoke, was suddenly harsh and devoid of all warmth. "Ah, so the lady plays at a whore. I presume you have some reason for it."

Elizabeth bit her lip nervously. Whatever warmth had been in his face earlier had vanished. He might have been a statue, and she found his chill silence as frightening as a rage. "Doubtless you will not believe it, and it matters not to me whether you do, for after tonight it will all be the same. But I am a woman of virtue."

"A virgin, in fact," he mocked in a deadly soft voice.

Her cheeks flamed. "Indeed, sir, I am. And as you will no doubt have your will of me tonight, you will find that out."

"And to what purpose do you sell your virtue? Surely you cannot hope to soften me toward your uncle."

"No, sir, I have no desire to do that," Elizabeth retorted, "no more than I have a desire to besmirch my name in your bed tonight."

"Indeed. Since you have so little liking for either of us, what are you doing here?"

"I came to warn you."

"Warn me?" His laugh was a harsh, disbelieving sound with no trace of humor. "Against your uncle's ire? Are you to inform me that he is too mighty to defeat?"

"No." Elizabeth linked her hands and steadied her voice, determined to remain cool headed even in the face of his scorn. At least he had not pounced on her yet. "I suppose, from the rumors I have heard of you, that you could defeat him easily, at least under normal, honorable conditions."

"Which of course will not prevail if your uncle has anything to do with it."

"That is true. I wished to warn you about my uncle's plot to attack you soon and unawares. He left a few days ago to hit you at Broughton Hall. I'm not sure when he will turn to this keep. But he will come."

Suspicion was clear on his face, although Richard did not voice it. "And what is your uncle's plot?"

"Sir Godfrey learned of your victory on Ballew's Field. A messenger from the Duke of Tanford told him. He decided to march on you now while you and your men are tired and weakened from battle, before you reach the security of Norcastle. He needed an excuse, though, so he would not fall into more disfavor with our gracious king."

"A wise idea. And what is to be his excuse?"

"That you dishonored me," she replied in a low voice, looking down at her hands, unable to face him.

He frowned. "I don't understand. I have not dishonored you."

"No. That was his original plan. He wanted to throw me in your path, hoping you would deflower me. Then he would attack immediately, excusing himself to the king by saying you had dishonored his niece and the Beaufort name, and he only sought revenge."

"He sent you out purposely to be shamed?" Disbelief threaded his voice. Norwen was a man of honor, despite his years at court. He could not believe that any man would send a woman of his family to certain shame. Women had respected positions in his home. His father was fond of them and enjoyed their company. Richard's aunt, his mother, his grandmother, even his father's mistress were honored and cherished. The only time his beloved Uncle Philip had struck him had been for a disrespectful remark to his Aunt Marguerite. It would have been unthinkable for a Norwen male to let the deflowering of one of his women go unpunished; and to send purposely one of his women to certain dishonor was beyond belief. Richard knew that such an attitude toward women was not common among his peers; however, even to them the despoliation of a woman of the family was a blot upon one's own name and honor. No man of honor would rest until he had avenged such a wrong; none could voluntarily bring it upon himself.

"Yes!" Elizabeth spat. "He doesn't care about the Beaufort name, and certainly not about my personal humiliation and pain. He thought it would help save his own neck, and that is all that's important to him!"

Richard stared at her in silence, trying to judge her

veracity. He knew Sir Godfrey was no man of honor. He had gained the Norwen possessions through vile treachery. He was an evil man in justifiable fear of his life; and it would be greatly to his advantage to attack Richard at this small, poorly fortified keep of an uncertain vassal, while Richard's men were still tired from battle. It fitted. It made a kind of slimy sense. "Why are you telling me this?"

Elizabeth, whose nerves were strained to the breaking point by his long silence, was swept with anger. "Just because I am a woman, am I unable to feel shame for my uncle's deceit? No doubt you will find it amusing, but I do have honor myself."

"And your honor places you here to be deflowered?" he asked sarcastically.

"I said that was Godfrey's plan. I did not say I agreed to it. I refused. When I wouldn't do it, he found a pregnant girl whom he hopes to pass off as me. He will say you got her with child, and that will be his excuse to fight you. He locked me in my room and set off to attack you. Once he has killed you, he'll go to the king with his lying story. He's threatened my brother with my death if Stephen does not vouch that the girl is his sister."

"He left you locked in your room. Yet you are here. You do not need to be deflowered for his plans, yet you place yourself in my path. Why? Why this burning desire to save my head?"

"I'm beginning to wonder," Elizabeth snapped without thinking, then stopped, horrified at her temerity.

But he did not reprimand or strike her. Instead, a ghost of a smile crossed his firm mouth. "I apologize. Am I discourteous? I am perhaps too used to the blunt ways of a soldier. How should I phrase it?"

"I don't care about the wording. It's the thought I object to. You ask why I should care that my uncle seeks to kill another man through treachery, or that he plans to blacken my family's name, as well as mine, by announcing to the world that I am unwed and with child.

Obviously you think I have no soul or honor, if you can wonder why I wish to obstruct his plans."

"I have never heard of Beauforts having either, milady."

"It is Sir Godfrey, not all Beauforts, who acts in that way. My brother is Lord Beaufort, and I am one, too. My father and his father before us were honorable men. It is only Sir Godfrey who has made our name vile in the mouths of men. But if you will not believe our pride is enough to move me, perhaps you will believe self-interest. I hoped that by warning you, you could prepare for his attack and defeat him. I want you to kill him—him and all his evil brood!"

Richard was taken aback by the pure hatred pouring from her eyes. "Bloodthirsty, aren't you?" he murmured.

"Yes," she hissed, stiff with long-nurtured hate and rage. "Yes, I would be nothing but happy to see them all killed before my eyes. My brother and I have been Sir Godfrey's wards for five years, and all that time we have been in hell. He despises us, reviles us. He's a cruel, wicked man, and I hate him!" She began to tremble as she tried to stop the flow of her violent words. She could not break down into hysteria before this cool, calm man. "I know the risk I take coming here. I know that you are as likely as not to take my maidenhead or beat me or toss me out of the keep after hearing my story. But I had to warn you in the hopes that you could end the terror under which my brother and I live."

The earl rose and went to Elizabeth, moved by her obvious fright and misery, but she retreated quickly. He stopped. "I will not harm you," he promised gently, as one might calm a frightened animal. "I won't touch you tonight, and neither will anyone else. Tomorrow you shall go where you want under my protection." Elizabeth glanced at him, startled. There must be some treachery here. Richard saw her expression, and for a moment his harsh face softened. "Now. Sit down and tell me about your brother and your uncle."

Shakily Elizabeth obeyed him. "My brother, milord, is named Stephen. He is thirteen, and I greatly fear for his life. If he should die, my uncle would inherit his lands and become Lord Beaufort."

"Then it is right for you to fear for his life."

Elizabeth fought against her sobs, refusing to break down, as she began her tale of their life with her uncle. Her shoulders shook, and the words came out in shuddering breaths; but she would not burst into tears. Richard felt a touch of admiration for her stubborn courage.

"It is my constant concern," she said. "They will not teach him the arts of war. I am afraid they will kill him if he is strong, so I have taught him to appear frail and not interested in fighting at arms. They laugh at him and say that I am more the man of the family than he, but at least he is alive. Only—he is thirteen now and cannot defend himself. How can he ever rule his land and vassals? What if they kill him before he reaches majority? My uncle rules his lands as if he were lord of them. Godfrey has even taken the lands my father set aside for my dowry. I would have had a substantial dowry, but what man would wed me without one? I am twenty-one years old and still not married because he will not allow suit for my hand from anyone. He fears to have me wed a strong man."

Gently Richard reached out to stroke her hair, and at that she collapsed into a storm of tears, as if his gentle touch was the one thing she could not endure. He pulled her to him to comfort her, but she was so stiff in his arms that he released her. Still she feared him.

He began to pace the floor, his mind turning over her information. She was a beautiful woman; she should have been an heiress. She had, if she were telling the truth, great reason to hate her uncle. He could not see how her telling him this could be a part of her uncle's treachery. Was it not more likely that she was telling the truth? Norwen had never really known Lord Beaufort; he had only hazy memories of meeting him once or twice when he was a child. By the time he returned to England four years before, Lord Beaufort was dead and his children in Sir Godfrey's hands. He did remember that his father had borne no ill will toward Lord Beaufort. He could recall faintly once seeing Lady Beaufort when he was about ten years old. She had looked much like this girl, now that he thought about it—a beauty, a true beauty.

He looked back at Elizabeth, biting his lip thoughtfully. "I think the answer to this dilemma is a wedding."

Chapter Five

ELIZABETH STARED AT HIM BLANKLY, HER SOBS HICCUPPING to a halt. "W—what?"

"Your brother's lands march with mine to the west and with Godfrey to the north. It would be good to have a friend on my flank and an enemy on Sir Godfrey's underbelly."

"Yes, I can see that, but his lands are controlled by my uncle," Elizabeth said, her expression confused. Was it that he was stupid and had not understood what she had said?

"For now, yes, but what if he were released from Sir Godfrey? What if he were made a ward of, say, his sister's husband instead of his uncle?"

Elizabeth stared at him, unable to take in what he had said. "What?"

"Elizabeth, I have no heir. My brother cannot inherit because he is illegitimate. I should marry. And who would be a better choice as a wife than a woman from

63

such a noble line as Beaufort, and an heiress as well? I mean you, milady."

Her knees began to shake. "Nay, please do not jest with me, milord. I am no heiress and my uncle—"

"Come, girl, think. You seem intelligent enough. You are here in my power, not your uncle's. Who is to stop our marriage? And you would be an heiress except that your uncle has stolen your dowry. What if your husband wrested your lands back from Godfrey?"

"You mean," she swallowed hard, "you want to marry me and then fight my uncle for my dower lands?"

"Exactly. The king will award me the guardianship of Lord Beaufort, I am sure, and we will take him from Sir Godfrey's hands. He will stay at Norcastle until his majority, and perhaps James and I can reform his education. Think what I will gain: lands and an ally. And more than that, it would give me an excuse to attack Godfrey. The king favors me, but he would not like it if I attacked Godfrey unprovoked. Yet I have to, for I have sworn to kill him. As for you, you would become the wife of a wealthy, powerful man. You are released from your uncle and your brother need no longer fear for his life. Cannot you see the benefit?"

Elizabeth wet her lips nervously. She must think, must not rush into anything. It sounded so perfect, this offer of freedom from her uncle. It was what she had hoped to achieve, but at the risk of her name; now the earl was offering not only what she wanted, but the saving of her honor as well. In fact, he wanted to give her even more than she had ever dreamed of asking for. He wanted to make her brother a powerful ally and train him in the arts of war. He wanted to make her his wife, the lady of Norcastle—not a castoff slut, but a woman of great position and wealth.

But why was he so ready to marry her, a woman he had just met, and under suspicious circumstances—a woman related to his bitter enemy, and one whose only wealth must be taken at sacrifice and danger to himself and his men? She stole a glance at him. Could it be that life with him would be worse than with her uncle? Was he given to strange perversions, that no other nobleman would offer one of his daughters to him? Or was it that he wanted to get Stephen in his power and then kill him? But, no, Stephen's death would not benefit him. The Beaufort lands would then go to Sir Godfrey. Only Stephen alive and his ally would be of use to Norwen. She could see that there were valid reasons for marriage on his part, as well. Of course, he wanted to attack Godfrey; and he, almost as much as Godfrey, needed a reason for the attack. No one could dispute that the Beaufort name had long been a noble one or that she would be a great heiress if he could obtain her dower lands.

She closed her eyes. It would not be a trap, then; perhaps there was none. But, even if it was, could it possibly be worse than living with her uncle? His strength frightened her, as did the look of lust in his face; but surely he would hurt her no more than Sir Godfrey and Geoffrey. After all, when she told him about her uncle's plans, he had not even raised a hand to strike her. Surely that showed a calmer, more just disposition.

The thing that held her back, she realized, was the fact that he would share her bed. She thought of her Cousin Geoffrey and the feel of his hands grabbing her, pinching her, sliding over her breasts and buttocks, and she shivered. Norwen had looked at her with the same hot lust in his eyes that Geoffrey did. She knew she would have to endure the same sort of painful, degrading attentions from him—only worse, because she could not slap his face or deny her husband his rights. She could not wriggle out of his arms and run away. She sneaked a glance at him. He was so big, so forceful. She remembered the weight of Geoffrey's body on hers, and she felt miserably certain that Norwen's huge body would hurt her more.

"Well?" he asked. "What ails you, girl?"

"I do not wish to share your bed," she said, shocked at her own courage. "Otherwise, it seems to be an excellent bargain."

"What?" He, too, was amazed at her boldness. Suddenly he laughed. What a daring chit she was, to deliver terms to him when she was obviously in no position to bargain. "And how, may I ask, would I get an heir that way?" His voice was amused, but when he spoke again there was steel in his words. "No, milady, do not mistake yourself. I am master of my lands and no one sets me terms to act by. No woman pipes a tune for me to dance to. Your beauty stirs me, and I desire you. And that sweetens the marriage agreement for me. I do not intend to forego that pleasure."

Elizabeth blinked back her tears and set a calm mask on her face. She could endure it. To save Stephen and to end their torment, she could endure anything, even this implacable man. "Yes, milord," she said, her tone and icy face belying the submission of her words. "It seems I have no choice but to accept."

He smiled a little, unbending, and reached out to touch her cheek with his fingers. "Don't fear, little one, I think you will find it not so bad."

She did not answer or look at him. Richard raised an eyebrow; what an unyielding little thing. He shrugged and turned from her. He had to make preparations for the morrow. He strode to the door and opened it.

"Fetch James to me at once," he said to the guard outside the door.

Elizabeth mused about the guard. How suspicious he had to be to have his room guarded even in the keep of his vassal. Had his past life held so much treachery? For a moment she reflected how nice it would be to have an army at your command, to be able to post a loyal guard outside your door so that none entered without your permission.

James's entrance into the room shook her from her

dream. He ran in, his face sharp and alert, his eyes darting suspiciously around the room. His hair was tousled and his chest was bare, but he carried a sword in his hand. Elizabeth's heart began to beat wildly; she stiffened in fear at the sight of him. His brother merely gave a snort of laughter.

"Good God, brother, is that how you bring so many maidens to your bed? And I thought it was a different sort of sword that attracted them," the earl said, his voice amused. Then he said to Elizabeth, "Forgive James, milady, he thinks himself always on the battlefield."

James's face darkened. "Did you bring me here to bandy jests? When your man bade me to come at once, I thought the lass had slipped a dagger between your ribs."

"Sorry to pull you from your sport, but my need is not inconsequential. James, I wish to introduce you to Lady Elizabeth Beaufort."

"Beaufort," he repeated, astonishment chasing all anger from his face.

"The niece of Sir Godfrey," Richard went on.

James looked at her, and Elizabeth felt the full force of his cold, blue eyes. "And what treachery brings her here?" James asked.

"Her uncle has conceived a trap for me, but I have a mind to turn it against him." Norwen turned to look at her also, and she felt her insides cringe at the sight of them, so big, forceful, allied against her. "Lady Elizabeth has told me that her uncle intends to attack us tomorrow, to exact my punishment for deflowering her. He has a pregnant lass with him, who he will claim is his niece, and she will name me as the father."

"I see." James's quick mind leaped immediately to comprehend the devious ploy. "Shall we race for Norcastle tonight or take a stand here?"

"Here, I think. The men are exhausted and it is more than a night's ride to Norcastle. They would be useless to me after that—and what if we ran into Godfrey's men on the way? Better to take a stand here. But tell John to pull the men from their drinking and whoring and put them to bed. The celebration will have to wait for a while. Send to Dorsey and Broughton for reinforcements. With luck, they could reach here by noon tomorrow. Send another message to Lady Marguerite; I will write out the message for him to take. When you have done that, come back; we need to plan."

James left, and Norwen immediately sat down to scratch out a brief message to his aunt. He was poor at writing, at best, and to state the complicated situation in a concise way taxed his skill. Elizabeth watched his frowning concentration, feeling that she and Stephen had been utterly forgotten. What were his plans for them?

"Milord?" she said tentatively, and he looked up at her as if she were a stranger. "What—what do you intend to do?" Suspicion touched his face, and she said, "Milord, please do not think that I would betray your plans to my uncle. I would cut my tongue out rather than tell him anything."

He smiled a little, his face relaxing. "I have a feeling that you would, indeed."

"I only wish to know what you will do with me and—and how you will treat Stephen."

His brows contracted as he studied her for a moment. "I dare not send you to Beldon Abbey, though that would be the easiest way to ensure your good name. You would be cut off from our protection there and Godfrey might seize you. No, you must stay here; although now, of course, you will be roomed in accordance with your proper station. I think we will fetch a nun from the abbey to sleep in your room; that should do much to protect your reputation."

Her knees went weak in relief. "You mean you will not—"

He stared at her for a moment in surprise, then said

harshly, "I am no Beaufort, madam; I allow no stain on the honor of Norwen, and in a few days' time you shall be a Norwen. I would do nothing to dishonor my wife. But let me warn you, I shall not allow you to dishonor my name, either. I'll have none of your Beaufort ways in my family. Should you lie to me or betray me or plot and connive against me, believe me, milady, I shall crush you. So think carefully before you wed me, for I mean what I say."

Not even her gratitude that he would not bed her that night, nor the fear his forbidding tone inspired, could suppress the anger that surged through her at this insult to her. "How dare you rank the name of Beaufort with cheats and liars! The Beaufort family has the purest noble blood, and never has our name been besmirched until my uncle. How can you accuse me so after I revealed my uncle's treachery?"

"I did not accuse you," he said evenly. "I merely warned you on the chance you have your uncle's characteristics. I know no Beauforts other than him, and he is always treacherous. Do you blame me for suspecting all Beauforts? As for your warning me about his plan, self-interest moved you to that."

"If you suspect me so, I wonder that you should want to marry me."

"It is a risk," he agreed, "but then all marriages are risks; and I trust that I am capable of handling my wife."

In fact, Richard felt much inclined to trust her because of her manner and because she flared up so in defense of her family's name, and because—most of all—she was so heartbreakingly beautiful. However, he was not fool enough to let himself trust her or to let her see how inclined he was to believe her.

"I am not a mare to be handled," she retorted, her fierce words a long-building cry of frustration at her impotence against the power of men.

"Are you not?" He smiled. She looked proud and

lovely, standing there facing him, her cheeks flushed and her eyes bright with anger. He rose and went to her. Elizabeth stepped back quickly, knowing such defiance would earn her a sharp blow from her uncle and knowing, too, that he often smiled at hitting her.

Her movement stopped him. "Do you hate all men, or is it only me?"

"I do not hate you; I do not know you."

"Then why do you flee whenever I approach?"

"I thought you were about to strike me," she said honestly.

"Strike you!" he ejaculated in astonishment and then laughed. "God's teeth, woman, am I so fearsome? Does even my smile look like the baring of teeth?"

"Some men smile before they strike."

"I am not so treacherous. Is that the way of Sir Godfrey?"

Elizabeth looked down at the floor and nodded silently, ashamed before the contempt in the man's voice. He came to her and this time she did not move, although she trembled a little as he raised his hand and gently touched her face.

"See?" he said, his voice soft as the fingers that traced the delicate bones of her face. "Is it so bad? Is it so painful to feel my hand?"

She shook her head, and the movement brushed her silvery hair against his hand. He drew his breath in sharply, and she looked up at the noise. His hard, brown face loomed above her, his black eyes hot and glittering in a way that made her throat constrict. His face came closer and she closed her eyes against it, and then she felt his lips against hers, smooth and soft and warm. Not like Geoffrey—not at all like Geoffrey. His arms closed around her and pulled her against him, and she winced at the pain of his hard arm against her bruised back. His kiss deepened and his lips pressed into hers, caressing, consuming.

Elizabeth felt weak and helpless and strangely light-headed. It frightened her, and yet she felt an odd elation. When at last he released her, she stumbled back. The earl looked at her, his breath coming in short rapid gasps, his black eyes aflame with desire.

"I think I had best take you to Sir Robert and his lady, or else I shall forget myself and take you here and now," he said.

Elizabeth stared at him, unable to speak. She was not used to men who desired but did not take. Such restraint was not the way of her uncle and her cousins. Moreover, his desire was different from Geoffrey's. He frightened her, but not at all in the same way that Geoffrey did. Geoffrey was like an animal, cunning and repulsive, but this man—he was powerful, commanding; she did not feel that she could outwit him.

After a moment, Richard continued lightly, "But what am I to tell Sir Robert? Why would my future bride have come here disguised as a whore?"

"Why must you tell a tale?" she blurted out, startled. Then, realizing she had questioned his actions, she blushed and finished lamely, "I mean, surely the truth would be enough. I came to warn you of my uncle's treachery."

"Your good intentions would not negate the fact that you spent several days on the road alone. That leaves your virtue very much in question."

Proudly Elizabeth drew herself to her full height. "I am no liar, sir, and I swear to you on the Holy Mother herself that I am a virgin."

A smile touched his mouth. "I believe you. Certainly I will learn whether you tell me the truth. And, trust me, I shall repudiate you if you are not. However, as I said, I will not allow even the shadow of dishonor to stain the Norwen name. No one must be able to question your virtue in any way. So I need to invent a story for those days you rode between your castle and here." He paused and continued curiously, "How, by the way, did you make it here? A woman traveling alone over that distance must make a tempting target."

"I dressed myself in my brother's clothes," she replied honestly.

A laugh rose in his throat. What a beguiling, daring wench! She seemed as brave as any man—more than most, truth be known. Quick, courageous, lovely—if only she were not a Beaufort, he would have no doubts. All the reasons that he had told her for their marriage were valid, but he had not added that the fire she set in his loins had been a prime consideration. Every moment he desired her more. How could he wait until their wedding day? Richard reminded himself that he must tread carefully. He could not let down his guard around her, for she was, after all, a Beaufort.

Elizabeth, emboldened by his smile, gathered her courage to offer an idea. "Could you not say I was guarded all the time by a group of your own men? That you had sent them to me here? They could have let me enter the keep alone while they rode in another direction to throw my uncle off the scent."

Norwen studied her. She had wit, which he admired. It was an added spice in a woman, but it quickened his suspicions, too. How like a Beaufort to invent a lying story. Was he shackling himself to a plotting, dangerous wife? "Lies come easily to your tongue."

Her hands trembled at his tone, but Elizabeth faced him calmly. "How else could a weak woman circumvent a man like my uncle?"

"You seem to have an answer for everything. So give me one for this: why would I have sent an escort for you?"

Elizabeth thought for a moment, then grinned. "Because I am your affianced bride. We shall say my father betrothed me to you many years ago."

"Betrothed a Beaufort to a landless earl such as I was then? Not likely."

"But who is to say it is not so? Certainly not my brother and I, and my father is dead. We could say that, when my uncle took my brother and me, he forbade the marriage and kept us apart. But you seized the opportunity of his absence and stole me from the keep."

"It would answer their questions, if we can convince anyone it is true. For one thing, it will take care of some of the formalities of marriage which we have overlooked— such as a betrothal contract and a period of betrothal. We shall say we had a contract, but your uncle tore it up. However, you and your brother intend to honor the verbal contract between your father and my emissaries." He twisted a heavy gold ring from his middle finger and tossed it to her. "Here is my signet ring. We shall say I gave it to your father to seal our bargain."

Elizabeth turned the large ring over in her hand. It was the initial *N* supporting the heraldic insignia of the Norwen family, a leopard couchant. Flourishes and curlicues extended the letter and encircled the whole. The earl used the ring to seal his letters. Signet rings were often used as betrothal rings because they symbolized the husband's bestowing his future wife with all his possessions. The ring was huge, far bigger than Elizabeth's largest finger. She would have to twist yarn around it to make it fit. Heavy in her hand, it thrust upon her the full realization of what was to happen to her. She would be the wife of one of the most powerful nobles of the kingdom, a man close to the king, a man of wealth and reputation. Never in her wildest dreams could she have imagined such good fortune dropping in her hands. Yet it frightened her almost to death.

Norwen went on thoughtfully, not noticing her expression, "Your idea is clever. We shall say my aunt and her husband escorted you here. Marguerite would never betray us, and it will provide you with an excellent chaperon, as well as protection, during the whole of your journey." He hardly knew whether to admire her quick story or to deplore it. He could handle her. He had no doubts about that. Even if she turned out deceitful, he could avail himself of her body and her land without revealing secrets to her. If it came to the worst, though he doubted he would have the heart to kill her, there were always isolated tower rooms where a wife could be locked away from opportunity to deceive.

But he wanted more than that. He wanted her a willing, loving bed partner, and a woman confined to her room was unlikely to be that. He hoped to God they would not be at odds—she stirred his blood unbelievably. Slowly, caressingly, his eyes roamed over her body. Holy Mother, she was lovely; fragile, graceful, her hair as fine as spun silver. She was as delicate as a fleeting dream. Yet her breasts were full and proud, and her mouth so firm, that he knew she would fill his arms, not shatter at his touch.

Elizabeth moved nervously under his gaze. Why did he have to look at her like that? Why did he have to feel the same way about her that Geoffrey did?

Her thoughts were interrupted by the entrance of a young man into the room. "Milord, I have come to take a message to Lady Marguerite."

"Oh, yes." Richard stirred from his thoughts and went to his desk to pick up the note he had written to his aunt. Quickly he perused it to make sure he had said everything that was necessary, added a hasty line, then poured the melted wax to seal it with the ring he had just given Elizabeth. "Here, then. Be off with you and travel quickly."

Just as the boy left the room, James reentered. "Well, brother, it is done. The men are away from their bottles and in bed—and all the maids out of them."

He swept Elizabeth with his gaze. "And what is to be done with her?"

His brother laughed. "Her? Why, she is to be my wife."

James laughed shortly, but the laughter died on his lips

as he looked at Richard's face. "Are you serious? You can't really mean—"

"Oh, yes, brother, that is what I mean."

"Good God, man!" James expostulated. "Can you really mean to take a Beaufort woman to wife? You'll be dead before the vows are said."

"Have you so little faith in me?" Richard replied jestingly. "Think you I am unable to guard myself against a mere woman?"

"A mere woman? A wily Beaufort, you mean, and her entire clan!"

"Now, James—"

"God's bones, have you so little sense, so much desire? Has she cast a witch's spell on you that you should want her so it overcomes your reason? Granted, she is a beauty—"

"A beauty, yes, but more than that. With her lies my reason to attack Godfrey. My wife's dowry withheld! All I need is my right arm—and yours—to defeat Godfrey. I can kill the villainous snake without recourse."

"We can find another reason to kill Godfrey. I will go to court and reason with the king. He's sure to see my way: grant it that I am a skillful diplomat."

"Ah, but there is more. Once we are wed and I have won back her dower lands, I'll have that much more land to my name. She is an heiress. Moreover, there is a brother concerned here, Lord Beaufort. He is now in the control of his uncle; but if we can take him back, he and all his vast lands will be our allies. Think of it. Sir Godfrey with an impossible enemy below him and beside him."

Elizabeth interrupted, made bold by her concern for her brother. "But, milord, he is in Sir Godfrey's hands. How will you get him away to make him an ally?"

"Now that is a problem I have not yet studied. Where is your brother kept?"

"He is with my uncle, milord. Sir Godfrey plans to bring him with him to battle, so that he can testify that the pregnant girl is me!"

"I see. That is lucky for us. We shall not have to breach Godfrey's castle to take the lad. I think the plan must be to make Sir Godfrey accept our wedding."

"Accept our wedding! He will never do that. He will know that it means his ruin."

"There we may need my brother's skill." Norwen looked pointedly at James.

The handsome man glared back at his brother, his face a mask. "What makes you think I will aid in your destruction?"

"Come now, James. Don't be so blind and stubborn. Surely you must see the advantages of it."

"I see that you are trying as hard as you can to get yourself killed—that's what I see!" James exclaimed. "You're as big a fool as our father ever was, risking your life for a pretty face. There is more than one wench that can fill your bed, and just as well as she."

"Have you not been listening to what I've said? This marriage involves land and power. I do not marry simply to tumble a maid."

"That's a good thing, since I doubt that you shall get a maid," James said pointedly.

Elizabeth sucked in her breath at the insult but did not speak. She had not liked this man from the very beginning, and now she liked him even less. He despised and suspected her; she knew that he would always be against her, and he had his brother's trust. She realized immediately that he would be her enemy. It seemed a hopeless situation. Her future husband suspected her already, and with his brother's constant compounding of his doubts she would not stand a chance. It was as likely as not that she would end her life locked away in some tower or, worse yet, murdered secretly in her bed. She remembered now her uncle's insinuations that the Bastard was in league with the devil; she was finding that much easier to believe now.

"I cannot allow you to insult my future wife," Norwen

said softly, but his voice held a chill in it that James had never heard.

James studied him for a moment. So the wench really had her claws into him. She was a beautiful woman, true, but James had never thought to find that Richard would fall prey to the same sort of weakness that his father had. Women were fine for relaxation, but they slowed your mind and drained your strength. Well, it was obvious that there was no point in arguing with Richard now; his mind was firmly set on marriage. There was nothing he could do at the moment—only wait until he could find proof of the girl's treachery and show it to his brother. James had little doubt that she would prove treacherous; he would trust no Beaufort—her or her brother.

"All right. I yield to you," James said, his voice calm. "And I will think of a way to help you get the brother within our grasp. But, as for now, I'm sure the lady is tired and would desire a little rest."

Elizabeth would far rather have heard their plan than take any rest; she was sure that as soon as they had her sent away, they would discuss what was to be done with both her and Stephen. She was not about, however, to raise their suspicions further by protesting at not hearing the plan; instead, she smiled graciously at James and said, "Indeed, milord, I fear it is true, I am somewhat tired from my journey."

"Come, then, I will take you to Sir Robert."

The two of them hurried to his castellan's room. Sir Robert's face registered surprise when his lord entered his room with the slut from the great hall in tow.

"Milord?" he said hesitantly, rising from his seat by the fire.

"I fear that I must reveal something to you. I hope you will not take it amiss that I have kept it secret from you until now."

"Of course not, milord. What is it?"

"It is this: Tonight this woman entered your home

alone," Richard began, carefully keeping his eyes away from Elizabeth, for fear he might laugh at the absurdity of what he said. "Of course, everyone took her to be a woman of little virtue, but such is not the case. I recognized her as soon as I entered the hall, of course, and sent for her immediately after dinner. She is, you see, the woman I propose to marry."

Sir Robert stared at them slack-jawed, unable to speak. Elizabeth felt an inappropriate desire to giggle at his expression. Poor man, he could obviously hardly believe his ears; yet he could not gainsay his lord.

"I realize this must seem somewhat unusual to you," Richard said in a massive understatement. "But, you see, there were important reasons for her disguise. Her uncle is my archenemy, Sir Godfrey. Lord Beaufort, Lady Elizabeth's father, betrothed me to her several years ago, before he died. Of course, when her uncle seized her and her brother and took their lands, he refused to countenance the marriage; he has held her prisoner these many years and retained her dowry for himself. But, a few days ago, my aunt and uncle, taking the opportunity of her uncle's absence, sneaked my betrothed from his keep and brought her here. Releasing her a few miles away, they veered off in another direction to confuse anyone who had followed them."

"I see, milord," Sir Robert hastened to say, though he suspected that his master must be a little mad.

"I trust that you will be able to explain this fully to your good lady."

"That may be a trifle difficult, but of course I shall."

Elizabeth doubted that it would be only a trifle difficult, for his lady looked to her to be quite a harridan.

"Send one of your men to Beldon Abbey and fetch a virtuous and truthful nun to us to stay with milady tonight. Considering her arrival, we certainly want no suspicion to touch upon milady."

"Of course, milord, of course."

"We have decided to honor you by holding the wedding here."

Again Elizabeth almost laughed at Sir Robert's expression; no doubt he felt the expense of a wedding was an honor he could easily forego. But he said nothing, only gulped and nodded his head.

"Also, we may expect Sir Godfrey and his family to attend the wedding."

"What do you mean?" Sir Robert gasped, shaken from politeness by his utter dismay. "Sir Godfrey here? That's not possible!"

"I admit they will not be the most welcome of wedding guests, but we can hardly turn away the bride's family, can we? Their manners, of course, will leave a great deal to be desired, but I hope that we can persuade them to leave most of their army outside the walls."

By now his knight was a pale shade of green. He had never expected his own keep to be the site of a clash between the forces of Sir Godfrey and the Earl of Norwen. He could see his home, his wealth—yes, even his life—draining away before his eyes.

"Don't worry, Sir Robert, we shall try our best to avoid a pitched battle; however, we must prepare for the worst. I have sent for reinforcements; and, if Sir Godfrey attacks, we must be able to hold out until they come. Therefore, let us make all preparations for a siege. Set your men to it at once. I shall inspect the walls and the preparations tomorrow morning."

"Yes, milord," Sir Robert said, his voice thin with fright. If there had been any way to get out of this predicament he would have done it, but he saw no hope of release. Knights like himself were merely pawns in the great lords' hands. There was nothing he could do but grit his teeth and do as his lord commanded—and hope that Norwen came out the winner. With a bow to Lady Elizabeth he hurried away to tell his wife of these strange events. After a few moments of an acrid exchange that could be heard all over the keep, the good lady of the house bustled into the room, her face wreathed with false smiles.

"Milady," she exclaimed, "forgive me for the treatment you have received. I had no idea, of course, that such a great woman came upon us unawares. I hope you will forgive me."

"But of course," Elizabeth said graciously. It was hardly the poor woman's fault that she had thought her a common whore; certainly she knew she had looked that part. "If I could just be shown to my room. I fear I am greatly tired after my trip."

"Of course, milady, of course."

Now that Elizabeth was taken care of, Norwen bade Sir Robert to inform him of the nun's arrival and then went back to his brother.

Chapter Six

IN DISCUSSION UNTIL LATE INTO THE NIGHT, THE BROTHERS obtained little sleep before they rose at dawn to inspect the defenses of the keep. They found the walls of the keep poorly kept up, but still strong enough to withstand a siege for a few days, at least; and, by then, their aunt and the others should be there with reinforcements. Buckets of oil stood ready to be heated and pitched down at the siegers below. Carefully James stationed all their best archers along the wall, but hid them completely from view. More men were stationed at the bridge to draw it up on a moment's notice; however, the bridge was left down as part of the lure to capture Stephen without a fight. After declaring themselves satisfied with the preparations, the brothers set to their breakfast with gusto.

Elizabeth, who had had little more sleep than they, was amazed at their appetite. Her own stomach was so nervous that she felt she would be lucky to ever eat again. How were they planning to free Stephen? She feared greatly that he would lose his life in the fray. How were they to withstand her uncle's siege? She had seen the size of her uncle's army and had also seen the smallness of this keep and the tiredness of her new lord's men. All was lost for her and Stephen if her uncle breached the walls. The next few days would decide her life for her, and she found it a most frightening prospect.

However, she hid her fright admirably, presenting a cool mask to the world. Few could have told that her face was calm with frozen terror, not confidence. Her future husband looked at her and thought her a cool one.

Sir Godfrey's army did not appear that day. Their only visitor was the village priest, whom Sir Robert had summoned to speak with the earl. When the black-robed man arrived, Richard quickly explained their situation, ending with a brief command, "So you will marry us within the next few days."

The priest returned his stare unblinkingly. "Milord, what you ask is impossible."

Norwen's face tightened. "Why?"

"The banns have not been read. They must be published at Sunday mass two weeks before the wedding. Therefore, it will have to be at least two weeks before you can be wed."

Sir Robert's face fell ludicrously at the idea of having his liege lord and men at his home eating his food for two weeks more. Norwen sprang to his feet. "I cannot wait that long. I have to return to Norcastle."

"Then take your lady with you and wed there, milord," the priest suggested calmly.

"Out of the question," Norwen thundered, and Elizabeth trembled inside at his expression. Had she been the priest, she thought, she would have quailed before those blazing eyes and dark face. It was obvious the earl was a man used to getting his way, and he did not brook any change in his plans. She dreaded to think what would happen to her if she crossed him or made a mistake. She was sure his anger, once aroused, would be terrible; and should he strike her, he might easily snap her neck. "I have to marry now, and I'll not let some puny village—"

His brother, James, cut in smoothly, stepping between the two men. "What my brother is trying to say is that it is very important that he be wed as soon as possible. I realize that the Church cannot bow to worldly considerations, but there are certain dispensations that can be issued. Surely it is in your power—"

"If there is need, certainly, but I've seen no indication of that here. Carnal desires are not considered a valid need by the Holy Mother Church."

The earl gritted his teeth and growled, "It is not a question of carnality and lust! But I must have the lady legally my wife before we travel. We have been betrothed for many years, as I think Sir Robert explained to you. Surely that is long enough. Another two weeks can't make any difference."

"Perhaps a donation to the poor of the parish," James inserted.

The man swung on him, his voice ringing with conviction. "The blessing of the Church is not for sale!"

James turned away, shooting his brother a wry look. Money and his honeyed persuasion had not eased the matter as they usually did. Norwen's hand fiddled at his sword belt. He would have liked to threaten force to make the man comply, but that was a sin too dreadful to contemplate. James was almost heathenish in his beliefs; but Richard, though not considered a religious man, was unswerving in his faith in the omnipotence of the Church. He could not blatantly oppose a man of God. He frowned and emitted a harsh sigh. "All right, Father. Then post your banns, and let's get on with it. We will be married as soon as you allow."

The priest bowed his head and glided from the hall. James sneered, "Save me from pious psalms singers."

Richard made a noise of disgust deep in his throat and sat back in his chair, his eyes sliding to Elizabeth. She was so lovely. Although it would be more expedient to marry

in the next day or two, it wasn't entirely necessity that
had spurred his bad temper at the priest's denial. He
wanted his bride-to-be in his bed. Every time he looked
at her, his pulse quickened. The thought of waiting over
two weeks to take her was sheer torture to nerves already
strained by waiting for the appearance of Sir Godfrey.

Stephen rode beside his uncle in the early dawn light.
Sir Godfrey was in a vile temper. The day before they
had arrived at Broughton only to find that their quarry
had moved to Emsford. They had traveled all afternoon
and arisen early this morning in order to arrive at the
keep at dawn. Sir Robert's keep, though not as large and
elegant as Broughton Hall, was a better fortress. Godfrey
wanted to attack as early as possible, feeling that now he
needed every bit of advantage he could get.

Stephen fingered the dagger slid up his sleeve. He had
his own plan should his and Elizabeth's scheme not
succeed. He knew there was every possibility that it
might not. It meant several days travel for her, and a
woman alone was in constant danger of attack. The more
Stephen thought about it, the less he believed that she
would reach her destination. At the time he thought of it,
it had seemed the logical thing to do. But he realized now
that it was highly dangerous. For too long he had thought
of Elizabeth only as his older sister. She had always been
the one who made their plans and told him what to do.
She was wiser, older, more experienced than he, and
Stephen had obeyed without question. But he was
beginning to realize that, because Elizabeth was a
woman, she was at a distinct disadvantage in the world.
Their roles had to change. He should be her protector,
not the other way around. Instinctively, he had assumed
she could manage to do what they had agreed upon. But
with time to think, he had realized it was wild and foolish.

If she wasn't killed or raped on the road, it was likely
that Elizabeth would be stripped of her honor when she
met Norwen. Although the man was a great warrior,

Stephen knew he was also a man subject to the same lusts of other men; and his sister was a lovely woman. She was alone and a Beaufort, both of which would encourage the Black Earl's taking her to his bed. There was no telling what he might do in his rage at Sir Godfrey's deception. But, even should Elizabeth escape unscathed, her reputation would be in shreds. Because she had traveled alone, spending several nights in a keep with an army of men, everyone would be sure she had been deflowered. Though they had intended to protect the Beaufort name from dishonor, it would nevertheless be stained.

Even worse was the possibility that she had not reached the keep, that she had been killed along the road. She would have died in a crazy attempt to save his own life. If he were half a man, it would have been he saving her, not the other way around! If they arrived and found the keep unprotected, then he would know she had been killed, or at the least injured or held somewhere against her will. After his uncle destroyed the keep, they would ride to London to present Godfrey's case to the king; and there Stephen planned to take his revenge. Standing before the king to affirm his uncle's story, he would pull the knife from his sleeve and plunge it into Godfrey's chest. Of course, he would probably be killed himself immediately, but it would have been worth it. He would have stopped his uncle from soiling the Beaufort name. He would avenge his sister's death and the years of misery they had suffered at Godfrey's hands. And he would reveal the treachery of his uncle. At least he would be able to clean the honor of two names, Beaufort and Norwen.

The keep came into view, the rising sun glinting off its harsh stones. Godfrey smiled tightly and urged his horse forward. The keep was obviously not expecting attack. Stephen's heart sank. Elizabeth had not arrived in time— or the earl had not believed her. The drawbridge was down across the moat, the heavy portcullis drawn up.

Godfrey pulled out his sword and whirled it above his head, signaling attack. Although he was not a man inclined to lead his army, he wanted to be at the forefront of this battle. He wanted to see the Black Earl's face when he realized his fate would be the same as his father's. He pounded forward, his sons Robert and Peter by his side. Geoffrey hung back, reluctant, as always, to place himself in any danger. But Stephen raced at his uncle's heels. He must see for himself what happened this day and discover why Elizabeth had not warned Norwen.

Norwen was seated in the great hall with his brother and Elizabeth, all of them tense and silent with waiting, when a guard rushed in. "An army is sighted approaching, milord."

James and Norwen sprang up and rushed to be fitted into their armor. First they put on a heavily padded garment known as a gambeson, and over it the hauberk of mail. The hauberk was a long tunic of chain mail reaching to the ankles and split up front and back so that the knight could mount a horse. Leggings of mail covered their legs. Long plates of armor, or greaves, fitted over the shins, and leather caps buckled over the knees. A cloth surcoat was dropped on top of the suit of armor, and last came the sword belt, which ran across the hips and over one shoulder.

As soon as they were dressed—a matter that ate up only minutes with the help of their experienced squires— the brothers ran for the battlements, their squires trailing them with shields and helmets. They did not intend for a full-scale battle to develop that day and, therefore, did not plan to use the shield and helmet; but should something develop to occasion a battle, they could quickly pull up the mail hoods over their heads, drop on the flat-topped barrel helmets and grab their shields. Elizabeth watched as they ran from the castle. She stood beside Robert's lady at the entry, ready to slam shut the heavy doors and bar them, should things go awry and a battle begin to rage in the courtyard.

Norwen took his place on the walkway around the battlements, the low wall making him clearly visible to those below in the courtyard. James waited in clear view for his signal. Extra men had been assigned to the great wheel that pulled up the drawbridge, and they watched James intently. Norwen stood beside a guard, his eyes fastened on the approaching army. It was close enough now that he could make out the arms on the shield of the man in front. Clearly it was Godfrey. Suddenly, Sir Godfrey spurred his horse forward, followed by three other riders close on his flank. Their spurt of speed carried them ahead of the rest of the army by several yards. Norwen smiled secretly. Godfrey was aiding his plan. The four horsemen neared the bridge, and Norwen raised his hand. James, intently watching him below, did the same.

The front-runners clattered onto the innocent-looking drawbridge and under the open portcullis into the courtyard. At their first step onto the bridge, Norwen's hand dropped. James signaled to the men at the wheel, and they threw themselves mightily at their task. The bridge was already rising when the first men behind the leaders pounded onto it. Their horses stumbled and slid on the suddenly uneven footing, and they tumbled over into the deep, dank moat. Immediately after them, horses crashed head-on into the rising bridge and fell, turning the approaching riders into a mass of churning, kicking, screaming horseflesh and humans. A rain of arrows from the embrasures of the battlements above and the cross-shaped arrow slits in the towers further increased the milling confusion. In haste, the men withdrew, leaderless and frightened, the heart suddenly shaken from them.

Inside, Godfrey reined to a halt, hearing the sounds of wild disorder behind him. In dismay, he and his sons saw the drawbridge rising and heard the screams of the horses and men. Sword upraised and a bellow dying on his lips, he realized in an instant of stunned dismay that he and his sons were alone and trapped within the bailey of his enemy, while his entire army lay outside. He was too far gone in shock to speak or move.

Before his thoughts could clear, a huge voice shouted down from the battlements, "Godfrey! Welcome to my keep!" Godfrey swallowed and looked up, shielding his eyes to see the massive figure whose outline lay black against the sun. The earl laughed harshly. "Yes, it is I. That boy whom you chased from a burning castle twenty years ago. That man whose father and family you most foully murdered."

"Norwen!" His one word carried all the fear swelling inside Sir Godfrey.

"Yes, Norwen." Richard ran lightly down the curving staircase. "May I suggest that you gentlemen dismount?" He glanced significantly at the battlements around them, where archers stood, hundreds of arrows pointed straight at Godfrey and his men. Godfrey licked his lips, then sheathed his sword and dismounted. He knew he had somehow been betrayed, though he couldn't fathom how; and he knew the earl held him in his power. But it was also obvious that he was not to be killed immediately, so Godfrey obeyed, hoping to buy time. "I am glad you could attend my wedding," Norwen continued brightly. "Oh, I'm sorry, I didn't introduce my brother. James?"

James stepped into the light, the rays of the sun glinting off his mail and blue black hair. His eyes were lazy, his lips almost smiling. He didn't appear to have a nerve in his body. "Sir Godfrey."

"And is one of you Lord Beaufort?" Norwen went on.

Stephen stepped forward. "I am, milord." He wasn't sure exactly what was going on, but things were clearly going against his uncle. And it meant that somehow Elizabeth had made it through.

"I am Richard, Earl of Norwen, milord," Richard gravely introduced himself to the boy, eyes twinkling at

Stephen's amazement at being addressed as "milord." Plainly such honor was not given him in his uncle's household. "My brother James." Stephen remembered himself enough to execute a very passable bow to both men. "I am pleased to meet you. I have heard much about you."

"From my future bride, I hope. Since Lady Elizabeth and I have been betrothed these many years, I trust she has spoken of me with fondness."

Stephen gaped while behind him Godfrey sputtered. "Betrothed! Damn your eyes, you were never betrothed to a Beaufort! You have dishonored my niece and I demand satisfaction!" He was confused, but tried to reestablish his plot line.

"You are in little position to demand anything," the earl reminded him crisply. "As for your niece's honor, I assure you it is intact, as a good nun from Beldon Abbey will be happy to attest, having slept beside her all last night."

Elizabeth stepped out of the door. Her brother let out a happy cry and ran to her. "Elizabeth!" She reached out to hug him tightly. "Oh, Elizabeth, you made it safely. Is everything all right?"

"Yes, more than all right." Tears choked her eyes and throat. Stephen was safe, protected by the wit and might of the Earl of Norwen. Gratitude and happiness vied for supremacy in her heart.

"I am glad you could come in time for the wedding festivities," the earl went on blithely. "It is always good to have family at such occasions. Of course, your method of arrival leaves something to be desired."

Stephen gazed at him wonderingly, then turned back to his sister. "Is it true?" he whispered.

Elizabeth nodded. "Yes. He means to marry me."

Stephen gulped hard as though swallowing the extraordinary idea. Not only was his sister unharmed, but the earl was bestowing on Elizabeth the title of Countess of Norwen, with all the wealth and position that entailed.

It was mind boggling, and Stephen stared at his future brother-in-law with almost worshipful awe.

Elizabeth felt a small pang of dismay. For the first time, her brother looked to someone else with love and devotion. She realized that what Norwen had done had made him forever a hero in Stephen's eyes. Stephen would be bound to someone else—how would he choose if Norwen were at odds with her? The thought of Stephen's possible defection was terrifying.

"Gentlemen," Norwen addressed Godfrey and his sons, "my men will see you to your rooms and keep anyone from disturbing you there. I'm afraid it will be two weeks before the wedding can take place. I trust you will not grow bored. Of course, you won't need your arms at such a pleasant celebration, so my men will take them and store them for you."

The earl's polite words were thinly veiled commands to disarm. Godfrey glared at Norwen impotently, but handed over his sword and shield and the spike-studded mace from his saddle. Robert and Peter followed suit. The three men were herded into the keep and down to their room in the storage floor of the keep, where the door was shut behind them and a heavy bar dropped into place. For a few minutes, Godfrey stormed around the room, venting his rage on the furniture, even grabbing Peter by the throat and shaking him until Robert pulled him off the young man. Finally the red wash of insane rage receded from his eyes, and he began to think more clearly. His first clear thought was that they were trapped. He knew his son Geoffrey well enough to know he would not rescue them. It would be to his advantage for his father and older brother to be slain. Besides, even if his army did storm the castle, Godfrey was certain he would be slaughtered as soon as the troops began their assault. His army was equally aware of that, and so would not act.

But he was being allowed to live to continue Norwen's charade until after the wedding. The earl wouldn't wish to spoil a wedding feast by killing the bride's family.

Perhaps he would even set them free. Godfrey clenched his fists at the thought of Elizabeth. Damn that witch! How had she gotten here? And how had she convinced the earl to marry her? "Of course! The dower lands!"

"What?" Robert glanced at his father, relieved to see that his fury had passed.

"The dower lands. That's why the Black Earl wants to marry her. He needs an excuse to attack me, and he'll use Elizabeth's dower lands! He'll marry her, demand the dowry her father left for her and attack me when I refuse." He grimaced, thinking of that eventuality. "Damn her soul to hell! That witch betrayed me! How did she escape? No doubt she talked your idiot mother into letting her out. She must have learned of our plan and ridden here to inform the earl." He paused, musing on her perfidy. "Perhaps she was in league with that devil all these years. I wouldn't put it past her." He thumped one hand into the open palm of the other. "I'll make her pay for this betrayal. I'll make her pay."

Above in the great hall, Norwen and James followed Elizabeth and her smiling brother inside. Stephen was eagerly asking questions, but a word from the earl stopped his chatter. "Lord Beaufort, I have a request to make of you."

Stephen looked at him, surprised. "Of course, milord. Whatever you wish."

"I must ask permission to wed Lady Elizabeth."

James, standing slightly behind his brother, had to smother a smile at the lad's expression. He obviously had never been asked for permission for anything before. It took Stephen a moment to recover and assume his rightful duties as Lord Beaufort.

But very quickly he inclined his head solemnly and said, "Of course, milord. A marriage alliance with Norwen is indeed a great event. You must know that my father and I have had no quarrel with you; it is only my uncle who acted against you, just as he has acted against milady sister and me. I hope that we two families can combine to defeat him."

Both Norwen and James were impressed at his calm and quickness of mind. Elizabeth was proud of the way he carried himself, although she was somewhat taken aback by his sudden assurance and maturity. She felt a funny pain; her little brother was no longer so little.

"I am sure you must be tired and wish to refresh yourself from your trip," Richard said to Stephen. "Lady Elizabeth will take you to your room."

He knew, but did not need to add, that the two would welcome a chance to converse together. Once they were alone, Stephen immediately began to ply his sister with questions. "What has happened? How did this marriage plan come about? What has Norwen done?"

Quickly Elizabeth explained the situation to him. She related how she had revealed to Norwen her uncle's dastardly plan and his counterplot.

"He is a great man, is he not?" Stephen breathed, his eyes shining.

"He is quick in intelligence," Elizabeth admitted, "and he is a strong warrior; but I would not put my full faith in him. And even less would I trust his brother. James opposed our marriage greatly. He claims that I am a lying, deceitful Beaufort and will murder Norwen in his bed some night."

Stephen said reasonably, "Knowing the nature of our uncle, I can readily see how they might fear that from a Beaufort. It will only take time to prove him wrong."

"Do not fall upon him with cries of joy. Do not trust him so easily and quickly. Every man is our enemy; you must remember that. He may be as full of deceit and treachery as Sir Godfrey. What if he holds you in virtual captivity as did our uncle? What if he refuses to train you in the martial arts? What if he takes our lands and locks you and me in some remote tower at Norcastle? Keep your eyes open, Stephen; don't trust him."

"I have seen nothing yet to indicate that he is so full of

treachery. He seems to me to be a man of great honor. After all, did he not rescue us and offer you his hand in marriage as well?"

"Do not forget that it will help him, too," Elizabeth cautioned. "After all, it gives him an excuse to attack our uncle. Not only that, if he can win them away from Godfrey, he will have my dower lands, which is not a small prize. Moreover, he can become your guardian and control your lands as well. And if you persist in this hero worship of him, he will be able to control them long after your majority."

"I am not a fool, sister," Stephen said with a certain sternness in his voice. "I am almost a man grown; he treats me as such. Did not you see that?"

"I saw a very clever ploy to gain your undying loyalty."

"Elizabeth! Why are you so set against the man? It seems to me that he has done you nothing but great good."

Elizabeth felt a pang of remorse at his words. He spoke the truth. The earl had done nothing but kindness to her so far; he had exceeded her wildest expectations. She was displaying an unseemly ingratitude. "I am sorry, Stephen. You are right, of course. It is just that I fear his brother, for his brother has great power with the earl and James does not like me. I am afraid to trust in him too much, for I know James will try to influence him against us. More than that, I fear trusting any man after our experience with our uncle."

Stephen took his sister's hand in his and squeezed it gently. "I know. I know. But don't forget I am a man, too. It is not all men who are treacherous."

Elizabeth smiled at her younger brother. How quickly he was growing up; how soon he would indeed be a man. He desperately needed a man's influence. He needed Norwen, even though it gave her a wrench of pain to think that he needed someone other than her. Dear God, she hoped that Norwen would be the proper man; she prayed that he would do what Stephen needed —teach him honor, warfare and, most of all, maybe a little happiness. Heaven knew, he had had little enough of that to learn in his short life.

"I know, Stephen, and perhaps Norwen is a man such as you are. I pray that he is. But, please, do not trust him overmuch, at least not until you have known him for some time."

"I will not trust foolishly, Elizabeth, I promise."

Chapter Seven

SOON THEREAFTER STEPHEN WENT TO BED TO SLEEP, for he had spent several sleepless nights in his anxiety over his sister. Elizabeth returned to her room to find there a maid with several bolts of lovely cloth.

"What is this?" Elizabeth asked the girl.

"Milord bade me bring them to you," the maid answered.

"You mean they are for me?" Elizabeth asked.

"Yes, ma'am, I guess so."

Elizabeth went to her bed, where the bolts of cloth lay. Hesitantly she reached out and touched one of them. They were beautiful, fine, expensive cloths in pale, glimmering colors. That pink would look beautiful on her, she knew—and the blue, or the green. But most beautiful of all was the rich, thick brocade; it was white and woven into it were tiny threads of silver and gold, giving it a shimmering quality very similar to the color of her hair. What a fine wedding dress that would make. Even as she thought it, she shook her head. No, it could not be for her. Surely Norwen would not so lavish goods upon her. Of course, it was up to him now to clothe her—but so richly? Her uncle was a tight man, and her new dresses had been few and far between and always of a dull, inexpensive material. Even her loving father had never given her this sort of cloth. On the other hand, it was said that Norwen was wealthy; and why else should he send the cloth to her? Who else could they be for? Himself, perhaps. Perhaps he meant that she was to make his clothes from these. But no, how silly; he would not wear that pale pink, that fragile blue or that delicate silver and gold brocade.

She was startled from her thoughts by the entrance of the earl himself into her room. She turned, barely suppressing a gasp.

"Milord?"

"Do not look so frightened. I did not come to harangue you."

"Of course not. I am sorry. Pray be seated."

He smiled a little at her nervous manner. "Thank you, I will. What is it that makes you all jumpy like a colt?"

"It is just that I did not expect you, milord. I did not know of any reason for your coming. Is there something I have done?"

"Nay. Is it so unusual for a future husband to visit his betrothed? I only wish to see you and speak to you, nothing more than that."

"I see." She hesitated for a moment, unsure of what to do.

Again he smiled at her and said, "Why don't you sit down? I think you will find it more comfortable than standing there shifting back and forth upon your feet."

"Oh, yes, thank you." She sat down quickly and then stared at her hands, trying to think of something to say. She had never been required to make polite conversation with a gentleman since she had come to live in her uncle's house. She tried to cast her mind back to her life before her uncle; but, even then, though she had sat at her father's table and entertained his guests, she could not ever remember facing a situation of sitting alone with a man and conversing. She had not really thought about having to talk to her future husband. From what she had seen of marriage, companionship never entered into it at all. When she thought of marrying the Black Earl, she had thought of the trials of the marriage bed, of bearing his children, of caring for his home, of sharing her meals with him. But she had never thought of sitting and talking to him as an everyday occurrence.

Richard looked at her, a little surprised at her nervousness. She was a difficult one to understand—at one moment angry and distrustful, full of harsh, sarcastic words, at other times so full of terror or, as now, so shy and uncomfortable.

"I have sent a messenger to the king," he began, to set her at ease, "to ask him to grant me guardianship of your brother now that I am to be his brother-in-law. I am sure that Henry will grant the wardship to me."

"But what if he does not?" Elizabeth asked, lifted out of her timidness by her concern for her brother.

"I cannot see why he would not. However, if he does not, I doubt your uncle will live long enough to take him back."

Elizabeth felt a little stab of fear at the coldness of his tone. "Do you—are you saying that Sir Godfrey will not leave this keep?"

"No, I do not wish to mar our marriage feast by the cold-blooded murder of your kin. I would gladly kill that snake without a single regret. However, it is my way to meet on the field of honor in rightful battle rather than in sly secret. It would impugn my honor for your uncle and cousins to die at our wedding feast, unarmed and alone, surrounded by my friends and relatives. And, anyway, the king would not like it. Better to wait until I have the opportunity to kill him with the law on my side. Henry is very great on the law. Your uncle will refuse to surrender your dower lands and that will give us our excuse. I do not think he can bear to let go of what he has gained, even if he knows it means certain death for him. Besides, he will always hope that even though I outman him he can defeat me through some trick or other. I am certain he will oppose me for your lands, and that will give me the opportunity to strike him down."

"What are your plans—I mean after the wedding?"

"Why, we shall go to Norcastle, of course—your brother and you and I and James. Winter fast approaches. I think that we shall rest and recuperate there for the winter, demand your lands from your uncle and, in the spring, after he has refused, take them from him by force. I hope to draw him into actual battle, so that I can defeat him with my own hands."

"Do you mean to kill him?"

"Yes." The word came out harsh and hissing. "I will never rest until he is dead at my feet. He destroyed my family, killed my father and grandfather, my mother, my sister—" His voice trailed off bleakly, and there was a blank, set look to his face that was frightening.

Elizabeth looked at him and considered for the first time the reasons he had to hate Sir Godfrey. Her uncle had made her life miserable for five years, had abused her, threatened her, kept her in constant fear that he might kill Stephen or her, or both of them, and had taken away her lands and wealth. But this man who sat across from her had seen all of the people he loved destroyed by her uncle. His entire family, except for his aunt and uncle and his brother James, had died at Godfrey's command. Sir Godfrey had taken away all of his wealth, his very home, and forced him to flee, at twelve, from his home, even from his country. He had lived in exile for fear of his life, penniless because Godfrey had confiscated all his wealth. He had had to make his way on his own: whatever he had now, no doubt he had had to pay a bitter price for. For the first time she realized how strong must have been his hatred for Sir Godfrey. Surely it exceeded even hers. And for the first time she really sympathized with the distrust he must have harbored about her since she was a Beaufort. No matter how untrue it might be, it was not an unreasonable thing for him to think. She could see that there was something to admire in him for having risen above that hatred enough to marry her. True, it was for his own best interests as well as hers, but how much easier it would have been for his rage at her uncle to have brought him to violate her or kill her, even. He had exhibited an iron control that was awesome, frightening. She wondered if it was really possible for one to ever breach the steel around him and reach the man beneath.

Richard looked up, shaking his head as though to clear it of his gloomy thoughts, and said, "We shall have a good few months of solitude to begin Stephen's training in arms."

"Indeed? Do you plan then to train him?" she asked.

"Of course. What use would he be to himself or you or me if he is a weakling, unable to defend his own property? What sort of an ally would that be? What sort of a safety could he offer you if something should happen to me? What kind of an uncle would he be to our children? No, I want him strong. He seems a quick lad, but as for his strength—I fear that that will take some working. He looks to be—forgive me—a sickly youth."

"He is not that, I can assure you," Elizabeth came hotly to her brother's defense. "It is merely his coloring that belies his strength. He is small but wiry, and he has never been sick a day in his life. He is not as strong as other boys his age, no doubt, because he has had nothing to develop his strength. But the raw material is there, I am positive."

He smiled at her. "Well, certainly we shall do our best to develop his strength. I promise you that. Of course, at his age, he should be a squire for a knight. But I presume he was never sent to another knight's home to be his page?"

Elizabeth shook her head sadly. "No. My father had

made arrangements with Lord Harold of Darcy before he died, but my uncle refused to honor them. He didn't want Stephen out of his power."

"Since he didn't start the process with other boys, he would be a fish out of water if we made him a squire now. Besides, he is so far behind in his training that he needs intensive work. It will be better for us to teach him."

"Milord, what are your intentions for Stephen's land?"

"As his guardian, of course, I could fight to regain his lands. However, I think it would be wisest for Stephen to build up an army of his own."

"An army of his own!" Elizabeth cried out. "But he is only a boy!"

"I did not say that he could lead the army yet, but when he is sixteen he will be in command of his lands. Better that he should have an army loyal to him than to begin then to build one up and not be capable of defending his own lands until he is nineteen. Someone else shall have to lead his army for him now. I think that James would make a good commander for his men. He will, of course, be perfectly loyal to me and therefore perfectly loyal to Stephen; and we need not worry about him selling out to Godfrey or trying to retain possession and control of the lands when Stephen should take them over."

"James?" Elizabeth questioned, feeling her heart sink within her. Of course, his brother would think him loyal and seemed to have no idea that James could be disloyal to another; but, even with the best of intentions on Norwen's part, she feared that James would be more than capable of taking away her brother's land.

But Elizabeth held her tongue. No use to speak against his brother now; he would not believe what she said, but would attribute it to her deceptiveness.

To avoid expressing her thoughts, Elizabeth changed the subject. "Milord, these bolts of cloth the maid brought in—"

"Yes. Do you like them?"

"Yes, of course. They are beautiful. But—"

"But what?"

"Why did you bid her bring them to me? What am I to do with them?"

"Do with them? Why, make them into dresses, of course. What else would you do with them? I thought this gold and silver one would do excellently for your wedding dress; if you and the maids set to it with will, you could finish it by the day of our wedding. They are part of my wedding gift to you. The jewelry, of course, that I will give you is at home in Norcastle. Are they not fine enough? Did you expect more for a wedding gift?" His voice grew sarcastic.

"Oh, no, milord, no. It is not that; it is not that at all. It is only that I did not expect this much. I did not expect these beautiful dresses or—and the jewelry—"

"Did you think I would not even give you a few bolts of cloth as a wedding gift? God's bones, woman, what sort of man do you take me for? Do you not expect me to give you the perquisites of your station? Did you expect me to allow you to dress in the sort of thing you wear now? I am not your uncle, madam." His voice began to rise with anger. "Do not presume that I am like him in any manner. I have pride in my name and in my family, and you will bear my name and be part of my family. You will not run about looking like a serf. Do I make myself clear?"

Elizabeth quailed at his tone. She had not intended to stir his anger. "I am sorry, milord. I—I have no other man to judge you by except Sir Godfrey, just as you judge all Beauforts by him. I never received any kindness from him; it surprises me to get it from any man."

His face softened at her words. She had known so little kindness. It was obvious that she had no idea that her beauty stirred him so that he would have given her far more than bolts of cloth if she had asked. No doubt her loveliness had never altered her uncle's attitude toward her, and she did not realize that she could tempt and tease a man into giving her what she wanted. Of course, that was just as well—he had no desire for her to try her wiles on him. The less she realized she had power over him the better.

"Well, remember this: what you expect from your uncle is not at all what you shall receive from me. I am a fair man, I think; and if you have needs, you must let me know and I will fulfill your wishes."

Elizabeth smiled a little, uncertainty written on her face; she did not know whether to fully believe him. Of course, all men were not like her uncle; after all, she had had the example of her father, who did not resemble Sir Godfrey at all. Yet it was hard for her to believe that any man without natural ties to her would be kind, especially one so dark and so fierce a warrior as this man. Certainly Elizabeth would let herself trust no one, no matter how fair his words. And yet—she looked toward the cloth on the bed—he had shown her nothing but gentleness and understanding. Could it be that she was wrong where he was concerned?

The earl studied her. How lovely she was in her obvious confusion. He reached out and took her hand and pulled her down into his lap. He nuzzled her neck, his lips working at the tender flesh of her throat. Lifting up her hair and wimple, he kissed the strangely sensitive nape of her neck, sending shivers down her backbone. One hand caressed her arm, then went to her waist and stole upward to cup her breast. His thumb circled her nipple, feeling the soft flesh become a hard button beneath the material. His cheek was suddenly blazing hot against her neck, and a muffled groan escaped him. He was pounding with desire, aflame with wanting her.

At his touch, she stiffened and, though she did not resist, there was no compliance in her body. He frowned; what was the matter with the girl? Did she, despite his assurances, still believe that he might force her and blacken her honor? Was it that she hated him—or hated all men? With a sigh, he released her, and she jumped quickly from his lap.

"I shall not harm you; I have given you my word on that," he said roughly. "Do you not believe me?"

She said nothing, only looked at the floor. She could not explain her automatic reaction to his touch. Rationally, she knew he would not take her against her will; however, it was not so much the loss of her honor that brought about her reaction, but simply fear of his touch. As soon as he touched her, she thought of her cousin and the unspeakable things he had done to her. She felt the cold hatred she felt for him and his father, and she felt the icy dread of what this man could do to her—and do legally. She did not know if she could bear it. From all her Aunt Maud had said, the marriage bed was the most severe trial a woman faced. It was full of pain and revulsion and, at best, boredom. She felt an awful panic at the thought that she would be his to do with as he willed, and no hope of ever escaping. At least she had been able to dream about being free from her uncle, but now she would have to endure this misery for the rest of her life. She hated herself for her cowardice. If only she could be brave and strong and face what all other women faced. She had to do it for Stephen—and for herself. She knew she only angered the earl by her actions, and it was foolhardy to anger him. Yet she could not seem to control the involuntary way she tightened at his touch.

Richard, watching her, felt desire wash over him. He longed to reach out and caress her slim body. Her breasts strained against the too-tight shift, and through the thin material he could see their hardening peaks. Suddenly he yearned to explore her with his hands and mouth, to pull her clothes from her and gaze upon her naked form. His loins ached with wanting her.

Hastily he stood up and said, "I shall leave you alone, since you seem to dislike my company." His voice was harsh with suppressed desire. He turned on his heel and strode out of the room, and Elizabeth followed him with her eyes.

She was a fool, she knew, to displease him. He would have full powers over her when they were married, but she could not bear to be the foolish, submissive thing her aunt was, or even her mother, though her mother had not been a cringing, whining sort like Maud. She had been a sweet, clinging, doting wife. She had adored her father and did as he bade, never questioning or objecting. Her mother had been well loved by her father, but Elizabeth abhorred the price she had had to pay. She could not act like that; she simply couldn't. To dance and smile and simper at his command—no, that was not the sort of life for her. She had saved herself and her brother from Sir Godfrey for five years with no help from anyone; she had used her strength and her wit, and she had no desire to give them up now just to be Norwen's property, no matter how much he might shower on that property if it pleased him.

Chapter Eight

THE DAY AFTER SIR GODFREY'S CAPTURE, THE EARL AD-
dressed Godfrey's troops, who waited outside the castle.
Climbing to a tower of the battlements, he called to the
commander of Godfrey's troops to come forward. Cautiously, Geoffrey approached to a point where he remained just beyond arrow range. "Sir Godfrey and his
sons are inside and will remain for two weeks to enjoy the
festivities of my wedding to his lady niece." Geoffrey
goggled in amazement, at a loss to understand how
Elizabeth was here marrying the Earl of Norwen when
they had left her barred in her room at home. However,
he was quick to realize that, since the earl had his father in
his power, Godfrey might very well be killed. If Robert
and Godfrey both died, Geoffrey would inherit. He also
recognized the thinly veiled hint in Norwen's voice. He
was notifying them that any attempt to rescue his father
and brothers would result in their immediate death. For a
moment Geoffrey contemplated attacking the castle in
order to bring about that result. However, his dislike of

battle outweighed his desire. If it happened, it would happen. He would not help them, but neither would he send them straight to their deaths. That way it would not be on his soul if they died.

"Of course, we wish it were possible for all of you to participate in the festivities; but there will not be enough food to supply such a vast army, especially since my vassals Broughton and Dorsey and my uncle and his troops will arrive tomorrow to attend also."

Again Geoffrey understood his meaning. Norwen was commanding him to return with his men to Fenwick Keep. If he did not, he would have to face the combined power of Norwen's troops, as well as those of three loyal vassals. "Of course, milord," Geoffrey called back, standing in his stirrups and sketching a bow. "We understand perfectly. We shall return to our keep immediately."

"Good. I will provide an escort for Sir Godfrey and his sons."

Geoffrey nodded and trotted back to his troops. Explaining to his captains that, if they attacked or even remained here, his father and brothers were certain to die, he ordered them to get the men ready to leave as soon as possible.

When the Beaufort army pulled out, Norwen had a few of his men follow them at a safe distance to make sure they didn't circle back for a sneak attack. When he was certain Godfrey's army was gone, the men of the castle went hunting. It would take a great deal of food to keep Norwen's troops and guests well fed for two weeks, and another massive amount for the great wedding feast. Besides, the almost daily hunting for deer, venison and wild fowl kept the knights busy and cut down on the boredom-induced brawls that were always a danger with a large group of fighting men confined in close quarters.

Elizabeth set to work on her wedding dress with the help of a maid and a nun from the abbey. They sewed constantly, leaving her room only to attend the meals. At the meals, she sat upon her future husband's left and, as was the custom, drank from the same cup as he. Although he acted with perfect courtesy, finding her choice bits of meat to eat and offering his goblet to her to drink, his manner was remote and formal. They carried on little conversation beyond that required by politeness and necessity. He did not come to her rooms again to speak to her, for Richard found that he could not be around her without his desire for her threatening to overcome him. Sometimes when they sat side by side at the table and her firm leg accidentally pressed against his, or he grazed her arm or breast with his hand as he reached for food, he felt tremors of longing shake him; and he knew that he could not be around her sweet, entrancing body for long without taking her into his arms. He longed to hold her and kiss her, but he knew that, once started, he might very well be unable to stop. The most effective means of avoiding this was, therefore, not to be around her at all until they had wed and he had the right to take her. Elizabeth noticed his absence but was rather glad of it, both because she had work to do and because she had no desire to face his strength and passion again.

The next afternoon Elizabeth was startled from her concentration on her sewing by shouts from the wall and the great creak of the drawbridge being lowered. Hastily she laid down her work and went running down the stairs and out into the courtyard, anxious to know what was transpiring. Her brother, not surprisingly, was there before her, standing beside the earl and James on the steps leading down into the courtyard. A band of men poured in across the bridge.

"What goes on?" Elizabeth questioned Stephen, grabbing his arm and pulling him to the side a bit.

"It is Sir Philip," Stephen said excitedly, "the earl's uncle. He and his wife led Richard and James to safety when their family was murdered by our uncle. The earl sent for him to attend your wedding and, of course, to have his strength of arms and his men in case Sir Godfrey had engaged him in battle."

"My, you seem to have learned a great deal from his lordship," Elizabeth said, a little miffed at her brother's excitement and interest in her betrothed's family.

"Oh, yes," Stephen said. "He has talked to me a good deal. It's so exciting!" Her brother's eyes flashed.

Elizabeth turned from him to watch Sir Philip dismount and take off his helmet, then begin to ascend the stairs. The earl rushed forward to greet him, and the two men embraced joyfully. Sir Philip patted his nephew upon the shoulder.

James followed right behind his brother, and the older man threw an arm about him and hugged him fiercely, too.

"I am glad to see you both alive and well. Your aunt and I feared that we might find this keep a smoldering ruin. What mean you wedding a Beaufort?"

Richard laughed and said, "Once you have seen her, uncle, and heard her story, you will have no doubts. Come, let me introduce you. But first, where is Aunt Marguerite?"

"I can see that you still do not think of your aunt as being a mere mortal like the rest of us. Did you honestly think that I would allow her to come into the middle of what might very possibly be a battle? She is a good distance behind us, cooling her heels at a friendly keep. She, of course, is no doubt fuming, since she considers herself as immortal as you apparently do. I shall send her a message to tell her that it is safe to proceed to this keep. Now, where is this bride? Come, man, let me see her."

"Come, sir. Let me introduce you to her."

They came up the steps to Elizabeth and stopped in front of her. Elizabeth stared in awe at this man who so easily laughed with and chastised the fierce earl and who did not hesitate to go against the earl's plans. She pulled herself together enough, however, to execute a sweeping curtsy to him.

"Uncle, this is my bride-to-be, Lady Elizabeth. Milady, this is my uncle, Sir Philip."

"Come, lass, stand up and let me look at you," the older man commanded.

Elizabeth stood and returned his gaze firmly. She knew it did not help to let a man see her fear. She saw that his ease with her betrothed and his happiness at seeing them had made her mistake him. There was no bluster or bullying about him. He was a tall, fair man with blond hair now graying at the temples. Gray showed in his beard, too, and there were deep lines about his nose and eyes. The years had taken their toll on him. But his blue eyes were soft and tranquil, and his face calm and composed. He was a strong man, but his strength was quiet. He studied her thoughtfully and finally smiled.

"Madam," he said and bowed to her, and made no further comment on her beauty or her name as other men were wont to do.

"And this is her brother, Stephen, Lord Beaufort." Richard directed him toward the blond young boy.

Sir Philip looked at him for a moment and a slow smile spread across his features. It was hard to resist her brother's fair good looks or his obvious hero worship.

"Milord," Sir Philip said gravely.

In his excitement at being thus addressed, Stephen almost forgot to bow in return and offer his greeting.

A messenger was sent to Lady Marguerite and the party went back inside the castle. Elizabeth quickly retired to her room to leave the men alone to indulge in the sort of talk that they enjoyed.

It was some hours later, after supper, that there was another clatter at the gate, and Lady Marguerite rode in with her small band of protectors. Elizabeth hurried down to the courtyard, curious to see a female Norwen. There she saw a tall, dark woman being aided in dismounting by Sir Philip. Close behind him stood James and Richard, their faces alight like schoolboys.

"Richard, you unpredictable lad." She threw her arms

around her nephew's great form and hugged him tightly. Then she turned to his half brother and engulfed him in no less fierce an embrace. "James, my love."

She looked up the steps to where Elizabeth stood and said, "Ah, this must be the lady. Introduce me, Richard."

The three walked up the steps, the two brothers each holding one of their aunt's hands. She was a pretty woman still, her olive skin barely touched by time, and her tall frame still slender. Her eyes were black and sparkling, and there was a vivacity to her face that gave it its prettiness. She had not the beauty that Elizabeth did, but she was intriguing looking and one always wished to know her better.

Richard introduced her to Elizabeth and she immediately swept the young girl into her arms. If she had any doubts about the proposed marriage, she certainly did not express them. For all her laughter and animated ways, Lady Marguerite had learned through experience that it was best to keep her own counsel. Now, like the commanding ocean, she pulled all of them into the keep after her, keeping up a constant chatter about the weather, her horses, her men-at-arms, the wedding to come and her own weariness.

Elizabeth liked her immediately; it was almost impossible not to. It was the first time Elizabeth had ever met a female quite like her. She was obviously worshiped by her nephews and her husband, who hung upon her words and chuckled at her witticisms. She was as fond of her nephews as they were of her. However, while she was quite pleasant to her husband, she did not hang upon him or cater to him; yet neither did she seem to fear him. Elizabeth had never before seen a woman who had such little concern for her husband's good will, and yet her husband seemed most infatuated with her—even after all these years of marriage. Was it possible, she wondered, for a woman to be cherished without groveling before a man?

Lady Marguerite immediately took charge of the keep.

She did not shout commands or disturb the regular order of the castle, but her very personality seemed to sweep through its halls. The castellan's wife, formerly haughty and overproud, suddenly bobbed and curtsied and simpered like a serving girl before the great lady. The maids scurried at her glance, and whatever she asked for was immediately before her. She infected the keep with excitement, and for the first time Elizabeth realized that her wedding was supposed to be a joyous occasion, her most memorable day. Her future aunt set to helping her sew with a will, although she laughed and insisted upon only sewing such stitches as need not be so fine. She was not, she said with a perky shake to her head, a skilled seamstress.

"Frankly, I was quite indulged by our father, and I never learned to sew really well. And then with those two boys on my hands, as well as my own lads, and a household to run—while constantly traveling, of course —somehow I never seemed to have the time to practice. Not," she added, "that that fact distressed me overmuch. I haven't the patience for it, I fear. But you, what lovely needlework you do!"

"Thank you, ma'am. My mother was an excellent needlewoman and she taught me well before she died."

"How old were you when she died?"

"About eight. She died in childbirth with my brother."

"'Tis a pity. So many die that way. My own sister died in childbirth several years ago." A look of sadness crossed her face. "All of them are dead now, except me."

Suddenly it occurred to Elizabeth that this woman had seen all the members of her family die, had lost all of her wealth and spent much of the rest of her life in exile; yet somehow she had retained her humor and her spirit. She had built her life on ashes and come to some sort of peace and contentment with her lot.

The older woman gently passed her hand across her face, as if the gesture would wipe away the troublesome thoughts from her mind, and smiled at Elizabeth. "Well," she began cheerfully, "no doubt you have some curiosity about your betrothed that I can satisfy—his likes, his dislikes, the tales of his harsh past."

Elizabeth realized that she had really thought very little about her future marriage as a reality. She had feared her betrothed, had wished that her marriage would not come about, had prayed for some divine intervention; but until this moment she had not really looked at it squarely in the face. It struck her now that from here on in she would be the mistress of Norcastle, the one who would see that the household operated smoothly, that the earl's favorite foods were served, that those he did not like were banished from the table. It would be she who sewed his clothes and chose the fabrics, who bound up his wounds, who bore his children and raised them. She would no longer be a Beaufort but a Norwen, and she had no choice but to concern herself with the things relating to the Norwen clan. And so, for the first time, her curiosity was piqued, and she wondered about the details of the fall of the Norwens and all her betrothed's past life.

"Could you—tell me about his family? What they were like? The others, I mean. His mother and father. I don't even know if he has other brothers or sisters."

A sad smile touched Marguerite's lips. "He did at one time, though they were all killed. He had three sisters, one a whole sister, the other two James's sisters. They were beautiful girls, especially James's sisters. Black hair, sky blue eyes. One was five years old and one six. Alys and Millicent." Marguerite closed her eyes. Elizabeth wasn't sure whether she was lost in memory or pain. Perhaps it was both. "Anne, Richard's sister, was much like him and their mother in looks—dark eyes and hair, tall. She was fourteen, older than Richard, and already very much a lady of the manor. She was betrothed to Harry Dorsey, Lord Dorsey's son. Richard's mother, Mary, was a tall, strapping woman, not uncomely; and Henry, my brother, was quite fond of her. But he fell deeply in love with Gwendolyn; and when he brought

Gwen into the castle, Mary was so offended she retreated to one of the tower rooms and refused to join the family until Gwendolyn was put from the castle. It was a contest of wills, and my brother had all the power. So she whiled away the rest of her life in her self-imposed exile, never venturing from her tower. My mother and I went to visit her often, and Anne and Richard lived with her, at least until he was sent out to be a page. After that, when he came home, he slept in a room near the rest of us. Mary was a proud woman, intelligent, but she was hurt deeply by Henry's infidelities."

"I—I can understand her feelings," Elizabeth ventured, not wishing to say anything against Marguerite's brother but strongly sympathetic to Richard's discarded mother.

"Oh, yes, so can I. It is not something I would put up with, though I doubt my solution would be to cut myself off from the world." Marguerite's eyes glittered, and Elizabeth thought with amusement that Marguerite's approach would be much more forthright and decisive. "I cannot excuse my brother, except to say that it is often the way of men. Even I don't expect faithfulness from Philip when he is away on a campaign and I am not there to—ah, satisfy his needs. But Henry was—" She paused and smiled, her eyes distant. "Oh, he was a lovely man. Handsome, bright, clever, bursting with life. One couldn't help but love him, no matter what he did. He did everything to the fullest—when he fought, he was a lion; when he loved, he loved to the depths of his soul. He loved to dance, to hunt, to match wits with me in riddles and guessing games. I've never known anyone who enjoyed life better or gained more from every aspect of it. It made it doubly sad when his life was cut short."

"How did it happen, Lady Marguerite?"

The other woman did not need to ask what she was referring to. "Your uncle had managed to plant a treacherous band of men among our own men. My brother did not know this, but was led astray by the influence of—well, Henry always had too much of a weakness for the fairer sex." It was the story she told everyone, including Richard and James. She had never revealed all the events of that night, for it would have only caused Richard needless suffering. Marguerite had heard a noise as she lay awake after lovemaking with her husband, and she had risen to investigate. Padding quietly down the hall, she had entered the staircase of Lady Mary's tower and there seen her sister-in-law, a fur-trimmed robe wrapped around her, stealing down the stairwell. Puzzled, she had peered out an arrow slit, watching the woman's movements as she ran across the bailey to a small, heavy iron door in the thick wall, which was used for quick and easy passage outside the walls when it was not necessary to open the full gates of Norcastle. Frowning, she saw Lady Mary unlock the door and slowly pull it open. Armed men slipped in the door and darted silently across the empty courtyard.

Marguerite had turned and run down the corridor, shouting to awaken her father and brother. Already the clash of arms sounded in the bailey below, and she could hear the creak of the drawbridge being lowered. Her father, brother and husband appeared in a flash in the hall, swords in hand. Quickly she babbled that there were enemy men inside the castle. They wasted no time with questions, but hastily donned their shields and helmets and ran toward the sounds of fighting. Marguerite had hurried to secure the castle itself, barring all entrances and setting servants at each door to open it if the men of the family or their soldiers were forced to seek shelter. Hurrying up the stairs, she burst into her sister-in-law's room. "What in the name of all the saints have you done?" she cried out in anguish.

Mary knelt at her padded prie-dieu. She turned toward her slowly, her black eyes aflame with an unholy light. "I have saved the earldom for my son."

"What are you talking about? I just saw you let traitors into the bailey. The earl and Henry and Philip have gone out to fight them, but unprepared and ripped open from the inside—my God, Mary, they are bound to lose the day!"

"Yes!" she hissed, and Marguerite realized that her years of isolation had pushed her over the edge of sanity. "Yes, he shall pay for the years of shame he's given me. He shall pay for the pain and humiliation!"

"With his life? With Norcastle? Does your pride require that much remuneration from all us Norwens?"

Mary smiled thinly. "None of you are my friends. You come to visit, yes, but you do not forbid *her* your rooms. You consort with her daily. I have seen you laughing and talking as you sat together sewing. You should have ostracized her. Before God, you are as guilty of sin as your wicked brother!"

"But, Mary, your son!" Marguerite cried.

"I have done it for him! William made me realize that Henry was so besotted with his whore he would abandon his rightful heir, my son, and give the lands and title to his bastard!" Her voice spit venom.

"Who? William? William of York?" She hazarded a guess at one of her family's enemies.

"Yes, and Sir Godfrey, the Beaufort. They have promised to give Norcastle and the title to Richard once Henry is defeated."

"You fool!" Marguerite shook with rage. "Why in the world should they give up what they've won to a mere boy? You have stripped your son of everything, madame. You have murdered him!"

She whirled to find Anne standing on the threshold of the room, frowning. "Mother?" She looked in puzzlement from her mother to her aunt. "What is wrong? What is going on?"

"Your mother has betrayed us all!" Marguerite barked without thinking. "She has gone mad. Come, Anne, we must hurry and get the others." She started past her into the hall, taking the girl's arm.

"No. Wait. What about my mother?"

Heatedly Marguerite started to consign Lady Mary to

the devil, but she stopped. After all, the woman was
Richard's and Anne's mother. She could not leave her
behind to suffer certain death. "Bring her with you. But
we must hurry."

When Anne tried to raise her mother from her kneeling
position, the woman refused, stubbornly insisting she
would be safe and protected, as would her children. It
was only Henry and his spawn of Satan, Gwendolyn's
children, who would fall under the sword. "I haven't time
to waste on you," Marguerite told her flatly. She could
hear heated battle outside and knew that the bailey was
overflowing with traitors. It would not be long before
they defeated the sleepy, half-armed troops of her
family. "Come, Anne, leave her here. Let her meet her
'friends.'"

Tears welled in the girl's eyes. "No, I cannot."

"What do you mean?"

"I am all she has in this world. I cannot leave her."

"But you must!"

"No. Go, save Richard and the others. I will stay with
her and slit her throat before they reach us. I will protect
her from that final humiliation."

"But, Anne, what about yourself?"

She raised great dark eyes to her aunt. "How can I
bear to live, knowing what my mother has done to us
all?"

It was her words that determined Marguerite never to
reveal Lady Mary's perfidy. She dreaded the effect it
would have on Richard. Shaking the dark memory from
her mind, she continued her tale to Elizabeth. "When Sir
Godfrey attacked, these traitors inside the castle turned
upon us. My father and brother were both good warriors
and had many loyal men; but with such a canker there at
the core of their men, they were defeated easily." Her
face looked stretched tight over her bones as she recalled
the sad event. "They were killed, both of them, and
Richard's mother as well. I tried to convince Richard's

sister to flee with us, but she refused to leave her mother. Finally I had to leave Anne in order to save the others. Richard was home visiting before he began his term as a squire. He slept in the top room of one of the towers. My cries did not waken him, but the sound of battle did; and he rushed into the hall, wielding that child's sword of his like a true knight. I awakened Gwendolyn and grabbed up the baby James. I managed to take a few of the family jewels, too. The little girls slept in the front part of the castle, and I ran to rescue them; but the battle outside burst in the front door and through the great hall before I was aware of it. By the time I approached their room, they were cut off from me by the fighting. Praying that the monsters would at least spare two little girls, I had to abandon them." Tears sprang into her eyes at the sad decision. "Of course, they did not. I've lived with that all my life. I should have wakened them sooner, gotten them away. I didn't think quickly or clearly enough. I—I was filled with rage at the betrayal." She paused for a moment, then continued. "We ran out the back door of the hall and across the bailey, taking a secret exit from the castle. Only we family members knew of it. It was our last resort, the method by which we could save the family name if all was lost. None of us ever expected to have to use it, although Henry and my father and I had at various times discussed how I would have to save the heir and slip him out of the castle if we should lose a siege. We escaped into the field beyond, and my husband, Philip, joined us, sent by Henry to guard us. So we fled Sir Godfrey—James and Richard and James's mother and I—with only Philip to protect us. It's a miracle we survived." She smiled briefly at the girl. "Much of Norcastle was destroyed. We had no army left to speak of, no wealth, and York and Sir Godfrey snatched up all the rest of our land. We fled England and went to the court of Mathilde. So, as you see, neither of my boys has led a simple life: almost killed, hunted like wild animals, and then having to endure the poverty we did and the intrigues of the court. We gambled all on our good King Henry's taking the throne and, Mary be praised, he did.

"But favor at court is a slippery thing; and if my nephew seems a little suspicious, that is why. They've known so much treachery in their lives. Sometimes I think that trust is a foreign word to James. At least Richard had the example of his father until he was twelve years old, had the warmth and security of our home. But James fled when he was barely three years old. He remembers little of that life before fear and the treachery."

"Well, he certainly doesn't trust me," Elizabeth said.

Her future aunt smiled mischievously and said, "Well, for that matter, nor do I trust you entirely. You are a Beaufort, you know."

"But—but, madam, you are so nice. I—" Elizabeth broke off and looked down at her hands, blushing. She had almost blurted out childishly that she had thought the other woman liked her.

"I don't condemn until I have all the facts," the other woman said. "Richard has chosen to marry you, and that is reason enough for me to accept you and be kind to you. I am much disposed to like you, but that does not mean that I don't reserve my trust. And I will tell you that I think you should do the same. You have little experience of the world. If what you have told Richard is true, then I think you will be an honest wife; so don't be misled by your naiveté into making some mistakes that will harm that honesty. I am speaking for your own good. Don't do anything that may appear suspicious."

Elizabeth looked at the other woman. She wanted to cry out that she was indeed honest and beg Marguerite to help her, to tell her what to do. She felt so terribly alone, surrounded by strangers, all of whom suspected her. It was as if she walked among hissing vipers, never knowing when a misstep might cause one to strike. But Lady Marguerite was obviously no more her friend than any of the others, and so she could not speak. Instead she gulped and clasped her hands together and willed herself to be calm and silent.

Marguerite looked at the girl's pale face and said, "Here now, don't be frightened of Richard. He is a good, kind man and will remain so if you do not cross him. Be a good wife to him and you shall have no problems. He is an honorable, upright man, a nobleman in the truest sense of the word. He will not harm you; he is gentle with children and women."

"Of course, milady," Elizabeth said, although the woman's words reassured her little. After all, the man was her beloved nephew, almost a son to her. She, of course, would see nothing wrong with him. Her recommendation was hardly one to be relied upon.

The time and the work passed quickly with Lady Marguerite there, for her light chatter made things speed along. Elizabeth noted that she said little of any real importance regarding Norwen's plans or military strength or wealth; rather, she chattered on about fashions and court gossip and all the latest romantic intrigue. Elizabeth, cut off from all such interesting things for the past five years, was more than happy to hear these tidbits. The greatest pleasure, however, was simply to be able to sit there and talk without constraint, to laugh and gossip over her work without constantly listening for the heavy tread of her uncle and without fearing what he might do.

The maids and Marguerite sewed Elizabeth's shimmering wedding dress while Elizabeth's nimble fingers set to work on a wedding tunic for the earl. She traded some of the cloth he had given her to the lady of the keep for a bolt of forest green velvet. Marguerite had brought her a bundle of tippet furs as a wedding present, and Elizabeth used them to trim the cuffs, neck and bottom of his tunic. When she had finished, she was very proud of her work—her uncle might be sending her penniless into this marriage, but at least she would not be shamed by not giving a wedding gift to the earl in return for his generous gifts.

Since Norwen had not sought her out again, Elizabeth was uncertain how to approach him to give him his tunic. It would have been unwise to seek out her uncle any time; one usually stayed out of his way and hoped he would not decide to visit her. Of course, the earl was not the same type as Sir Godfrey, but still—she certainly did not want to incur his wrath by going to him if he did not wish to see her. He might think her presumptuous to seek him out when he had not sent for her—or he might feel that she was spying on him.

She thought of sending the tunic to him by a servant or of asking his aunt to give it to him. However, both those ways were the coward's way out. It was fitting that she give him the gift she had made; anything else seemed a disrespect either to her future husband or to herself. And since her marriage was to take place the next day, there was no time to dither around about it. She had to take the bit in her teeth and approach him.

Her heart was pounding and her clenched hands were clammy with the sweat of fear as she left her quarters and went down to the great hall to find Norwen. What would she do if he was in his room or at his men's quarters below? It never occurred to her that he might not take offense if she sent a servant to him to request that he visit her; her uncle would have beaten her for daring to tell him what to do.

Fortunately, she did not have to face this dilemma, for he was seated by the roaring fire in the great hall. When she saw him, however, she halted and almost turned and fled. Norwen sat leaning against the wall beside the fireplace, his legs stretched out in front of him. He held a goblet in his hand and his face was slightly flushed. He was drinking—and there was nothing more dangerous than a drunken man. His half brother lounged beside him, a mocking smile on his face as he spoke to Norwen. They were the center of a group of men, all laughing and talking loudly and drinking ale. The noise and the overwhelming masculinity of the scene frightened her. Norwen would probably dislike her breaking in on this male camaraderie, and no doubt the presence of the other men would force him to be stern and unyielding.

Elizabeth stood for a moment, uncertain, and Norwen looked up and saw her. Too late—she was caught now. She sucked in her breath, waiting for the explosion, but none came. Instead, a half smile touched his lips and he motioned for her to come forward. She swallowed hard and obeyed him, although it made her stomach knot to walk defenseless into that group of men. However, they all moved aside for her to pass and Richard stood up to greet her with no anger on his face.

Thankfully, she swept him a deep curtsy, but he bent and pulled her up.

"Milady, I am honored by your presence. What brings you into such rough company?" His voice was light and mocking.

"Milord, I would talk to you," she said, still too shy to raise her head. When he said nothing, she added in a rush, "Privately, if it please your lordship."

He chuckled and said, "Then privately it shall be. Excuse me, men, my lady has need of my presence elsewhere."

Richard held out his arm to her and escorted her from the hall. Behind them she heard James's smooth voice and then a burst of ribald laughter. Elizabeth stiffened at the sound.

"I am sorry," he said and patted her hand. "You have little patience with jesting, have you?"

She glanced up at him, not sure what to say. "I—I am unused to it, milord."

"Well, what is your news?"

"Oh—well, actually none—that is, I wanted to give you something. It is upstairs in my chamber."

"Indeed?" He smiled down at her, his curiosity piqued.

She looked at him and felt her tense muscles loosening. It was all right. He was not angry with her or even irritated; in fact, he was actually smiling. He had not even treated her coming to him unsummoned as unusual. On light feet she led him to her room.

When they reached it, she took his tunic from the chest where she had put it and held it out to him. He looked at her in surprise.

"It is my wedding gift to you," she explained.

"But—I did not expect this; I did not mean for you to sew my wedding tunic. That was not why I gave you the cloth—but, wait—this is not from any bolt I gave you. How did you get it?"

"I traded Lady Gertrude one of my bolts for it. The fur Lady Marguerite gave me."

"But why?"

"Why? It is customary, milord. I have some pride; I could not come to you without even a gift."

"Would it burn your tongue to say my name? It is Richard. I am tired of 'milord' this and 'milord' that, as if we did not know each other." He was touched by her gift, given at the cost of time and effort and some of her meager possessions. Yet, at the same time, he was curiously irritated that she had done it not from any feeling for him, but because it was customary, because it touched her pride. So he snapped at her to ease the tangle of feelings in him.

Tears stung her eyes at his tone. "I—I am sorry, mi—I mean, I did not intend to offend you. I thought you would dislike the familiarity."

"Familiarity!" he exclaimed in astonishment. "We are to be wed tomorrow; you will share my bed, have my children, live with me for the rest of our lives—and you do not want to be overly familiar?" Suddenly he threw back his head and began to laugh.

At last he stopped laughing and said, with a little half sigh, "I am sorry, Elizabeth. I should not have been rude to you. It is just that I am irritable and overready to take offense."

Elizabeth stared at him, amazed. He was apologizing to her! That was totally outside her realm of experience. She had no idea how to react.

He smiled at her and said, "Of course, it is all your fault, you know. 'Tis my unsatisfied passion that makes me so."

At those words, she braced herself for another physical onslaught from him. But he only took her hand and kissed it.

"Don't worry; I do not intend to put myself in temptation again—your virtue is safe for another night. But I must go now, or it will not remain so." He paused, not letting go of her hand. "Thank you for the tunic; it is lovely, all the more so because I know how much it cost you. I shall wear it with pride." Again he raised her hands to his lips and then left her.

She watched him go, baffled. How did one deal with a man like this? He was so big, so dark, so overwhelmingly masculine, so uncompromising on some matters—and yet he could be kind, apologetic, generous, thoughtful. Not at all like her uncle. There were nice men; there had to be—her father had been a reasonable man, gentle and loving to his wife and children. But, then, neither had he been a strong man. He had been only a passable warrior, having the skill, but not the inclination. He never quarreled if he could avoid it, never attacked, only defended. He had retained his lands but certainly had not gone out to acquire further land or wealth. What she could not reconcile was that Richard seemed nice, and yet he was so forceful. Most of all, she could not reconcile his kindness with his passion. That lust in his eyes—inwardly she shuddered. How on earth was she to bear it?

She spent a troubled night before her wedding, tossing and turning in her bed, dozing only to have a frightening dream and awake from it to worry about Richard, his nature, her future life, Stephen and, most of all, the first night of her marriage. By the time daylight came, Elizabeth was exhausted.

Her maids bustled in to help her dress. They combed out her fine-spun hair, leaving it to flow loose—the sign of a virgin—down her back in a glimmering waterfall. She donned her white underdress, then the heavy silver, gold and white brocade kirtle over that, loosely belted with a long, golden chain that hung around her waist and fell smoothly down the front of her dress to her ankles. The chain was brought to her by Marguerite, who smiled and said she did not need it and had realized that it was just the thing to finish off that gown.

It was lovely with the dress, Elizabeth agreed, and she could not be so rude as to refuse it; but it pulled heavily at her waist—it and the thick brocade weighing her down. Encumbering, frightening—like the family, even Marguerite, hard, strong, suspicious, ever ready to gobble her up.

With Marguerite by her side she at last went down to the chapel, and there they stood waiting for her: his men; his big blond uncle; James, sleek and forbidding, and Richard, so tall, so dark, so handsome in the rich green velvet she had made for him that he seemed overwhelming to her. He would crush her, she thought, moving forward mechanically. And there were her uncle and cousins, let out to attend the ceremony and to give their forced approval. They glared at her with hatred, and she shivered under their gaze. That way was certain death; she had no hope but Norwen!

It seemed to take forever under everyone's unbending gaze, but at last she reached the earl's side. He took her hand silently and they faced the priest. The wedding mass was long and exhausting. Elizabeth's knees hurt from kneeling and her back and shoulders ached from the weight of her dress. Toward the end, she began to tremble; and Richard's arm went around her to hold her up. When it was over, he pulled her to her feet and, supporting her firmly, led her down the aisle.

Somehow she managed to smile at their guests as she walked and even at the serfs outside who shouted their blessings upon them. They entered the hall of the keep and, thankfully, she sank down into her chair beside Richard at the head of the table.

A sumptuous feast followed the wedding, but Elizabeth's stomach was too knotted to partake of the many foods lying on the table in front of her. Roast boar, venison, pheasant, goose, cheeses, meat pies, candied fruits, sweets weighed down the boards; but none could tempt her appetite. She barely nibbled at what Richard laid upon her plate and sipped sparingly of the heavy mulled wine in their shared goblet.

There were jugglers and jesters for their entertainment, and then music for dancing. The others entered into it wholeheartedly; but, after one dance with her new husband for form's sake, Elizabeth demurred. She felt only weariness, and the mirth and merriment just frayed her nerves. She wanted only to get away from it all, to face the coupling and be done with it. Richard, however, seemed to feel none of her reservations. He partook liberally of the wine and food, laughed heartily at the jesters and danced with his aunt and the ladies of the household. Elizabeth watched him, resenting his ease.

Sir Godfrey surveyed the gathering with an even more jaundiced eye than his niece. The gaiety contrasted harshly with his own ill mood. Norwen had soundly defeated him, not only foiling Godfrey's plans to defeat him, but also gaining a claim on lands Godfrey held. He had no illusions that the earl would not attack him for Elizabeth's dower lands. Nor did he delude himself that Norwen would not defeat him in open battle. The earl and the Bastard both were renowned fighters, and they had a large, well-trained army and enough land and wealth to sustain them. The best he would be able to do was stave them off.

No, it was obvious to him that the only way he could defeat Norwen was through treachery. The earl's security around himself was inpenetrable, almost impossible to get an assassin through, and it would be certain death for him after the deed; so it would be difficult to find one willing to risk it. Far better someone on the inside, who could do it secretly and not be discovered. But who? Which of the earl's men would assume the risk and dishonor for the reward—and what a reward it would have to be! Thoughtfully he looked around the hall— where was the potential traitor among all these smiling, loyal faces? Sir Robert, the castellan, would be the easiest, but Godfrey doubted his courage; besides, he was not close enough to Norwen—the earl would soon leave his keep and probably not see him for a year or more. It must be someone in his retinue, someone—but wait! Over and over his eyes had slid past one man, dismissing him as too close; but there—he looked at him closely—there, in all this ludicrous swell of fellowship and harmony, was the one jarring note: James.

James sat looking at the newlyweds, and out of all the warm, friendly faces only his was cold and clear as a statue's. Of course! That had been his very first idea—to turn James into a traitor. In his concentration on Elizabeth, he had forgotten it. Illegitimacy always carried with it the dark shadow of envy and discontent. James must have stood there all those years in his brother's shadow, much more a physical replica of their father, and yet not entitled to his name or any of his possessions. His mother had been a whore, and he must have endured the torments of a whore's child. Handsome, skillful, intelligent, with Norwen blood running through his veins, he must have bitterly watched as his brother gained title to all the lands they had won together.

It was obvious that he did not favor this marriage; he watched the bride and groom with eyes like marble. The earl had to be thirty or thirty-two—rather late to be marrying. Perhaps James had come to believe he would not marry and produce an heir. Of course, James could not inherit the title; nor could he legally inherit the land. But, as no legitimate heir was closer than a second cousin, it was not at all inconceivable that he could claim the land by force of arms. With Richard's blessing, with the fact that he had been second-in-command and could hold the obedience of Richard's army after his death, with the fact that he would be sitting there at Norcastle, already in possession, and any true heir would have to attack, he could more than likely hold the majority of Norwen's land—but only if Richard did not have a son. A son would have the lands, title, and army—no chance for a bastard brother then.

Perhaps he had some feeling for his legitimate brother (though that was hard for Godfrey to conceive of, having hated his own full brother all his life); certainly he had no liking for Elizabeth. Surely he could, at the worst, be persuaded to harm Elizabeth and Stephen. And, since Elizabeth had so foiled his plans, Godfrey had a burning desire to see her ruined and killed—no one could cross him and not pay for it. But if he was fortunate, with the possibility of an heir to displace him, James would be willing to betray his brother as well.

Sir Godfrey made his way toward James and said casually, "Norwen entertains well for such a hasty wedding."

James turned to him and appraised him coolly. "We Norwens believe in doing everything well."

Godfrey sketched a bow. "But, of course, the earl can afford it. We younger brothers do not fare so well."

"No, I suppose not." The beautifully molded face was devoid of expression.

"I was somewhat surprised, I confess. But then my niece is a very convincing wench. I remember her mother could always wrap my brother around her finger." No harm in adding to James's suspicions of Elizabeth.

James studied him, and under his gaze the older man felt the same queasy flicker of fear he felt when a serpent slid across his path.

"You do not sound overly fond of your niece."

Sir Godfrey shrugged. "She is biddable only when it suits her self-interest." He smiled maliciously and said, "But, then, we Beauforts are known for cunning and wit, not loyalty."

Some wild flame leaped in the hazel eyes and died immediately. "Yes, I know something of Beaufort traits."

"Come, come. I have heard of your ambitions and schemes. You are for yourself. Can you say that you would not have taken a ripe plum like Norcastle? Your father's licentiousness and weak will ruined him and his entire family. Women were his downfall—and that seems to be a family trait."

For a moment, he feared that he had gone too far, for the Bastard's whole body tensed as if to spring and his face flamed with hatred. But then he relaxed and his face settled back into its customary mask.

"What is your point?" James asked crisply. "I know you are not just wanting to chat with me."

"Just this: my niece has thwarted my plans—and I suspect that she has hurt yours somewhat, too."

"What do you mean?"

"Well, now she will provide Norwen with an heir, and you will have no chance at the Norwen lands."

"You forget that I cannot inherit, regardless," James said bitterly.

"You know you could have retained at least some of the land if Richard had no heir, title or no title."

"Well, that is past history now."

"Not necessarily. Not if we join forces. Your brother might not have an heir."

James looked at him for a long, chilling moment. "You mean kill Norwen?"

Sir Godfrey could hardly suppress a smile. He had

leaped to assume Norwen must die, not Elizabeth; that meant killing his brother was already lurking in his mind.

"God's blood, man, you are daft!" James continued. "Murder my own blood kin? I am no saint, but— fratricide!"

"Calm yourself. I did not suggest such. But what if Lady Elizabeth was dead? Or, better yet, kidnapped and in my possession but still alive, so he could not remarry and produce a legitimate heir?"

"Why should you wish to harm your niece?"

"She betrayed me. She thought up this plot to ruin Norwen, and then she enslaved his passions and so betrayed me. I want my revenge on her.

"But more than that. I need her dower lands and Stephen's lands. I need Stephen in my possession and Elizabeth, too. And I need a friend who has the earl's ear and can counteract the evils she will plot against me. In return, I can pay you—and I know a bastard is always in need of gold. Moreover, I'll put Elizabeth out of your way and keep the earl from producing a legitimate heir."

"Don't be a fool. I would not betray my brother in any way," James said quickly.

Too quickly, Sir Godfrey thought. He's denying his wishes. "Think, think," he urged him. "Could you not use the gold? What harm would it be to the earl to rid him of those two?"

James looked at him thoughtfully. "It would really be a service to Richard, would it not? He would be better off without her and that weakling brother."

"Why, yes—and there would be no heir."

"No heir." For a moment he seemed about to give in, but then he stopped and said, "No, no, I must give this some thought. You are a snake, Godfrey, and I have no wish to be bitten."

Elizabeth glanced around the room. Her eyes chanced to light on James and her uncle in deep conversation, and a chill of fear went through her. Even when James turned and walked away, she did not feel easy; there had been no animosity on his face, only a thoughtful expression. What if they were conspiring? Was James as loyal to Norwen as his brother thought? Certainly a meeting between those two boded her no good. And perhaps it endangered Norwen as well. If the earl fell, she and Stephen were without hope.

Sir Godfrey looked up and saw her eyes upon him, and he started toward her. Hastily she turned away, seeking some group of people as a refuge. She did not feel that she could stand her uncle, not today, already so weary and anxious as she was. But before she could find a haven, he was by her side, taking her arm in his hand and squeezing until it hurt.

"Well, niece, you think you have played me a fine trick, don't you?"

"I don't know what you mean," Elizabeth replied coolly, refusing to cry out at his grip.

"Don't play the fool with me. I know you and your treacherous ways. You betrayed me."

"How dare you talk to me this way! I am the Countess of Norwen now; my husband could squash you like a bug," she said, with a good deal more bravado than she felt. Just the sight of Sir Godfrey filled her with the familiar icy dread.

He dug his fingers into her arm harder and she winced at the pain. He decided it would not hurt to let her feel some of the old intimidation and fear. Besides, it might help to make her suspicious of James; nothing would suit him better than to have the two brothers fighting each other instead of him.

"Don't think you are too safe, wench. Kin are not always loyal, especially bastard ones. There are those inside this castle who are friendly to me."

Elizabeth felt the blood draining out of her face. It was as likely as not that her uncle lied. And yet she had just

seen them talking together quietly—it was possible.
James had despised her from the beginning. Would he
hesitate to engineer her death? Was he really even loyal
to his brother, the earl? His face was so cold and
unreadable; he could mask all manner of treachery.

"You are his dupe, then," she said to disguise her fear.
"You are a vicious, evil man, uncle; but, more than that,
you are a fool, and you shall certainly die a fool."

His free hand lashed out and slapped her cheek, and
her head buzzed with pain.

From across the room, Richard saw Sir Godfrey
approach his bride. He saw him clutch her arm and saw
her evident pain and fear. Immediately he excused
himself from the conversation he was engaged in and
walked toward them. When he was halfway across the
room, he saw her lift her chin and say something to her
uncle; and her uncle responded with a slap across her
cheek. With a primitive, inarticulate cry of rage, he ran
toward them, his hand instinctively flying to his sword. It
was not there, for on this festive occasion he had left off
his weapons; so, snarling, he hurled himself at Sir
Godfrey, his huge hands fastening upon the man's
throat.

Elizabeth screamed as he hurtled past her, tearing her
uncle away and throwing him against the wall. His hands
dug into Sir Godfrey's throat, and Godfrey flailed at him
in vain. For an instant everyone stood stunned, and then
suddenly they lurched into action. Two men-at-arms ran
to Elizabeth to stand on either side of her, swords drawn,
guarding her from attack. James and several men ran to
Norwen and pried him loose from Godfrey. It took four
of them to pull him away and restrain him until the red
rage left his brain. Sir Godfrey slid to his knees, purple in
the face and gasping for air.

At last, Norwen took a long breath and stopped
straining against his captors. James, seeing that reason
had returned to his eyes, loosed his hold and nodded to

the other men to do likewise. Norwen stood, still sucking in calming breaths, until he was again fully in control of his anger.

Then he spoke. "I will not mar my wedding day by letting blood. But let me give you fair warning: should you ever again raise a hand against my wife, you will be dead on the spot. I swear it by the Virgin Mother. She is no longer in your brutal care. The Lady Elizabeth is now my wife, the Countess of Norwen, and any offense to her is an offense to me. Is that clear?"

Weakly Sir Godfrey nodded. Richard turned and signaled the silenced musicians to begin again. Then he turned and walked to Elizabeth.

She stared at him in amazement. It did not surprise her that Norwen would not like Sir Godfrey interfering with him in any way, including striking his wife. But his ferocity in attacking her uncle, his anger, his fierce protectiveness—those things surprised her very much, indeed. What had sparked such wildness? It was frightening to see that power unleashed—what would he do to her if she angered him? Yet it was gratifying, too, to be defended so; it showed she had value and proved she would be protected from outside forces. It showed—well, it showed that he cared for her. Didn't it?

"Are you all right?" He bent over her solicitously, and she could feel the heat emanating from him, hear his still uneven breaths.

Elizabeth nodded, a little afraid to look up at him. He touched her shining hair.

"You are so beautiful. It makes me sick to think of one such as he daring to hurt such loveliness."

So he did not want her pretty face marred by a blow. Well, that was understandable, since that was one of the things he had wanted to buy with this marriage, she thought bitterly. She could smell the liquor on his breath. He had been drinking heavily. She had forgotten that; that explained his enormous reaction to the blow. He was drunk and therefore excitable and vicious, as men so often were when drunk. For some reason, she felt disappointment.

"I am fine," she said crisply and looked up at him.

The look in his eyes almost took away her breath. His fine dark eyes blazed down at her, black as coal and yet burning, whether in anger or in passion she was not sure. The intensity of his feeling shook her, and she forgot what she had intended to say next.

"I think I am ready for bed." His voice was a little unsteady. "I will tell Aunt Marguerite to begin the bedding ceremony."

Abruptly he turned and left her. Elizabeth stared after him. Forgotten was the sting of her uncle's hand; she could feel only the cold knife of fear that pierced her vitals at his words. At last it had come; she could no longer avoid it: he was going to take her now. Fear turned her numb; she stood rooted to the spot, afraid she might break down right there in front of them all. When Marguerite came to her and took her hand, she looked at the woman as if she were a stranger. The panic that encased her made her feel very far away from the Norwen woman.

"Why, child, your hands are like ice," Marguerite exclaimed, taking one hand in both of hers. She leaned in toward her sympathetically. "Are you afraid? There, now, don't be; it does not hurt overmuch. I know my Richard; he will be gentle. You will discover that it is—oh, quite wonderful. Really. Well, I can see by your expression that you are too scared to even comprehend what I am saying. Come along; the best thing to reassure you is to just get it over with."

She put her arm around the girl and guided her from the great hall. Marguerite, raised in the security and love of her father and brother, had no inkling of the abysmal fear that engulfed Elizabeth, of the bone-chilling terror of pain and domination that turned the girl waxen and stiff.

The other women of the castle fell in around them, eagerly chattering and giggling and enviously remarking on the wealth, handsomeness and broad proportions of Elizabeth's groom. Their noise buzzed around the girl, swelling her panic, until a stern look from Marguerite quelled them all into silence. They escorted her to the bridal chamber and helped her to disrobe. Marguerite brushed her long hair until it floated like spun gold down her back and front, barely concealing her full, pink-tipped breasts. Everyone exclaimed over her pure white body, slender and unmarked by blemishes, dainty yet firm and rounded.

The men burst into the room, laughing and making coarse comments, Richard in the forefront, belt and tunic already removed. Elizabeth blushed and stood stonily staring in front of her, her numbness blessedly isolating her from much of the embarrassment she would have felt normally at the frank, admiring stares directed at her naked body.

Marguerite shot a meaningful glance at James and her husband, and quickly the three of them shuttled the crowd out the door, leaving the couple finally alone. Elizabeth remained rooted to the spot, and Richard's hungry eyes lingeringly moved over her. She was so delicate, all ivory and pale gold, her hands and feet and face so fragile, her eyes grave green pools. Yet how enticingly she was put together, her arms and legs smooth and firm, her narrow waist flowing into her smooth, creamy abdomen. And above her waist her fine golden hair barely concealed her full breasts, the pink nipples peeking through the golden veil. And there, where legs and torso joined, the soft tuft of glinting golden hair that hid her womanhood, the center of her femininity, soon to be revealed to him in all its secret splendor.

"God's blood, you are lovely," he said at last, his voice choked and tight, and hastily began to remove the rest of his garments.

Her heart pounding, Elizabeth kept her eyes modestly

on the floor while he undressed. But when she heard him move toward her, she looked up. His lean brown body was fully naked now, and she could see how spare and muscular he was, leather tough, without an ounce of fat or softness anywhere. His chest was wide and covered with hair as black as that on his head; his arms were heavy, and his legs long and corded with muscles. Power and masculinity exuded from him like a scent. But Elizabeth did not notice the lithe, animal beauty of his body nor feel any stirring of sympathy for the raised, light battle scars that creased his body here and there.

All she could see was his distended manhood, stiff and swollen with desire for her. Like a spear it hung between his legs—the huge male weapon he would use to defeat and degrade her. With a cry she stumbled back from him. It terrified her to think how he would pierce her with that shaft, would humble and humiliate her.

Richard stopped in surprise. Although desire ran through him like liquid fire, clouding his mind and pushing him forward, he saw the real terror in her eyes, and it halted him. What had he done that was so frightening? Surely she had to know what the marriage bed entailed; surely she had seen a naked man before. The times were rough and hard, and life and sex were neither one prettied up and sugar-coated. Sir Godfrey certainly wouldn't have taken care to shelter her.

Some fear he could understand—facing something one had not experienced before—was always a little frightening. But that wild panic on her face went far beyond normal fear.

"Am I so fearful?" he said lightly. "Come, what frightens you so?"

Elizabeth could not speak, only backed further away from him. Slowly, softly, he followed her, careful not to startle her, speaking to her in a low, soothing voice. He had spoken this way before to a horse maddened by blood and fear, or to a lad almost paralyzed at the sight of his first battle. Steadily the girl went backward until she ran into the bed, and then she stopped, a look on her face like an animal backed into a corner.

"Shh. I will not harm you. Come, lass, I do not want to hurt you. There, now; there, steady. You are far too lovely to look so beleaguered. Let me help you." He moved slowly toward her until at last he was close enough to reach out and grasp her arm.

With his hand securely around her waist, he breathed a little sigh of relief. For a moment he had been afraid that she would run screaming out the door. Gently he made her lie down on the bed with him and wrapped his arms around her for comfort and warmth.

"What is it that makes you fear me so? Is it my anger downstairs at your uncle? I did not mean to frighten you. I was furious when I saw him strike you. To see him hurt you—you so frail and pretty, and he such a filthy, sneaky beast—it enraged me; I wanted to kill him. But I would not act that way to you; it is not my normal manner.

"Do you fear that I am like Sir Godfrey? Do you think that all men are of his ilk, and that I will beat you whenever you displease me, or that I will take my anger at others out on you? Believe me, it is not so. I have never struck a woman, even a maidservant. Even in a rage like this afternoon, I know how mismatched a lady is against me."

His tone calmed Elizabeth, although his words only half penetrated her brain; and she was able to regain the self-control that had almost slipped from her grasp entirely. He could sense the change in her, although she remained stiff in his arms.

"Is it this that frightens you?" he asked, stroking her arm softly. "Marriage? A husband? Sex? You told me at the beginning that you did not wish to sleep with me. Why? Am I more fearsome than other men?"

Silently she shook her head, and he continued, "Then all men frighten you? Because of Godfrey?"

She did not answer, and he sighed. He was a kind man

and hated to frighten her. But lust for her was throbbing in him; the feel of her soft, sweet flesh in his arms excited him almost past bearing. He had wanted her for days now and had waited patiently to take her, so that her honor would be undamaged. He was a man used to succeeding, accustomed to taking what he wanted. Now he wanted her, and she was rightfully his; and to have to abstain from taking her was frustrating, maddening— worse, almost impossible to do.

Richard did not understand her fear and reluctance, and it irritated him that she would not explain it. Like his aunt, he had no experience with her situation. Because of his size and prowess with a sword, he had never been physically frightened and intimidated. If blows were exchanged, he was always the winner. When he was a lad and had been chased from England by Sir Godfrey had been the only time a powerful force had almost crushed him; but then he had been too filled with rage and horror and bitter sorrow at the loss of his family for fear to gain control of him.

He bent to kiss her neck, then nibbled lightly at her ear. The sweet scent of her was dizzying, and he ached to part her legs and enter her secret, sealed inner self.

"It is not unbearably painful, I understand," he said, his breath hot and rasping against her ear. "It is a brief hurt when I pierce your maidenhead, nothing more. Once it is done, you will take pleasure, I swear it. There's nothing for it but to do it. It is over in an instant, and then you need no longer fear." It seemed to Richard that the best thing he could do was go ahead and get it over for her. It was always that way with battle; once you were into it, the nervousness and fear would vanish. The unknown was always more frightening.

Elizabeth, again in control of herself despite her fear, knew he was right. She might as well go ahead and endure it. It was something she was going to have to do for the rest of her life. She chastised herself for her weakness; surely it was not too high a price to pay to save herself and Stephen. She had struck a bargain with him, and this was her payment. Although she was still stiff with fright, she knew she had to bring out her courage and give him what he wanted. Norwen had been amazingly patient with her, but she would be a fool to struggle or beg him to not take her, thereby angering him.

"Yes, go ahead, then, please," Elizabeth said through bloodless lips.

Richard smiled and bent to take her mouth in a consuming kiss. Under the force of his lips, Elizabeth's lips parted, and his tongue slid into her mouth, eagerly probing the warm cavity of her mouth. His big hands roamed over her body, delving into the silken mass of her hair, caressing her legs and stomach, cupping her breasts and hardening the nipples with his battle-hardened fingers. Again and again he kissed her until she was breathless, while his hands sought out every part of her body. At last his mouth left hers to travel to her ears and gently nibble at her lobes, then trail kisses down the soft skin of her neck. He kissed her breast, sucking gently at the nipple, making lazy rings around it with his tongue.

So isolated was she by her fear that Richard's kisses and caresses had no effect on Elizabeth. His lips tickled against her ears and neck, but the pleasurable sensations died before they could reach her brain. Despite his efforts, she remained cold and unyielding beneath him.

Richard slipped his hand between her legs and gently opened them. His fingers trembled at the feel of the soft, silver-gold fuzz between her legs, and his turgid manhood throbbed with desire. He knew she was not ready for him, but he could wait no longer. He rolled on top of her and spread her legs wider with his own legs; slowly, as gently as he could, he entered her. Her tender tissue tore under his pressure, and Elizabeth bit back a cry of pain. Quickly he rode out his passion, thrusting into her repeatedly. Every thrust was painful to her, and she longed to cry out to him to stop as she tightened every muscle against the hurtful invasion.

When at last he shuddered to a stop and then rolled off her to fall asleep beside her, she lay awake in her pain and humiliation. How awful, how degrading to lie like that beneath him, split, pierced, helplessly speared upon his staff like a fish who cannot wriggle free. Oh, God, to have to endure that whenever he wished to take her. Fiercely she wished that she were a man so that she could fight for her lands and protect her brother with her own strength and skill, instead of being doomed to purchase those things with her shame and degradation. Slowly a hot tear slid from her eye and rolled onto her pillow.

Downstairs the feasting continued. Godfrey, recovered from his close brush with death, balefully watched the merriment. Unfortunately there were a few men who drank nothing and stuck close to Sir Godfrey's side—his guards, he thought bitterly, parading as participants at the feast to preserve the image of a wedding with his consent, but nevertheless obviously his wardens.

Everyone else in the hall was swilling down liquor—most noticeably, James. At last, as the lights in the sconces lining the walls guttered and dimmed as the evening wore on, James made his way unsteadily toward Sir Godfrey. At a glance from him, the guards fell back.

James sat down beside him and said in a low voice, "You are right. My brother is better removed from Lady Elizabeth's influence. Tonight, the insane way he attacked you, it proved to me how deeply in her sway he already is. She should be removed, and Stephen, also. My brother would be better off dead than tied to her."

Godfrey gazed at the other man, savoring the satisfaction. James was obviously drunk and just as obviously needed to rationalize his actions. He could not admit to himself his real reasons for doing what he did, could not accept his hatred of Norwen and his desire to see him dead and the lands in his possession. But Godfrey knew that he had him. Once James was ensnared in his web, Sir Godfrey could lead him in deeper and deeper. Before long he would have all of them—Richard, Elizabeth and James—at each other's throats.

"All right," he said at last, "then let us get down to business. Once I am at home again, I will let you know how I will need your help."

"When do I get paid?"

"When the work is finished."

"And the amount?"

Sir Godfrey smiled a little at the other's eagerness. "It depends on what you do for me. For information the price is less than for an actual deed."

James glowered at him darkly. "Don't think that you can cheat me, you knave. I'll slit your gullet if you try to cheat me."

"I will not cheat you—as long as you are honest with me," the older man said smoothly, and rose. "And now I think I shall take my escort to my chambers. The festivities have wearied me. I shall be in touch with you soon."

He strode away, leaving James sitting by himself. His face expressionless, James stared down into his cup of wine. The dying light slanted down across his face, eerily lighting the bones and making his eyes great pools of shadow, turning his features into something chillingly handsome and yet almost inhuman.

Chapter Nine

ELIZABETH AWAKENED, FEELING ABNORMALLY WARM AND cozy in her bed. For a moment she did not remember where she was or why it felt this way. And then in a rush it came back to her—the pain of the night before, the fright. Cautiously she turned over to look at her new husband; he lay close beside her, sprawled in sleep. His great body emanated heat; that was the reason the bed felt so warm. At her movement, he woke up and looked at her. Elizabeth froze, not wanting him to repeat what he had done to her the night before, and yet not knowing what movement on her part might cause him to do that again. Richard smiled at her, unaware of her feelings, and reached up to take a strand of her hair between his fingers.

"Your hair is the color of the dawn coming through that window," he said softly, and then smiled a little with embarrassment. "You make me wax poetic. It is not something I am accustomed to being."

141

Elizabeth felt irritated at his cheerful good spirits when she herself felt so awful. She moved slightly in her irritation, and the bed covering slipped lower to reveal one rounded breast. Norwen grinned and looked unabashedly at her exposed body. He reached out to touch her and instinctively Elizabeth scooted back from him. Immediately she feared she had angered him; but he said nothing, merely looked at her and frowned in puzzlement.

"Am I still an ogre to you?" he asked. "Don't be that way; you know me now, and that pain you had last night—it will not come to you again. That is finished. From now on you will taste only the pleasures, as I do."

He moved toward her, sliding his arms around her. She winced at the feel of his arms upon her back, and he drew away from her.

"What is amiss? Why do you flinch from me like this?"

Elizabeth hastily said, "It is not you, milord—I mean, Richard. It is just that to force me to go along with his plans my uncle beat me. My back is still sore from that."

Richard's brows drew together fiercely, and he commanded her to turn around so that he could examine her back. At the sight of the purpling bruises and the welts raised by her uncle's belt, he cursed long and loud.

"I ought to kill him!" he burst out. "He is an animal to use you thus. I should have throttled him last night. It is no wonder that you fear men so. You have no reason to know that I am not like your uncle. What else has he done to you? What force did he apply to make you come to me?" Earnestly he seized her wrists and held her so that she had to look at him. "What did he do to make you fear my bed so much? Did he tell you that I was cruel, that I practiced some form of perversity in bed? What? What did he tell you about me?"

"I swear, he did not tell me that."

"Then why do you fear me so?"

Elizabeth gulped, not knowing what to say. Anything she might say could anger him, and yet if she did not answer it would anger him as well. "It is only—only that it was so painful. I felt—" Tears welled up in her eyes against her volition. "Please, milord, I know that it is a woman's lot in life. I swear that I shall grow accustomed to it. I promise not to flinch and pull away."

"By the Virgin, you are a stubborn wench!" he exclaimed. "Why will you not simply answer me straight out?"

Angered, Elizabeth snapped back, "Because you frighten me! You are so huge, so strong, you could crush me in an instant like a bug. I am wholly in your power. Is that not enough to make me afraid? What you did to me last night—it was ugly, disgusting. Like Geoffrey."

His face darkened. "And who is this Geoffrey?"

"Sir Godfrey's other son, the one who remained outside the walls with the army. He always looked at me in the same way you do. He waited for me in the halls and would kiss me and fondle me. He—" Suddenly, to her amazement and embarrassment, Elizabeth began to cry.

"He what?" her husband demanded, his face stony.

"Whenever he could catch me, or when his father allowed him to in order to punish or frighten me, Geoffrey would run his hands over me and pinch me—on my breasts or the inside of my thighs, everywhere it was most painful. He threw me to the ground and ground his body against mine. He said that when his father allowed him to take me, he would do terrible things to me, hurt me, abase me. And when he tired of me, he said he would offer me to his men to use." The memory rose and flooded out in tears. Her body was wracked with sobs.

The earl stared at her for a moment in shock, then leaped from the bed roaring, "God damn him—damn his soul to everlasting hell!" His face was contorted with rage. "I'll kill Godfrey now; I'll run him through this instant! What kind of a brute is he to allow his son to do such a thing to you? He is insane. And, as for Geoffrey, when next we meet, I'll kill him with my own hands. I'll spit him like a chicken. I'll cut out his heart."

Richard stormed around the room until finally his rage cooled and he was able to speak more rationally. He came to Elizabeth and sat on the bed beside her, and pulled her into his arms to hold her gently until her tears subsided.

Then he said, "It will be all right. You are safe now, Elizabeth. Nothing like that will ever happen to you again, I swear it. Now, wipe away your tears and wash your face; otherwise everyone will think I have been cruel to you." He smiled at her and she managed a watery smile in return.

She rose and went to wash her face as he requested. She also washed the blood on her inner thighs and tried not to think about the soreness there. She called her maid to help her dress and braid her hair. Then she covered her head with the fashionable wimple, though her husband laughingly protested at her covering up her hair.

When they were dressed, they proceeded downstairs. There Marguerite immediately whisked Elizabeth away from Richard and took her back to her rooms to continue their sewing on Elizabeth's other dresses. With a wink, she handed Elizabeth a little vial of cream and told her that it would soothe where Richard had hurt her. Marguerite, sensing that something was wrong, pressed the girl to confide in her. But Elizabeth, even though she felt a desire to let out her anxiety about the pain she had felt the night before and what she feared to feel in the future, about her fear of men in general and what her life would be like with Richard, could not talk to Marguerite about it. There was no doubt in her mind that Marguerite would accept no criticism of her beloved Richard. She was too ashamed to tell Marguerite of her uncle's iniquities and too afraid that Marguerite would turn against her if she complained about Richard. So she maintained her silence, despite her new aunt's probing questions.

Meanwhile, Richard settled himself in the great hall

and sent for Sir Godfrey and his sons. His anger had burned down to a cool flame; it did not show in his manner but strengthened his determination to thwart Sir Godfrey. When the men were ushered in, he acknowledged them coolly and said, "I am certain that you gentlemen will wish to leave immediately now that the festivities are over. We will miss you, but of course you are free to go. However, I think that you will agree with me that it is only fit that your nephew Stephen remain here with his sister and me. I think his new brother is a far better guardian than an uncle, don't you agree? I have already sent a messenger to the king requesting him to make Stephen my ward. I am sure he will give his consent; after all, your education of Lord Beaufort has been somewhat lacking, has it not? I have found that the lad knows nothing of fighting or arms or how to govern his own property when he reaches his majority. I believe that the king will agree that you are not a fitting guardian."

Anger flamed in Sir Godfrey's face. "You cannot keep him! Unless and until the king changes it, I am Stephen's appointed guardian, not you. It violates the laws for you to keep him; he must return with me!"

"I would not allow a dog to remain in your care, much less a child," the earl said fiercely. "Be careful how you tread with me today, Sir Godfrey. My wife has told me of the ways you used to try to persuade her to do your evil deeds. God knows, I never bore you any love, but today it is almost more than I can do to refrain from having you drawn and quartered right here. I suggest that you be thankful for your life and get you and your sons out of my sight as quickly as possible. Oh, and another thing: I want to make you a promise. It is this: I am letting you go today because you are my wife's kinsman, and I do not wish to spoil our wedding festivities with your death; however, in the future I promise you that I will show you no leeway. I promise you I will not rest until I have killed you with my own hand. You are a filthy creature who does not deserve to live, and I shall take it upon myself to remove the blot of your presence from this world. Do I make myself clear? Now go back to your castle and sit there and shake in dread, for I will come after you."

Godfrey swallowed; he felt sick at his stomach. He had no doubt that Norwen would do as he said. He was a man of unswerving purpose. Godfrey could see his doom stretched out before him. Quickly he turned and left the room, his sons following upon his heels.

While Elizabeth and Marguerite sewed, they talked of many things, but not of what concerned Elizabeth most. Elizabeth had never confided in anyone, except perhaps Stephen; it had always been too dangerous. And, just as Marguerite did not completely trust her, Elizabeth felt that she could not trust Marguerite in anything regarding her nephew. So Elizabeth maintained her silence about her married life with Richard, about the night that caused her pain and anxiety, about the fears and worries she had concerning her new husband.

The following night Richard tried to be as gentle and slow with Elizabeth as he could, keeping in mind the agony she had suffered with Geoffrey and the way it must have set her against all men. His desire was like a flame that grew ever hotter; it did not decrease with possession of her body, but rather grew more and more each time. The beauty of her slender body, her perfectly molded face, her flowing silver-gold hair never failed to entice him. He found that he thought about her all the time, even when he was away from her. And, by the time night fell, he was always burning with passion for her. He felt sorry for her, but he could not refrain from wanting her. Carefully he tried to build passion in her, caressing her, kissing her, lingering over her body until he felt that he would die with wanting her.

His efforts were not without success, although he saw little evidence of it. Each night the pain when he entered her grew less and less. Gradually, as she grew familiar with him and came to realize deep inside her that he would not ultimately hurt her as Geoffrey had, she began to relax more and more. And, as her muscles grew less tight, the pain grew smaller until at last, after several nights, she did not feel pain at all. However, neither did she feel any pleasure. She lay passively beneath him, enduring his attentions. Try as he would, Richard could not bring her to pleasure; and he found that it was harder for him to reach fulfillment if she felt nothing.

Secretly he hoped that matters would be different between them once they were back at Norcastle. There she would feel more secure from her uncle and all others, more protected. There she would be the mistress of her own household and could occupy herself happily. Once they were settled together, it would be better; it had to be.

After a week of waiting, the party set out for Norcastle. Elizabeth found herself strangely reluctant to leave Marguerite. She had become attached to the woman and feared being left alone with the male household of her husband. She astonished both herself and Marguerite by hugging the older woman fiercely and crying that she did not know what she would do without her.

Marguerite patted her sympathetically and said, "There, there, child. I promise I shall come to visit you when you bear Richard a child. That will be a good time. I shall come then and see you through the birth of your first baby."

That did not ease the girl's fears any, for she feared that she might fail in her duty and not produce an heir. On the other hand, she also was afraid of bearing a child, for she could remember well that her mother had died in childbirth with Stephen.

No one else shared her apprehensions about leaving. James and Richard were anxious to be home and secure in their fortress once again. And Stephen looked forward with glee to living in Norcastle with his idols and there learning all the arts of war that he had been so long denied. Looking at his happy face, Elizabeth reminded herself how much she had gained. She had done the right thing; there was no doubt about it. She might be uneasy about James, and she might dislike her duties in the marital bed; but nothing would ever be bad for her and Stephen, as it had been when they lived with Sir Godfrey.

It took them three days to reach the fastness of Norcastle; and, although Elizabeth was well cared for and had a tent to sleep in at night and a litter to carry her when she grew tired of riding her horse, she was quite weary by the end of the journey and very much relieved to see the fortress loom up in front of them. Stephen was riding beside her on a horse that Norwen had chosen for him when they first caught sight of Norcastle.

"There it is!" he cried, pointing. "Oh, Elizabeth, isn't it wonderful? Richard told me that he and James will begin to teach me as soon as we settle down; and, with the winter coming on, he says we will be able to practice a good deal."

"Yes, how wonderful," Elizabeth said, feeling a little spurt of jealousy at Stephen's obvious attachment to her husband. No matter how much she reasoned with herself, she could not quite accept the fact that she was no longer Stephen's whole world.

As they rode closer, Elizabeth could see how gigantic the castle really was.

Limewashed, it glittered a stark white in the autumn sun, dominating the countryside around it. Norcastle was built to guard the entrance to a valley and stood on flat ground. A wide moat surrounded the thick walls, and trees had been cut down around the castle to provide a bare "killing ground" for enemy troops. It was built in a square, with a fat bulge at one corner where the old keep lay. A wide, flat, bare piece of land jutted from the old round keep to the moat beyond. Diagonally across from this bulge, on the opposite corner of the outer walls, lay the drawbridge and gatehouse. Since part of Norcastle had burned, the earl had rebuilt when he took it over again, and he had employed the most modern defenses in his renovation. The walls already had been widened twenty feet thick on the outside base, the plinth slanting up and in, narrowing until it reached the original wall. More arrow slits, called oilets, had been added to the towers. They were in the shape of crosses to fit either longbow or crossbow, with rounded corners to ease the turning and aiming of the bows. Across the crenelated battlements atop the walls, shutters had been added to many of the embrasures, providing more protection for the archers who shot from them.

The party clattered across the narrow drawbridge and entered the dark tunnel of the gatehouse. The gatehouse was in reality two towers that joined overhead to create a long, narrow entry tunnel. Should enemy troops manage to breach the heavy bridge, they would have to fight in narrow, constricted quarters, giving the advantage to the defending army at the open end. At the end of the tunnel the heavy, wooden, iron-studded and barred doors opened into the inner courtyard.

The hall was a long, rectangular building, also white-washed with lime, which backed onto one side of the outer wall. If one faced the hall, the left-hand tower was the old keep. It was the place where the occupants of the castle could make a last-ditch stand during a siege. There was no opening in it until the second floor, and one entered the door by climbing a rope ladder that could be pulled up after him. The walls were thick and sturdy, windowless except for narrow arrow slits. It was rough but livable. A well was sunk in the ground floor, so that the defenders would be assured of a supply of water, the most precious commodity in a siege.

The right-hand tower was the prison tower, used to house enemies and miscreants. The remaining tower was used for storage. The kitchen was detached from the main hall—a custom left over from the days when towers were wooden and, therefore, removed as far as possible from the open fires on which meals were cooked. Next to the kitchen lay the huge bake oven, where bread was cooked for the castle. It was also used by the Norcastle serfs and neighboring village. Beyond the oven lay another well, the one commonly used by the castle. On the wall opposite the main hall lay the small, elegant chapel built by the earl's grandfather for his wife. Across from the kitchen stood the granary and stables. Norcastle was a self-sufficient community and built to withstand long sieges. Only treachery could have breached its defenses, as had happened twenty years before.

The earl dismounted and helped his bride from her horse. Her hand on his arm, he led her up the steps and into the great hall. Huge beams arched far over her head. Rushes crunched underfoot as they crossed the large room. Elizabeth gazed at the heavy Oriental tapestries lining the walls—obviously prizes from Norwen's days in the Holy Land. A woman hurried down the wide staircase to greet them.

Although middle-aged, she was still a stunningly beautiful woman. Her hair, not entirely concealed under her wimple, was a bright flaming red with only a sprinkling of gray in it. She was tall and fine figured; and, though her fair redhead's skin was crumpling under the stress of time, her features were finely molded and still quite handsome.

"James! Richard!" she cried. "Where have you been; I was expecting you days ago?"

She threw her arms first around James and then around Richard, and glanced curiously at Elizabeth. Elizabeth returned her gaze, wondering who she was.

"I'm sorry, Gwendolyn. I should have sent a messenger to you, but there was not enough time for you to attend. I have been delayed because I have been married. This is my new bride, Elizabeth, Countess of Norwen."

Elizabeth dropped the woman a curtsy, unsure of her station; the other woman stared at her in surprise, then said, "Oh, excuse me, I did not mean to be rude. It's just that you caught me so by surprise. Welcome to Norcastle, Lady Elizabeth."

"Elizabeth, this is Gwendolyn, James's mother," Richard explained to his wife.

Elizabeth froze at his words. This beautiful red-haired woman with whom he seemed so much at ease was the illegitimate James's mother! She must have been his father's leman, a woman who had no doubt been his mother's enemy and the cause of pain and humiliation to her; yet the woman seemed to be quite friendly with Richard and to have the run of the household. It was puzzling that he would act this way toward her. But to introduce her to his new bride! That was a direct insult to her. No man would introduce his father's whore to a lady, let alone his wife. It reminded her forcibly of the sort of humiliating thing that Sir Godfrey took great pleasure in putting upon his wife.

Color flamed high on Elizabeth's cheekbones. Coldly she looked straight through the woman, then turned away and said to her husband, "Richard, will you show me to my room now?" She must let him know from the very beginning that he could not get away with such things with her.

The color drained quickly from Gwendolyn's face at Elizabeth's direct cut to her. It was not something she was unused to, but it was certainly something she had never encountered within the family. She had been greatly loved by Richard and James's father, Henry, and had always been a friend of Marguerite, who adored Henry. Ever since Henry's death she had continued to live with Marguerite and James and Richard as a part of the family. So it was a trifle shaking to her to suddenly have an enemy in the midst of the family.

To get away from the awkward scene, she turned to her son James and said, "Please come up to my chambers, James, and tell me what you two have been doing all this time. Excuse me, Richard, milady." She did not look at Elizabeth as she said this.

James, who had witnessed the entire scene, shot Elizabeth a look of pure hatred, then offered his arm to his mother to take her upstairs. As soon as they were out of earshot, Richard turned furiously upon her.

"How dare you act like that!" he thundered. "Gwendolyn is a respected member of this household. She has been the lady of Norcastle since James and I returned to it. I will not have any of that overweening Beaufort pride in this household."

Elizabeth held her head high against his words; she could not allow him to intimidate her. "And I have never been forced to meet a woman of low virtue either! No gentleman would do that to his wife. It is a thing typical of Sir Godfrey to humiliate his wife so. I refuse to be treated so. I will not address that woman as if she were an equal."

"Oh, yes, you shall, if I so order. Gwendolyn was the person my father loved most in all this world and for that she will be respected. I don't care what you may think of her or what others may think of her, she has always been a respected person in the Norwen household. She is a friend to my aunt and has always been a friend to me. I will not tolerate your rudeness to her."

"How can you say that about her? Don't you realize what she must have done to your mother—the humiliation, the shame she brought upon her? She took away your mother's lawful husband. Think of the nights your mother must have spent weeping in pain and shame because Gwendolyn was so much loved by everyone in this house."

"My mother brought much of her loneliness and pain upon herself. She had no understanding of my father. For all his faults, he was a wonderful man, and he loved her and his children. He did all he could to keep her from hurt, but she was uncompromising. Many nights she could have had his company but refused it. I remember that. I know my mother's pain far better than you, and God knows there are times when I still cannot forgive my father for it. But Gwendolyn is not a slut because she loved my father enough to be his mistress; nor is she lowbred. She is the illegitimate daughter of a knight." He did not add that her mother had been the daughter of a wealthy Jewish merchant. That would really have set Elizabeth off. "She has never been anything but kind to me. She never tried to influence my father against me or set James up in my place. After my mother's death, she helped Marguerite raise us. She is a kind and loving woman and has been much hurt over the years by the pride and cruelty of others. I do not care what your pride demands from you; I do not care how much you dislike her or her position. You have gained much by marrying me, and I do not think I am a hard husband; but I do demand this one thing of you: I will not have any more rudeness to Gwendolyn. Do you understand?"

Elizabeth looked at him stonily. His words had been cutting and harsh. She hated him for what he demanded of her. He was just like other men, although he had seemed kinder. He expected complete obedience, no matter what the slight to her. He insisted that she submit to his wishes despite the insult to her. He wanted to humiliate her by forcing her to do something so repugnant.

"I will not obey you," she said, her voice trembling a little.

"What?" His eyebrows rose dangerously. "You are my wife, madam; do not forget that. You have vowed to obey me. I expect you to maintain the sacred vows you made on our wedding day."

It was all Elizabeth could do to keep from flying into a rage. What was so horribly frustrating was that she had made a sacred vow in church to obey him. On the other hand, she could not let herself become the sort of wife that Maud was, completely dominated and in fear of her husband and obeying him in everything no matter how painful or humiliating to her. It was horrible; she could not defy him. He was her husband; he had all rights over her, not to mention the fact that he could physically make her do whatever he wished. It wasn't fair, she railed inside; it wasn't fair. But, fair or not, everything was against her.

"I refuse to be friendly with her. I will speak to her, but no more than that. I will not be friends with that woman. You cannot make me."

"I do not ask you to be friends; I only demand politeness from you," Richard said, his voice cold and clipped. "Now, I shall show you to your chambers."

Elizabeth's bedchamber was a large, airy room. Facing the inner bailey, it had a window to allow in light. In winter, wooden shutters closed out the cold; but now they stood wide, letting in the pale autumn sun. There was a large bed against one wall, high off the floor. Heavy curtains hung from its top frame and could be drawn against the winter chill. When Elizabeth sat on the bed, she realized it had a luxurious feather mattress. On top of the rushes on the floor was laid a beautifully designed rug woven in shades of blue. It, too, was Oriental and part of Richard's booty from the Crusade. An X-shaped chair with a back and a stool sat beside a low table. A cupboard stood against the far wall beside a stone washbasin. Elizabeth glanced around the room, warmed by its loveliness and spacious qualities. However, after her argument with her husband, even the lovely chamber could not lighten her heart.

After their row that afternoon, it did not surprise Elizabeth that Norwen did not come to her bed that night, but slept in his own chambers. Certainly she did not mind his not being there, but she could not help but know that it was a sign of his displeasure with her. She did not know what sort of hold Gwendolyn had over Richard, but it was obvious to Elizabeth that she was not to be the mistress in her own household. For a while she had thought that she would enjoy her new position as Countess of Norwen, but now she realized that it would be an empty title. No doubt Gwendolyn would continue to operate the household—and very poorly she had operated it, Elizabeth thought with a mental snort. Gwendolyn had obviously gotten by all these years on her charm and beauty, not on her household skills. No doubt Richard's mother had run Norcastle and Marguerite had run their household in exile. Gwendolyn was obviously a sloppy housekeeper. The reeds that covered the floor were dry and stale, but she had not replaced them. The maids appeared slovenly, and the food was tasteless and, Elizabeth feared, a trifle spoiled. She knew she could set it right if given the chance, but her husband favored Gwendolyn. She would no doubt spend her life as Richard's mother had, sewing away in her lonely tower room. On that great flood of self-pity, Elizabeth burst into tears and, curling up in her bed, cried herself to sleep.

The next morning Elizabeth got calmly up, ate the breakfast that was sent to her on a tray and set about tidying her clothes, which had been wrinkled on the journey. She could see the courtyard from her room, and as she looked down she saw James there instructing Stephen. The boy looked at the older man with shiny awe in his eyes as James discussed the sword he held in front of him. With a pang, Elizabeth thought: they will even take away Stephen from me, and then I will have nothing left.

It was then that Richard entered the room. "I apologize for my anger yesterday. As Marguerite told me, it would never do to have both you and Gwendolyn in the same household; but foolishly I did not believe her. I still hold to everything I said, but I should not have raged at you. It is just that I am fond of Gwendolyn, and it shocked me to see you react in such a pious manner. I did not think you were the sort. However, I do not want to let this matter come between us. I have come to give you the keys to Norcastle."

"The keys?" she repeated.

"Yes. You are the chatelaine now; you will need the keys."

"But what about Gwendolyn? I thought that she was the mistress here."

"She has run our household, yes; but she would not continue as chatelaine with my wife here. The Countess of Norwen would, of course, run the household." He smiled teasingly. "Did you think you were going to do nothing but loaf?"

Suddenly she smiled that radiant smile that so few saw, and it almost took his breath away. "It is just that after what you said, I—I thought you wanted her to remain in charge. I did not expect to—I mean—oh, thank you. Thank you, Richard."

He held out to her a ring that was heavy with keys. "Gwendolyn will show you which doors all these keys fit. And, here, I have brought you the remainder of your wedding present."

He turned and called to a servant waiting outside, and two men entered carrying between them a large wooden box. It was beautifully carved, and a trace of a spicy scent drifted up from it.

"How beautiful!" Elizabeth gasped. "What is it?"

"It is something I got during the Crusades. Go on; open it."

Gingerly she raised the lid and gasped at the sight of its contents. Inside lay a gleaming mass of jewels, rings, necklaces, bracelets, anklets, diadems for her head. The glittering sight was almost too much for her eyes.

"How beautiful! But what—you mean you are giving all of this to me?"

"Yes; you are my wife, are you not? These jewels belong to the Countess of Norwen. Some were my mother's." He reached in and picked out a heavy golden ring with a bright garnet stone. "This was my mother's wedding ring. It is one of the jewels that Marguerite grabbed when we fled the castle, and we managed to avoid having to sell it. And this gold bracelet was hers also. And this I got long ago in the Orient; I always intended it for my wife."

He handed to her a heavy golden belt, studded with jewels that shone like golden fire. The belt was made of joined squares of gold, and in the front a heavy chain swung down from it. Elizabeth took it; it was heavy in her hand.

"Milord, it is—I don't know what to say. It is the most beautiful thing I have ever seen."

"Yes. I seized it when we conquered a heathen castle in the Holy Land. It was lying in this very box among beautiful fabrics that looked as rich as jewels themselves. This heavy perfume that lingers hung over everything in that room; I remember it well." He shook his head as though to rid himself of the memories, and said, "I thought it was fine enough only for the Countess of Norwen, so it is yours. All of these are rightfully yours, and I give them to you."

Elizabeth was speechless. She had never expected him to shower such wealth upon her; never had she seen so many beautiful jewels. She was astounded at his generosity. Only moments before she had thought herself an outcast in the house, a person relegated to the back room; but now here he was giving her all the Norwen jewels, turning the household over to her care, setting her up as the full mistress of Norcastle. Suddenly, in a burst of feeling, she threw her arms around his neck.

"Richard, I am sorry for what I thought, for all the things I said. I continue to compare you to my uncle. I expect all men to act like him. I was afraid you were trying to humiliate me by forcing me to your will. I cannot understand your reasons for wishing Gwendolyn to be here, but I promise I will be polite to her as you request."

Richard swept her into his arms and hugged her tightly against him. It was the first spontaneous display of affection that he had seen from Elizabeth, and it touched him deeply. With her pride, he realized how much it cost her to consent to his demands. Somehow it strengthened his determination to completely win her over.

Elizabeth set out immediately to get the household in order. She and Gwendolyn toured the castle, both aloofly polite, and Gwendolyn showed her which keys fit all the doors. Elizabeth got her maids together and told them what to expect from her. She declared that she would demand their full obedience and, more than that, their efficiency. In return she promised to be a kind and just taskmaster. She ordered the maids to clean out all the rushes and to lay new rushes on the floor, then to take down all the tapestries, carry them outside and beat the dust of years from them. Linens were to be all washed, and all the furniture was to be dusted.

She then turned her attention to the kitchen. Here she swept through like a cyclone, declaring that all pots and pans must be scrubbed completely and demanding that the cook institute better standards of cleanliness in his domain. She laid out her menu for the week to him and told him how she wished her food prepared, and then she roundly threatened them all with back lashings and worse if the food were carried so casually from the kitchen that it arrived in the great hall cold or even dirty.

Next she toured the cellar storehouses, carefully looking into all the barrels of salted fish, meal, water and other necessities that were stored there. She found, to her great dismay, that the water that would have to serve them if the castle were besieged was brackish and unfit for consumption. She immediately ordered it poured out, the barrel scrubbed and fresh water stored. She discovered rot among many barrels of fish and weevils in the grain. This she felt was due to their pouring new supplies of fresh fish or grain in on top of the old without using the old up first. In this manner, the old would contaminate the new; so she carefully instructed the cook that all the old supplies had to be used up first or thrown out if they were spoiled.

Within a couple of weeks there was an amazing change in the castle. Brass and gold ornaments sparkled with cleanliness. The food was warm and better tasting, and no longer with a tinge of spoilage. The rushes beneath their feet were fresh and sweet smelling from the herbs sprinkled among them. The tapestries, bed linens and furniture were all cleaned, and even the kitchen sparkled. Bowls of lavender seeds were placed around the castle to sweeten the air.

Richard had never really noticed the sloppy condition of the castle, until he saw the changes that his bride had wrought. There was so much more to Elizabeth than her beauty; he was realizing that more and more. She had wit; she knew how to get the castle in order and running smoothly; she was courageous. After all, hadn't she dealt bravely with her uncle all those years that she was under his power? She had endurance and strength of character. Daily he felt more inclined to trust her, was more convinced that she was not a lying Beaufort. He would have been a very happy man had it not been for the nights. Although she no longer seemed to dread and fear him, Elizabeth remained passive in his arms. Nothing he did seemed to excite her; never did she indicate any desire for him. Richard discovered that this diminished his pleasure greatly. He yearned for some sort of response from her; it seemed to him that that would make his enjoyment all the more complete.

She did things for him very well; she ran his castle efficiently; she did not nag or whine; he was certain she was never unfaithful to him. She was, in fact, the model wife—except that she had no feeling for him. He could have been anyone else, he felt, and she would have acted just the same. There was no tenderness in her for him, no love, and that was what he wanted most. He remembered the way Gwendolyn had felt about his father, and his father about her. He knew that, although his aunt was anything but a clinging wife, there had been a deep current of feeling between Marguerite and Philip. That was what he wanted for himself. He longed to have that same deep love that he had seen among his family. God knows he had seen a great deal of life, the vanities and infidelities of court, the arranged marriages, indifference, even hatred between husbands and wives. He was suspicious of nearly everyone and unlikely to easily let any woman through that armor of suspicion; but, despite all these things, what he wanted most desperately in his innermost being was to have the close loving relationship that he grew up with.

Realistically he said that he did not expect the sort of closeness that lay between his aunt and uncle, but surely some feeling was possible. After all, he felt a great deal for Elizabeth, even though he might still be somewhat distrustful of her. He found her beauty exciting, her qualities intriguing; he enjoyed being with her in conversation or in bed. Perhaps he did not quite love her, but he was close to it. Perhaps he was not bound to her as Philip was to Marguerite, but he felt great emotion for her. If only she returned some of that emotion!

While Elizabeth set about putting the castle in order and Richard began straightening up the financial records and management problems of his domain, James began to teach Stephen the skills of warfare. Daily he had lessons for Stephen in the use of a sword, a shield, a lance, and in the art of riding. First Stephen had to be taught how to ride a horse skillfully; later he would learn how to use the horse in battle: how to guide his steed by the pressure of his knees without the use of reins, how to use his mount as another weapon, how to turn him in conjunction with sword thrusts or parry with his shield, how to keep from being dismounted and how to remount if he were downed in battle.

Stephen lacked strength from the years of inactivity,

and so James set him exercises to do daily to increase his
strength. Hour after hour James taught him how to
handle the sword; over and over again they practiced
different types of blows. The sword that a knight used
was a very heavy weapon, not sharp pointed and used
for thrusting, but sharp along the edges and used for
slicing and hacking. They were used to crush, to cut
deeply, to stun, and therefore had to be heavy. However,
the weight of a normal man's sword was far too much for
Stephen to use; he could barely lift the thing, let alone
execute any blows with it. Therefore, James had a much
lighter sword made for Stephen and used it to teach him
the various blows. He also concentrated on how to wield
a knife. A dagger was a far more effective weapon at
close quarters than a sword, and also much easier for
Stephen to handle.

Stephen needed to become well versed in the rudiments of self-defense in order to protect himself as much
as possible now. Swordplay would be of use to him in the
future, when he had gained the age and strength to really
use a sword. The same thing applied to other heavy
weapons, such as the lance or mace.

Often Richard would join them in the courtyard for a
little exercise, and sometimes he and James would
demonstrate various fighting techniques. When James
was not teaching him warfare, Stephen would tag along
with Richard, riding with him to inspect his lands, watching him mete out justice to his serfs on their court days,
when they came to their overlord to resolve their problems. He also observed Richard checking over the books
that his clerk kept, and James taught him the use of
numbers, how to add and subtract, how to make the
mystifying world of books comprehensible and thus
enable him to check the work of his clerk. This was
something that many lords were unable to do, not being
well versed in anything intellectual, knowing only how to
fight and ride a horse.

All of this was a delightful new world to Stephen, who

had been thirsting for such knowledge for five years. He soaked it all up eagerly, never missing an opportunity to listen to James and Richard as they talked, and learned in this way about his fellow nobles and their intricate politics. He learned of long-standing feuds, of the honor of some nobles and the treachery of others, of the tendencies they displayed toward courage, cowardice, fidelity, lying, kindness or cruelty. Every word that they said was important to him, every opinion immediately the final word. They were his idols, the very opposite of his uncle and cousins: manly, courageous, honorable and, most of all, kind to him. He could not remember ever having a man to admire as he admired these men.

Daily Stephen grew healthier and happier. Although he would always be pale in coloring, he lost his sickly look. Daily practice and riding in the sun gave his fair skin a healthy golden tone. From exercise and the huge amount of food his adolescent body consumed, he began to fill out, his muscles strengthened and he took on weight. His eyes and face were now animated with enthusiasm and interest.

Elizabeth was pleased to see the changes in Stephen; yet she could not help but feel a pang of regret that she no longer had him for a companion. She felt the pain a mother feels when she has to let go of her son. More than that, she was jealous that James and Richard should receive so much adulation from Stephen. She was only being careful, she reasoned with herself. Stephen should not become so attached to these two that he would do anything they said. Much more than Richard, she worried about James's influence on her younger brother. She knew James hated her and feared that he meant to do her harm through Stephen. Might he not try to convince Stephen that Elizabeth did not have his best interests at heart? Might he not persuade Stephen to hand over too much authority and land to him? Richard said that James was fond of Stephen, that he used him as a replacement for Marguerite's boys, whom he had doted on. Personally Elizabeth found it difficult to imagine James being fond of anyone; most particularly she found it hard to believe that he would like Stephen, mistrusting and disliking her as he did.

Elizabeth remembered the comment her uncle had made on her wedding day regarding James: "Kin are not always loyal, especially bastard ones." He must have been referring to James, hinting that he was likely to betray Richard. Of course, anything that her uncle said was as likely as not a lie; yet she knew how much James had been against the wedding. He certainly did not like her, whatever his loyalty to Richard. One day, as she came from the kitchen, she chanced to see James standing in the hallway talking to a servant. The servant looked vaguely familiar and yet somehow out of place. It was not until she had reached her chambers that she suddenly remembered who the servant was. It was a man who served Sir Godfrey; she was certain of it. Quickly she ran back downstairs, but James and the man had already left. She was certain it was one of Godfrey's men, and that made her even more uneasy than before. What could James have to say to a man of her uncle's that was not treasonous, or at least dangerous, to her or Stephen?

For a moment she thought about running to Richard to tell him that she had seen James conversing with the man, but she discarded that idea quickly. It would serve no purpose except to make Richard angry at her. She knew he would not believe that James could betray him or would plot to harm her or Stephen. He was too loyal to his brother; he would not believe her, and it would make him suspicious that she was telling tales against James for some devious plot of her own. No; the best thing to do was hold her tongue and see if she could find out enough to circumvent whatever James had in mind. Only with complete, substantiated proof against James could she hope to sway his brother.

Elizabeth was not wrong in her recognition of the man. He was, in fact, a follower of Sir Godfrey and had been sent by him to give instructions to James. Sir Godfrey had decided, the man told him, to take Stephen back; only with him in hand would Godfrey feel safe in his possession of Stephen's lands. He must act now, since Stephen was still officially his ward, although chances were he would soon be given by the king to Richard. Therefore, Godfrey was sending James a small purse of gold to aid him in kidnapping the boy.

James watched him silently, a slightly sardonic expression on his face, as if the other man amused him. It irritated the fellow, and he wished that Sir Godfrey had chosen someone else as a conspirator. There was something unnerving about this man, who was as handsome as Lucifer before the Fall and about as friendly as a rock.

"And what is your master's plan to grab the boy?" James asked.

"He wants you and Stephen to ride out alone tomorrow toward the village, and when you come to the crest of the hill where there are bushes on either side of the road, I and several other men will be there waiting in hiding. We shall leap out and attack you and take Stephen off with us. Of course, you will probably have to put on some show of fight so that your story will be believed."

James smiled. "Don't worry. I think that I can keep up my end; it is whether you and your men shall succeed that worries me."

It was then that Elizabeth walked past and saw them. When that happened, the messenger declared that it was best he be going along now; there was too much traffic around here for his comfort. James watched the man scurry off, wondering if he went to meet Lady Elizabeth. Perhaps her walking past had been a signal for him to come to her. It was quite possible that Sir Godfrey played a double game, scheming both with him and with Lady Elizabeth. For a moment he was tempted to follow him and see where the man went, but then he shrugged the idea aside. He was hardly unobtrusive enough to do any spying, and it was too late to call a servant and set him on the man's trail. The best thing to do was just to prepare for the morrow's kidnapping.

It was nearing noon the next morning when James and Stephen set out to ride toward the village. They often rode together this way, practicing Stephen's horsemanship. James mounted gracefully. His face showed nothing to indicate that this was to be anything more than the daily ride. Only if one looked closely and knew him well could one detect a sparkle of excitement in his dark eyes. Stephen seemed to be in a little less than his usual high spirits, but James did not point that out. The huge iron-studded gates opened for them and they left at a canter. It took twenty minutes for them to reach the hill, moving along as they did at a leisurely pace. When they came in sight of the hill, James imperceptibly tightened his grip on his reins for a moment and loosened his sword in its scabbard. Slowly they started the climb to the hill.

Almost halfway up, there was a thunder of horses behind them and Norwen's strong voice came wafting through the air. "A moi! A moi! A trap! A trap!" In one fluid motion, James dropped the reins of his horse and pulled his sword out. As quickly, Stephen wheeled his horse around and started at a run back toward the approaching band of men. The ambushers at the top of the hill, startled, flew into action. They came rushing toward James. With one quick blow he knocked their leader off of his horse with the flat of his sword, sending him breathless to the ground. Then, wheeling, he laid about him effectively with his sword.

Beside him the man he had struck down struggled to remount, crying, "Lay off! We must recapture him."

"Fool! I cannot look as if I knew of this plot. No doubt you betrayed us somehow. Run. Run. It is over."

Norwen and his men had split to surround Stephen and thundered on. They were now upon the group that surrounded James, and the shock as they rammed into them shoved Godfrey's men backward. Norwen fought his way to his brother's side, and in the face of their combined skill Godfrey's men scattered quickly. Norwen's men went in pursuit of them, striking each of them down as he fled. James dismounted and knelt beside the leader of the men, who lay upon the ground bleeding but still breathing.

"Well, this one is dead," James said.

"Good," his brother replied. "Thank God we caught you in time. Fortunately one of our men saw that blackguard in the castle yesterday. When he came to me and told me that, I realized that you and Stephen were in danger of being ambushed today on your ride to the village. I was afraid I would not catch you in time."

James smiled at his brother, an amused grin that suddenly lit up his face. Norwen returned the smile and winked. Behind them Stephen cried, "Wasn't that magnificent? I've never enjoyed anything as much."

When the party returned to Norcastle, Elizabeth heard the hubbub below and wondered what was its cause. She sent one of her maids down to find out what had happened. The girl returned quickly, excitement written all over her face.

"Oh, milady!" the girl cried out. "Lord Stephen and Sir James were attacked by Sir Godfrey's men as they rode to the village! But fortunately the earl found out about the plot and he rode to save them. Isn't that exciting?"

Elizabeth jumped to her feet, the color drained from her face. "Is Stephen—is he all right?"

"Oh, yes, milady, perfectly all right. Milord and his brother killed all of Sir Godfrey's men."

Elizabeth drew a deep breath and sat down shakily. Dear God in heaven! Stephen had almost been killed. She should have known that Sir Godfrey would try something like that. The only hope he had of benefit now was to kidnap or kill Stephen—preferably kill, since that would bring all of Stephen's lands rightfully into his possession. One of the ambushers must have been the man she had seen yesterday talking to James. And James and Stephen had been the ones who rode out this morning. James must have been in on the plot! No doubt he was to ensure that Stephen would be at the correct spot to be attacked. Thank heavens Norwen had somehow discovered that Stephen was to be ambushed. What made her numb was that she had seen Sir Godfrey's man, yet had not told Norwen about it, for fear of incurring his displeasure. By doing so, she could very well have been a party to Stephen's death. If Norwen had not found out about the ambush, she would have had the vital information that could have stopped the attack, and yet would not have given it. She felt sick to her stomach. Stephen could have been killed; he could have been killed! She must not let these attacks continue against him. She realized now that she had to tell Norwen about his brother.

Quickly Elizabeth hurried down the stairs where she found Stephen, Norwen and James standing among a group of men recalling their adventure. The earl looked up and saw her, and went to her.

"Milord, I must talk to you privately," Elizabeth whispered urgently.

"Of course. Let us retire to your chambers."

Quickly Elizabeth went back to her rooms with Norwen on her heels. Once inside she turned to him and blurted out, "Richard, James betrayed my brother!"

Norwen's brow drew thunderously together. "What? Do you realize what you are saying?"

"Yes, I realize. But I must speak out to save Stephen's life."

"James risked his life to save Stephen. He stood off all the attackers alone until we could reach him. You wrong him, Elizabeth. You wrong him."

"Nay, I do not. Please believe me. I swear to you that I am telling the truth. I knew he was somehow involved yesterday, and I should have spoken out then. Much to my shame I did not because I feared your wrath."

Norwen opened his mouth and then closed it. For a moment he studied her. He wanted to trust her, to believe that her motives were of the best and that she truly believed what she said. But what if she lied? What if this was part of some plan of hers to drive a wedge between him and James? God knows she had suffered at the hands of Sir Godfrey, if what she said was true; but he knew just as certainly that she had no feeling for him. His pain would cost her little. She had lived for years in the tainted atmosphere of Sir Godfrey; it seemed more than likely that she would have absorbed some of that evil. He could not confide in her, dared not refute her. He had learned the bitter way not to trust anyone except his family. He could not be sure that she was not plotting against him, trying to make him suspect the one most trustworthy person he knew.

"I will hear no more, madam. You may as well save your breath. If you fear for your brother, trust me in this: James is loyal. Moreover, he is fond of Stephen. No harm will come to your brother, if James and I can possibly prevent it. But I will not hear these irrational accusations against my brother. That is all I have to say."

Elizabeth stared at him helplessly. He would not listen to her; he would not listen to her at all. There was no hope. James would destroy Stephen, and her husband would not lift a finger to help.

"Yes, milord," she said stiffly, and turned away.

Chapter Ten

THE DUKE OF TANFORD STARED ANGRILY AT SIR GODFREY and drummed his fingers on the table. "You are a fool," he said dispassionately. "Only a fool would try to kidnap Lord Beaufort right out of Norcastle, and only a fool would think that the Bastard would go along with you."

"But, Your Grace, he did. My man tells me that he saved his life. It was not he who betrayed us, just some man who recognized my man," Sir Godfrey pleaded. The Duke of Tanford always managed to reduce him to a foolish child pleading with his elders. Godfrey resented it bitterly, but Tanford was so often right—so coldly, methodically, evilly right.

The duke sighed with impatience. "Why am I doomed to dealing with men like you? Now, the Bastard—he would be a challenge to my abilities. You—" the duke broke off and shook his head. "Now try to think logically. What possible reason would James have for helping to kidnap Stephen? It benefits him not at all. Supposing he does hate your niece; I'll accept that. He might very well go along with killing her. But why Stephen? He gets no land, no wealth, except the paltry sum you bribed him with. What is that compared with risking his brother's finding out? Besides, even if you had managed to get Stephen back, what good would that have done? Norwen would have been on you like a hawk. He is twice the warrior you are and has a better army. What chance would you have? I'll tell you: absolutely none. If you had Stephen back, you would have gained nothing. You have already possession of Stephen's land, and you still have the right to defend it until Henry makes Richard Stephen's guardian. You did not need to actually have the boy. And having possession of his lands obviously doesn't improve your army. Richard will still crush you."

"I did not know what else to do," Godfrey said sullenly.

"If only you had consulted me before going off on this harebrained scheme, you would have known what to do. Obviously Richard must be killed. It is the only way to save yourself and the only way for me to keep the two fortresses I got from Norwen. It is also the only reason James has to betray his brother. If his brother dies, James could control much of his land—we all three know it—even though he is illegitimate. For James's purposes, as for ours, Richard must be killed quickly, before he can get an heir in Lady Elizabeth. Moreover, as you know, you and I need a reason to attack Richard. We have none. My plan is this: James is to kill Stephen in Norcastle, making it look as if Richard murdered him. Then you will have an excuse to attack; I can support you with my men, and James can betray Richard from the inside. Then all three of us can divide the Norwen lands, and moreover, feel perfectly righteous to have slain the murderer of a child. Now doesn't that make more sense?"

"Yes, milord," Sir Godfrey mumbled. Damn the man! Why did he always have to have such excellent ideas!

"There. Now if you had only asked me before, you wouldn't have had all this trouble and lost your men." The duke rose. "I suggest that you persuade James to our new plan. This must be resolved quickly, you understand."

"Yes, Your Grace."

"Well, I must be on my way now. See to it that nothing goes wrong this time." The duke swept from the hall and out into the courtyard. He preferred never to spend the night inside anyone else's keep, even if he was an ally. He liked to conduct his business and remove himself from even the danger of any control over him.

Sir Godfrey bowed him out of the hall and, once he had left, vented his rage on stools and dogs and any unwise servants who got in his way. At last he threw himself down in his chair, shouted for a cup of ale and began to think. He would have to send another messenger to James or, better yet, meet with James himself some place outside of Norcastle. He had to present this plan just right so that James would help him. He could see now that the duke was no doubt right; James probably had betrayed him about Stephen. He would have to persuade James not only to kill his brother, but to do it quickly, before Elizabeth had an heir.

But wait. Suddenly he stopped in midthought. There was no reason for him to want Richard to die before Elizabeth was with child. With Richard dead, Elizabeth would obviously be his ward once again. Moreover, he would be the logical choice to be the guardian of any babe that she might have. So if he could stall until Elizabeth had conceived or, even better yet, actually borne an heir, and take Elizabeth and the babe at the same time that he killed Norwen, that would be the answer. He would outwit Tanford and James.

Sir Godfrey burst out laughing and wrung his hands with glee. He could imagine nothing more satisfying than outwitting the Duke of Tanford. If he took his time to get

James on his side and to persuade him to kill Richard, but
to hold off until Elizabeth was pregnant, and then got
James to kill Stephen and make it look as if Richard had
done it, then it would be easy to get Elizabeth, James and
Richard all at each other's throats; and he could easily
conquer Richard and take away Elizabeth, leaving James
with nothing, as befitted a bastard.

For a while, Elizabeth admitted, she had felt a growing
fondness for Richard. He had seemed a kind man, had
seemed to respect her, had helped Stephen, had not
misused his power over her. She thought how she had
grown to enjoy talking to him, had become accustomed
to his humor. She had even once or twice in bed felt a
tremor of pleasure run through her. But now she realized
how foolish she had been. She had believed that he
respected her, enjoyed her, yet had feeling for her. But
now he had made it clear that she and Stephen had no
importance compared with James. He would hear nothing from her against his brother, would not even consider
the possibility that James was treacherous rather than
she. She had no doubt that Richard would try to protect
Stephen, but only up to the point where it interfered with
his protection of James. As always, it would be up to her,
ultimately, to save Stephen from those who wished him
dead.

But how? What was she to do? Stephen trusted James;
Richard trusted James; everyone trusted him except her.
He was strong and she was weak. Well, for one thing, she
had to convince Stephen to be on his guard against
James. She knew that was an almost impossible task,
considering the way he felt about him; but she had to try.
She had to do it very carefully, of course, but surely—
surely Stephen would trust her after all the years she had
been his only hope. Aside from warning Stephen, she
could see nothing else to be done except to kill James
before he could kill Stephen. As soon as she thought that,

her mind skittered away from the subject. There had to be something else she could do; there had to be. She could not kill a person—well, Sir Godfrey perhaps, or Geoffrey. Yes, those two she would have gladly killed, if she had had the strength and ability. But James was another matter. He had never brutalized her, as the other two had. She would not be killing him in a fit of anger, but coldly calculating his death. And yet—what else was there to do? She could not let him kill Stephen just because she was too afraid to act. She had to be strong; she had to firm her resolve. Stephen's death was the price she would pay if she did not.

But how to kill him? She knew nothing of poisons; and how else could a woman kill a man, having inferior strength? At night, perhaps, when he was asleep, she could sneak in and stab him as he slept. But that way she was as likely as not to be discovered. She might very well awaken him; and he always had some lass in his bed, from what she heard. There was no way she could do it and get away unseen. No; poison seemed the only answer. But how did one obtain it? Witches, she knew, brewed such things; but she knew of no witch in the area to whom she could go. There were certain trees and plants and mushrooms that were poisonous, but she was not sure which ones. Perhaps she could go out and pick mushrooms and surreptitiously put them in his food, and hope that they would be the poisonous ones. But that seemed an awfully chancy venture. With an angry sigh, she threw herself onto a stool. She would never be able to do it. Never! She did not know the means and did not have the courage. She wanted suddenly very much to cry—to have come so far and kept Stephen safe from harm, and now to have this unexpected danger to him. It seemed so wrong, so unfair.

After a few minutes, Elizabeth pulled herself together and went to Stephen's room. At least she could tell him to beware of danger; she could watch out for him as she always had in her uncle's household. And maybe, by some stroke of good fortune, she would find a way to solve her problem.

She found Stephen in his room, quietly practicing with his sword. She had to smile at the sight of him. So young, and so intent upon the steps he took and the movements he made with his little sword. He whirled at the sound of her footsteps and then smiled.

"Good day, sister," he said. "I was just practicing. Look, let me show you this."

She watched, smiling, as he performed his sword skills for her. She hated to disturb his secure happiness, but she knew she must.

"Stephen," Elizabeth began hesitantly. "Stephen, I know this will be hard for you to accept, but I must warn you: you must be very careful and watchful."

"For what?" Stephen asked, instantly alert.

"James, the earl's brother," Elizabeth said.

"James! Whatever are you talking about?"

"I saw him not long before they tried to kidnap or kill you. He was talking to one of Sir Godfrey's men."

"Yes. What about it?" Stephen nodded.

"Don't you see, Stephen? He must have been in on the plot to kidnap you. Why else would he be talking to Sir Godfrey's man? Moreover, Sir Godfrey said to me that James would be disloyal to Norwen."

"Sir Godfrey lies all the time, Elizabeth. You know that. What good is a hint from him?" Stephen pointed out.

"But, Stephen, don't you see, when I saw him talking to one of Godfrey's men, I realized it must be true. Why else would he talk to him? The man must have been telling James to lure you off on that road that morning so they could ambush you."

Stephen stared at her in amazement. "God's bones, sister, what are you talking about? Do you mean to tell me that you did not know?"

"Know what?"

"That James was in on the plot to double-cross them. You see, Godfrey approached him on your wedding day and offered him money if he would help Sir Godfrey. And James pretended to go along with him, but he only did it so that we would know of any plots against us. He pretended to be ready to betray me or Richard in order to betray them. Don't you understand?"

"How do you know all this?"

"Why, James told me. The evening before they tried to kidnap me, James came to me and told me that I must do something very dangerous. He explained to me what he had been doing, that he was pretending to be a traitor. He said that it was far better for him to play this game and draw out and destroy any plots, than to try to guard against them without any foreknowledge of them. Anyway, he told me that one of Sir Godfrey's men had given him a message to take me out riding on the road to the village; and, just beyond the top of that hill, Godfrey's men would ambush us and take me off. So James had told Richard about it, and they decided to attack the men and James and I would be the bait." Stephen's eyes sparkled with remembered excitement. "I had to pretend not to know what was going on. And then, as we rode along, I listened for Richard's cry; and when I heard him shout, I was to turn and gallop back to Richard. Then, protecting me, they attacked Godfrey's men. I did just as I was told, Elizabeth, and Richard said that I had done very well."

Elizabeth stared at him, mutely. So James had only pretended to be a traitor, and Richard knew of the whole plot. Richard knew and had not told her.

"So you see, James is not a threat to me at all," Stephen continued. "He is playing a very dangerous game. If he is caught, you know what Godfrey will do to him. Moreover, for a while there, he alone was holding off Godfrey's men while I fled. He risked his life for me."

"Norwen did not tell me of this," Elizabeth said.

"No doubt he did not wish to alarm you. Not knowing that you had seen James with Sir Godfrey's man, he would not think you would suspect James of betraying me. And not knowing that you would worry about it, he surely thought that it would be less worrisome to you not to know of James's intrigues."

"But, Stephen, he knew that I suspected James. He knew that I feared James was trying to kill you, and yet he did not tell me otherwise. Why? Why would he do that to me?"

Stephen looked at his sister, troubled. "Richard and James are very distrustful. No doubt they would not have told me if they had not feared that I would not run for safety when I was ambushed."

Elizabeth hardly heard what he said, for she was seething with anger. Knowing how frightened she was for Stephen, her husband had callously not told her why she need not fear James. He had left her to stew in her worries and fears. All of her former terror for Stephen's life was now transformed into rage at Norwen. Without considering her actions, she stormed from the room and went in search of Norwen. She found him in the counting room, where he was tallying his clerk's figures. He looked up, mildly surprised at Elizabeth's quick entrance.

"How could you! How could you do that to me? Stephen just told me that James was in on the plot to betray Sir Godfrey. He also told me that you knew about the whole thing. And yet, knowing that, you did not tell me. Knowing how I feared for Stephen's life, you would not give me the information that would allay my fears. I had thought my uncle was a cruel man, but now I realize that you are his match! To leave me in such torment when you had the knowledge to ease my fear!"

Richard was unused to be so upbraided, and he replied hotly, "I believe I am in charge here, madam! I did as I thought best to preserve your brother's well-being and my own. I started to tell you, but then I realized that I did not know to whom you might tell the tale. I could not endanger James, and I did not trust you not to tell your uncle of James's double cross. We went to some trouble to leave one man alive and to let him think that someone else had warned me of the plot. I wasn't going to ruin that by letting you know the truth."

Elizabeth, who had been pacing about the room feeding her anger, stopped and stared at him; his words made her so furious that she could hardly speak. She began to tremble with anger and it took her a moment to get enough control over herself to say, "You think that I would tell Sir Godfrey? You think that I would endanger my brother's life? You say that you are in charge of his protection; and therefore you will decide not to tell me things, because I might reveal them to Sir Godfrey and thereby contribute to Stephen's death? Who do you think has protected him all these years? Me! I have lied and pretended and risked my own life to protect him, and now you say that I am not trustworthy, that I might betray him! I would give my last drop of blood to save Stephen, while you send him out to be ambushed! You knew where those men were; you could have attacked them. You did not need to send Stephen in the forefront. He could have been killed!"

Richard jumped up from his seat, anger exploding in him. Damn her, she cared nothing for him. She gave no thanks to him or James for saving Stephen; she had no concern that he might have been killed fighting for her brother's life. Oh, no, every thought was for Stephen. Everything she did was for him: she had even made the ultimate sacrifice of marrying him and enduring his unwanted advances to ensure Stephen's life. That thought cut through him like a knife, and he slammed his fist upon the table and bellowed, "By the Virgin, you would coddle that boy to death! If I had simply charged up the road and attacked them, many of the men would have gotten away. This way Stephen lured them down the road toward me, and I was able to kill them every one, except the one that we wished to escape. If Stephen did as he was told, I knew there would be no danger to him. And, thank God, your brother is more reasonable than you! He is nigh onto being a man, and he must begin to act like one. Stephen wants to learn to fight, to carry arms, to be a knight as he should be. But you must baby him; you would keep him in swaddling cloth until he dies if you could. I think that all those years you had him play his weakling role, not so much in fear of his uncle, but because you would keep him close to you!"

Rage poured through Elizabeth at his words and her control snapped. "I hate you!" she screamed and flew at him, striking out wildly.

Richard raised his arm to ward off her blows, taken aback by her attack. Elizabeth was not easily thwarted, but continued to rain blows upon him until at last he was able to pull her to him and wrap his arms around her tightly, so that she could not lift her arms to hit him. Still she struggled, wiggling ineffectively in his arms. Richard smiled; he rather liked their struggle; even her anger was better than her usual indifference to him. At least he had touched some emotional chord in her. Her vain struggles to get free rubbed her body against his, and the movements aroused him.

He began to kiss her ears and neck, and his hands came up to shove her wimple from her hair and send the golden mass spilling across her shoulders. Richard plunged his hands into her silky hair and turned her face up to kiss her. This freed her and she pulled away from him, but he grabbed her with one arm and pulled her back and buried his lips in hers. For a while Elizabeth continued to struggle; but then suddenly a strange new feeling swept her, and her arms crept up around his neck. Her rage had broken through her passivity and control. For the first time her emotions and her senses were opened to Richard's touch. His lips and tongue aroused her, sending strange flickers of desire throughout her body. Hardly knowing what she was doing, she pressed closer to him, her lips moving against his, her tongue softly creeping into his mouth as though to find the secret of this wonderful new feeling.

A tremor shook Richard at her response, and eagerly he began to caress her body. Her clothes impeded him, and impatiently he tugged at them. Elizabeth suddenly wanted to feel his hands upon her bare flesh, wanted him to look at her naked body with those hot, black eyes. She pulled away from him and with trembling hands untied her kirtle and sleeves and let them drop to the floor, then pulled her underdress off over her head and threw it in the pile at her feet. For a long moment, Richard gazed at her, savoring the event, until his hot pounding desire overcame him; and he took off his clothes and added them to hers, then knelt and pulled her down on the floor beside him. And there, lying on their clothes on the floor of the counting room, Richard took her for the first time in mutual passion. He kissed and caressed her body until she moaned with pleasure. Her breasts and loins tingled at his touch, and she ached to feel his hardness inside her. At last he slid into her, and she sighed with content. He filled the yearning void inside her and with each pounding thrust filled her again, until at last he trembled and cried out and plunged into her as if to seek out the core of her being. Elizabeth wrapped her arms about him tightly and held onto him for dear life. Gradually he relaxed and shifted his weight from her and, holding her, slipped softly into a shallow sleep.

Elizabeth lay awake beside him, floating in her newfound emotion. Never had she dreamed that this could happen; never had she imagined that anything could be this pleasurable. How silly and stubborn she had been to hold herself aloof from this man, when his lovemaking could bring her to these wild, beautiful feelings. She trembled a little; it was almost frightening, so new and strong were her emotions, so inflamed were her senses. But—she smiled mischievously—this was certainly one time when she would welcome the fright.

Chapter Eleven

RICHARD WAITED IN THE GREAT HALL FOR HIS BROTHER TO come in from the courtyard. He had a plan for the fast-approaching winter that he wished to discuss with James. Before long James entered and strode to the fireplace to stand before it, baking the chill from his body. Stephen tumbled in after him and curled up on the ledge beside the fireplace. Richard looked at him and smiled; it was hard to resist Stephen's pleasing ways and open adoration of them. He was developing daily, not only in his physical appearance, but also in his personality. He was learning to laugh and make jests, whereas before he had been unnaturally solemn. He was picking up puns and joking comments from James; but what was, on James's lips, sarcastic and biting became softer when Stephen said it and lacked the barb. Now his eyes often had a merry twinkle to them, and he was even beginning to indulge in mischievous, boyish pranks. It pleased Richard to see him this way; he liked the lad, both for himself and for his resemblance to his sister. It was good for him to acquire some merriment and youth, but Richard also knew that Stephen never forgot his heritage nor his danger. He would work himself to exhaustion trying to catch up in his education, and he fully realized the responsibility that lay ahead of him.

It was for these reasons that Richard did not send Stephen away while he talked to James, but included him in his conversation.

"James, how would you like a new position?" he began lightly.

"What do you mean?"

"Well, I think you should be the commander of Stephen's forces."

James looked at him, his eyebrows rising in amusement. "Indeed. And precisely where are these forces you speak of?"

Richard smiled. "Well, now, that we have not supplied yet, but they will be there someday. That is part of your job."

"Oh, I see." James turned to Stephen. "And what do you think of this, Stephen? Shall I be your captain?"

"Oh, yes!" Stephen exclaimed. "That would be perfect."

Richard explained his plan. "I think, James, that you should go to Melton Keep. It borders on Stephen's land. Therefore, I think we should make it our base from which to launch our attack against Sir Godfrey for Stephen's land."

"But Melton Keep is hardly in any condition to shelter an army. Any concerted effort against it would crumble it," James interrupted.

"That is why I wish you to go there. You can while away the long winter months repairing it and stocking it with ample provisions. Make it as impregnable to attack as you can, and also make it fit as the base for our expansion into Beaufort land. Also, you will need to start building an army for Stephen. Hire the best mercenaries and get a few good knights you can trust."

Now it was Stephen's thin voice that interrupted him. "But, milord, I have no gold. How can I purchase an army?"

"For the time, I shall support it," Richard said. "Of course, it will cost a good deal if we cannot offer them loot when they conquer a keep. We want no ill will felt by the locals against their returning lord. Therefore, we shall have to recompense the mercenaries for their loss of ransacking the villages and castles. However, once you have regained all your land, you will not need to maintain so large an army; and you will have enough revenues from your land to support your men. Let us hope you have some faithful vassals in your keeps. After all, since Godfrey is your guardian, it is not evidence of their disloyalty that they follow him. Some, I think, will be safe for you to keep; the others you can get rid of and reward some of your followers with their castles.

"After a few years of rebuilding and regaining your rightful position, both on your land and at court, you will probably be able to repay me. If not," Richard shrugged, "then I do not think I will consider it too severe a price to pay for your help in defeating Godfrey and your loyalty as an ally. After all, you are my blood kin now; and I hope someday, between you and me and James, we shall be an indestructible force."

James's eyes glittered; he far preferred rebuilding a fortress to spending a winter sitting and drinking in boredom around the fireplace. "I approve of your plan. It will also get me closer to Sir Godfrey and make it easier for him to take me into his confidence."

"When winter is over, I shall attack in the north where Elizabeth's dower lands are, and you can attack from Melton Keep in the south. That way, Sir Godfrey will have to split his forces to fight us both or allow one of us to make easy gains in the territory we seek."

"Am I to go with him?" Stephen asked.

"No, I think not. James will not have the time to train you; and, although it would be good for you to see all the things he does, I think it is more important that you continue your basic education in defending yourself. I have caught up with my accounts now and have things running pretty smoothly at all my castles. Therefore, I will have the time to train you. Besides, you will be in less danger here, as we are much better fortified and armed than Melton Keep; and it will take away James's time if he has to watch out to see that you are not kidnapped again."

Stephen looked disappointed but said nothing. What James was going to do sounded far more exciting to him than spending the winter here. And James was really his favorite; although he liked and respected Richard, it was James who spent the most time with him—who had tutored him and laughed with him and teased him. Richard was older and sterner and a little forbidding, while James was exciting, intriguing and fun.

"I think it will be safe enough at Melton that you can take Gwendolyn with you to set the household in order," Richard said. It had occurred to him while they were talking that this would offer Gwendolyn a chance to again have her own household. Although Elizabeth had been polite to the woman, as she promised, she had not been at all friendly. Also, Elizabeth had taken all the household duties upon herself. And, although he realized after Elizabeth took them over that Gwendolyn was not an excellent housekeeper, he felt that she must be bored, having no home to keep up.

At his words, James felt a stab of suspicion. It occurred to him that Richard's plan was a polite excuse to send him and his mother away. He knew Elizabeth disliked them both, and he wondered if she had cajoled his brother into getting them out of her way. Certainly Richard had seemed extraordinarily caught up in Elizabeth lately. For a moment, he almost began to argue with his brother; but then he remembered Stephen's presence and stopped. After all, Elizabeth was his sister, and Stephen was very fond of her. He could not say anything about her in front of him without hurting him or making him distrust James. And James had no desire to do either, for he had a great deal of feeling for Stephen. Stephen was young enough and so obviously admiring that he was one of the few people that James did not mistrust. He was a hardworking lad and not at all proud—never once had he made a remark about James's parentage. Though few would have believed it, James liked children; and he found in Stephen both a child and a pattern for an adult whom he could admire.

So he clamped his teeth shut over what he was about to ask concerning Elizabeth and her role in their departure. Anyway, even if it were true, it would do little good to take Richard to task for it; he was infatuated with Elizabeth and would do almost anything to please her. And, even if the scheme was spawned by Elizabeth's dislike of him and Gwendolyn, the idea was still a good one, and the fortification of Melton Keep should be done. He certainly was not about to get into an argument with his brother over it. He would just have to go ahead and do what was asked of him, and set one of the maids to spy on Elizabeth so that he could be kept informed of her movements. That way, if she was planning something against him, he could find out about it and return to Norcastle to thwart her plans.

"I am sure my mother would like to accompany me," James said, and Richard wondered a little at the coldness in his voice.

Preparations for their departure were immediately begun. James and Richard picked a few men as guards to accompany James and Gwendolyn. Cart after cart was loaded with provisions to keep them through the winter. The castellan of Melton Keep had been poor, and it had been neglected through the years. James felt sure that it would be poorly stocked, even with food. Gwendolyn went about packing her clothes and linens with great happiness. Elizabeth had never been rude to her since that first time, but Gwendolyn never felt comfortable around her. She knew Elizabeth disliked her and was polite to her only because Richard demanded it. Gwendolyn in return had very few good feelings about Elizabeth. She thought her a cold, proud thing, and felt sure that she dissatisfied Richard in bed. Certainly she was not pleasant to be around and converse with. Gwendolyn had avoided her company; but that made Norcastle seem rather cramped, for she had to spend much of her time in her room. It would be far better, she felt, to have her own keep to look after and not have to bother with Elizabeth.

Within a few days' time, James and Gwendolyn were packed and ready to leave. As their entourage left the castle gates, Stephen and Richard felt a pang of sorrow at their leaving. Richard and James had rarely been separated since James was a child, and it made Richard feel rather as if he were missing some part of his body when James was not there. As for Stephen, he would bitterly miss this man who had become his most beloved person, next to Elizabeth.

However, Elizabeth felt none of their sadness. She was quite frankly pleased that James and Gwendolyn were gone. Somehow she never felt quite secure when James was there. Even though she had been wrong about his betraying Stephen, she still believed that he was capable of doing almost anything. She knew he disliked her, and she had seen that dislike stronger in his eyes the past few days. Sometimes she feared that he would do her some wrong, and always she feared his influence over his brother. No matter how much Richard delighted in her company in bed, she knew she could not hope to prevail if James set out to make Richard mistrust her. Elizabeth had little tolerance for Gwendolyn. She had tried to be polite to her because Richard wanted it, but she could not like her. She could not forget that the woman had been the mistress of Richard's father, and her presence seemed an insult both to her and to Richard's dead mother. Besides that, she had been a bad housekeeper and, once Elizabeth took over the running of the household, had not offered to help in any way. Elizabeth felt she would like her life much better when Gwendolyn left it.

Heavy winter soon fell upon them, isolating Norcastle from the rest of the world. The inhabitants of the castle did not mind their enforced solitude, however. Ever since that day in the counting room, Elizabeth and Richard had been very happy together. Having once broken through the ice around her, Richard was able to show Elizabeth the delights of love. Their nights were spent in pleasant mutual discovery. Richard could now explore Elizabeth's body without feeling that he violated her. He could stroke her, tease her rosy nipples to hardness, trace lazy designs on her skin with his fingertips.

Every time he made love to her, Elizabeth enjoyed it more and more. For the first time in her life, she was realizing that the bonds between a man and a woman could be highly pleasurable. In other areas, their lives changed also. Elizabeth, better pleased with her husband, more secure in her position as his wife, began to lose many of the misconceptions about men induced by her uncle and cousins, which she had used as a shield against Richard. Now she admitted that he was kind to her, that he was gentle and generous, that he had saved herself and her brother. More than that, he had given them much; he had given her jewels and the full charge of his castle, not to mention numerous bolts of cloth for her dresses. He was spending a great deal of time and effort training Stephen and preparing him to rule his own lands one day. Unlike Sir Godfrey, he tried to enable

Stephen to meet all the problems he would face as a great landholder. She could accept these things now without fearing that they were pretenses and part of some plot to ensnare her and Stephen.

As for Richard, he found himself daily slipping more and more into love with her. He realized that he had never met a woman quite like her—so beautiful, so honorable, so quick-witted. Now that she seemed to return his affection, or at least took pleasure in him, there was nothing to impede his growing feeling for her. Sometimes in the evening, as they sat in the great hall by the fire, he would gaze at her, mesmerized by her beauty, and his chest would swell with emotion. He had never trusted anyone outside his family, but he found now that he had to trust her. He could not bear not to. He was beginning to realize that, if she was unfaithful or disloyal to him, he might as well be dead. With so much at stake, he had no choice but to give in and trust her and let happen what would.

December passed quickly, lightened by the merriment of Christmas festivities. The Christmas season began early in December with Advent, which started on the Sunday nearest the feast of Saint Andrew. During the first week of Advent, the plum pudding was made in a huge batch in the kitchen. By custom, everyone in the household had to help stir. Elizabeth and Stephen, deprived of the merriment of the season during their stay in Sir Godfrey's household, went about hanging holly, ivy and mistletoe. Stephen also hunted with Richard, and even Elizabeth accompanied them sometimes, although not when they hunted the dangerous wild boar. Much food had to be laid in and prepared for the Christmas feasting, and the castle hummed with activity.

On Christmas Eve, the yule log, a huge tree trunk complete with roots, was hauled in and placed with great ceremony in the fireplace. Superstitions abounded regarding the log, and the Norwen clan followed them carefully. It had to be lit with the ashen faggot left over from the year before, in order to keep the house from burning down. It also had to ignite on the first try, lest trouble follow. And it had to be kept burning for twelve hours for the members of the household to have good luck. After the lighting of the yule log, there was singing and dancing in chains, called caroling. It was often condemned by the Church as a pagan practice left over from the Druid days, but the happy custom was kept by most people despite that fact. When the log had burned down, the last charred piece of it was carefully wrapped and stored for next year's ashen faggot.

During the night, about three o'clock, the family, including Philip and Marguerite, who had traveled to Norcastle for the holidays, gathered in the chapel for the Missa in Nocte. Later, about dawn, they rose again to celebrate the dawn mass, or Missa in Aurora. After mass, they sat down to eat a bowl of frumenty, traditionally the first thing consumed Christmas morning. It was a cereal of hulled wheat boiled in milk and seasoned with cinnamon, sugar, and other spices. The bells of the chapel and of the village church sounded throughout the day to celebrate the birth of Christ. After the day mass about noon, everyone settled down to an afternoon of eating, drinking and merriment. There was a wassail bowl of mulled cider, from which everyone drank liberally as they played games and riddles and watched the mumming.

The main meal began with the ceremonial carrying in of the roasted boar's head, caught and killed two days before by Sir Philip. Along with the boar's head, there was mutton, bacon, peacock (roasted and then magnificently refeathered), plum pudding, capon, goose, a haunch of venison, mallard, pigeon, meat pies, and the Christmas delicacy of mince pie. The mince pie was cooked in an oblong-shaped pastry made to resemble the manger. It was filled with chopped spices and meats, and an image of baby Jesus adorned the top. Presents were exchanged, Stephen receiving a shining set of chain mail from Richard, and Elizabeth getting a sparkling sapphire necklace that nearly took her breath away. She gazed at her husband in delighted awe, and he smiled, heavy-lidded with desire and contentment.

"What I have for you seems so little," she murmured, handing him a rolled tapestry. She had worked on it for weeks, applying every bit of her artistic and sewing skills. It was a depiction of Norwen's victory at Ballew's Field. In the center, dominating, stood Richard, sword upraised in triumph and his foot on the neck of his enemy.

Hooking a hand behind her head, he drew her close to kiss her. "It is beautiful, and I will honor it. Your time and skill make it more precious than any jewel."

She smiled shakily. As the evening progressed and the drinking continued, the riddling became more and more bawdy, until Elizabeth blushed and declared that she must retire to bed. Her husband rose immediately. His eyes glittered, though he showed no other signs of drunkenness. His smile was wide and warm. "Then I must depart, too," he commented suggestively, "for our wit has inspired another part of my body."

Elizabeth's color deepened, but she smiled back, no longer hurt or dismayed by a lewd remark. She had learned that they meant her no harm. Curtsying to her new aunt and uncle, she climbed the great stone stairs to her bedchamber, Norwen at her side, one arm lazily encircling her waist. When they stepped inside the door, he pulled her to him, kissing her deeply, his tongue plunging into her mouth to seek its sweetness. "I need no honey, only your kisses," he murmured huskily.

Elizabeth giggled and moved away, teasingly swaying her hips. "Yet I notice that you ate first. It would seem to be the more important hunger."

"Wench." His lazy voice held no reproof. He enjoyed seeing her like this, responding to him with a woman's wiles, laughing and delighting in their love play. He tugged at the laces of her bliaud. "It seems our servants are making merry. Shall I serve as your dressing maid?"

She glanced up at him provocatively through lowered lashes. "Have you the skill, milord?"

He inched her outer garment off her shoulders and down over her hips until it crumpled to the floor. "I have been known to undress a few women."

"Indeed?" she said, raising one eyebrow as she set to work on his clothes, sliding them from him slowly, letting her hands caress his tough skin as she removed his clothes. Casting the wool tunic aside, she played her fingers across his bare chest, hard as rock and muscular from swordplay. Light as a feather, she drifted across the white ridges of old scars. "And is that where you earned these scars? From women who were displeased with your skills?"

He grinned, sucking in his breath at her touch. She had never toyed with his body before, never explored and aroused him. "More like jealous husbands."

"Hah! I know you knights. You don't choose the wives of sword-wielding fighting men. Oh, no, it's the company of sluts and bored merchant's wives for you." She ran her fingers through the mat of hair upon his chest and slipped down to the laces of his chausses.

"Since you became my wife," he said seriously, his face flushed with passion, "I have had no woman, lady or merchant wife."

"Not even a slut following your army?" she mocked.

"Least of all that." His hand was trembling as he placed it on her hair. "Lord, you stir me beyond belief."

"Do you—enjoy my touch?" she asked curiously. "Am I not too bold?"

He chuckled hoarsely. "I love your boldness. I have yearned for you to *want* to touch me."

She smiled and rolled his chausses down his legs, then led him to the fire. Warmed by its glow even in the winter cold, they stretched out on the lovely rug before it.

Elizabeth wriggled out of her hose and woolen shift. He watched her unbraid her hair. "Elizabeth?" he began hesitantly.

"Yes?" She shook loose her flowing mane of hair.

"Would it please you to touch me? I would like for you to, if you feel you would not mind. I want you to make love to me."

"Of course, milord. I am, after all, your willing handmaiden," she replied, her eyes gleaming wickedly.

He gripped her shoulders. "I don't want your obedience. I want your passion."

Suddenly she bent and nipped his shoulder, and he shuddered with delight. Kissing, sucking, lightly tracing with her tongue, she ran down his iron-hard arm, imitating his sweet handling of her body. He groaned at the touch of her mouth on his flesh, never felt before. Elizabeth was drunk on her new sensations, suddenly yearning for him, burning as she never had, eager and hungry, wanting to know every part of his body intimately. Her hands trailed across his abdomen as her lips feathered over the soft inside of his elbow. Gently her fingers folded around his burgeoning manhood, stroking the velvet rod. Richard groaned and twisted his head, clenching his fists helplessly.

"What?" Elizabeth whispered close to his ear. "Have I made the great warrior tremble in fear?" She moved her head down his body, sliding her silken hair across his skin until he was wracked with shudders.

"Yes!" His whisper was fierce, his bright eyes anything but submissive. His hands settled on her hips, and he moved her until she sat astride him. "You are my conqueror. Now ride me, as a good conqueror should."

Elizabeth blinked, surprised. She had never imagined a man might allow a woman to be on top. "But I—how?"

His hands pulled her pelvis down onto his hard, hot shaft, thrusting upward to meet her. Elizabeth smiled at the new sensations coursing through her. She began to move atop him, circling, pumping, slowing, then speeding up, swaying from side to side. His hands twined in her hair in a wild agony of pleasure. "Elizabeth, Elizabeth."

Something swirled at the edge of her consciousness—a delightful, pushing something—and when he stiffened and cried aloud his pleasure, the cords of his neck taut, she wished they could continue to move. She sensed there was something more for her, but she did not know what or how to ask for it. So she remained silent, contenting herself with the pleasure of his filling her.

January came, and the twelve days of Christmas ended with the Epiphany, or Twelfth Night. On Twelfth Night a cake, baked the day before, was cut and eaten. The one who found the bean in his slice of cake became the King of the Bean and was set up as the mock ruler of the household, or Lord of Misrule. This year the honor fell to Stephen, and he exercised his wits to the fullest in thinking of merriment for them to do and jokes to play on each other.

A few days later, the joyful season over and hard winter upon them, Philip and Marguerite returned to their home. Life at Norcastle fell back into a norm. January that year was a bitterly cold month, and everyone spent much of their time huddled by the fire in the great hall. They wore layers of heavy clothing, and Elizabeth found that her hands were too numb with cold to even do her sewing. At night, Richard and Elizabeth slept warmly, however, entwined in each other's arms.

Elizabeth and Richard passed much of their time in talking. Now that there was no longer sexual tension between them and they were happy in one another, they found that they could sit together and talk freely without strain. More than that, they discovered how enjoyable it was to sit and talk. They spoke of their childhoods, their parents, events that had changed them or meant a great deal to them. Richard talked about the time spent out of England in exile from his home. He spoke of the sacrifices Marguerite and Sir Philip had made and of the many hard times they had experienced. He told her of his experiences in the Crusades, of the hot, dry land of the East, of the perfumed, dark-skinned women and of the beautiful jewels and fabrics.

One evening late in January, as they sat by the fire in Elizabeth's quarters drowsily listening to its hiss and pop, Elizabeth asked Richard how he had acquired his wealth. He glanced at her and laughed.

"What have you heard about that?" he asked.

"Well, that it was given to you by satisfied noble ladies, or that James is a witch and conjured it up out of nothing," Elizabeth teased.

Richard threw back his head and laughed. "A little far off the mark. James would have been very useful when we first left England if that were the case. As it was, we lived hand to mouth. Sir Philip fought in tourneys and hired out as a knight to noblemen to fight in their petty feuds in France and Germany. Sometimes we went with him, but most of the time we remained at Mathilde's court. We were forced to sell the jewels that Aunt Marguerite brought from home with her. The only one we kept was that ring that belonged to my mother. After a few years, when I got old enough and strong enough to fight, I followed the tourney circuit like Uncle Philip. After I was knighted, I joined a French count who was going to the Crusades to fight, and I acquired many jewels and much gold there. When I returned, that wealth enabled us to live in a better style. I was able to outfit James and myself and Uncle Philip with good armor and several good war-horses. Also, I was able to hire and support several good fighting men. But I saved most of my wealth for our return to England; I knew that that was when I would need it in order to regain my lands.

"After we returned with King Henry, James acquired quite a bit of money for us through the Jewish money-lenders. Gwendolyn's mother was the daughter of a rich Jewish merchant in London, so James and Gwendolyn contacted her cousin. At that time there was rioting in the

Jewish section, and they were greatly in fear for their lives. James and I and our men protected them. We cleared the mobs from the streets and let it be known that these people were under our protection. In return, they paid us a great deal of money. With that, I was able to hire and train and sustain the army that I used to take back my land. Does that appall you, that I got my money from the Jews?"

Elizabeth studied him for a moment. She realized that it probably should be abhorrent to her, but she found that she could only think how resourceful he was, how well he had taken care of himself and his family, and how much he had gained through his own efforts. Here was a man who would not allow himself to be discouraged, but had struggled throughout the years in many ways to overcome all the things that had been done to him.

"No," she said, "I think that I am rather proud of you. What other knight has had such courage as you?"

Richard took her hand in his and pulled her over onto his lap. It thrilled him to hear her say that. Did not that show that she had some regard for him? Might not pride for him give way to love? At least she was beginning to feel something for him, whereas before she had felt only indifference. Gently he kissed her, and she returned his kiss, matching him touch for touch, kiss for kiss, passion for passion. Playfully she nibbled at his ear while her hands ran over his clothed body, until finally, with a groan, he wrapped his arms about her and rose, picking her up. Richard carried Elizabeth to the bed and, divesting himself of his clothes, lay down beside her. Quickly Elizabeth wriggled out of her own garments and tossed them aside. She snuggled up against him, delighting in the feel of his smooth bare skin, and let herself float along on the waves of her passion. He cupped her breasts and kissed them, flicking the nipples to hardness with his tongue. His hand crept between her legs and caressed her, and she sighed with pleasure and let her legs fall apart so that he might reach that most secret and wondrous place. Easily he fanned the flame of her passion and then entered her. He plunged into her again and again, delightfully hard and filling inside her. As his strokes grew quicker and deeper, Elizabeth felt a wild, glorious something growing in her loins, rising and swelling with his strokes until finally it burst within her, sending waves of pleasure throughout her body and throwing her into a complete peace that she had never known before. When she reached that pinnacle of pleasure and all her muscles tightened, she felt him rock above her and come to his fulfillment, also.

For a time, she lay completely stunned beneath him. What had happened to her? She felt the most beautiful, languid peacefulness, the most complete satisfaction. When he rolled off her, she turned her head to look at him. He seemed suddenly golden and beautiful, and she felt in that moment as though there was nothing she would not do for him. Gladly she would melt at his feet. Blissfully she laid her head on his shoulder and went to sleep.

When she awoke the next morning, Richard was already gone from the bed. For a moment, she contemplated what had transpired the night before. Never before had she felt that way. She wondered if men always felt that wild burst of pleasure she had felt that night. Did other women usually feel it? She smiled to think that she might feel it again. But then a cold wave of fear swept over her, as she remembered how joyous Richard had made her feel, how she had wanted to do things for him, to sacrifice for him, to live in and through him. She realized suddenly that the real danger a man presented was not that he might physically harm her or abuse her in lovemaking; no, she had learned to take that at her uncle's house and live with it and still be herself. The really frightening thing was that, as Richard had done, a man could give one so much pleasure, so much delight, that one could fall madly in love with him. She wanted to give in and love him, immerse herself in him—and lose her own identity. Once she loved him and wished to obey him, then he truly had great power over her. No longer would it be a question of him forcing her to do his will. She would voluntarily submit, and her desire would be not to do as she wished, but to discover what he wished and do that. She would be lost then, lost, forever an extension, a possession of Richard—never herself, Lady Elizabeth, but Norwen's wife and the mother of his children.

Elizabeth thought about her mother, so willing to please her father, so overjoyed at seeing him, so eager to be with him, never having any thought, opinion, or mind of her own. Elizabeth did not want to be like that, could not stand to be like that. She much preferred to be the sort of woman Marguerite was. Marguerite was herself, with her own opinions, who did her own deeds, who did not beg for permission or ask her husband's advice. She was certainly not crippled by love. Her face when she looked at Sir Philip betokened, if anything, only mild affection. She did not cling to him, but went her own way. Elizabeth could not remember ever seeing her hang on to his arm or look to him for help. She was independent and in control. And the reason—she did not love her husband. She gave him none of those sugary looks or sweet giddy smiles nor did any of the other things that were the hallmark of love, and that was what Elizabeth wished to be like.

Never, Elizabeth swore, never again would she give in to that feeling. She had been wrong to feel this pleasure and leave herself open to be taken advantage of. Her response had scared her, and she vowed never again to give way to it.

That night when she and Richard went to bed, he found to his surprise that the willing, joyous bed partner of the past two months was gone. When he kissed her,

her lips were firm, but unresponsive. Her tongue did not creep out to play with his, nor her mouth press sweetly into his. A little surprised, Richard renewed his efforts, deepening his kiss, gently working his lips over hers while his hands strayed down to caress her breasts, his callused fingertips stroking the nipples to hard buttons. He bent to take her nipple in his mouth, sucking, licking, flickering wildly over it, but none of his efforts brought a groan or tremor or even a quickened breath from her. He pulled back, his forehead knotted in puzzlement. "Elizabeth, what is the matter?"

"Nothing," she replied, struggling to keep her voice calm and cool. His kisses had stirred her far more than she wanted to admit, even to herself. She longed to wrap her arms around him and return his kiss. She wanted to explore and caress his body and feel again the thrilling release of the night before. But she knew she should not. In this one thing she had to remain firm, or she would be lost forever. Elizabeth stiffened herself to his advances, sternly forcing her mind to dwell on unappealing things and praying that soon it would become easier for her to ignore the flames he ignited in her body.

"What do you mean, nothing? You are as different as night from day. What happened? Do you feel ill? Is it the time of your course?" Mutely she shook her head. "Then what? Why are you suddenly so stiff and cold? Last night you were a wanton, wild little thing." He smiled, remembering. "How you wriggled and moaned. You nearly took the flesh off my back with your nails."

Elizabeth blushed, shamed at his reminder of her helpless, uncontrolled passion. He delighted in her complete subjugation to him. It was just like a man. That irritating thought helped sustain her in her silent battle; and, when Richard resumed his lovemaking, she remained passive beneath him. Finally, in a fury of passion and despair, he took her, raging inside for the love he had known the night before and which had suddenly vanished. As soon as he was finished, he tore away, his anger spilling out. "Damn you! Why have you turned cold again?"

"I am sorry if I displeased milord husband," Elizabeth responded tonelessly.

Richard turned to her, almost gnashing his teeth in fury. "What is the matter with you? Are you trying to drive me mad?"

"No, milord."

"Have I offended you in any way?"

"No, milord."

"My name is Richard!" he roared, and she quailed before his anger. He hated himself for frightening her, but he could not tamp down the boiling frustrations within him. He clamped one hand around her frail wrist. "You shall tell me, before God. I'll not let you go until you do."

"It is an early Lent this year," Elizabeth began, her mind racing frantically. "Shrove Tuesday is not far away."

"What the devil does that have to do with anything?"

"We must give up such sport for Lent," she explained. That should cool his ardor—and her own. Lent was a time of sadness and penance, when pleasures should be given up. If she could get him to agree to this period of abstinence, by the time Easter came, perhaps she would have brought her flagrant desires under control.

A muscle jumped in his jaw. He knew it was a common practice to abjure sex during Lent, but the idea rasped his nerves. "And that is why you have turned cold? To drive me from your bed during Lent? I had not realized you were such a religious woman," he remarked sarcastically. "Perhaps you should have become a nun."

"No doubt I would have been happier serving a spiritual master than an earthly one," she retorted sharply, stung by his tone.

"No doubt." He swung out of bed. "So you wish to

begin Lent a few days early. All right. I shall not grace your bed again until after Easter. Perhaps by then you will have recovered from your sudden saintliness." He wrapped his fur-lined robe around him and stalked from the room. Elizabeth watched, unhappy and cold, alone in her great bed.

As the days passed, Richard grew paler and thinner. He looked almost ready to sicken. In truth, it was more an emotional turmoil than any physical illness. He slept little and dreamed of Elizabeth when he did sleep, awakening hard and panting, aching for her lithe young body. Yet he had promised to stay out of her bed throughout Lent, and he would not break his promise. But, by all the saints, it was the hardest penance he had ever had to endure. At times he thought he would go mad thinking about her, wanting her, and knowing he could not have her. He had to get away from her soon.

Therefore, he sat down and wrote out a demand of Elizabeth's dower lands, which he gave to a messenger to take to Sir Godfrey. He knew what Sir Godfrey's answer would be; and, so as soon as the message was sent, he began to make preparations for the coming battle. He wrote a letter to King Henry that explained his reason for fighting Godfrey in order to recover his wife's dower lands, and that he planned to dispatch as soon as he received Godfrey's negative reply. He made his battle plans for besieging the keeps of her land and set his soldiers tasks to ready their physical strength and skills.

Elizabeth saw the increased activity, but did not think it wise to question her husband as to the reason; he was touchy enough with her as it was. So it came as a complete surprise to her one afternoon in late February when he strode into her room and said, "Madam, I demanded your dower lands from Sir Godfrey, and I've received today a reply from him."

Elizabeth was a little surprised that he had already demanded the lands; however, she had no doubts as to what her uncle's answer was. "I presume that he refused to give them up."

"Yes. He says that he did not countenance our marriage; he did not give his permission, and therefore we are not legally wed and I am not entitled to the dower lands. I have already sent a messenger to King Henry with a letter explaining my position and my reason for attacking Sir Godfrey. I have been readying my army ever since I sent Godfrey my demands, so that we would be able to leave as soon as he refused and thus hope to surprise him by a few days. The servants are today finishing stocking our carts with provisions for my men and fodder for our horses. We should be able to leave at dawn tomorrow."

Elizabeth rose, staring at him in mute surprise. When at last she found her tongue, she said, "But, milord, Richard, what can you mean? It is not even spring yet. The weather is still damp and chill. The spring thaws are just now coming, and within a few weeks you will have to face the awful mud that they will bring. Your carts, your horses will all sink and be difficult to remove. Your travel will be much impeded."

Richard looked at her coldly, his eyebrows rising. "Are you presuming to speak to me on military matters? Do you think I have not already thought of these things? My plan is to move my men in carts now, before the thaw begins, and take the first keep while Godfrey is still napping. From there I will have a base of operations to take the other keeps, and will not need such a large entourage of heavily laden carts."

Elizabeth could hardly believe her ears. This did not sound at all like Richard to be so impulsive and indifferent to the dangers. "Richard," she said, "be reasonable. Your men cannot fight in such cold; many of them will grow sick. You increase your chances of losing. Why, you yourself may catch a chill or fever and succumb to it. What would your men do then without a leader? What would any of us do without you? Please, Richard, reconsider, I beg of you. Stay here with me until the spring is full upon us. You know that James is not yet ready to fight for Stephen's land. You will have nothing to distract my uncle. Godfrey will be able to turn his full forces against you for several months."

"Oh? It sounds as if you are worried," Richard said, a sneer in his voice. "I assure you, madam, that I shall not fail; I believe I know how to fight better than you give me credit for. At any rate, should I die, James would be more than capable of carrying on my battles and protecting you and Stephen. No doubt that is your only concern in this matter, since it is obvious that you have no regard for me."

"Richard, you are mistaken."

"Am I? I think not. Let us not pretend, at least not with each other. We both know that for the past few weeks you have wished to have nothing to do with me. For a while I had hoped that we might achieve some sort of accord between us, that we might have the sort of bond that lay between my father and Gwendolyn or between my aunt and uncle, but I see quite clearly now that it is not to be. I do not hope to know what happened to you to change you so; I only know that something did happen and that you are different. You are a cold, indifferent bitch, and living with you has become like living with a block of ice. I would rather take my chances in the cold outside than remain here with you."

Elizabeth stood frozen, staring at him; his words lashed through her like a whip, yet she could say nothing to refute them. Suddenly she felt lost and helpless; she had no idea what to do. Richard looked at her for a moment, and when she made no reply to his words he turned swiftly upon his heel and left.

That was the last Elizabeth saw of him until the formal leave taking the next morning. She bid him farewell from the steps of the courtyard at dawn the next day, and offered him a goblet to take a final drink before his journey. He took it and drank and handed it to her, with no change of expression upon his face. She felt as if she did not exist. She watched sadly as he and his men rode out of the courtyard, their horses' hooves clattering across the wooden bridge.

Chapter Twelve

JAMES LOOKED UP FROM HIS WORK AT THE SERVANT'S ENtrance into the room. "What is it?"

"A visitor, sir," the man said. "He would not give his name, but he gave me this and said that you would recognize it."

The man held out a small object to James. James took it and examined it; it was a small square piece of silver, a brooch with the insignia of the Duke of Tanford upon it. James looked at it for a moment, tossing it in his hand.

At last he said, "All right. I will see the man. Send him in."

In a few moments a small, fair-complexioned man entered the room. He bowed to James and greeted him, but all the while his eyes darted about the room, searching, looking, recording it in his mind. He reminded James of some small curious animal—a ferret, a weasel. His hair and eyebrows were bleached out, almost white; his skin was paper thin and dotted with reddish freckles.

It was certainly not the duke himself; James presumed it must be some man of his.

"What do you want?" James asked bluntly. "Does the duke wish to negotiate concerning the two keeps he stole from us?"

"Indeed, sir, you wrong His Grace, the duke. He is a just, fair man, not one inclined to thievery. He did not take those keeps from you; they were simply up for grabs to anyone who had the power to maintain them. The duke happened to have that power."

"Ah, yes, I see the difference," James said sardonically.

"His Grace, the duke, asked me to bring a message to you from him. He has grown weary of dealing with such fools as Sir Godfrey. This last attempt to kidnap Stephen —such idiocy. The duke can hardly countenance that sort of thing."

"Well, I can only say that I approve of the duke's decision."

"Nay, there is more to it than that. His Grace knows that you were involved, or at least pretended to be involved, in that plot with Godfrey; is that not true?"

James shrugged silently.

"Of course, the duke realizes that Godfrey acted foolishly, as always, believing that you would betray your brother or Stephen for such a pittance. Not all men are as venal as Sir Godfrey. His Grace is sure you would not sell yourself for such a low price."

"Do you mean that His Grace feels that I would sell myself for a higher price?" James's voice was amused.

"No, of course. Not sell. His Grace realizes, however, that you must act in your own best interests, and the duke feels that it would be in your self-interest if your brother did not produce an heir."

"Do not be foolish. I am illegitimate; I cannot inherit."

"Don't you take me for a fool. We both know that you could gain much of your brother's territory upon his death if he did not have an heir."

"And why should the Duke of Tanford be so concerned that I should inherit rather than Richard's rightful heir?"

The other man waved his hand airily. "You do not understand my master. He believes very strongly in maintaining the present balance between the lords of this land. He feels that no one should gain too much property, wield too much influence. It is for this reason that the duke does not wish to see Godfrey and his niece succeed in their plan. He would much rather that Norwen keep his land and that you inherit after him."

James went suddenly still. "What do you mean? What scheme between Godfrey and his niece do you speak of?"

"Do you mean you have not got wind of it yet? His Grace will be sadly disappointed to find that you do not have the excellent spy system he had heard you kept. Oh, well, never mind. The plot is really quite simple, although rather devious, as befits Godfrey's mind. He and Lady Elizabeth concocted a scheme whereby she was thrown into your brother's path with a very sad tale about the cruelties of her uncle. She appeared to betray her uncle's wicked plan and thus win your brother's sympathy. Being a lovely wench, it did not take her long to convince him that the best tack to take against Sir Godfrey was to marry her and seize her dower lands. Godfrey, of course, pretended anger at their marriage. He even went so far as to cook up a plot with you to kidnap Stephen. No doubt he will make a good show of defending Elizabeth's dower lands against Norwen, but in the end it matters little to him whether Norwen seizes them or not. For you see, once Lady Elizabeth bears Norwen an heir, it is their plan to murder him and seize Norcastle. Then Godfrey and Elizabeth can rule all of Norwen's lands as the guardians of the child." The man studied James. "That makes a little better sense, doesn't it?"

James's face did not change expression, but inside his

brain raced. He had had no inkling of this plot, and he doubted that it was completely true. However, sifting the truth from the lies in one of Tanford's stories was almost impossible. In a way, the story made sense. James had never trusted Elizabeth, and he thought her a woman who could lie coldly and steadily with a straight face. And it sounded like a scheme of Sir Godfrey's to gain back the Norwen land through treachery. But it made little sense for Tanford to be informing him of the plot.

"What value is it to the duke that I know of this plan? Why should he betray his ally thus to me, who has no bond with him at all?"

"Ah, there, you see, you think only of the present. His Grace is much more farsighted. Right now there is no bond between you, but he foresees one."

"What are you speaking of?"

"The duke has a younger brother, whose name is Simon. Simon has an eleven-year-old daughter, named Clarissa. The duke feels that the man who will take over all the Norwen land would be a proper husband for Clarissa, even though he be illegitimate. His Grace wishes to betroth his niece to you. That way, he will be blood kin to the ruler of all the vast Norwen lands; and it is so much better to have such a one as an ally than an enemy."

"But Sir Godfrey is already his ally," James pointed out.

"Yes, but the duke does not wish to have an ally who owns Beaufort land and Norwen land both. He fears that he will be far too mighty. You, on the other hand, shall hold title only to the Norwen land, while Godfrey will retain the Beaufort land. So you see, it all works out."

"Yes," James agreed, "I can see how it all works out for His Grace."

"And for you, sir, for you, too. You could not look higher for a bride than the niece of a duke, being a bastard as you are. She will carry with her a pleasant dowry, as well as her name. Moreover, you will stand to inherit your brother's lands, if we foil Sir Godfrey's plan."

"And exactly how does the duke propose to do that?"

"Why, it is very simple. Only one person must be taken out of the picture, and that is the Lady Elizabeth."

"So you mean that I am to kill my brother's wife. That is a grave sin you ask me to do."

The other man smiled. "Come, come, sir. I would not put it quite so bluntly. You are simply looking out for your interests. You are simply saving your brother's life by getting rid of the woman who would murder him. You know that he is too infatuated with her to ever believe you if you told him of the plot."

James said nothing, but he knew that it was true. And look at the way Richard had sent him to this remote keep. He had always suspected that Elizabeth had had a hand in that. While certainly his rebuilding of the fortress made sense, it also fit in very well with the scheme of Elizabeth's to murder Richard and seize his lands after she had borne him an heir. With James so far away, he could not prevent Richard's death, nor return to Norcastle in time to keep it from falling into Sir Godfrey's hands.

"No doubt a great deal of your story is made up of lies," James said.

"Oh, no." The man shook his head vigorously. Actually he had very little idea about how much the duke said was ever true. He knew that the duke was serious in his betrothal offer and that he wanted Lady Elizabeth killed. He also knew that that was because the duke suspected Sir Godfrey of delaying murdering Norwen until after Elizabeth had had an heir, so that Godfrey could kidnap her and rule both her and her child. The lady was not in on the scheme, of course; but it was close enough to the truth that no doubt James, who obviously disliked the woman anyway, would seize upon it and believe it. Of course, the betrothal offer, while completely legitimate now, might someday be easily forgotten if it seemed advantageous at that time to forget it.

James stared at the wall thoughtfully, drumming his fingers on the table before him. At last he said, "Tell your master that I accept his plan. I will think of a way to carry it out. Also, I shall draw up my wishes regarding the betrothal contract and send it to him."

"Oh, thank you, sir. Thank you. I am sure His Grace will be most pleased when I return to him with this news. He has told me that he would love to meet you in person sometime in the future, if that meets with your approval," the other man said, rising and bowing out.

"Of course. I should like that as well," James said.

The man nodded and backed quickly through the doorway. James remained for a moment, staring after him. He felt uneasy about what he had just done. It was the first time he could remember entering into a plot that could harm Richard. Richard was so infatuated with the woman that he would no doubt grieve if she died. Any move against a man's wife was a move against him. However, that would be far better, certainly, than standing by and allowing her to murder Richard. Of course, he did not know that what Tanford's man had said was true; but the more he thought about it, the more likely it seemed to him. His spies had reported no unusual behavior on Elizabeth's part, but that would fit in with this plan. She would not be contacting her uncle until she had borne an heir and it was time to kill Richard and seize Norcastle. He knew that he would really be saving Richard by killing Elizabeth. He would feel more comfortable if he had better proof, of course; but he did not see how he could obtain any proof until the plan was set into action, and then it would be too late. Besides, he could think of no reason why Tanford should turn against Godfrey in this way unless he did really fear that Godfrey would seize Norwen's land. And the plot he had laid out before him was the only realistic way that Sir Godfrey could control those lands. It must be true; it had to be true. Elizabeth must die.

The idea of wedding Clarissa appealed to him. It did

not bother him that she was a mere child; he had none of Richard's dreams of a wedding of love and companionship. He had been too young when Henry died to remember his father's relationship with his mother. Of course, he had grown up with Marguerite and Philip's marriage; but he saw Marguerite as far too perfect a person to compare with anyone else. The fact that Marguerite and her husband adored one another scarcely meant that that was possible for anyone else. He had never hoped to find a woman like his aunt, for in his eyes she was a saint. And, though he loved his mother, his feelings about her were far too mixed and ambiguous for him to truly like women. None could live up to Aunt Marguerite; his mother was much more typical, and she had by his very birth hurt him too greatly for him to truly trust women. All he wanted from a marriage was the most property and the best name he could obtain in order to improve his own status, and he agreed with the duke; he could certainly look no higher than a duke's niece.

Tanford would be a slippery one to have as blood kin, but James felt that he was more than able to handle him. Of course, as soon as Elizabeth was gone and he had married Clarissa, the duke would then want him to kill Richard, too. However, he felt confident that he could thwart that plan. Once he had Clarissa and her lands in his control, he would feel no compunction about double-crossing the duke.

He was certain he could handle that. The important thing was to get Richard out of Elizabeth's clutches as soon as possible.

It was almost two weeks later that James's spies reported that the relationship between the earl and the countess had deteriorated rapidly. Norwen was apparently angry with his bride and had in a storm of rage departed from the castle and gone north to retake Elizabeth's dower lands. No one knew precisely what had caused the disagreement. James could not understand why his brother had already left to fight Godfrey; it was still bitterly cold and the spring thaw had not even arrived yet. When it did, roads would be horribly muddy and almost impassable. Moreover, although he had spent his winter well and acquired several good men for Stephen's army, he certainly had not yet had time to turn them into a well-trained fighting force. Richard must know that by fighting now he would be taking Godfrey on alone, for James was not yet ready to attack Stephen's property.

Also it bothered James considerably that Elizabeth had been left alone in charge of Norcastle. Although he doubted that she would do anything against Richard until after she had borne him an heir, it worried him for her to control the Norwen seat of command. So he was rather pleased when he received a messenger from Richard some days later asking him to settle his affairs as quickly as he could at Melton Keep and return to Norcastle. His brother's letter was terse and did not explain his reasons for attacking Sir Godfrey earlier than they had planned. He only said that he had gone and that he did not like to think of Elizabeth and Stephen alone at Norcastle and unprotected. Therefore, he hoped that James could finish training the army and rebuilding the keep so that he could return to Norcastle and take command there. James immediately stepped up his training of the men, for he wanted to do as Norwen bade as quickly as possible.

After Richard's departure, Elizabeth waited for word from him, worried that he might meet with disaster on his campaign. He had left too early because she angered him; and if anything happened to him, it would be her fault. She was almost sick with fear that he would be killed. If he was, she and Stephen would be in serious trouble. That fact justified her nightly prayers for her husband's safety—at least to herself. She would not admit to any concern for him based solely on his own welfare. It was simply that she and her brother would be up for grabs if Richard died, with James and her uncle snarling over them, both out to help themselves at Stephen's expense.

To add to her misery, Elizabeth fell ill. It was a peculiar sickness. When she arose in the morning, she felt well; but as the day progressed, she grew dizzy and sick at her stomach, though never quite to the point of vomiting. Throughout the late afternoon and evening, she was forced to retire to her bed to reduce the nausea. Even the *thought* of food made her ill. After a week, her misery gradually lessened, for another week and then another, hanging on but growing lighter.

"Oh, Peg," she moaned to her maid, a sturdy girl, and attractive in a frank, open way. She was pleasant and devoted to her new mistress, always concerned for the poor, fragile thing's health. Her mistress had not been well since his lordship left. "I feel so peculiar, so sick. Do you suppose it's a punishment upon me?"

"For what, milady? You hardly ever say a cross word, you go to mass daily, you never strike anyone. You're generous and kind."

She smiled weakly. "Why, thank you, Peg." She couldn't tell the girl that she meant a punishment for throwing her husband into the teeth of battle by refusing him her bed. Even now the audacity of what she had done amazed her. She had not really expected Norwen to give in to her. She had thought he would growl and keep her in his bed; but, instead, he had gone charging off to battle like some demented creature, placing his life in jeopardy—all because of her selfishness, her independence. Perhaps God was punishing her for not being a proper wife—a humble, submissive woman as the priest said she should be.

"Besides, milady, I told my mother about your sickness, and she said 'twasn't a sickness at all."

"Indeed? Then what is it?"

Peg smiled conspiratorially. "She said sounds like you're with child."

"What!" Elizabeth sat bolt upright, and immediately regretted her sudden movement as the bile rose in her throat. "No, it couldn't be. I feel better in the mornings. You're supposed to feel sick in the morning, aren't you? Not the evening."

"Not everyone, my mother says."

Elizabeth knitted her brow in thought. "It's true, I haven't had my monthly course as I should. But I thought it was simply the change, the excitement of Norwen's leaving." She stared at her maid, her eyes beginning to shine. "Oh, Peg, what if she's right! An heir for Norcastle. My lord will be so pleased!" She didn't add that it might make him forget his bitter words on leaving and his anger at her denying him his marital rights.

As the days passed without a sign of bleeding, she grew more and more convinced her serving girl was correct. She hugged the knowledge to herself. This was too personal, too intimate to dictate to a priest to write her husband. No, she would wait until he returned and tell him in private. Smiling to herself, she realized that her sickness began to seem less onerous. Her future was suddenly bright and rosy. A son. An heir for Norwen. Her position would be much more secure. Richard would be very happy with her.

"Milady!" She glanced up from her dreamy contemplation of the future to focus on one of the serving wenches.

"What?"

"There is a messenger below, milady, from the earl. He carries a letter for you."

Elizabeth sprang to her feet, heedless of the bout of dizzyness such motion usually brought. "Fetch the priest to me in the great hall. I shall see the messenger there."

She hurried downstairs to take the folded parchment from the dusty messenger, and sent him to the kitchen for refreshment. Impatiently she awaited the arrival of the priest, studying the seal of wax and the scribbling across the front. Oh, if only she could read and did not have to wait for the priest. If only she could rip open the seal and understand the words written by his hands, could know what he said to her. It seemed so unfair that she not be allowed to learn the mysterious art because she was a woman.

"Milady," the priest bowed gravely.

"Father John." She sprang up and handed him the missive. "I have received this from the earl, and I wish to know its contents."

"Of course, milady." He broke the seal and perused the letter, then began, "Your lord husband says that he has taken the first of your dower castles. Apparently it fell quite easily."

"No, no," Elizabeth interrupted impatiently. "I want you to read the letter to me, not summarize it. I want to know every word he says."

With a frown that clearly said the vagaries of the female were beyond understanding, the priest went back to the beginning of the letter. " 'My lady wife,' it begins. 'I pray that things are well with you and that God protects you from all harm.' " Elizabeth clasped her hands tightly. Was that merely a typical formal address in letters, or did he truly mean it? " 'I have taken the first of your dower castles, Derry Slough. It fell into my hands like a ripe plum, being poorly equipped and taken completely by surprise.' " Elizabeth smiled. How much better it was to hear his exact words. She could almost see him writing it, almost hear his voice. " 'Now I shall set about reinforcing the keep and making it strong to use as my base in our enemy's territory. I'—here he has crossed out something and then wrote—'regret my bitter words on parting and hope that you will not be displeased by my return. Your lord and husband, Richard, Earl of Norwen.' "

The black-frocked man looked over at her curiously, obviously awaiting an explanation of the last lines. Eliz-

abeth gazed back with a trace of defiance. Surely he had
no right to know everything that passed between herself
and her husband, even though he was a man of God.
She wished again, quite desperately, that she could read.
She would like to keep the letter by her side to peruse
again and again, to ponder the significance of each word.
Had he forgiven her? Would he be pleased to return? Did
he worry about her safety? "Father John, I wish to dictate
a letter in reply to my lord husband."

"Yes, milady." He trotted off and returned after what
seemed ages.

Elizabeth knew she could tell her husband little real
news. She couldn't expose her joyous expectation of an
heir to the curious priest. Her husband must hear it from
her own mouth. She wet her lips nervously. "My lord
husband, may this letter find you in good health and
withstanding the rigors of the cool spring. I am most
pleased to receive your news, though I had every faith in
your ultimate victory." She couldn't explain the great
flood of relief on finding her actions had not sent him
precipitously into disaster. Norwen was a wise campaign-
er. He had been correct in making a surprise attack on
Godfrey. It was a well-thought-out plot, not merely anger
at her, that had propelled him from the castle. "We are
well here at Norcastle. Stephen is growing apace." She
halted, uncertain what else to say. "May God watch over
you and protect you. Your . . . devoted wife, Elizabeth,
Lady Norwen."

She wished she could have asked him to return
quickly. She felt so lonely nowadays, and she worried
about giving birth. She remembered that her mother had
died when Stephen was born. Although Richard could
not save her from such a fate, she knew she would feel
more secure if he were with her. But she could not ask a
fighting man to forego his battles and fly to her side
because of foolish womanly fears. It was the lot of a
nobleman's wife to bear her loneliness and fear in silence.
To badger Richard to neglect his duty would only create

further friction between them and lower her in his esteem. So Elizabeth bit her lip and sealed the letter as it was. When the messenger was fed and had slept, she would send him back to the earl with her reply.

Two more weeks passed before she received another letter from Richard. This one informed her that the second dower keep had been taken. Elizabeth listened eagerly to the priest's dry voice reading her husband's words, and tried to imagine how Richard had looked as he wrote the message. She recalled the way he had bent over the parchment when he had written to his aunt, his forehead creased in concentration, his teeth chewing at his underlip. Pain slashed through her, and she was afraid she might burst into tears. Whatever was the matter with her? Did carrying a babe, as she was now certain she did, make a woman a weeping fool?

The reading of the letter was interrupted by Stephen's excited voice: "Elizabeth! Elizabeth!" He rushed into the room, not noticing the priest seated on his stool. "I was up on the tower and I saw men approaching!"

"What? Who?" Her heart jumped wildly, her first thought being that the earl was returning home. "Norwen? Is it Norwen?" Her face changed. "Or is it our uncle?"

"No, it was the earl's colors! I'm sure of that."

Elizabeth almost ran from the room, yanking open the huge outer doors and hurrying into the bailey, her brother on her heels. The drawbridge, kept up for protection during her husband's absence, was being lowered. Elizabeth swallowed convulsively, her hands twisting together, as the first horse trotted onto it. She shaded her eyes against the sun, trying to see the tall figure astride the mount. There was something different about him, something . . . Her heart plummeted as the man swung off his horse and pushed back his mail hood, his black hair damp with sweat. James! It wasn't Richard at all, but his brother, whom she hated and feared.

Suddenly the tears that had threatened earlier overwhelmed her. They welled in her eyes and spilled over onto her cheeks as she watched James approach. She clapped her hand over her mouth, but could not suppress the sob which burst from her. Disappointed and embarrassed by her tears, she wheeled and ran into the castle, darting up the stairs to her room and collapsing on her bed in tears. Stephen and James stared after her, mouths open. Finally Stephen turned back to the tall man. "I—I am sorry, James. I don't know what's wrong with Elizabeth. She's been acting strangely of late. I told her it was Norwen's colors, and she expected Richard. I guess —I guess she didn't want you to see her cry," he finished lamely.

James shrugged. Elizabeth had been rude to him, but it was little more than what he expected. She had made it clear from the first that she disliked him. Breaking into tears and running seemed a bit extreme, but . . . He picked up Stephen to hug him, groaning in mock dismay at the boy's growth. "You're waxing fat!" he accused. "I can see my brother does not exercise you enough."

"Then you shall have to take me hunting, won't you?" Stephen laughed, his astonishment at Elizabeth's peculiar actions vanishing from his mind. James joined in his laughter, and they entered the hall, arms about each other, in jovial friendship. James changed and cleaned away the dirt of travel while Stephen hung about, chattering and soaking up his idol's words. Finally, when James was dressed in a soft woolen tunic of deep blue and clean chausses, a wide leather belt with a jeweled buckle fastened around his slender waist, they returned to the great hall. It was time for supper to begin, and they waited for Elizabeth to appear.

She did at last, her face splotched and red from crying, her eyes lowered in embarrassment. She came to where they stood and curtsied gravely, not lifting her face, humiliated that James of all people had witnessed her emotional outburst. She could not even excuse herself with her pregnancy, for she refused to tell James the news before her husband. "I am sorry, sir, that I indulged in such unseemly behavior when you arrived. I was quite overset that it was not my lord husband who returned, as I thought. I pray you will forgive me."

"Certainly, milady." His voice matched hers in courtesy and coolness. He privately doubted that Elizabeth would be so anxious to see her husband that she would cry if she found out he had not arrived. However, he supposed she might have wanted to beg a favor from Richard and was disappointed that James had arrived instead. Expecting one whom she could twist around her little finger, it must depress her spirits to discover that their visitor was a man whom she could not influence at all.

Elizabeth glanced up at him through her thick, downcast eyelashes. His cold, blue black gaze on her sent a shiver down her spine. More than ever, she was certain he wished to harm her. Her feelings were supremely accurate, for James was considering what method he should use to get rid of her. He could not let suspicion fall upon himself or Richard. It would be best to have it done when neither of them were in the castle, but that would entail hiring someone else to perform the deed. James didn't like the idea of there being another person involved, for he might reveal that it was James who wished her dead. That would be disastrous if somehow Richard learned of it. His brother was so besotted with the woman he would never understand why James had had to kill her. The best method would be poison that he administered himself. But, if he was in the castle when she died, suspicion would immediately fall on him, even though nothing could be proved. James didn't want the canker of doubt eating away at his brother's love for him.

"James has come to guard Norcastle until Richard returns," Stephen informed his sister excitedly. "Isn't that wonderful? Now I can start my lessons again. I'll bet he'll be amazed at how much I've learned, won't he?"

"Yes," Elizabeth replied colorlessly. "Milord is an excellent teacher."

They sat down to eat, Stephen, whose rank was the highest, at the head of the table. He carved meat for his sister and placed it on the slice of manchet bread before her, offering her goose and fish, as well as a venison pie. Elizabeth still felt rather nauseated most evenings, and she ate little, her turbulent stomach worsened by James's presence. Looking at her pale face, James realized she was thinner than when he saw her last, and he wondered if she was ill or worried. For an instant doubt flashed across his mind. Should he believe Tanford's story? Was this woman really dangerous to his brother? She looked unhappy and she had cried when her husband hadn't appeared today. She had all the markings, in fact, of a lonely wife miserable without the presence of her husband. James frowned.

"I trust your mother is enjoying Melton Keep," Elizabeth remarked politely to James, attempting to create a conversation between them.

"Quite well, milady." James stiffened, wary at Elizabeth's touching upon his mother. He had never forgotten or forgiven her slight upon the woman when she first arrived. He remembered her pride, her coldness, her Beaufort blood. His doubts of a moment before flew from his mind. He could not allow Elizabeth's acting skills or sweet face to influence him, James reminded himself. She was plotting to destroy his brother.

He thought of Clarissa's dower lands and bloodline. He remembered the years of barbs about his paternity and the strange hunger he had felt all his life, knowing that the titles and pride and lands that were Norwen rightfully belonged to Richard, not him. No matter how he loved his brother, it ate at James to always live in Richard's shadow. Only this haughty woman stood between him and Clarissa's lands—this proud woman who had sneered at his mother and convinced Richard to

send him away to Melton Keep so she would be free to
work on Richard. She had tried to separate him from his
brother. Didn't that prove Tanford's story? She wanted
James far away, where he couldn't warn Richard or help
him when she betrayed her husband to Sir Godfrey.

James's face blackened, and suddenly the perfect
method sprang into his mind: he could put poison upon
her sewing needle. Needles were hard to come by, and
even a great lady had only a few. It would be easy to
poison them before he left. She was bound to sometime
prick herself with one; but he and Richard would be away
by then, so no suspicion would fall on them. And there
would be no accomplice to betray him. If he chose a
strong enough poison, she would die from even a small
stab. He studied Elizabeth's smooth, shuttered face. It
would be for Richard's own good. He would hurt at first,
but eventually even he would know he was better off
without Elizabeth.

Richard sat alone in his tent, his cloak wrapped tightly
about him, feeling miserable. As always lately, he was
berating himself for having left Norcastle so early to come
fight. He had, as he had predicted, caught Godfrey by
surprise, and the keeps had fallen quickly into his hands;
but he was not sure it was worth it. The weather had
been chilling and was still cold at night. Several of his
men had succumbed to fevers and chills. Fighting, now
that the spring thaws had arrived, was messy and
difficult. All the roads were turned into quagmires; men
and horses sloshed along slowly, and the heavy provision
carts often got stuck to halfway up their wheels.

They were besieging their fourth and final keep now;
the other three had fallen to him. This one, however, was
better supplied and manned than the other three had
been. Moreover, Godfrey had sent his reinforcements;
this castellan had refused to surrender, and they had
been camped here in the mud and muck for several
weeks now. The spring rains had begun, adding to the

mess. Richard's men were short-tempered and irritable; daily their grumbling grew. Although the fighting had not been difficult, their morale was quickly falling apart under the poor weather conditions and lack of any real fighting.

Richard sighed. He was going to have to do something soon to make the keep surrender. It simply was not feasible to sit out a long siege and starve those inside into submission. His men might begin to desert; Godfrey might attack him as he waited; and he needed to join James's attack against Stephen's lands. It was already April, and James would need to launch his offensive soon.

Mentally he cursed himself for having begun his campaigns against Elizabeth's dower lands too soon. If only he hadn't allowed her to get under his skin so. If only he had been more patient and understanding when she suddenly turned cold to him again. He had been an impulsive fool, not only militarily, but also personally. Hardly a day went by that he did not think of Elizabeth and wish that he were with her. He remembered her voice, her pale silky hair, her firm, lithe body. He ached to touch her again, to have the feel of her in his arms, to kiss her and stroke her and sink deliciously into her flesh. He had pushed her too hard, been too impatient. He remembered all the terrible things that had been done to her by Godfrey and Geoffrey; it was no wonder that she should fear and dislike men. He should have realized that the weeks when she had been responsive to him were not likely to continue unbroken. It was not at all surprising, really, that she should suddenly draw up short and return to her old suspicious ways. That was the way people were; it took them some time to get over things. One might, for a while, feel better and then suddenly revert to one's old depression, but the reversions would grow shorter and fewer as one got well. He should not have expected Elizabeth to get well at once. He regretted bitterly his actions. His raging had done nothing but frighten her further; and certainly his separation from her had not done him any good, and he doubted that it had helped her any either. He wished heartily that he had not done what he had.

Thoughtfully he chewed on his lip. He must bring this keep down quickly. He needed to return to Elizabeth; he felt that instinctively. He longed to see her and, more than that, he felt that she needed his help. Richard rose and went to the door of his tent. He called for the captain of his men, William St. John.

When St. John entered, he said, "We must take the offensive. I cannot let my men just sit here for several weeks waiting for the keep to fall."

St. John nodded, for he agreed with him entirely.

"We must attack the castle. Tomorrow take a group of men out of sight of the keep, cut down a tall tree and fashion a battering-ram. Set the other men to checking our rope ladders to make sure they are not frayed. As soon as the ram is completed, we will attack the keep."

The following day, St. John and his group of men went far back into the forest and cut down a tall tree. They chopped off all of its branches and at the end chopped away part of the trunk until it became a sharp point. This they would use to batter down the heavy gates of the keep.

The day after the large ram was completed, Richard roused his men before dawn. A selected group went into the woods and fetched the battering-ram and brought it back to the camp. In the icy predawn chill, the priest blessed them, and they began their attack. Ever since they had first set siege to the keep, their catapults had been hammering away at the walls. Daily they shot huge stones against the firm walls. Whatever breaches they had made had quickly been repaired, however. Richard chose not to use them in this attack, as they would alert the keep to the coming danger; instead he left them sitting motionless.

The men with the battering-ram began first. Theirs was the most dangerous job, for they could wear no armor, as it would have weighed them down too much for them to run with the heavy ram. Therefore, Richard thought it best that they begin under the cover of darkness. They picked up their burden and moved forward toward the castle. When they were some yards away from it, they ran and shoved their ram hard against the door; then they retreated and ran at the gates again. The heavy pounding quickly awoke all the castle. Torches flared on the battlements, and archers began to shoot down at them; however, in the dark it was almost impossible for any of the archers to hit his mark.

Now, to draw fire away from the battering-ram, Richard's troops moved forward. Carrying their shields above their heads, they marched in close formation, thereby forming a metal cover to deflect the arrows aimed at them. The men ran forward, trying to get close enough to the castle to hurl up their grappling hooks, to which were attached rope ladders. Richard had pinpointed three areas where the castle walls seemed weakest and most poorly defended. He divided his forces into three and sent them at these three points. The archers, who had been concentrating on the men at the battering-ram, were forced to leave their posts and circle the castle battlements to fire at the oncoming troops. When the troops reached the castle walls, they threw up their ladders; the metal scraped against the stone and caught, and the men began to climb quickly. This was the most defenseless part of the battle for a soldier. His shield slung over his back so that he could climb, he was protected only by his mail and helmet. The heaviness of his accouterments slowed him in his climb, exposing him to the merciless marksmanship of the archers for a longer time. It was then that you were most likely to get an arrow in the throat, or for one to slip in between the chinks of mail and pierce your skin, or go through the eye openings of your helmet and kill you instantly.

As they climbed, the soldiers at the top were trying frantically to chop through the rope before the men could reach the top. For the last few moments of the climb, it was a heart-stopping race between the soldier at the top and the ones on the rope; for if they managed to cut through the heavy rope, all of the soldiers climbing would go tumbling back to the ground, causing serious injury to those who were near the top. There was a pause as the soldier at the top drew his sword and went on, for at the top he was met with armed resistance. He had to break through the men and create a little space for the men following him to stand and fight. For this reason the first man or two was always the best of the fighters. St. John led one group and Richard led another, giving the third group to a knight of his who always exhibited both skill and bravery.

Richard scrambled up the ladder quickly, drawing his sword as he climbed. He was faster than most at this and consequently reached the top long before the rope could be sawed through. As he came over the top, the soldier left off hacking at the rope to swing at Richard's head. Richard parried the blow and struck him hard with the flat of his sword, sending him tumbling. This gave him enough time to leap over the top of the battlement and assume a fighting stance against the three men who rushed upon him immediately. One of Richard's men came over the side and took his place at Richard's back, so that the two men were able to ward off the approaching soldiers from both sides. The knot at the top grew, and Richard's men began to push the others steadily back.

The archers went down quickly, for they were not armed or armored to combat with soldiers. Most of them fled before the oncoming men, leaving the troops below unharassed to continue to climb up the ladders and over the side. As Richard fought, he heard the groan and crack of splintering wood, and he knew that the gates had been breached by the ram. With renewed vigor, he called to his men, shouting that the gates were opened; and they pushed forward. The others fell back before them and soon began to panic, running for the steps that led down from the battlements. Richard and his men charged after them, and the steps became a tangled mass of fighting men. Once they had pushed the men completely down into the courtyard, Richard sent several of his men scurrying after them; and the rest he took back to the battlements to run to the other points and help his other forces.

Quickly the battlements were cleared and his men swept into the courtyard, taking everything before them. The remainder of Richard's forces were pouring in through the gates, having left the more difficult ascent over the walls. They pushed the others back to the doors of the house itself, which were barred against them. The men, trapped before the doors, surrendered quickly, and the battering-ram soon brought down the heavy wooden doors. They took the house quickly, rounding up frightened servants and putting down any resistance they found.

Godfrey's vassal, who controlled the keep, they found with three other men at the bottom of the stairs to the tower; quickly they were dispatched. Although Richard had shown mercy to some other vassals who had held the other keeps, he had none for this man who had resisted him. The others could be brought under his control, but not this man.

Once these last guards were dead, Richard went storming up the stairs and burst into the room at the top, finding there, as he expected, a collection of the vassal's wealth and the cowering women and children of the castle. For a moment he considered throwing the women to his men, but he decided not to. He would give the chests of valuables to them to repay them for their efforts and make them content in his army, but he did not wish to create the sort of ill will among Elizabeth's people that violation of women or killing of children would bring. He turned to the men behind him, telling them to take the women and children to the dungeon, guarding them on the way. He singled out two of them and ordered them to pick up the chests and carry them down to the men below. There he would distribute them.

As his men hurried to do as he bade, Richard wiped the sweat from his face and drew a deep breath. As soon as he had taken care of his men and had made sure this castle and surrounding countryside were secure with his own forces in control, he would be able to return home. He was done here, and he could go back to try to mend what was broken between him and his wife.

Chapter Thirteen

THE NOISE OF THE HUGE BRIDGE AT NORCASTLE DESCEND-
ing and the heavy gates being pulled open awakened
Elizabeth from her deep sleep. It took her a moment to
realize what the sounds were, and then she sat up in
alarm. Whatever could be happening? Why were the
castle gates being opened to someone? Hastily she threw
on a garment over her underdress and shoved her feet
into shoes, and, picking up a small dagger, she went
hurrying out into the courtyard to demand what was
going on.

When she reached the steps of the castle and saw the
weary men riding in through the gates, she recognized
the large figure in front; it was her husband returning
home with his forces long before she had expected him.

"Richard!" she cried, forgetting her public manners.
"Richard, you are home!"

She ran to his horse and took hold of his stirrup.
Looking up at him, she inquired anxiously in a low voice,

"Richard, what is amiss? Are you all right? Have you been hurt?"

Richard shook his head, a slow, tired smile touching his face. "No, it is all right. There is nothing wrong, I swear it. Just let me get down from here and I shall tell you."

He dismounted and handed his reins to a servant to lead his horse away and bed it down. Once he was on the ground, he drew Elizabeth into his arms and hugged her tightly. How good it was to feel her soft, warm body again in his arms. He did not think he could get enough of it.

"Richard, please, come inside," Elizabeth said at last, feeling a little anxious as to his mental state. He had to be horribly weary or stunned from battle, or both, to be standing out in the courtyard like this clinging to her.

At her words, Richard released her and they went into the castle, his arm about her shoulder. Richard had pushed his men hard to reach Norcastle, and he was very tired; but as he climbed the steps with Elizabeth he found his weariness giving way to desire. Her sleep-tumbled hair, the hastily donned dress that was slightly askew made him think of her in bed, and passion began to vibrate through him.

"Why did you bring so few troops back with you? What happened to your men?" Elizabeth asked.

"I left most of them behind guarding your dower castles, my dear," he said. "I shall tell you all about it tomorrow. Right now, I have other things on my mind." He stopped and drew her into his arms and kissed her. It had been so long since he had felt her lips beneath his, and their velvety softness made him tremble with desire too-long suppressed.

"Oh, my love," he groaned, "it has been so long." Quickly his hands swept over her body, and then he picked her up in his arms. "I must have you."

His eagerness dismayed Elizabeth, but she lay acquiescent in his arms as he carried her into her bedroom. He put her down and pulled the clothes from her, exposing her pale body to his gaze. Hungrily his eyes moved over her body; she seemed heavier, thicker around the waist and stomach. He reached out and gently stroked her slightly rounded belly. "You have taken on weight since last I saw you," he joked. "Do I burn that much off you?"

"No, milord, it is just—" Elizabeth bit her lip, somehow shy about telling him face to face. She drew a deep breath and said, "I am with child, Richard. I am carrying your child."

For a moment he stared at her uncomprehendingly, and then his tired face lit up. "Are you sure? Do you mean it?" Suddenly he threw back his head and laughed aloud. "So we are about to be blessed with an heir, eh? By the Cross, Elizabeth, that pleases me to know my son is curled up in there—"

Gingerly he touched her abdomen again. On his face there was a look of wonderment. Carefully, as though she were precious glass that might break at his touch, he leaned down and kissed her. "You have made me very happy, Elizabeth."

He kissed her again; and his kiss deepened as his passion returned, combining with his joy to swell in him and grow in him until, at last, he picked her up and laid her in the bed. Lovingly, his lips traveled over her skin, lingering on her breasts. He bent and softly kissed the inside of her thighs. She flinched at the intimate touch, and yet it sent a tingle of excitement through her. Tenderly he entered her and took his pleasure of her until at last his joyous passion flooded out of him and into her.

They awakened slowly the next morning, lazily stretching and lying abed to talk.

"I think that I must teach you how to read and write," Richard said, folding his arms behind his head. "It is too restrictive knowing that what I say to you in a letter must be fit for a priest, and that what you say to me must be entrusted to him, also. Far better, I think, for our safety and privacy if you could read my letters and write to me directly."

Elizabeth turned toward him, excitement in her eyes. "Do you mean it? Would you teach me how to read and write? I would like that better than anything, but Sir Godfrey would never allow us. I know no woman who writes."

"Well, the Countess of Norwen is different, I can assure you. She will be able to read and write," his tone mockingly self-important.

"When can we start?"

"Soon. Soon," he laughed. "At least let me tell you what I have done with your dower keeps."

"Oh, yes, please do, Richard. I would enjoy that very much," Elizabeth urged him, pleased that he would include her. Her lands were his now, and many men would not think of even telling their wives what they did with their dower lands.

"Well, the first three keeps fell like ripe plums. The fourth one I had to bombard and take by force; therefore, it suffered some damage. I have left soldiers and workers there to repair the walls and gates. Also, we must send some provisions to them to replenish their supplies. At that keep, Lindale, which is the most northern of your keeps, I did away with the vassal who ran it. He was a man of Sir Godfrey's, put there by Sir Godfrey after he took over your lands. He had no loyalty to you and resisted my taking over. Therefore, I felt it best to do away with him.

"But at the other three keeps I kept the vassals who ruled them; all three were your father's men originally, and merely knuckled under Godfrey's authority because he was your guardian and uncle. They pledged their swords to me, and I think that they shall be faithful. Of course, I heavily augmented their troops with mine to ensure their fidelity. I left St. John at Lindale to oversee the rebuilding of that keep. It is the most strategic of your castles, being closest to Sir Godfrey's home. So I think we need a strong man there, one loyal to you and me. I have a knight, Sir Gawain, who is a very loyal, steadfast man. He is a sturdy fighter, but a man more inclined to follow than to lead. I thought we could reward him for his faithful service to me by giving him Lindale to maintain. I think he will do well there. He is not quick enough to cheat you or to enter into any treason. He is a very loyal, honest man, and I think that is what we need there—one who will always look to me for guidance and not go off on some tangent of his own. He will keep me very well informed of what goes on, and that is what I wish.

"We shall have to keep a close eye on the other three, of course. I do not wish to stir up any discontent among your people by replacing one of them if it is not necessary; however, I do not trust them to be loyal vassals of yours until we have observed them for a time.

"I had thought to take you on a procession throughout your lands, to let the people see you and the vassals see my power. I think that your resemblance to your father and the actual presence of a Beaufort will do much to make the people cleave to you. I doubt that Sir Godfrey was a very just or kind master; so I do not think it would take much. But, of course, now that you are carrying a child I dare not let you travel so much. Perhaps I shall take Stephen; it might have the same effect, and he needs to grow used to dealing with his underlings. What think you?"

Elizabeth looked at him a little startled and tried to compose her thoughts. It surprised her that he should ask her opinion, even in this matter concerning her. Kind he had always been, but she had never before found him overly concerned about her opinion on a matter. "Why, I think it would be an excellent idea. He resembles my father greatly in looks and coloring. He is very close-mouthed, so I think he will never let anything slip to the wrong people; and you know he would do exactly as you tell him. I think it would be very good training for him."

"Good. I agree." Richard took Elizabeth's hand and held it. "I am well pleased, Elizabeth. Many is the time I have lain awake at night, lying there in the wet or the cold or the muck or the desert heat, and have wondered if it was worth it, agonized over how to get the gold I needed to retake my land, how to get the king's approval, how to maneuver and fight and—" he broke off and sighed. "In a way, I never really imagined I could have this much; but having it, having Norcastle back again, and you and a family now, a son to give it all to, to plan for—I have something to build here, something that will grow and be greater than I am and yet be a part of me. Do you understand how I feel?"

Elizabeth nodded, impressed by his feelings. He smiled a little and shrugged. "It may not seem anything but normal to others who have had it all their lives, but to me—to me, it seems everything I could want."

"Then I am glad, I am truly glad that you are happy."

Later that morning, Richard rose and dressed and went to tell James his news. He found his brother waiting for him in the great hall. At sight of him, James rose.

"Good morrow, brother," James said lightly. "Did you think we were the enemy to come sneaking in upon us at night?"

Richard smiled and said, "Nay. I just hoped that way I could be saved from having you plague me with questions."

The two men embraced one another and sat down by the fire. "So," James began, "tell me about your campaign. Was it successful?"

"Yes, but I shall tell you about that in a moment. First I have much greater news."

James's eyebrows raised questioningly. "More important than a successful campaign?"

"Yes. Elizabeth told me last night that she is with child. Soon I will have an heir, James."

James stared at him for a moment and then turned his lips into a smile. "Congratulations, Richard. I am pleased for you." On the inside, his mind raced. That would spoil his plans for the moment. Of course, he had never really contemplated being the heir himself, as Tanford had suggested. That would happen only if Richard never married again and had children, and that was unlikely. What it did do was delay him. He could not do anything now to Elizabeth while she carried Richard's child. He certainly could not destroy his brother's heir and give Richard such double pain. He could not do anything to harm his own nephew; he could not poison his own blood. Therefore, he would have to wait in patience until after the child was born.

James returned to Melton Keep to finish preparing Stephen's army for the battles ahead. Within a month he had brought them into a fairly cohesive unit, and he began to lead them on forays into the Beaufort lands, nibbling up the nearby villages and farmland and taking, almost without battle, the smaller keeps. Godfrey was holding himself aloof and safe in the fastness of his own castle.

At Norcastle, Richard spent most of his time with his wife, teaching her the rudiments of reading and writing. She was eager to learn and worked at it very hard. It pleased her husband to see how quickly she picked it up. "Good," he encouraged Elizabeth as he watched her carefully move the quill over the parchment, the tip of her small tongue peeking out between her lips as she concentrated on her letters. "I think you are fooling me and already knew how to read and write."

"No!" Elizabeth denied quickly, then flushed when she saw his smiling face and realized he was jesting with her. "Oh. Well, I want so much to learn. That's why I've done it quickly. I have always wished I could read. And when I got your letters and had to listen to Father John read them, I hated it. I couldn't say what I wanted to you, and I wasn't always sure he told me everything. At first he tried to merely relate the sense of it to me, without reading every sentence; but I made him read it word by word—or at least I hope he did. I would far rather know for myself what you say without having anyone else see it, too!"

"And I would rather others not see it, also." He smiled, his fingers stealing out to curl a lock of her sunny hair around his fingertips. "There are things I would like to tell you when I am campaigning that are not fit for a priest's ears."

Elizabeth swallowed, her heart beginning to pound. Since her husband had returned, she had found it increasingly difficult to withstand his sexual advances. Her expanding body and the new life within her had made her more languid, but it had also increased her passion. She found herself eagerly awaiting their nights together. She enjoyed looking at his long, lean-hipped male body, and often wished she could caress his chest and run her fingers down his muscular legs. "What would you like to write me?" she asked now, her face unconsciously provocative.

"That I dream of you at night," he replied in a low voice, raising the lock of hair to his lips. "And I awake as hard and pounding as a young boy. That I burn to touch your body, feel the tips of your breasts against my chest." He nuzzled her neck, his mouth searing her skin. Fizzles of excitement shot along her nerves, and Elizabeth was aware of an almost overwhelming desire to let her hand slip beneath his tunic to stroke his hips and knead the tough muscles of his thighs, even to take his manhood in her hands and feel it grow with desire. Sternly she repressed her longings.

Richard nibbled at her earlobe, his tongue stealing into the shell of her ear to lightly tease her senses, tracing its convolutions. "I want you," he murmured, his breath blazing against her skin. "Oh, Elizabeth, my Bess, I want you so. Let me taste your delights."

"You are my husband," she answered. "It is your right."

"I want more than my 'right.' Touch me as you once

did, let me feel your pleasure again." His hand roamed over her body, arousing her sensitive skin through the material of her bliaud, creeping beneath it to feather his calloused fingertips over her naked flesh. A moan rose low in her throat. Elizabeth tried to twist away, but he held her fast. His fingers moved to the soft joining of her thighs to explore and arouse, hurtling her into a swift spiral of almost painful passion. She closed her lips against the panting breaths rising from her. It was just a strange by-product of her pregnancy, Elizabeth told herself. When she had delivered, she would no longer want him. But that didn't help her now, when her whole body ached to feel his power.

Richard heard the moan, could feel the sudden heat of her flesh. He was certain she wanted him, but he could not make her say so. Although he yearned to take her, he pulled back. She opened her eyes in amazement as he stood and walked a few feet away. She was pulsing with desire, so much so that she almost reached out and called him back. But she managed to refrain. He waited for her to say something, and when she did not, his shoulders sagged. He had hoped she would admit her desire. He would have to hold off longer—let her feel unsatisfied lust, let it build and grow inside her, and perhaps next time . . .

But, the next time, Elizabeth was more in control of her body, and he was unable to stop the flood of love that carried him along like a tide. He thrust into her again and again, pouring out his passion with a hoarse cry. When their lovemaking was over, and he rolled aside, pulling her into his arms, Elizabeth chuckled and took one of his great hands to place it on her belly. She was in her seventh month now, and her abdomen was firm and rounded. The life within her quivered and pounded against her belly, and Richard jumped to feel it under his hand. "Is that our child?" he asked in awe.

Elizabeth nodded, smiling. "He is often thus after you take me."

He frowned. "You mean it disturbs him?"

"I don't know. He seems to jump and kick more."

Richard sat up, suddenly uneasy. He remembered his aunt's first birth, and the prospect of that happening to Elizabeth filled him with dread. Until now he had been so filled with excitement over the prospect of his child that he had not thought of the ordeal waiting for his beloved, delicate wife. Marguerite's first labor had been long and hard. Her cries had resounded throughout the small house. He had been thirteen years old then, and James was four. He could recall vividly huddling with his little brother in the hall outside her room, holding James, who was white-faced with fear, while Sir Philip paced frantically up and down the hall, completely oblivious to their existence. If a woman like his aunt, with the large frame of the Norwens, who was always bursting with good health, could suffer so much, think of what would happen to Elizabeth. "You are so small to bear a child," he murmured.

"I have little choice," she answered, smiling at his masculine worry.

But he did not see the smile. He stared at the wall, seeing only a horrible vision of Elizabeth torn and bleeding, her life seeping out in the long struggle to bear his child. She had no choice. That much was true, certainly. He had forced the lovemaking on her. She never asked for it, just as she had not asked for it that night. He sucked in his lower lip between his teeth. What if he was harming her or the babe by his avid lovemaking? What if he was too rough or used her too often? The sweat of a fear he had never known before popped out on his upper lip. He was certain suddenly that his nightly lovemaking could make her miscarry. He knew no one he could ask about it, but he didn't know what to do. Racked with guilt and worry, he rose and began to pace the room.

Elizabeth stared at him, confused, wondering what had caused this sudden change in behavior. Only a moment before he had been relaxed and sated, heavy and almost asleep. "Elizabeth," he began gruffly, and she tightened at his tone. Had she done something amiss? "I am wrong, I think."

"Wrong? About what?"

"Taking you like this."

"I don't understand. You are my husband."

"Yes. But what if I harm you, what if I have done so already? Think how the babe kicks after I make love to you. It disturbs him." Elizabeth opened her mouth to protest, then shut it. After all, she didn't know that he wasn't right. The child did seem to bounce and thrust and jump about more after a vigorous session of loving. Was it harmful? She was fully as ignorant as her husband. "I—I have decided to stop," Richard went on. "I could not live with myself if I caused you to lose the child."

Not a word about herself, Elizabeth thought with irritation. His only concern was the son, the heir. He didn't want to lose the child. She clamped her mouth shut. This was what she wanted, wasn't it? She would no longer have to suffer the temptation of his touch. She could not protest his decision, but it left a funny ache in her chest.

For a few nights Richard continued to sleep with her, because he wanted to be close to her. However, it soon became obvious to him that he couldn't continue that course. Simply lying beside her aroused him past bearing. Her soft, succulent body, her breasts enlarged by pregnancy, even the mound of her stomach tempted him. He could not sleep, and it was all he could do to keep from reaching out for her. Therefore, after a few days, he began to sleep apart from her in his own room.

Elizabeth missed their quiet talks in bed; and, more than she would admit even to herself, she missed him physically. However, the situation was much harder on her husband. Merely seeing her at dinner soon began to arouse his desire. He found himself watching her hungrily as they sat at the dinner table. Looking at her neck and arms, imagining the shape of her body beneath the dress, straining to see the outline of her breast against the material of her dress, he longed to hold her and caress her; and there were times when he was afraid that he might reach out and run his hands over her in full view of everyone.

At night, he tossed and turned in his bed and lost much sleep thinking of her and longing for her. Before long, his nerves were frayed to the utmost and he became very nervous and irritable. The servants and even his men began to avoid him, for he snapped at everyone and found displeasure everywhere.

Finally he decided that the only course for him to take was to leave Norcastle. He hated to leave Elizabeth during her pregnancy, but he was afraid that if he stayed he would go mad. So in May he left to take Stephen on a tour with him over Elizabeth's dower lands. They traveled slowly, spending weeks at each castle so that the people and vassals could become familiar with Stephen and recognize the true Beaufort qualities in him. Stephen matured quickly, acquiring polish and ease with his people.

However, Richard found little surcease. Although he did not have Elizabeth's actual physical presence to inflame him, he found that he thought of her constantly. He worried about the state of her health and the condition of his child. But, most of all, he missed her. Achingly he longed to be with her, to hear her voice, to see her smile, to feel her small body in his arms.

Elizabeth was at first relieved that she had been released from bedding Richard. With him gone, she felt, she would not have to face any of the conflicts he seemed to rouse in her. But she soon found that the castle seemed rather lonely without him. She thought about him much more than she ever had before. She remembered his many kindnesses to her, the things he had done for Stephen, the gentle way he had treated her, how he had taught her to read and write. There were few husbands who were so generous and thoughtful. She had enjoyed their conversations together and she missed that. Moreover, she began to experience some tensions herself. She remembered what Richard had done to her in bed. Often at night, she dreamed about sleeping with him again. Sometimes just thinking of him set her flesh to tingling. She would remember his kisses and her flesh would grow hot.

Daily she grew heavier and more irritable. Everything seemed to annoy her. She snapped at her maids for their incompetence; and once, when one of them clumsily pulled her hair while she was combing it, Elizabeth burst into a tirade against her that ended by her slapping the girl and then dissolving into tears, herself. Once she had prided herself on never crying or showing signs of distress, but now it seemed that she cried constantly. The slightest thing was enough to make tears well up in her eyes. She grew quite moody and often sat for hours at her needlework without actually doing anything, meditating self-pityingly on all the wrongs done her. Irrationally she grew angry at Richard for not being there, even though when he left she had been glad to see him go. She decided he had stopped sleeping with her not out of concern for her, but because she had grown ugly and fat. In particular, James made her nervous. Having chewed off a good chunk of Beaufort lands, James had returned to Norcastle to protect it while Richard and Stephen were gone on their procession. Elizabeth could not stand to be around him. His quiet voice, his catlike walk, his unreadable blue eyes all served to make her jumpy and nervous.

Elizabeth could not understand why she was so moody and on edge and miserable. She put it down to her pregnancy, and refused to even think about why her irritation always seemed to surface more after one of her nights of dreaming of Richard.

Richard had informed his aunt about the coming birth and when the babe should be due. Therefore, Marguerite decided to come and help Elizabeth through the birth. She came during Elizabeth's seventh month, when the heat of July had descended upon them, making everything seem far worse than it was. Marguerite immediately sensed the burgeoning tension within Norcastle. Elizabeth she understood easily; her husband was gone and she was heavy with child, and naturally nothing would seem quite right to her. But Marguerite could tell that there was some trouble where James was concerned, and this she found more inexplicable. For once James refused to talk to her about it. She questioned him about his unusually silent mood, but he simply shrugged and muttered something about not feeling like talking. Marguerite was not usually perturbed, particularly where her nephews were concerned, and she tried more than once to pull some information from James; but James was adamant in his refusal to admit that there was anything wrong with him. For once he found that he could not tell his aunt his plans, and that thought troubled him.

Marguerite took over much of the operation of the castle, thus relieving Elizabeth of her heavy duties. Elizabeth was glad to hand over the reins to the other woman, for she was finding it increasingly difficult to even maneuver up and down the stairs, let alone run a household the size of Norcastle. It was becoming clear to Elizabeth that Richard had left Norcastle simply so he would not have to endure these months. He did not want to look at her swollen body and bear with her black temperament. It seemed to her the height of cowardice that he should do so. It also seemed to her dreadfully important that he should return. By August she was beginning to fear that he would not do so. She told herself that the coward had decided not to return until after the birth. That was typical of a man, she thought— to not be there exactly when one needed him. She conveniently forgot that she had vowed she did not need him. She knew things would be better if he were here; she just knew it. She would feel safe from James, and Marguerite would talk to Richard instead of plaguing her; and he would come and entertain her, tell her pleasant witty things and ask her opinion. When she grew too tired going up the steps, he would help her; probably he would carry her. It was most unfair that he was not here, she decided.

One day, as she sat staring at her embroidery, a messenger entered Norcastle and came to kneel at her feet.

"Milady, the earl is coming; he is no more than five miles behind me. He stopped to rest the horses and bade me come forward to tell you that he will soon be here."

Elizabeth thanked the messenger kindly, for the first time in several weeks feeling a thrill of excitement and pleasure. Richard would be here in a few minutes! Hastily she clapped her hands for her servants and told them to prepare food and drink for their master and his troops. Then she sat impatiently awaiting his arrival. It was announced by the clatter of horses hooves on the wooden bridge. Elizabeth rose as quickly as she could and hurried to the front door. Richard was already dismounting and going up the steps.

"Richard!" Elizabeth cried and held out both hands to him.

Richard was up the stairs in a flash when he saw her do that. Her arms went about his neck and she hugged him warmly.

"I am so glad you are home! Now everything will be better," she said, her voice excited, almost joyful. Richard wrapped his arms around her and clung to her. He had not expected such a pleased greeting from Elizabeth; this was far more than he had hoped for. He had merely wanted to see her again, to be able to sit by her and watch her and make certain she was safe; but to have her throw herself into his arms like this and cry that she was glad to see him home—that was enough to send him reeling. Did it mean—was it possible that she had developed some feeling for him after all? Surely such a warm greeting proved that she had liking for him—nay, more than liking, some tenderer feeling. Perhaps, perhaps she was beginning to love him.

Chapter Fourteen

ELIZABETH AWOKE IN THE MIDDLE OF THE NIGHT, A CRAMP-
ing pain bringing her upright. It had begun.

It was a little sooner than she had expected, but she
had no doubt that her labor had begun. She called for
her maid, who slept outside her door. Quickly the girl
came, her eyes wide and frightened—she realized what
this call in the middle of the night must mean.

"Go wake Lady Marguerite, Peg; tell her that my pains
have begun."

"Yes, milady," the girl said, then bobbed a curtsy and
left the room. She was frightened for her mistress. She
liked Lady Elizabeth, for, though she was stern and
demanded that things be done correctly, she was always
fair and just, and rarely ever slapped a servant. So she felt
great sympathy with her as she faced childbirth. Peg had
gone through that ordeal, and she knew how painful and
debilitating it was, even for a big, healthy girl like herself.
Just think what it would do to a frail little thing like
Elizabeth! Everyone knew, including the master himself,

that it was as likely as not that Elizabeth would not survive it, as narrow hipped as she was.

Cautiously she tapped at Marguerite's door. "Milady. Lady Marguerite."

"Enter." The woman's voice was instantly awake and alert.

"It is Lady Elizabeth, ma'am. She's started her pains."

"All right. I'll be right there." Marguerite left her bed immediately and began to dress. "Go tell the earl that it has begun; he will want to know. Then fetch my maid to me."

The girl nodded and scurried away. Marguerite calmly dressed and went down the hall to Elizabeth's room. She was not as anxious about the countess as everyone else was. Lady Marguerite had seen worse things than childbirth, and she would not be surprised if Elizabeth had, too. True, the girl was slim hipped. But then the baby was earlier than they had thought; probably it was small. And Marguerite realized that, despite her pale, delicate looks, Elizabeth was a very healthy, sturdy young woman. Marguerite's first birth had been difficult, but she had survived it. It had not left the scars on her that it had on her young, impressionable nephews. She had not seen her mother die in childbirth as Elizabeth had; in fact, until her own childbirth, she had not attended a birth. Therefore, she was more practical, less fear ridden than most.

Peg's message, however, sent the earl's heart into his throat, and hastily he scrambled into his clothes and hurried down the long hall to his lady's chambers. He arrived there only seconds after Marguerite did. His aunt took one look at him and decided that the bedside was no place for him. At the moment, Elizabeth was scared, but admirably calm; and she certainly did not need Richard's wild-eyed, distraught face to unnerve her. So Marguerite took his arm and hustled him from the room.

"There is nothing you can do in there," she told him sternly. "You will only be in the way and distress Elizabeth with your mournful face. One look at you and she would be certain she was on her deathbed. I will send for James to come keep you company. Now go down to the great hall and just keep yourself in peace."

Richard nodded numbly and did as she said, and Marguerite returned to the room. She sent her maid to waken James and send him to sit with his brother. Then she turned her attention to the birthing. Elizabeth's contractions were still a good distance apart; it would be some time yet. She had the maids tie ropes around the bedposts for Elizabeth to pull on, and wrapped a piece of linen into a roll for her to bite on. Nor did she forget to follow the custom of placing a knife underneath the mattress to cut the pain. Then she washed her hands with soap and water and made her maids do the same. If there was one thing Marguerite cherished above all else, it was cleanliness. She had had enough of dirt and mess and stench to last her a lifetime during their escape from Sir Godfrey many years ago. Her first child had been born in a tiny, airless room, and she could still remember the filth of the midwife who attended her. Ever since, she had demanded cleanliness from all her attendants. Although it earned her the dislike of local midwives, at any birth she attended Marguerite required scrubbed hands, and always removed the bed linens afterward and put clean ones on. It was more customary to leave the mother lying on the same old bloody sheets during her weeks of recuperation; linens were dear and not often changed and washed. But when others sniffed at her finickiness, she was quick to point out that she had never lost a woman to childbed fever afterward.

Elizabeth found that the pain was great, but not unbearable. The bad thing was that it came more and more frequently, and it never came to an end. Her labor was long and weakening. Through the hours it drained her strength. She lay drifting in a haze of pain, racked by contractions, feeling herself gradually slipping away. Once or twice she lost consciousness, and the rest of the time she floated in a fog, her thoughts confused and unclear. Memories of her mother's death came back to her: the feeble cries she had heard from her room and then her father telling her that mama had left them; the sight of Stephen in his bed, repulsively red and hairless. It scared her, and her breaths came in pants. She felt a cool hand on her head and a calm voice telling her to breathe deeply and relax. Marguerite. Richard's aunt. That thought gave some structure to her world, which had become formless and timeless in her long pain.

Elizabeth fixed her mind on Richard as something to hold on to. He would keep her from drifting away into that frightening nether land. She pictured his face: the fierce, hawklike eyes, the strong jaw, the wide cheekbones. How strong he was, how brave and determined; he would not let anything happen to her if he was here. But he was gone, gone because she was fat and ugly. He wrote to her, but that wasn't the same; she was lonely. She wanted him beside her, wanted his arms around her at night. Why was he not here when she needed him?

"Richard," she whimpered. "I want Richard." But he was gone; she had driven him away with her heavy body—no, with her coldness and her disagreeableness.

"Richard," she moaned aloud.

Marguerite was instantly by her side. "He is downstairs, dear."

"No, he's gone; he's gone. I drove him away."

"Nonsense." Marguerite frowned. The length of the labor was beginning to alarm her, and now Elizabeth seemed to be getting delirious. "He is with James in the great hall, waiting for us to announce the birth of his child. He is right here in Norcastle, and he is very concerned about you. So bear down, Elizabeth, bear down."

"Richard! Richard!" Elizabeth screamed out as the pain cut through her like a knife.

Below Richard paced the stone floor anxiously, his face strained and his eyes red with lack of sleep. The night had passed and most of the morning, and still no word from his aunt. He envisioned Elizabeth dead or dying in agony—because of him, because of his lust for her. She had never wanted him in her bed.

James joined him quickly and cajoled Richard into drinking a cup of mulled wine to calm him. It had no effect on him. He continued to roam the room like a caged animal. James downed one glass and then another. He could think of no place he would rather not be. Childbirth touched a deep, almost unconscious terror within him because of Marguerite's experience when he was a child. Only for his brother would he come this close to it. And then he felt the desperate need for a drink. Without it, his mask might split and fall.

Neither man talked as night changed to day and the day wore on endlessly. Stephen joined them as soon as he arose, and learned what was transpiring in his sister's chamber. When he stepped into the room, his fear was not as great as Richard's, for he still felt deep inside that his sister was invincible, as he had when he was a child. However, one look at the other men's pale, lined faces, and he knew something was seriously wrong. His heart leaped into his mouth, and he sat down on suddenly weak knees, too fearful even to ask how things went. Just before noon, Lady Marguerite came down to them, her face drawn; for once she looked her age. Richard stared at her pleadingly, unable to speak.

"She is all right, Richard, but it is a slow, painful birth. Her belly is narrow and her bones, small; there is little room for the babe to come out."

Richard's face turned ashen at her words. James saw the distress on Richard's face, the awful fear and anguish, and his stomach knotted in sympathy.

"She is not going to die, is she? Aunt Marguerite, tell me she is not. If she dies—I am lost."

"No, I do not think she will die. She is a healthy lass and can hold her own. But it will take a while. I am sorry; I must get back to her now."

Richard sank into a chair, his face drained of expression, his eyes black pools of terror. Watching him, James realized that, if she lived through this, he could not harm her. No matter how dangerous she was, he could not hurt Richard so.

The two men jumped at a cry from above. Then, faintly but distinctly, they heard Elizabeth call, "Richard!" Immediately Richard leaped from his chair and ran from the room. He bounded up the stairs and burst into Elizabeth's room. The women all whirled around at his loud entrance.

"Richard, please—" Marguerite began in irritation.

But she was interrupted by Elizabeth, who struggled vainly to sit up and said, "Richard? Oh, Richard."

In mute appeal, she extended her hand to him, and he was instantly at her side. Tenderly he took her hand, and she clung to his hand as if for dear life. Marguerite said nothing further; she knew he was about as movable as a castle now. Besides, if it comforted Elizabeth and gave her renewed strength . . .

Throughout the rest of her labor, Richard stayed by his wife like a rock. Whenever the pains were upon her, she dug her fingers into his hand. Her fingernails cut fiercely into his hand; but he did not even notice, so concerned was he with her welfare. Icy fingers of dread clutched at his stomach. She looked so pale; she had so little strength yet. The sight of her in pain sickened him, and he wanted to scream with frustration at his inability to help her.

Suddenly Marguerite said excitedly, "There! His head is coming out. Oh, Elizabeth, he's coming. Push, child, harder."

Elizabeth strained, her hand like a vise on his. Richard did not look at the child, only at his wife's contorted face.

"There, I have him! Good lass, Elizabeth, you can rest now."

Marguerite slapped the silent baby soundly on the rump and it set up a howl. Quickly she wiped the slippery child and placed it on a blanket. There was a slight look of consternation on her face, but neither parent paid any attention. Elizabeth sank into her pillows, exhausted; her eyes closed and her hand slipped from Richard's grasp. Slowly, dazedly, Richard rose. He knew it was over, that Elizabeth was not dead; but nothing really seemed to register. He turned and walked toward the door. Marguerite intercepted him, holding out the baby for him to view. He paid no attention to her, did not even glance at his newborn baby, just walked right past her into the hall.

Marguerite bit her lip and stared after him for a moment. Then she shrugged her shoulders a little and carried the baby to its mother. Weakly Elizabeth's eyes fluttered open and she looked at her child. A girl!

"No!" she wailed. "Oh, no, it is a girl!" She began to cry in anger and frustration. She had failed utterly, had produced not the desired heir, but a female child. Not only had she failed in her duty to Richard, she had inflicted upon her own child the subordinate place in life that she herself had endured. Somehow, she had never imagined having anything but a son—a son to meet Norwen's dynastic needs, a boy she could watch grow tall and straight as a reed, a son to have all the power and strength that she had never had. But now she had doomed this mite to servitude, misery and pain. Elizabeth turned her face into her pillow and cried herself to sleep.

Richard stumbled blindly down the hall to the winding tower staircase. Almost running, he went up the stairs and out onto the roof. Desperately he sucked the fresh air into his lungs, trying to dispel the odors, sights and sounds of the childbed from his mind. He had been deeply shaken by what he had witnessed below. He knew that he had come to love Elizabeth, but he really had not realized to what extent he loved her until just now. Suddenly he knew that he could not bear to lose her; she was dearer to him than anything he had ever known. What if she had died? What if she died even yet? Many women died from childbed fever. He did not know how he could bear such a thing.

He had seen many bloody deaths in battle, had seen men die horribly in torture, but nothing had ever frightened and appalled him as much as Elizabeth's pain. What made it all even more unbearable was the awful knowledge that he was the cause of it all. He had wanted an heir; he had desired her; he had not paid the slightest attention to her wishes; he had let nothing stand in the way of his getting what he wanted. She had never wanted to sleep with him. Never! He had forced her, really—oh, not physical force, but using his marital rights as a club. Because of his willful selfishness, she had almost died; because of him, she had been put to that pain.

It would not happen anymore, he vowed to himself. Never again would he take her against her will, never again would he bed her. He could not bear to lose her or cause her more pain.

"I swear it," he said, clenching his fists and gazing out across his land. "I swear it."

James soon returned to his campaign against the Beaufort lands. Having made his decision not to cause Elizabeth's death, he found that he wished to get far away from Norcastle. He knew he was putting to death his hopes for Clarissa's hand, and somehow that seemed easier to bear on the battlefields. This time Stephen accompanied him; Richard and James felt it would be good for him to witness battle tactics and for his troops to see and get to know him. After all, in a few years he would have to lead these men himself.

Stephen, of course, was highly excited about getting to go to battle. Elizabeth had her reservations, but she swallowed her fear and bade him farewell. She knew that he must grow up now, that he must make up for all the years he had lost with their deception of Sir Godfrey. Besides, she felt too weak and too overcome with other problems to protest about Stephen's going to battle.

Because the birth had been so difficult, it took her a

long time to recover from it. Although she did not fall prey to the dread childbed fever, she was very weak; and it was almost three weeks before she was able to leave her bed. While she lay in bed idle, she agonized over what Richard must have thought about her producing a girl. They had all been sure it would be a boy; no other thought had ever entered their minds. It was very important for him to have an heir; a female simply would not suffice. Elizabeth felt that she had failed him and that Richard must hate both her and the baby. His demeanor with her did little to dispel that feeling. Whenever he visited her, he was stiff and almost curt. She did not realize that this came from his desperate effort not to drown her in his love. He wanted so badly to hold her and kiss her and whisper about the beauty of their child that it was all he could do to restrain his affection; but he had sworn no longer to inflict himself upon her, and he felt that such demonstrations of affection would be offensive to Elizabeth. His effort to hold back made his manner formal and stiff.

In actuality, Richard was almost mad about his daughter. He had been shocked when he was told the babe was a girl, rather than the expected heir; but once he had recovered from the initial shock and went into the baby's room to look at her, he hopelessly lost his heart to that tiny scrap of flesh. She was a little baby, even for a newborn. Her arms and legs were thin, and there was hardly an ounce of baby fat anywhere on her. Her head was covered with a fine, golden fuzz, and her eyes were great blue pools. Her tiny face was perfectly formed, every feature delicate and beautiful. Richard realized that she was going to look very much like her mother, with those huge eyes and blond hair; and for that reason he could not help but adore her. Moreover, he delighted in her personality. Fragile though she might be, there was nothing sickly or listless about the child. Her hands and feet were in constant motion, and she squalled loudly. Feisty little thing, he told himself—

just like her mother. He discovered that, whenever he went into her room and bent over her crib, she would grow quiet and still; and if he extended a finger to her, she would wrap her tiny fist around it.

She recognizes me, he would think, and fall even more deeply under the little thing's spell. After a while, he ventured to reach in her crib and pick her up, and found that it did not disturb her; rather, she seemed to fit in his hands or in the crook of his arm. And always she would gaze at him trustingly. He crooned to her and talked nonsense, and she seemed to enjoy it. All the frustrated love he felt for Elizabeth he poured into his feeling for this child. It was silly, he knew, for a father to be so crazy about a mere daughter; and he was embarrassed that someone might realize it. Therefore, he sneaked into her room at times when he knew maids were not around, to pick her up and play with her. He wanted badly to talk to someone about her, but he could think of no one who would not laugh at him. He guessed that Elizabeth would at least understand his feeling, but he was afraid he could not rave about his daughter to her without revealing his feelings for Elizabeth herself. The only indication of his feelings that he revealed was his decision to name the girl Mary, after his mother. Because he loved Marguerite and was fond of Gwendolyn, few people, including Elizabeth, realized how close he had been to his mother; but when he was about seven or eight, after Gwendolyn came to the household and his mother had retreated in indignation to her tower, he and his sister had been her whole world. The love that her husband had killed in her she gave to her son, and he had visited her daily to comfort her and to give her all the news of the castle and the world. So deep was his feeling for her that, in later years, he hardly ever spoke of her. And, though, when he was grown, he thought her foolish for the haughty way she had thrown away all happiness with his father and retired to her rooms, he still could not help but feel anger and shame for his mother's humiliation and exile.

Because this memory was so strong in him, despite the fact that he had not visited his wife's bed in several months, he would not relieve himself with any of the women of the castle or any local whore. He could not bring such shame upon his beloved Elizabeth.

So his frustration mushroomed. He lay awake at night thinking of Elizabeth and his feelings for her, remembering the feel of her velvety skin, the softness of her breasts, her small, vulnerable mouth. Such thoughts, of course, sent desire coursing through him, and he tossed and turned in his bed, vainly seeking to sleep. Even worse, however, was actually to be around her, to get a whiff of the delicate fragrance that surrounded her, to watch her move about the room and know how she would look without her clothes. He wondered what changes the child had wrought in her body. He longed desperately to reach out and take her in his arms, to feel again her lips beneath his, and he would begin to tremble with passion. It was all he could do to keep from taking her and took all of his self-control to turn and leave the room. Therefore, Richard tried to avoid being around Elizabeth as much as possible. Of course, after she recovered from the birth and resumed her household duties, he had to see her at meals and when she came to him regarding household problems; but he never went to her bed at night, and he spent as much time as possible during the day gone from the castle, so that he would not meet her by accident in the halls. At times when he had to be with her, he was careful not to touch her or be too close to her. Many times he ached to break his vow and take her, but he did not. It was only for his gratification that he made love to her, and it caused her pain; no longer could he do that to her. Moreover, he was too much a man of honor to break his solemn vow.

Elizabeth could not understand why her husband had suddenly deserted her bed. Even after she had recovered from the birth, he had not visited her at night. She felt that it must have been because he was so filled with anger at her for not producing an heir that he no longer even wanted to touch her. Of course, it was really a relief to her that he did not push his attentions on her, she told herself. After all, she had no desire to go through those nightly ordeals again. It was just that she did not want to be in disfavor with him. She did not want to lose her position. Before, because he had wanted her physically, she knew that she was secure as Countess of Norwen; but, now, he might very well bring in a mistress as his father had done to his mother, and Elizabeth would no longer have any power in Norcastle. She and her daughter would be helpless, ignored. How easy it would be for James to set Richard against her now, when he was already angry and undesirous of her; how easily he might be persuaded to do away with her, who could not produce boys—and then what would happen to her daughter?

Even though Elizabeth had cried out in anguish because the baby was a girl, she loved her dearly. No boy could have been any more precious to her than Mary was, and the only satisfaction that she could find these days was in playing with the child. It filled her with terror to think of Mary being left alone in an unfriendly household. She told herself that it was for Mary's sake that she wished Norwen would return to her bed. Her restlessness, that funny ache in her loins were things connected with having given birth, she was sure. Certainly they had nothing to do with Norwen or his avoidance of her.

One evening after supper, as Elizabeth sat doing mending in her room, she heard a sound in the baby's room next door. Knowing that the wet nurse was not in the room, but downstairs partaking of supper, she felt a sudden stab of fear. Who could be in the room? Anxiously she laid aside her sewing and crept down the hall to the door of Mary's room. There, a most unexpected sight met her eyes. She saw her husband standing by Mary's cradle, holding her daughter in his hands. The little girl was hardly bigger than one of his hands, and she nestled very comfortably there. The huge man was bending over her, talking to her softly. Mary exhibited no fright at this great looming creature who held her; rather, she smiled and cooed with pleasure. And, when he bent to kiss her face, she giggled. Astonished, Elizabeth stared at her husband's face; Norwen's hard, stern features were soft and alight with love. He was smiling and whispering lovingly to his daughter, obviously totally enraptured with her.

Elizabeth stepped backward, not knowing exactly what to do. Norwen heard her and whirled to face her. His face was aflame with embarrassment at being caught, and he stood there awkwardly for a moment looking at her.

"Richard, whatever are you doing here?" Elizabeth asked.

A little sheepishly, Norwen said, "Just visiting with my daughter."

"But I thought—" Elizabeth began, and then halted.

"Thought what?" Richard asked.

"Nothing. It is just that since Mary was a girl, rather than the heir that you wanted, I thought you were displeased with her."

Norwen's brows shot up in surprise. "Displeased with her! How could I be displeased with her? Why, she is beautiful and already so clever. Look, see how she will grasp my finger? Surely not all children can do that."

Elizabeth burst into a sunny smile. She felt warmed and touched by Norwen's love for her child. "I am so happy, so pleased that you feel that way. I cannot tell you how frightened I was that you would reject her, that you would think of her as less than nothing."

Elizabeth's voice broke on her words, and tears flooded her eyes. Upon seeing her distress, Richard quickly laid Mary back in her cradle and went to his wife and pulled her into his arms. "There, there, Elizabeth. It is all right. I love the child; truly, I do."

The feel of her soft, flexible body inside his arms, the

scent of her perfume, the silkiness of her hair against his face as he bent his head to hers all struck him like a blow. He wanted her, immediately, desperately; he began to tremble all over. If he remained here another instant he was certain he would take her, vow or no vow. As if she were hot lead, he pulled away from her, cleared his throat and tried to say something, but was unable to. As she looked at him, puzzled, he quickly moved past her and out of the room.

Elizabeth stared after him, her heart plummeting in her chest. Why did he suddenly dislike her so? It was obvious that he could not even bear to touch her; look at the way he had recoiled from her. She wondered if James had convinced him that she had done him some terrible wrong. Perhaps he had made him believe she had been unfaithful to him or had tried to plot against him; but surely, if that were the case, he would at least confront her with it and take her to task for it. Surely he would warn her never to do it again. She could not imagine that he would not even remonstrate with her. Nor could it be the babe. His obvious love for her child, his tenderness with Mary touched her and filled her with a great glowing feeling for him. But it also made her realize that he must not hate her for bearing a female child.

Slowly, hot tears began to pour down her face. It must be that he just wasn't interested in her any longer. His passion must have cooled for some reason. Perhaps it was her swollen body during pregnancy, or perhaps it had been that the sight of her during childbirth had sickened him. Or perhaps it was just that with the passage of time he had grown tired of her; she had been told that that was the way of men. But somehow it seemed so unfair. So unfair! She ran back to her room, sobbing bitterly.

After that night when she became convinced that Richard simply did not desire her anymore, the thought of whom he did desire began to plague her. He was a man of great passion, and she had no illusions that he would remain celibate simply because he was married and no longer desired his wife. No, it was a common occurrence for a man to be unfaithful to his wife, though his wife was severely punished for any infidelity on her part. It was quite common for a noble to tumble the maids in his home and the serf women in the fields. Moreover, there were always whores who followed the troops, and of course he could have his pick of those. Some men took a full-time mistress; and there were those, like Richard's father, who set their mistresses up with style and position in their own households. Elizabeth prayed fervently that that would not be the case with her. She could not bear to be so shamed and humiliated before the whole world. Many women expected it as a matter of course; and there were women, like Maud, who would far prefer that their husbands visit a mistress rather than themselves. But Elizabeth felt she simply could not bear it. She had too much pride, she told herself, to live that way.

So far Richard had not done that, obviously; however, there was nothing to say he had not been bedding one of the servants or some serf. Any of them would be proud to be favored by the earl.

Suspiciously she began to look at all the maids. Her own Meg was a young lass and not uncomely. And two or three of the maids who worked in the kitchen or served the table could be said to hold some allure. There was one in particular—a pert, saucy little redheaded wench—that Elizabeth felt any man would be willing enough to bed; certainly she seemed willing enough to bed any man. Perhaps Richard had a preference for redheads as his father, Henry, had. She found herself searching all the women's faces, looking for some flicker of contempt or superiority. Which one of them could hold it over her mistress that the earl favored her more than Elizabeth? Which one knew that Elizabeth displeased the earl and that she pleased him? There were times when Elizabeth felt she would go mad thinking on it.

However, Elizabeth would never admit, even to herself, that the sharp pangs that stabbed at her were pangs of jealousy. Why should she be jealous, except of her position? After all, she did not love her husband. Of course, she woke sometimes at night from those hot lascivious dreams about him; and there were times when she sat beside him at supper that she felt her very bones would melt under his hot, black gaze, and she found herself all too often remembering the feel of his skin against hers, the hardness of his muscles and bone, the sheen of sweat on his skin when he made love to her—but that was all animal passion, just animal passion. Everyone—all sorts of people—felt that. That was not at all the same as love. She did not love Richard; she was not jealous. But then something inside her wailed: why did she have this awful ache deep within her?

Chapter Fifteen

RICHARD RECEIVED A MESSAGE FROM ONE OF HIS VASSALS
that he was being plagued with robbers. He snapped up
this opportunity to leave Norcastle. It would be so much
easier to live away from Elizabeth, where he would not
have to see her all the time and run the risk of touching
her or smelling her perfume. His eagerness to leave was
obvious, and Elizabeth felt a cold, hard lump in her chest.
He could not wait to get away from her.

When Norwen mounted his horse and rode away at
the head of his troops, Elizabeth felt something tug at her
and snap, as if there were some invisible cord from her
attached to him. For days afterward everything about
Norcastle seemed gloomy, and she moped about. Her
only source of comfort was the letter she received from
the earl. Freed from her disturbing presence, he could
more comfortably share his thoughts with her; and he
wrote her several letters during the few weeks that he was
gone. He discussed his luck and lack of it in chasing down
the bandits marauding his land, inquired constantly

about his daughter, Mary, and told her of the news he received from Stephen and James. Elizabeth was pleased to receive his letters, and even happier to exercise her new skills in reading them and writing back to him. However, she felt rather piqued that he would talk so freely to her on paper but would hardly visit her when he was home.

Stephen and James were proceeding well against Sir Godfrey and were at present besieging their third fortress, Merwen Keep. James's spies reported that there were movements in Sir Godfrey's castle, which indicated that troops would likely be marching from there to relieve the besieged castle. On hearing this, he sent a messenger posthaste to his brother, asking him to intercept the army that would be coming. Norwen, although he had not entirely put down the bandits, left the mop-up operations to his vassal and moved his troops in a line to intersect Sir Godfrey's army.

The first leg of his journey was back to Norcastle to replenish supplies and gather more men. His unexpected arrival brought Elizabeth hurrying into the courtyard, her face flushed and her eyes alight with pleasure.

"Milord!" she cried. "I had not expected you. Where —why—"

The earl chuckled at her confusion, feeling a lift in his spirits at the excitement on her face. Quickly he dismounted and went inside the castle with her. Upstairs in his room, she helped him off with his armor and ordered a bath for him, while he explained to her the reason for his sudden visit. Her heart began to pound when he told her that he would march to ward off Godfrey's army; it wasn't until later that Elizabeth remembered in amazement that her first fear had been for Richard's safety, not for the safety of her brother besieging the castle. However, despite the fear, it was very pleasant to be once again talking with Richard in this manner and acting out the role of a wife. It was not until the maids brought the tub and buckets of water and Elizabeth reached out to untie his tunic that things returned to the unease of the past few weeks.

Richard recoiled from her touch and said gruffly, "Nay, leave me. I will bathe myself."

Tears sprang into her eyes at his curt tone, and Elizabeth turned quickly and hurried from the room. She did not see him again that evening. He was busy overseeing the preparations of his troops for the morrow's journey. And Elizabeth's wounded feelings made her not go down to the great hall for the evening meal but have it sent up to her on a tray in her room. Richard noted her absence at the table, and his stomach twisted inside him at the thought that she avoided his presence when he would be here only a few hours more. She did not think he might be killed during battle and she would never see him again. She did not care, and it was painful to him to meet with that realization.

When he was certain that everything was in order for the journey the next morning, he went up to his daughter's chambers to say his farewell to her. As always, his spirit lightened when he looked down at the child. She had changed while he was gone. It amazed him that a child could change so much so quickly. Her fuzzy blond hair was longer, her eyes more alert, her arms and legs more under her control, and she was gaining weight, turning plump and happy. With a smile, he bent and picked her up; and, even though it had been weeks that he had been gone, she did not cry out as if he were a stranger to her. Instead, she smiled at him and gurgled and cooed, and he fell more in love with her than ever. He cradled Mary in his arms, and talked softly to her and listened to her baby noises, jiggling her a little now and then when she turned restless. It was so comforting to hold her thus, to feel her warmth and let his love pour out. It was such a thankful release from his thoughts about her mother.

She fell asleep in his arms, and softly he laid her down and turned away from her. As he did, the pain flooded him again. He bit his underlip and leaned against the wall, fighting back the tears that threatened to unman him. Dear God, how long would this horrible feeling inside continue? Why did Elizabeth not love him? What more could he have done than what he had done? He ached to hold her and tell her of his love and show her how much he loved her; yet, because he loved her so, he could not do that. Though it brought continual pain upon himself, he could not inflict hurt upon her; but he felt like a starving man who must withhold himself from food. Why must he be punished like this, loving a woman who did not return his affection?

Sternly, he made himself straighten up and walk from the room. He knew he ought to go to Elizabeth's room and take his leave of her, but he walked straight past her room. He could not bear it; he simply could not look at her and want to take her so, and have to refrain from doing so. He hurried back to his room, as if by reaching his room and going to bed he could get rid of all the demons that pursued him.

When he stepped inside his room he saw a dim figure there in the dark, and his hand went immediately to his dagger. But then the figure rose and the moonlight caught her hair, and he saw that it was Elizabeth who waited for him in his room. Surprised, he quickly lit a candle.

"Elizabeth. What are you doing here?" he asked abruptly.

His words made her feel nervous, but she was determined to go through with what she had decided to do. That evening in her room by herself, she had realized that she must take some action to heal the rift between them, if that was possible. She had to at least know what it was that was wrong.

She advanced toward her husband and, as she reached him, sank down on her knees before him, her head bowed in supplication. Richard looked down at her, silent in his astonishment.

"Milord husband, I have come to find out, if you will tell me, how it is that I have displeased you."

"Displeased me? Whatever do you mean?"

Elizabeth looked up at him, beseeching him with her huge liquid eyes. "You no longer visit my bed. Since long before Mary was born, you have not slept with me. I know I must have done something to offend you, but I know not what it is. Therefore, please tell me so that I may right whatever is wrong."

A huge lump rose in his throat, making it almost impossible for him to speak. Her words made his heart pound in hope, and yet his brain cautioned him to go slowly. "There is nothing wrong, Elizabeth. You have done nothing to offend me."

"Then why is it that you no longer desire me?" Elizabeth asked, her words ending almost in a wail.

"Not desire you!" he ejaculated. "Woman, are you mad? I lie awake at night and shake, I have so much passion for you."

"Then why do you avoid me?" Elizabeth cried out in frustration. "I thought you hated me for bearing a lass, but you love Mary; so that cannot be it. Have I grown ugly to you since the babe? Has someone turned you against me? There must be a reason for it!"

"I cannot bear to hurt you anymore!" he thundered. "What kind of a brute do you take me for? When you bore Mary, I saw the kind of agony you went through. Why, I still bear the marks of your nails on my hands. You screamed like someone tortured." Richard's face contorted with the anguish of his memory. "I shall never forget it—never. And the whole time, I knew that you were suffering because of me, because I was so hungry for you that I took you again and again when you did not wish it. Every pain you felt was the direct result of my own heedless, selfish desire!"

Elizabeth stared at him in wonderment, slowly rising to

her feet. "You mean—you want to bed me? And you restrain your desire because you don't wish me to have to bear another child?"

"Yes. God's bones, Elizabeth, how could I not want to bed you? You are the most beautiful, desirable woman I have ever seen. Your hair, your mouth—just the sight of your breasts pressing against the cloth of your dress—make me flame with desire. That is why I cannot bear to be around you long."

His wife smiled at him, and a warm, glowing feeling filled her chest. How kind he was, how self-sacrificing, to suppress his desire because he did not wish to hurt her. No other man would do half so much. She reached out and laid a hand on his arm. His skin was hot as fire, and he recoiled from her touch.

"See?" he said bitterly. "Even now I am hot for you, like a stallion for a mare in heat."

Elizabeth stared at him, perplexed. Somehow she had to coax him back into her bed. She did not pause to wonder why she had to do that, when for so long she had wanted to get him out of her bed. Her pride would not permit her to admit, even to herself, that she burned for him, too.

"But, Richard, you must have an heir. We need to have more children; we need to have a boy."

"I care not. Mary is enough for me. No boy could please me more. What do I care about passing on my title? I am strong enough; I will force everyone to accept her as heiress to my lands. And James and Stephen will be here to protect her when I die. It is not a calamity."

"That is a wild proposition, and you know it," Elizabeth retorted. "You need a male heir."

"No! My mind is set."

He strode away from her and flung himself down in his chair. Elizabeth chewed thoughtfully on her lip; it was obvious that she must try a new tack. Perhaps the best thing was to point out that cessation of their marital relations was not necessarily a benefit to her.

"Even so—putting aside the need for a male heir," she said, following him to stand before him. "Have you thought how this reflects on me? Everyone must gossip about your absence from my bed. They must all think I have fallen from your favor. Soon I will have no more authority with the servants. They will snicker and think it all right to defy me because you prefer some kitchen maid to me."

"What are you talking about?"

"I am talking about the affairs you are having and the ones you will have in the future! Do you not realize how it hurts me, how it shatters my pride to have you sleeping with some serf or some maidservant instead of me?"

"I am not sleeping with any maid or serf girl. Who told you that?"

"No one told me. They did not need to. If you are not making love to me, then you must be taking your passion elsewhere."

"I have not been unfaithful to you."

Elizabeth was openmouthed with shock. "You cannot mean you have been celibate all these months. Why, no man goes without sex when he desires it."

They looked at each other in silence for a moment, and then he said with finality, "I have."

Hastily Elizabeth sat down on a stool, trying to collect her swirling thoughts. He had been filled with desire for her all these months but had not taken her—and had not taken any other woman either! What manner of man was this?

"Did you honestly think I would do that to you? Throw you open to the scorn and laughter of the servants? Scatter my seed all over the castle and fields so that all your life you would be faced with the sight of my bastards? Take some woman as my mistress and allow her to lord it over you?

"Never! For years I saw that happen to my mother. My father was a handsome and engaging man; no one could help but love him, least of all I. But I hated him, too, for what he did to my mother. All my childhood, I saw replicas of myself all over the castle—stable boys, serfs, kitchen lads. It seemed as though he fathered half the children in the castle. And I saw my mother's pain when she looked upon them. I saw the insolent, smirking looks she received from serving wenches that my father was favoring at the time. I saw the shame and humiliation she felt at his infidelity and at all the reminders of it he set before her. She was crushed when he set Gwendolyn up as his mistress and gave her honors equal to his own wife's. I do not blame him or Gwendolyn; their passion for each other was immense. Nor was my mother entirely without blame."

He paused and took a shaky breath. "It is pointless to talk of fault. All I say is that my lady mother suffered greatly, and I bear you too much love and respect to ever inflict that upon you. Never, never would I subject you to that humiliation!"

Elizabeth was shaken by his words. What a good, kind man he was. She would never have imagined that any man would remain faithful to his wife if he did not have sex with her. The idea that he held such feeling, such respect for her was overwhelming, and for a moment she could do no more than put her hands on his in a gesture of gratitude and comfort.

"Thank you, Richard," she said at last. "You have no idea what that means to me. I never met a man who had so much honor and kindness. But there is no need for you to remain celibate. Return to my bed—please."

He swallowed, torn between his desire and his love. "No, Elizabeth, pray, don't tempt me. I do not want you to sacrifice yourself because of gratitude or pity."

"But, Richard, bearing children is a woman's lot. I will not pretend that I did not have great pain, but it was not too great a price to pay for such a one as Mary. They tell me that the first is always hardest; the others will be much easier. Other women are capable of doing it; surely I am able to, also."

"Damn!" He jumped from his chair and walked angrily away from her. "Why must you tease and tantalize me so? Can't you see that your very presence makes me quiver like an untried lad? It would be different if you wanted me. But you do not; and as long as you don't, I am risking the pain of childbirth for you and forcing you to endure something you dislike, just for my selfish pleasure! I made a vow, Elizabeth, and I will not break it: I have sworn not to take you when you do not want me."

So it had come down to it, Elizabeth thought. She could no longer hide behind excuses; her pride must tumble if she was to get her husband back.

Calmly she rose and, gazing straight into his eyes, said, "You can bed me, then, without breaking your vow, for I want you." Her mouth turned up into a deliberately provocative smile. "Mayhap I would like to feel you quiver inside me."

For a moment he stared at her, unable to believe what he had heard. Then, suddenly, like a prisoner released from his chains, he rushed to her and swept her up in his arms. They clung together, their bodies melting into one another, their mouths blending in an interminable kiss. Their passion mingled and grew until they were panting and trembling in their haste to join. Quickly they tore off their clothes, and Richard picked Elizabeth up and carried her to his bed. He lay down beside her and caressed her with his hands and mouth. Eagerly she returned his caresses, stoking the fire of his desire to the point of explosion.

"Come into me," she whispered in his ear. "Now. Please, Richard, please."

Her words aroused him past reason, and he plunged into her. Again and again he thrust into the soft inner recesses of her body, and she writhed beneath him, reveling in the feel of his velvety hardness filling her. A wild, wonderful warmth was building in her loins, growing, expanding at his powerful strokes. He pushed into her as if he would spear her heart, and suddenly the warmth exploded, washing over her with breathtaking pleasure. Wordlessly she cried out, and in a brief, wild moment of mutual splendor he gasped and shuddered at his own peak.

Elizabeth clung to him, floating in a mist of exhausted pleasure. She was aware only of his breath against her neck and the thud of her own heart. In that unthinking state, with her emotions open and exposed, she knew she loved him and was not complete without him.

"I love you," she whispered, but he was already asleep and did not hear her.

Early the next morning, Elizabeth awoke to find Norwen stretched out beside her, supporting himself on one elbow while he gazed down at her. It took her a moment to remember where she was and why; and, when she did, she blushed prettily, which caused him to laugh. But it was the rich, throaty laugh of pleasure, not scorn; so she did not mind it.

He stroked her shining hair and said, "Your hair is so lovely, like dawn sunlight—spun silver and gold entwined."

She smiled and cuddled up against him. She remembered what she had felt the night before, and she wanted to tell him that she loved him; but she was embarrassed and still too scared. He might be a man of honor and very kind, but that did not mean it was safe to give him such total power over her. Some last vestige of reserve would not allow her to so completely annihilate the barriers built up over the years. Instead, she tried to express her feelings by stroking his body tenderly. It was strange, she thought, how much she had changed—now she could caress and feel little embarrassment. She was no longer reluctant; rather, now she was eager. She actually enjoyed the feel of his body.

At her touch, his manhood began to swell. Richard

chuckled and said, "See what an effect you have on me?"

Hesitantly Elizabeth reached down and touched it, and his organ grew more at that. Elizabeth smiled a little.

"Funny how the sight of that used to frighten me so; it seemed a huge, horrible weapon to me. How silly; for, in truth, it pleasures me," she said, and then surprised them both by bending down to kiss his turgid manhood.

Richard drew in his breath sharply at the feel of her lips on that part of him she had most feared and hated. His delight was almost too much to bear; he wanted her again desperately, immediately. He pulled her up against him and kissed her, and she wrapped her arms about him and responded passionately. Once more they made love with full, happy abandon, and came together in a wild crescendo of pleasure that left them satisfied and exhausted.

For a few minutes they were able to doze in each other's arms, oblivious of the world around them. But then they had to awake to their duty. Richard's men were ready and he had to march to James's and Stephen's aid. No longer could he be just Richard; now he had to be the Earl of Norwen.

So they arose and dressed. Elizabeth sent her maid for a tray of breakfast for her husband, while he went to bid his baby daughter one last farewell. After he had eaten, Elizabeth helped buckle him into his armor, and then followed him downstairs. Out in the courtyard, their priest blessed the departing troops. Then Richard rose, pulled his wife to him in one last crushing hug and turned abruptly away to mount his horse.

Elizabeth stood as pale and still as a statue as he mounted his horse, glanced down at her briefly with his heart in his eyes, then wheeled and trotted through the gates at the head of his troops. Desperately she longed to reach out and bid him stay, to pour out her unrevealed love to him. But she did not—this was no time to unman him with such words, in front of his men and with a necessary battle looming before him.

She watched the last man cross the bridge, then she scurried into the house and up the steps to the tower, where she watched them until they were out of sight. Bitter tears clogged her throat as she went back to her room. What if he never returned? There was always a possibility that Richard might be killed in a battle. If he was, what would she do? How would she live without him? And she had not even told him she loved him—he could die not knowing that she loved him!

Inside her room she flung herself onto her bed and burst into bitter sobs.

Chapter Sixteen

A BAND OF RIDERS APPROACHED THE CASTLE CAUTIOUSLY.
They halted in the closest copse of woods and watched
the fortress. Norcastle lay silently in the moonlight like a
slumbering giant. It was obvious that none inside expected any attack, for the drawbridge lay down across the
moat and all within slept securely. It was the bridge that
the hiding riders watched, looking at the wide iron-
studded gates for some expected sign. Deep within the
castle all the servants slept, except one red-haired kitchen
maid who quietly rose and left her sleeping companion
on tiptoe. Quickly she scurried down the stairs and down
the hall and into the baby Mary's room. The babe slept in
her cradle, and in a bed beside her slept her wet nurse.
Carefully the redheaded girl approached the cradle, bent
down and picked up the baby. The movement made the
baby stir and turn her head fretfully, and the woman
stood breathless for a second, fearing that it would
awake. Then quietly she backed away and went swiftly
down the hall to the very end, where she entered the

earl's bedroom and slipped the child into his bed. There—she thought with satisfaction—that would get her gold from Tanford.

Now to take care of Godfrey's men. . . . She turned and went downstairs into the kitchen. There she went to the bin of flour, where she had earlier that day secreted a bottle of wine. She pulled it out and took out the cork, then brought a little vial of powder from her skirt pocket and carefully poured it in. She recapped the wine and waited until the powder had disappeared, then picked up the bottle and hurried through the door into the courtyard. Her destination was the guardhouse that stood beside the gates. She knew that two guards sat within and two stood above the house on the battlements. She had to lure all four to drink her drugged wine. Before she reached the guardhouse, she paused and smoothed down her dress and fluffed her hair. Then she put her provocative smile in place and darted up the steps. Two guards whirled and challenged her. She giggled softly.

"Why, 'tis only I, Alys." Her teeth flashed in the dark and she tossed back her bountiful red hair. "I thought you might enjoy some wine on your long vigil."

"Wine, eh?" one guard said and laughed. "Mayhap it is something else you seek."

"Indeed, and what might that be?" the girl said flirtatiously and walked toward him, her hips swaying with her movement.

The guard swallowed as he watched her. Everyone knew that Alys was a saucy, provocative wench, not one above a tumble in the hay every now and then. "Perhaps you are seeking a man to relieve your boredom."

The other guard laughed at his witticism. Alys smiled and held up the wine.

"Well, will you come down to the guardhouse with me and drink of it?" she asked.

The other guard said crudely, "Does it take four men to satisfy you, then?"

Alys grinned and said, "Perhaps so. One man has never seemed quite enough to me."

The soldier licked his lips and glanced hesitantly at his partner. "Nay, we two must stay up here to watch; the earl would have our hides if we forsook our duty."

"Oh, pooh," the girl pouted prettily. "How is the earl to know, may I ask? He is not even within the castle. You know no army is going to come upon us tonight. How silly to spend your time in the cold night air when you could be inside and warm—with me."

The two men conferred in a glance. The same thought was in both their minds: it would not take long to have a little wine and get beneath this maid's skirts. They would only be gone a few minutes in the dead of the night; what could possibly go wrong during that time?

"All right," one of them said, "just for a few minutes, though. Let's see what you have to offer."

The redhead laughed and skipped down the stairs before them. The two guards inside found it equally difficult to resist her allure, and soon all four of them were sitting joking and swigging deeply from the wine bottle, while they speculated upon the pleasure before them and fondled the girl avidly. Before long the men began to grow sleepy; and gradually, one by one, their heads lowered to the table, and they slept the heavy sleep of one drugged. Alys then slipped out to the huge gates. A heavy bar lay across them, and she heaved and tugged at it. For a moment she was afraid that she would not be able to move the thing; but at last, with one final shove, she made it rise. She threw all of her weight against one gate, and gradually it opened inch by inch until it was wide enough for a man to slip through. Then she stepped back and waited impatiently, constantly looking over her shoulder to make sure no one was watching. The four men who hid in the woods saw the gate open a little and left their cover to run for it. Softly they hurried across the bridge and into the gate, then pulled it behind them.

"Where is she?" whispered the one who seemed to be their leader.

"Come, I will show you," Alys said, and started forward. One man was left to watch over the guards, and the other three followed the maid into the castle and up the stairs to Elizabeth's chambers.

Lady Elizabeth lay asleep peacefully in her bed, her golden hair spread across the pillow. The men approached her bed, and one reached out and put his hand over her mouth while the others began to tie her feet and hands together. Elizabeth awoke immediately; when she saw the masked stranger looming above her she screamed, but no sound came out for the hand that was clamped across her lips. Fiercely she struggled, but her strength was as nothing against them; and they quickly gagged and tied her.

"Where is the baby?" the leader whispered to the redheaded girl. Elizabeth's eyes grew wide with terror at his words, and she began to struggle again in vain.

"In the room next door," the girl said, and Elizabeth looked daggers at her.

The leader exited the room and returned a moment later, his face red with anger. "The child is gone," he whispered fiercely at the maid. "Where is she?"

"I do not know," the girl said. "That is where she sleeps."

"Well, she is not there now."

"Well, ask her nursemaid. Perhaps she heard you here and hid her."

"That one?" he said scornfully. "She is sound asleep and snoring."

"Well, I know not, then. You will have to look for her."

"We have not the time to waste. Any moment some guard may come to replace those, and we will be trapped here inside the castle." Angrily he turned and left the room, motioning to the others to follow him.

One of them picked Elizabeth up and flung her over his shoulder, almost knocking the breath from her. The men went into Mary's room, where their leader had already awakened the nurse and was holding a knife to her throat.

"Now tell me, where is the lass?"

The nursemaid choked and gurgled, too frightened to even speak. He brought the palm of his hand heavily across her face and she gasped out, "I know not! I know not! She was here when I went to sleep. I did not mean to fall asleep. I just—"

The man pushed his knife deeper against her throat, and a trickle of red began to run down from it. However, she could not answer his questions, but only gasp and flutter. Finally, with a gesture of disgust, he plunged the knife into her throat, and she gurgled and then went limp. Elizabeth swallowed back the bile that rose in her throat at the sight.

The men began to tear apart the room, looking under the bed and in cupboards, but could find the baby nowhere.

Finally the redheaded girl volunteered, "Perhaps they have hidden the child away somewhere. No one ever sees Mary except her mother and her wet nurse. Perhaps they have sent her to Lady Marguerite, or perhaps they really keep her in another room somewhere."

Elizabeth shot the girl a look of gratitude; she knew that she did none of those things, and that therefore the girl could be the only one responsible for hiding Mary.

"Damn!" the leader swore softly. "I do not have the time to search for the babe. Sir Godfrey shall just have to take this one by herself. Come, let us go."

He left the room, with the other men hot on his heels. They carried Elizabeth out of the castle and across the courtyard, where the fourth man joined them. Quickly they slipped through the gate and ran for their horses, hidden in the woods. Elizabeth felt as if all the air would be pushed from her body, as it jolted against her carrier's shoulder. When they reached the horses, the men untied her legs and threw her on a horse, and tied her hands to the pommel. Then one man took the reins of her horse and led him.

The leader of the men looked at Alys, who had followed them, and asked gruffly, "What are you doing here?"

"I cannot stay there. They will know I was in on the plot because I drugged the guards. I would most assuredly be killed. Besides, they would probably torture me, and I would reveal to them who you are," Alys said cleverly. She had no desire to stay behind in Norcastle, for she knew she would be quickly discovered. She did not worry about the babe; someone would find it the next morning when it started screaming for food. She certainly was not about to stay in order to place it back in its bed. She had done her job, and now wanted to be away from Norcastle and to get her reward.

The man studied her for a moment, and then said gruffly, "All right. Get up behind me then."

The girl mounted behind him and they set off. All night long they rode as fast as it was possible. When dawn came, they left the roads and took out across the country. Elizabeth guessed that they did this so no one would see them and be able to track where they had gone. As they continued to ride, Elizabeth grew more and more tired, hungry and worried. She had no idea where they were taking her or what they planned to do with her. Why did Sir Godfrey want her? Did he hope to ransom her to Richard? Or did he hope somehow to ensnare her husband in some wicked plan of his—perhaps keep him from attacking Godfrey while he held Elizabeth? Anxiously she wondered how her daughter Mary would fare. She did not know where the girl had hidden her. What if she had hidden her too well, and no one found the baby and she slowly died of starvation? Even if she was found, what would happen to her with Elizabeth gone and her wet nurse dead? Would anyone take care of her properly? What would happen to her if Elizabeth was killed? What did her uncle have in mind? What would Richard do when he was told that she had been kidnapped? Would he pursue them? Was Godfrey perhaps hoping that Richard would abandon James and Stephen while he searched for his wife?

Finally they drew close to a keep. Elizabeth did not recognize it. She supposed it belonged to Godfrey, but it was not one in which she had ever stayed; certainly it was not his home. They rode up to the entrance, and at the sight of them the gates were slowly pulled back to allow them entry. Inside the courtyard the men cut the bonds that tied her to the horse, and set her down on the ground. Immediately her knees buckled beneath her; the strain of riding for so long had robbed them of all feeling and strength. She knelt there in the dust of the courtyard, too proud to ask for any help and unable to rise. The door of the keep opened and she looked up. There stood her Uncle Godfrey and, just behind him, her Cousin Geoffrey; her old, familiar terror began to rise in her throat. Her months with her husband and his kindness and protection of her had done away with her old fears; but now, like a nightmare, they swept down upon her again. In fact, they seemed even worse compared with her recent security. She thought of the way her husband lovingly handled her body, and suddenly she shook with fear and sick dread at the thought of Geoffrey violating it. Somehow it seemed worse now that it was a source of pleasure for Richard.

"Well, niece, I see that we meet again. You thought you could deceive me by your clever little plot with Norwen. You see now, I'm sure, that you can not ever deceive me," Sir Godfrey said, and walked down the steps toward her.

Elizabeth cringed away from him, not knowing what he intended to do and unable to rise to her feet to try to escape. He bent down and grabbed ahold of her hair and pulled at it. He laughed when she cried out in pain, and then with his knife cut off a lock of her hair. Elizabeth looked up at him, not understanding what he did.

Holding the lock of hair in front of her, he said, "Think you that this will bring your loving husband running to me?"

Richard walked through his camp, briefly talking to his men and checking to make sure that everything was in order. He knew how important it was that his men not arrive at battle weary and uncomfortable. He also knew how important it was that there be nothing wrong with their horses or armor or weapons. His scouts had told him that Robert, Sir Godfrey's son, and his army were camped not very far from them. Immediately Richard had set up his own camp and posted guards around it to try to catch any of Robert's scouts. He wanted to get them by surprise the next morning. His scouts informed him that the army was not overly large, and he felt sure that his men could defeat it easily, especially if he had the advantage of surprise.

He stopped to talk to one of his men and was interrupted by his captain at arms, St. John, who came running up to him with a black, suspicious look on his face.

"What is it, St. John?" he asked, somewhat alarmed at the other man's look.

"I must tell you in private, milord; it is rather serious, I am afraid!" the man replied.

Now really concerned about what was troubling his captain, the earl followed him to his tent. There he found a dusty, weary man waiting for him; he recognized him immediately as one of his own men.

"What is it? What has happened?" Richard barked, fear gnawing at his vitals.

The man knelt before him and said, "The Lady Elizabeth has vanished, milord."

"What! What do you mean, vanished?"

"Her maid found her bed empty when she went in to wake her. Thinking she was next door with the baby, she went into the Lady Mary's room; and there she found the cradle empty and the nursemaid's throat cut."

"The babe is gone, too?" Richard clenched his teeth against the cold bile that rose in his throat at that thought.

"No, milord; she soon set up a lusty scream and they found her in your bed. She now has a new wet nurse and there is a guard posted at her door. But no one knows where the countess is! The gates were open a trifle, and the guards were fast asleep in the guardhouse. Drugged, apparently. When they were brought to, they said the kitchen wench Alys lured them with wine and offers of her favors, and that after they had drunk some they fell asleep. The wench is gone, too."

Richard buried his face in his hands—dear God, Elizabeth kidnapped! Perhaps she was already dead. For an instant he almost gave way to his deep terror and grief, but then he shook his head and pulled himself together. He certainly would not help Elizabeth that way.

So he swallowed hard and clenched his fists and said, "Were there any tracks?"

"Yes, milord—there were tracks of feet from the gate to the wood southeast of the castle. It looked to be several people; I would say four or five."

"And in the woods?"

"The tracks of horses, sir; we followed the tracks to the road, where they headed east. One of your men followed the tracks for a ways, but they soon became too mingled with other tracks."

Norwen sighed and rubbed his face with his hands, deep in thought. Finally, he turned to St. John and said, "Rouse the men and get them ready. And send a man to me so that I can send a message to James."

"Yes, milord," his captain said and left the tent, taking the messenger with him.

Richard sat down on his camp stool and tried to bring himself to some kind of order. He hated to leave James without aid, but he saw no alternative. If Godfrey's plan had been to distract Richard from helping James and Stephen, he had certainly been successful. James might have to retreat if Robert's force was too superior to his, but he had enough time to do that safely. It would set back their plan to retake Stephen's land; but, once Richard was able to help them, they would still be able to do it. And what was a delay compared with Elizabeth's life? First and foremost, he knew he must save her—if she was still alive. There was always the possibility that Sir Godfrey had taken her merely in revenge, rather than to hinder Richard or extract some promise from him. If so, she might be dead already.

That thought was more than Richard could bear, and he pushed it away angrily. He could not let himself think that way, or he would go mad. Instead, he took a piece of parchment and a quill and set about explaining the situation to James, informing him of the size of Robert's army so that he could judge whether to retreat or stand his ground.

After he finished the message, Norwen debated his own course of action. If he returned to Norcastle to wait for a message from his enemy, he was forcing himself further away from Sir Godfrey; and that would mean a costly delay if he must attack him. He felt sure that it was Sir Godfrey who held his wife, and he was inclined to march directly to his castle and confront him. But what if he missed Godfrey's messenger with a demand for ransom if he did not go to Norcastle? He would then be risking Elizabeth's life by attacking, when he could have used gold to retrieve her. Besides, what if it was not Godfrey, but Tanford, or even a band of robbers who wanted only the money; if that was the case he would be throwing himself in the wrong direction. He must weigh the odds and take the risk, as he always had. Except that this time, the stakes were so much higher.

St. John came back into the tent, followed by a messenger. Richard gave the man the message for James and bid him speed to James at Merwen Keep, admonishing him to skirt Robert's forces carefully. When the man left, he turned to his captain.

"The men are ready, sir."

"Good. Send a messenger to Norcastle and bid them inform me if they receive any news regarding the countess. We will move north to attack Sir Godfrey."

Quickly, silently, the men moved through the dark. It was an eerie time to march, and the men did not like it; but if their earl had told them to march to hell and back, they would probably have done it. However, by dawn they were weary, and by noon could barely stumble along for their sleepiness. Richard saw that his men would have to have a rest when they stopped for their noon meal. He felt as though he might never sleep again, but he knew it was foolhardy to head for battle with exhausted troops.

So he called a halt for the meal and dismounted to stretch his body and walk the circulation back into his legs. He forced himself to eat a little, although the sight and smell of food almost made him gag. He even wrapped his cloak around himself and settled beneath a tree close to St. John to rest. However, his muscles remained taut, and he was fully awake when the messenger approached their camp.

The man wore the colors of Sir Godfrey, and the guard who had halted him threw him before the earl with great contempt.

"What says your master?" Richard asked, his heart pounding fiercely.

"He bade me bring you this." The man extended a gloved hand, and there, nestled in his palm, lay a soft curl of fine, light-gold hair.

Richard swallowed hard and took it from the man's hand. "What does this mean?"

"Sir Godfrey said it would prove to you that he has the lady."

"Yes." His hand closed convulsively over the lock of

hair, and he wanted insanely to tear the man apart. The thought of his sweet, fragile Elizabeth in the hands of her uncle horrified him; the images his mind conjured up were almost more than he could bear.

"My message is this: Sir Godfrey says that he will kill your lady if you approach in force. You must come alone with me and bargain with him. If you do not, the countess will die tomorrow at sunset," the messenger continued.

For the first time St. John, who sat behind the earl, spoke up: "Milord, you cannot accept such conditions— that snake will kill you if you meet him alone."

"You heard him. If I do not, Godfrey will murder Elizabeth."

"But what good will you do? You know that once he has you in his grasp, he will kill the countess, as well as you. Why should he spare her life, if he has already lured you into his trap?"

Richard turned to him, his face set and bleak. "What choice do I have? He will certainly kill Elizabeth if I do not go. What use would it be to me to live, if by doing so I put Elizabeth to death? I have no choice; at least this way there is some remote chance that I could save her. I must go."

St. John's shoulders sagged hopelessly. He knew there was no changing his master's mind.

"Put him under guard," Richard said, motioning to Sir Godfrey's man. "Then have my horse saddled."

His captain led the man away none too gently, and returned to the earl. Richard was buckling on his chain mail, his face grave.

"Well, St. John," he said, "it does not look too hopeful. If I do not see you again, I want you to know that you have been a good and faithful servant. I ask you to follow James and serve him as well as you did me. Above all, you must protect the Lady Mary and see that she does not come to harm. Get her under James's care as quickly as you can."

"Yes, milord," the other man said, barely able to hold back his tears.

"So long as he does not hold Mary, Godfrey can profit little by my death. I think he may actually wish to bargain with me. If so, I have a chance of saving milady, perhaps even myself. I want you to send a messenger to James and alert him to what has happened. Then I want you to follow me with my men; keep discreetly behind, of course, so my companion will not know we are followed. When you discover where I have been taken, hang back and send for James. When he arrives, attack the castle. I will try to delay in there until you do, and I shall try to keep milady and myself safe when you do."

"It seems terribly risky to me," St. John said, doubt written on his face.

Richard smiled. "But of course. It is good for your soul. You have become too complacent lately."

The captain grimaced, but said nothing. Richard bent and slipped a thin dagger into his boot. Another small blade he slipped up the arm of his mail.

"Well," he said, "I am as ready as I can hope to be. Pray for me—and for milady wife."

He strode off, his step firm and sure; at least now he had some plan of action, however flimsy. St. John, watching him walk toward his horse, felt a chill in the pit of his stomach. Never had he known a man as brave and good as the earl. And now he doubted that he would ever see him again.

Chapter Seventeen

As they approached the keep, Richard speculated on what it could be. It was not Sir Godfrey's home; so it had to be one of his other possessions. There were really only two other fortresses in his hands besides Stephen's holdings, and it was not far enough south to be one of Stephen's. From the distance and direction they had been riding, it had to be Fenway Watch. It was the closest to Merwen Keep, so it should not take James longer than half a day to reach it, if that much, once he found out where they were.

The problem, of course, was how long it would take him to find out. It would probably be a good two hours before St. John would send James his whereabouts. That would mean evening before the messenger set out, and the middle of the night, at least, before he reached James. Then James would have to mobilize, and then ride back to Fenway—tomorrow afternoon at the earliest would be when he arrived. That meant that Richard would have to somehow keep Elizabeth and himself alive for another twenty-four hours.

Slowly the gates were opened to admit the two men. Richard felt a thrill of apprehension run through him as his horse stepped through the gates. Delivered into his enemy's hands, he thought.

Two soldiers came forward, swords in hand, and demanded his weapons. Reluctantly he handed over his sword and the long dagger at his belt. They then escorted him into the house, where Godfrey sat waiting for him. Richard knew Godfrey felt it a show of his strength that he had the earl brought to him, rather than his going to the earl. For a moment Sir Godfrey said nothing, savoring the pleasure of forcing Norwen to stand and wait on him. Richard stared stonily back at him.

"Well, Norwen, now we are on a little more equal footing. You do not seem so haughty now."

"Where is Lady Elizabeth?" Richard said, ignoring the man's remarks.

"Why, where else should she be, but below in the dungeons, as befits a traitor to her family. Don't worry; you will get to see her shortly. But right now you and I have a few things to discuss."

"We have nothing to discuss," Richard said bluntly.

"Ah, but I think we do. I think it is time we put a stop to the war your brother is waging against my lands."

"Against Stephen's lands," Norwen corrected.

"Against the lands that I hold as Stephen's lawful guardian."

"You know as well as I that you shall not hold that position long."

Sir Godfrey shrugged. He found he really did not enjoy standing here bandying words with the earl. He was too calm and unfrightened to really enjoy baiting him. What Godfrey had really wanted to do was kill the man. Nothing would give him so much pleasure as torturing both Norwen and Elizabeth to death. But those fools had been unable to kidnap the baby, and now it would not help him to kill Norwen. Without the girl, he would have no claim at all to Norwen's lands. No doubt the Bastard would seize Mary and would control the lands for her. And he and Stephen would still take back Stephen's lands, and probably they would eventually kill him. And what better excuse could they possibly have than his murdering their siblings? So, however much he might dislike it, he had to bargain with Norwen rather than kill him.

"Well," Godfrey said, "it really matters not to me who actually has the wretched boy, so long as I retain his lands."

"James shall have them from you before winter; surely you realize that."

"Oh, no, not if you and I declare a truce."

"A truce? Don't be absurd."

"Absurd? Hardly that—unless you consider your life and your wife's absurd."

"That is the bargain then?"

"Yes. If you will agree to stop your siege of Merwen Keep and return the two fortresses the Bastard has already taken, and if you swear never to attack me in any way again, then I shall set you and Elizabeth free."

"What makes you think I would keep the agreement once we are free?"

"Because you must swear an oath not to attack me, and I know you will not break a solemn oath sworn before God."

"If you know me so well, then you must know that I will not swear such an oath."

"Not even to save Elizabeth's life? I did not know you were so cruel, Norwen, as to give your wife up to torture. Oh, yes, it will not be a quick or easy death. First, I believe that I shall hand her over to my son. Geoffrey, come here; I do not believe the earl has ever met you, since you did not attend the wedding." Godfrey's voice was heavy with sarcasm.

Geoffrey stepped forward from the shadows behind his father's chair. Richard had not even noticed him before, but now he studied him carefully. So this was the man who had so shamed and hurt his beloved Elizabeth. The red fires of rage began to build in his head, and he would have liked nothing better than to choke that leering smirk off the young man's face. Even though he was unarmed and surrounded by his enemy's men, the hatred flaring from Norwen's eyes made Geoffrey step back a little. If it was at all possible, there was one person Richard would do his utmost to slay before he died.

"And after Geoffrey is through with her, no doubt she could still provide a little amusement for some of my men. If that is not enough to convince you to bargain with me, we shall have to show you how some of the instruments in the dungeons will affect the countess's looks. Are you really that stubborn and prideful, Norwen?"

Though Richard's eyes flamed with an unholy red light, his face remained immobile; he was not a man easily intimidated.

"What assurance do I have that Elizabeth is even alive? I certainly have no intention of bargaining with you for her life if she is already dead," Richard retorted calmly.

"Oh, by all means, let us show her to you, then. Perhaps the sight of her will convince you that I mean what I say."

The thought that they might have already hurt Elizabeth made Richard seethe inside, but he looked at Godfrey impassively.

"Take me to her, then," he said.

With the guards beside him, Richard followed Sir Godfrey down the winding stone steps to the dungeons. At the bottom of the stairs stood a heavy wooden door locked and bolted on the outside. Beside it sat the heavyset jailer, who held the keys to the door and to the cells on a ring attached to his belt. At Sir Godfrey's bidding, the man unlocked and unbolted the door.

They stepped inside the dank, dark hall and walked toward one of the cells that lined the walls. It was cold and damp and evil smelling in there, and Richard burned with anger at the thought of Elizabeth being put in such a place. They halted before a small cell, in which Elizabeth sat huddled up. Still clad in only her night-robe, she shivered in the cold. Her hair hung loose and uncombed about her, and her white face was set in a look of cold, despairing misery. Richard's heart wrenched inside of him at the sight of her.

Elizabeth heard their footsteps approaching, but she did not look up. No doubt it was Geoffrey come to leer and gloat over her; for some reason, his father was making him wait to have his fun with her, for he did no more than look and talk. That was bad enough, however; she certainly did not want to encourage him by paying any attention to him.

"Elizabeth!" Richard could not help but exclaim when he saw her pitiful condition.

She looked up at the sound of his voice, and for a moment her face lighted up. "Richard, oh, Richard," she cried out, her joy propelling her up and forward.

Then she realized what his presence here must mean— somehow her uncle had captured Richard, too. Her face fell, and she said dully, "Oh, no. How did they manage to get you, too?"

There was no response from her husband, but Godfrey laughed and said, "Why, by using you, how else? Surely you don't think that the magnificent Earl of Norwen would not ransom his countess—even if it meant surrendering himself?"

"Oh, no," Elizabeth groaned. "Oh, Richard, I am so sorry."

"Nay, it was my own fault; it was my protection of you at Norcastle that failed."

"Yes, but—" Elizabeth's eyes filled with tears as she looked at him, "it is my eternal shame that members of my own family should do this to you."

Richard smiled briefly. "Unfortunately, one cannot choose one's own kin."

"Well?" Sir Godfrey impatiently interrupted them. "Are you ready to swear a truce with me, Norwen?"

"A truce! Oh, no, Richard!" Elizabeth burst out.

Richard said quietly, "No, I cannot do that."

Richard's cool demeanor filled his antagonist with rage, and he turned to his son. "All right, then. Geoffrey, get in there with the lady, and let us see if you can change the earl's mind."

The jailer unlocked the door, and Geoffrey stepped eagerly inside. Elizabeth raised her chin and firmly held her ground. She was trapped and could not avoid him; there was no point in adding to Richard's pain by exhibiting her fear and running about like a trapped rat.

Roughly Geoffrey pulled her garment from her and exposed her lovely white body to the eyes of the watching men. Slowly, savoring her humiliation, he moved his hands down her body, then shoved one hand roughly between her legs while he cruelly pinched and squeezed her breasts with the others.

"What would you like for him to do, Norwen?" Godfrey taunted. "Where shall he prod her? Her mouth? Her ass? Geoffrey, set her down and spread her legs so that we all might see what the earl enjoys nightly."

Geoffrey snickered lewdly and dragged her back to the wall and pushed her down to the floor. Richard, whose face had drained of color when Geoffrey first touched her, now went wild. Insanely he flung himself against the bars, then whirled and jerked the keys from the jailer and tried to open the door to get at Geoffrey. Before he could complete his goal, the guards were upon him. He flung them off and swung the door open; but by then Sir Godfrey, the jailer and the two guards threw themselves upon him. Richard struggled furiously, but even he, with all his strength, could not prevail against four men; and finally they pinned him to the floor.

Roughly Sir Godfrey pushed the earl's head to the

side, so that he had to watch Geoffrey chain Elizabeth's arms to the wall so low she was forced to sit. Then he attached chains to her ankles, pulled the right leg far to the right and fastened the chain to a ring in the floor. He did the same thing with her other leg, painfully spread-eagling her. The guards muttered lascivious remarks, and the jailer whistled appreciatively.

"Don't worry, men," Sir Godfrey said, "you shall have your chance at her, when Geoffrey has finished with her."

Geoffrey bent over her and roughly kneaded her breasts, then shoved his hands down her front, moving inexorably to the joinder of her legs.

"No!" Richard cried out hoarsely. "God damn your black soul, Geoffrey. I'll have your head for this."

"You are hardly in any position to threaten," Sir Godfrey laughed. "But I am still willing to strike a bargain."

Richard closed his eyes. "Let me think about it."

Sir Godfrey cackled and repeated, "Let you think about it! Why, Geoffrey is as hard as a log; he wants very much to proceed. He is impatient, I know, but I am an indulgent father."

"Please, I beg of you, give me tonight to think it over."

It swelled his vanity to hear his proud enemy beg something of him, and Godfrey considered his request. The threat was everything; once it was done, if Richard had not broken, the threat of a repetition was much less effective. Perhaps it would be good to give the earl a night to dwell on the horrors that would befall his wife if he did not give in. Particularly if he was thrown into the same cell with her and had to listen to her fearful tears all night. Besides, there was really nothing to lose. They were too far from Norcastle or the earl's army for them to relieve him; and James no doubt was little inclined to save his brother, whose death would benefit him. Even if they could reach him in time, they had to know any attack would seal his death inside the castle. So there was no harm in letting him go one night, and it might just be the thing to sway him.

"All right," he agreed, "I will let you have one night with your lady; perhaps she can persuade you not to put her to such degradation and pain. And you can contemplate what you will see tomorrow if you do not agree. No doubt Geoffrey will be up half the night searching out sticks and candles and iron bars and such that he can use to plug her when his own rod is worn out."

He stood up. "Put our guest in the cell with his wife. Come, Geoffrey, unfasten her and leave her. Tomorrow you shall have your chance with her."

Reluctantly, his son undid Elizabeth's chains and left the cell. The two guards hauled Richard to his feet and threw him into the cell with Elizabeth. Elizabeth flung herself into his arms, and he held her tightly to him. For a long time they clung to each other, and Elizabeth sobbed against his chest. Finally, they pulled apart, and Elizabeth wiped the tears from her face.

"I—I am sorry, Richard, to give way like that. Usually I am not so weak."

He smiled faintly and said, "It is all right for even you to be weak sometimes."

She smiled, and shakily began to pull her clothes back on. Richard watched her, admiring her indomitable courage. He was certain that no man had ever had a wife such as she. He looked around them, making sure there was no one to spy on them. Then he cautiously reached up his sleeve and pulled out the knife that was hidden there.

"Here, my love, take this knife and hide it about your person. If the worst comes, and they rape and torture you, it would be better to take your own life. First, however, plunge it into Geoffrey. I shall attack the one nearest me, for I, too, have a dagger." He took off his boot and pulled out the knife to show her, then hid it up his sleeve. "We shall try to make an escape. Let us hope that we will be able to take some of them with us. If we are without hope, I shall try to stab you myself so that at least you will not die with the sin of suicide on your soul. But if I cannot reach you, you will have to do it yourself."

Elizabeth reached out and took the knife from his hand. She looked at her husband admiringly; she knew how much it would cost him to take her life, and she also knew he would go to his death with the mortal sin of murder on his soul. Yet he was willing to do it to save her the sin of suicide, and also the painful slow death that her uncle had in mind for her.

"Thank you," she said, and her eyes spoke her deep feeling for him. She knelt beside him and said, "Richard, I want to tell you something. I wanted to tell you days ago, but I was too proud, too frightened, too determined to not give you the means with which to control me. And now—now that we are about to die, now that you have given yourself up to death because of me, I realize how foolish I was, how stubborn and blind.

"Richard, I love you. For a long time I would not even admit it to myself. But it is true; I love you so much. You are so good, so kind, so strong and honorable. You have treated me well—perhaps better than I deserved sometimes. You taught me pleasure; you gave me respect. I love you with my whole heart."

She paused, a little breathless with emotion. Richard looked at her, taken aback. He had waited for this so long, so hopelessly; now that she had told him, he almost could not believe it. Slowly he rose and went to her. Lovingly they came together; their arms wrapped around each other tightly, and their lips touched. The kiss deepened, and gently they slid to the floor. And there, in that cold, dank cell, with death and fear all around them, they found each other. In mutual love and passion, their bodies melted together, and for a little while, the world receded and nothing existed for them but themselves and their love and the perfect union they created.

* * *

When at last they reluctantly fell apart and rejoined the real world, Richard sighed and began to apply himself to their escape. Now, more than ever, he wanted to live, to return to Norcastle and live out his life happily with his wife and daughter. The first thing he did was go around the cell, testing all the bars and searching the floors and the stone wall.

"What are you doing?" his wife asked.

"I am trying to find some weakness in the bars or stone that we could work on to escape. But there is none; I really did not expect there to be. But all is not lost, Elizabeth—if only I can buy us enough time."

"How? What do you mean?"

"Sir Godfrey wants me to declare a truce with him—give up my fight to regain Stephen's lands and agree never again to attack Godfrey."

"Why do you not just agree?" Elizabeth asked.

"Because he would make me swear it, and I could not break an oath. I would have to abide by it, and that would mean I would have to break my oath to avenge my father's death. Moreover, I would have to let Godfrey retain your brother's lands; in good conscience, I cannot give away Stephen's lands like that. Why, if I were to do what he asks, I would be completely violating my honor. I cannot do that to your brother or to myself; I refuse to give in to Sir Godfrey like that."

Elizabeth grasped his hand, her heart swelling with pride.

"However," Richard continued, "I can buy us some time by pretending to consider Godfrey's proposal. Already I have gained one night. Tomorrow I can begin to bargain with the devil, saying perhaps I would agree if he would make this concession or that. If I am clever enough and Godfrey is so sure of us that he will waste time that way, I might be able to hold off until James can get here."

"James?"

"Yes. I sent a message to him when I received God-

frey's message that he had you. I told him I was going to
you, and I had my men follow me. As soon as they
discovered where I was taken, my captain sent a message
to James. So James will be coming to our rescue; we are
not completely without hope. However, it will take him
some time to get the messages; that is why I must delay."

Cold fingers of fear darted through Elizabeth. Richard
was so trusting of his brother; she certainly was not going
to plague him with doubts about James when they had
so little time left to live. But Elizabeth doubted very
seriously that James would come; or, if he did, no doubt
he would delay his arrival. He was a cold, calculating
man; he hated her and she doubted that he had followed
Richard through anything but self-interest. What use
would it be to him to hurry to save his brother, when
delay meant that the earl and countess would die and he
could take over the Norwen lands? The men would
doubtless follow him, especially since he could become
little Mary's guardian and claim he acted in her interests.
He could even rule Stephen's lands, for Stephen trusted
him absolutely, just as her husband did. There would be
no one to oppose him, no male heir to grow up and take
the lands away—only a frail girl who could not inherit the
title or most of the land. No, there was no reason for him
to rescue them—and all the reasons in the world not to.

James knew of the kidnapping and Richard's whereabouts long before his brother's messengers reached
him. He was told the news by a man of the Duke of
Tanford, who had reasons of his own for betraying Sir
Godfrey. It was late one afternoon when one of the
guards brought the man to James. He was dressed like a
poor beggar, but there was something about him that
belied his costume. James dismissed the guard and
watched the man warily.

"You are no alms seeker," James said. "Who are you?
Speak up."

"I bring you something from the duke." He reached inside his clothes and James stiffened.

The other man chuckled mirthlessly. "Nay, not a knife. A betrothal contract."

He extended a piece of parchment, and James took it and perused it carefully. His eyebrows rose and he pursed his lips in amazement; it was a very generous contract, indeed. Clarissa would bring with her the two keeps Tanford had taken when the old earl fell, as well as one of Simon's fortresses. Of course, she was Simon's only daughter; but nevertheless that was a very generous offer. It cut through him like a knife to know that he would never receive it.

"His Grace bade me tell you this as well: he has discovered through his spies a certain plot by Sir Godfrey against Norwen."

The man paused for a moment, and James said lazily, "Indeed?"

"Sir Godfrey had a plan to kidnap Lady Elizabeth and her child after Norwen left to come to your aid. He was to lure the earl to Fenway Watch by threatening to kill the mother and babe. Once Norwen was in his hands, both he and Elizabeth would die. Then Sir Godfrey would take over Norwen's lands as the babe's guardian."

James looked at him and shrugged. "Why reveal all this to me? It sounds to me as though Sir Godfrey has it all ready."

"Oh, Godfrey has already set it into motion. Even now the earl and the countess are in Sir Godfrey's hands. It suits the duke quite well for them to die. But for Godfrey to have the Norwen lands—that thought he gravely dislikes. Thinking it would be far better for his future nephew to have the lands, he bribed the maid whom Godfrey had bribed to help in the abduction. Because of this, the lass hid the baby Mary before she let in Godfrey's men. Therefore, they took Elizabeth, but not her child."

"You are to return to Norcastle to protect the babe; you can take over all the Norwen lands in your own name and as guardian of the lass."

"And what makes him think my brother's men will support me after I callously allow Sir Godfrey to murder him?"

"Oh, but to them it will appear that you bravely defended the earl. Merely delay for a day or two; then cry that you have received word that Norwen has been captured, and march to Fenway Watch. Of course, you will arrive too late to save them, but in revenge you can attack Sir Godfrey and defeat him."

"Why should the duke desire the defeat of his ally?"

"Because his ally did not consult him in this, but acted on his own. Sir Godfrey was a little too sly and greedy. He hoped to become as powerful as His Grace with this maneuver, and so he hid it from the duke. And, above all, the duke will not stand for treachery from his allies."

James studied the man for a moment. Obviously, Tanford had a great deal to gain by this ploy. James would be his ally through his marriage to Clarissa, and he would rid himself of a treacherous ally. But, more than that, he was insuring that those around him remained weak, by laying the ground for continued warfare between James and Sir Godfrey's sons. A very clever man, the duke.

"So as a prize for following his schemes, the duke offers me this generous betrothal contract," James mused.

"His Grace bade me tell you one other thing: you see what happens to those who betray him. So if you have any foolish notions of saving the earl, forget them. Your only hope lies in following the duke's instructions. If ever, in any way, you deceive him or betray him, he will crush you like a nut. Your power is as nothing against his. He knows everything, his spies are everywhere, and he never forgets a wrong. Should you be a traitor to him, someday for sure he will have you in his grasp, and you will rue the day you betrayed him."

James picked up the parchment and studied it, then laid it down and went to stand at the door of his tent. For several minutes he remained there motionlessly, watched the approaching dusk. He thought of his brother and of his brother's wife who disliked him; he wondered how long it would take her to turn Richard against him. He thought of Clarissa and her lands, and of the power and wealth his birth had denied him. He thought of Sir Godfrey and of the baby Mary lying in Norcastle; and he thought of the powerful duke, who plotted and moved men about and brooked no disobedience to his commands.

Slowly, the sun sank in a fiery red blaze, and James watched it burn lower and lower. At last, he turned and crossed back to the betrothal contract. Carefully he selected a quill from his camp desk and inked his name across the bottom.

"His Grace will be most pleased," the other man said, taking the parchment and stuffing it back into his tunic.

James did not reply, and the messenger left the tent. James strolled back to the tent flap and went outside; he watched the red sun slide inexorably below the horizon.

Chapter Eighteen

RICHARD AND ELIZABETH DOZED FITFULLY ON THE HARD, damp floor throughout the night. Several times they awoke, then settled back in each other's arms and slept again. Toward dawn they were awakened by the sound of feet and the clatter of keys. They looked at each other and stood up. Their fate was approaching; that day it was more than likely that they would both die. Richard took her hand in his, and stonily they stood waiting.

There was the flare of torches coming down the hall. Soon they discerned five or six soldiers coming toward them, and in front of them marched the jailer. Richard squeezed Elizabeth's hand, which was cold as ice; he felt the same coldness in the pit of his stomach. No one spoke as the soldiers halted, and the jailer unlocked the door and swung it open. Elizabeth and Norwen stepped out of the cell, and the soldiers closed around them. With the portly jailkeeper leading the way, they walked back through the dungeon. The two prisoners stared straight before them; Richard did not even satisfy them by turning to look at the soldier who was amusing himself by poking Richard in the side. Finally the man extended his foot and made Richard stumble, and furiously Richard turned toward him.

Norwen found himself staring straight into the blue black eyes of his half brother. James! Richard's eyes widened with delight. James winked at him; but when Richard opened his mouth to speak, he frowned and nodded toward the back of the jailer. Richard said nothing, but nudged Elizabeth and pointed toward his brother. Elizabeth stared at James, completely stunned. Her first thought was amazement that she had been so wrong about him. It took a few moments for her to realize that suddenly there was a ray of hope for them. James had come to rescue them!

They marched through the dungeon door and, leaving the jailer behind them, went quickly up the steps. Servants turned to eye them curiously as they walked boldly through the great hall and out the doors into the courtyard.

Once they were in the open, James whispered without turning his head, "The guards on the east battlement are my men. We will go there and climb over the wall, then run to the woods straight across where I have hidden our horses."

Quickly they strode through the yard, trying to appear purposeful and yet unhurried. While in the courtyard, no one questioned them; but once they began to climb the steps to the battlement, they were exposed and obvious; there was no reason for the prisoners and their guards to be climbing to the battlements. From then on, every moment was fraught with danger. Elizabeth clung tightly to her husband's hand, trying desperately to control her fear.

Two guards stood across their path, and Elizabeth's heart pounded as they approached the men. As they reached them, the two men stepped aside to let them pass.

"Thank God, you are here, sir. We had almost given you up," one of them said.

They had been standing in front of a tangle of rope. James picked up the rope and flung it over the wall. Elizabeth then realized it was a rope ladder secured to the building by grapple hooks, the sort of ladder used by soldiers storming a castle. James tugged hard on it to make sure it was secure, then turned to her.

"Come, Lady Elizabeth. Just kneel on the ledge here above the ladder, turn around and feel for the first rung. Then the next and down you go," James said.

Elizabeth gulped and walked forward. Cautiously she crawled up onto the edge of the battlement, with Richard supporting her. She looked down at the rope she had to take, and sick terror washed over her. It was a sheer drop to the ground below—one misstep on the swaying ladder and she would fall, to be smashed on the ground below. Elizabeth turned to Richard, her face drained of all color.

"I—I cannot," she pleaded.

"You have to!" James exclaimed. "How else are you to escape?"

"But, please, not first."

"James and I must stay here while you and the men run for the horses. We have to guard your escape. You have to go first," Richard said.

Elizabeth closed her eyes and took a deep breath. They were right, of course. There was no other way, and her foolish terror was endangering everyone. Numbly she turned to face Richard and, holding onto the stone wall for dear life, she sought with her foot the first rung. She found it and lowered her other foot. It took a supreme effort of will to move her hand from the wall to the rope. One by one, her feet traveled to the next rung, and she pulled her other hand from the wall and put it on the rope. The ladder was then free swinging from the wall, and it swayed precariously beneath her. Elizabeth froze, clinging to the swaying rope, and closed her eyes and prayed inarticulately to the Virgin Mary.

"Hurry, Elizabeth. Godfrey's men are coming!" Richard hissed down at her.

There was the pounding of feet, and above her the men turned to fight, bunching up with their backs together to form a solid front. James handed Richard a sword from one of the guards they had overcome. He was not well protected, having no shield and wearing his chain mail, not full armor. But it felt so good just to have a sword in his hand and be able to defend himself that he fought like a madman.

Elizabeth hung in midair, mesmerized by the clash of arms above her. Her hands were clenched around the rope so hard that they were growing numb. She could not make herself move, and she realized with rising hysteria that soon her hands would bloodlessly, nervelessly fall from the ladder and she would tumble to the ground far below.

Richard and his men gradually pushed the others back; and, as they did, their tight group loosened and fell apart. They moved farther and farther away from one another, the fighting falling into small personal battles. Before Elizabeth's horrified eyes, one of Godfrey's men felled a Norwen man with a crushing downswing of his sword. Then he turned and glanced about, and started unwaveringly for James's unprotected back. James, busy with another man, had no inkling of his approach until he heard the whistle of an upraised sword. Instinctively he ducked, but the sword would have sliced into his shoulder anyway had not Elizabeth been suddenly galvanized into action by James's swiftly approaching death. In a flash, without thinking, she scrambled up the two ladder rungs and over the wall, hurtling into James's attacker and knocking his blow sideways, so that it fell harmlessly on thin air. James caught his opponent as he rose from his sudden crouch, gutting him on the upswing, then turned to parry the second blow of the man behind him.

He shot Elizabeth one quick look of gratitude before he counterattacked viciously. Elizabeth, freed from her paralysis by her instinctive leap to save James, returned to the ladder and began to slowly, steadily descend it. Gradually Richard and his men were defeating the knot of Sir Godfrey's men; and, as more and more of Godfrey's men fell, one by one, Richard's men descended the ladder after Elizabeth. Once safely on firm ground, Elizabeth ran to the woods, where she found the horses tethered. Swiftly, she found the one intended for her, for there was only one with a sidesaddle. She led it to the edge of the woods, where she could see what happened on the castle wall. She watched Richard's men climb down the wall and run as she had for the horses. Before long the last man of Godfrey's fell, and all seven or eight men went over the ladder.

James and then Richard were the last to leave, of course; and when they were almost halfway down, to Elizabeth's horror, another enemy soldier appeared on the battlements. Quickly he drew a sharp dagger and set to work sawing at one rope. Feverishly he worked at it while James and Richard scrambled toward safety. At last one side snapped, and the ladder jerked and swung crazily, sending James tumbling to the ground. Richard clung fiercely to the wildly swaying rope. Elizabeth watched with her heart in her throat as the soldier set to work on the remaining rope.

Below Richard, James staggered to his feet; he had been low enough on the rope that the fall had merely knocked the wind from him. Richard, however, was several feet above where James had been; and James feared that, if he fell, Richard could break a limb. That would be nearly disastrous for their escape. Frozen, he watched the contest on the rope. Richard's feet had slipped and the rungs hung limp and useless with one side cut. So, dangling in the air, he came down hand over hand as quickly as he could on the violently swinging rope. Above him the man sawed frantically at the rope. Suddenly it snapped and, like a huge snake, fell coiling to the ground.

Richard, only feet from the ground, landed lithely on his feet and started off on the run, with James matching him stride for stride. A band of archers reached the battlements and sent arrows raining down upon them. However, the two men had a head start on them, and in a few moments had outdistanced the archers. They reached the edge of the woods and flung themselves into their saddles.

"St. John and your men are hidden over the south crest in front of the castle. I am sure Godfrey does not know they are there," James said to his brother, panting from his exertions.

Richard's eyes lit. "My whole force? Good. Then let's ambush them. We shall ride close to the castle instead of on the edge of the woods. That should pull them out after us."

He positioned Elizabeth in the middle of the group, so that there would be less chance of her getting hurt. Then, spurring their horses, they charged out of the woods, cutting across toward the castle. Archers lined the walls and spewed down arrows upon them. With a scream, the horse in front of Elizabeth went down, an arrow protruding from its neck. Her own horse stumbled and fell over him, and Elizabeth would have been tossed beneath the feet of the running horses had Richard not seen the front horse fall and immediately thrown his arm out and swept Elizabeth from her saddle. She threw her arms about him and clung on desperately as they pounded past the castle, across the meadow and up the crest to the south.

As they passed, the huge wooden gates opened, and Sir Godfrey's forces came thundering out in hot pursuit. Richard's band galloped over the crest and down the other side, for a few moments hidden from the view of their pursuers. As they topped the ridge, they saw an open space straight in front of them, with a stretch of trees on either side. Here lay St. John and the army, half on either side, barely concealed in the woods. Richard sent his small band straight forward; and behind them

Godfrey's men crested the ridge and followed them, their attention so focused on Richard that they entered the mouth of the trap before they became aware of the woods on either side. Then the jaws of the trap snapped to.

Godfrey's force was crushed between them. With attackers suddenly and most unexpectedly ramming into them from both sides, the army was immediately thrown into confusion. Mounts were brought up short, and both horses and men went tumbling to the ground. Frantically they reached for their swords and turned to fight, but many were felled before they could even pull sword from scabbard. Desperately Godfrey's men tried to fight through the mass and retreat to the castle, but none could make it.

James wheeled and charged back into the battle. Richard deposited Elizabeth on the ground in the woods and left the men with her, instructing them to care for her and get her to safety should the battle go the wrong way.

His page came running toward Richard leading his destrier.

"Your horse, milord!" he called. "Your horse and armor."

Richard dismounted and, taking his sword and shield, mounted his own horse. "Give me my helmet," he said. "I have not the time to put on the rest of my armor. My mail will have to serve." He saluted Elizabeth briefly and whirled to rush back into the melee.

Quickly Godfrey's men were defeated; only a few managed to break through and gallop desperately for the castle. Richard and his men poured after them. The gates stood wide open. Too late did the guards realize that their men in front were desperately fleeing and that the mass on their heels wore Norwen's colors, not Godfrey's. The guards rushed to crank the heavy gates to, but they were too late: before they could get them even half-closed, the army came storming into them.

The archers turned and fired down onto the milling

enemy, but a few of Norwen's men ran up the stairs to the battlements. The archers, unable to defend themselves close in, fell quickly. From all over the castle, the remaining troops came running out to defend their home.

Richard was a madman all through the battle, striking recklessly all around him. Constantly his eyes roamed over the men and courtyard, seeking his special prey. Geoffrey and Godfrey—that was all he wanted. He would not rest until the two of them lay dead at his feet. But he could find them nowhere. They did not come out into the courtyard to fight beside their men.

It did not take them long to conquer the courtyard. They spread out along the battlements, taking them, too. Richard ordered the gates closed so that Godfrey could not escape, and then methodically he began to hunt them down. He divided his men into smaller groups, and assigned each of them to clean out various outbuildings and parts of the castle. Like the well-trained machine they were, his men moved through Fenway Watch, seeking out all pockets of resistance and quickly squelching them.

James, Richard and the majority of the men took the castle. The huge front doors were barred against them, but they took heavy hammers from the blacksmith's and pounded steadily on the doors until they splintered beneath the blows. They found inside the last desperate contingent of armed men. The men fought like trapped animals, but they were no match against the superior numbers.

It was here that Richard found Geoffrey. He ran straight at the young man, the fire of killing in his eyes. It was too much for Geoffrey; he broke and ran for the stairs. But Norwen was on him in an instant, and he reached out with one long arm and whirled Geoffrey around to face him.

"No mercy, Geoffrey!" he roared. "I swore to kill you and I shall!"

Richard swung, but Geoffrey had wit enough to parry his blow. Geoffrey was not a prize swordsman; but he knew he was fighting for his life, and he fought with a skill he had never before exhibited. The battle was all defensive on his part, however; he could manage to do little except retreat step by step, warding off Richard's blows. The larger man was too much for him, and with one heavy blow with the flat of his sword he knocked Geoffrey flat. He raised his sword high and plunged it down into Geoffrey's throat, slipping between the protection of his armor and helmet.

He turned to find the rest of his men victorious. At his command, they spread out through the castle. Taking James and two others with him, Richard headed for the tower. He suspected strongly that it must be there that Godfrey hid. A heavy wooden door blocked the entrance to the tower, and they had to break it down with hammers as they had the front doors. Then up the steps they raced to the door at the top. It, too, fell before them, revealing its lone occupant: Sir Godfrey.

"Leave us," Richard said to his companions, his black eyes drilling into Sir Godfrey. "He is mine."

James and the men retreated, though they went no further than the stairs behind them. James was not about to leave his brother with that treacherous man; there was no telling what trickery he might have up his sleeve.

But Godfrey had reached the end of his rope; for once, he had completely run out of tricks. Warily the two men circled each other. Richard wanted to savor this moment fully. At last Godfrey could no longer stand the tension and he moved in. He was a better swordsman than his son, though certainly no match for Norwen. Heavily their swords clashed again and again until Godfrey's arm was numb from the blows. In a last desperate attempt, Godfrey dived suddenly at Richard's knees and sent him crashing to the floor. Godfrey quickly pulled his dagger from his belt and thrust at Richard's neck, but Richard grabbed his wrist with both hands. For a moment they hung there motionless, and then Richard's strength forced his arm up and away. With a final burst, he shoved his enemy away. Norwen leaped to his feet and picked up his sword and went after his prey.

Over and over his sword slashed down and thrust up, each time being met either by Godfrey's sword or his armor. At last one sweep of his sword sent Godfrey's weapon flying from his hand. Triumphantly Richard raised his sword with both hands and brought it down hard, biting deeply into the man's neck. Blood spurted, and Sir Godfrey slumped to the floor. Richard looked down at him, sucking in the air in great gulps.

Softly he said, "This is for my father and my mother— for my sister and grandfather and all the other Norwen people you foully murdered. And, above all, that is for the years of suffering which you inflicted upon my wife."

Chapter Nineteen

DUSK WAS FALLING AS THE WEARY MEN RODE SLOWLY back from the castle. Elizabeth, standing with her guards at the edge of the woods, watched them anxiously, straining her eyes in the fading light. At the beginning of the battle, Elizabeth had seen the men charge into the castle. Then she had waited, hearing the faint cries of battle. Then all sound had died, and she stood tensely through the long afternoon.

Elizabeth knew the castle had been taken. Otherwise, Godfrey's men would have ridden out in search of her by now. But that did not mean that Richard was alive. James could have led them to victory. And Richard's being alive was the one thing that really mattered to her.

So now she peered at the returning soldiers, looking for his familiar form. Then, at last, she saw them: the two brothers, topping everyone else in height, riding side by side. Relief washed over her, and for a moment she was unable to speak or move. Then she started forward; and, as they drew nearer, she increased her pace until she was running to greet her husband, her face shining with joy.

"Richard! Richard!" she cried, and Richard smiled to see her, despite weariness and aching muscles.

He leaned down to her, and she caught his hand and held on to it fiercely. In that one moment, he felt he had reached the pinnacle of his happiness. His greatest enemy, the last of the men he had sworn to kill in vengeance, lay dead in the castle behind him. And his wife—his lovely, brave wife, who had remained cold to him so long—now gazed up at him with the fires of love in her eyes. His heart swelled with love for her. She was so beautiful, so fine; never had he thought to feel this complete love for any woman.

"Are you all right?" she asked.

He nodded. "Merely a scratch here and there. Your uncle is dead. And Geoffrey. I made sure of that. Never again will those two cause us any pain."

She squeezed his hand silently. He understood the flood of emotions inside her that was too great for words.

Slowly she walked beside him back to their camp. There Richard dismounted, and Elizabeth helped him remove his bloody chain mail. Richard and James made a fire against the evening's chill, and wearily stretched out beside it. Elizabeth went to find their provisions and obtain a little food for them. It took her some while to locate the pack horses and get enough to eat; and, by the time she returned, both men were asleep.

Gently she awakened them, and they dug into the bread and meat with gusto. For a few minutes they ate eagerly, too hungry to indulge in any talk.

After a while, when their hunger had been somewhat assuaged, Richard paused long enough to say, "Now, James, tell us how it was you came to rescue us. My messenger could never have reached you so quickly."

"Lord, no. I never saw any messenger from you. No, it was Tanford who let me in on the plot to kill you. I had some months ago worked into his scheme to get you. I was to kill Lady Elizabeth, then doubtless you, too, and then take over your lands, since you would leave no heirs."

"What good would that do him?" Richard asked, puzzled.

"I was to marry his niece Clarissa; so I would be his blood kin and ally. Also, he did not want Godfrey to seize your lands as guardian of your child if you died. He foiled Godfrey's plans by paying a maid to hide the babe so Godfrey could not take her. Then he sent a man to me who told me of the plan to kill you and Lady Elizabeth. I was to allow that to happen, get the child in my possession and claim guardianship of her, and attack Godfrey for foully murdering you.

"The problem with Tanford is that he tells you about things only after they have gone so far that you can't change them. So I was unable to stop the kidnapping. There was nothing for me to do except ride for here and hope that I reached you in time. I left most of the troops there with Stephen and took a small force with me that could travel fast and light. Fortunately I ran into St. John and your men not far from here, and they aided me."

"But how did you actually get into the castle?" Elizabeth asked.

"Mostly by luck. We scaled the wall of the castle and crept along the battlements, silently overpowering the guards one by one. We dressed in their uniforms, and six of us went down to the dungeons to get you while the rest patrolled that area of the battlements. It was sheer good luck that we weren't discovered."

"Is Stephen safe, besieging Merwen without all his men?" Elizabeth queried, concerned for her brother.

"Yes. I took very few men. He has more than enough."

"And I am sure that, once Robert receives word that Godfrey is dead and I am alive and this keep taken, he will beat a hasty retreat and sue for peace. He is too good a warrior to think he can win against our combined forces without Sir Godfrey's troops to aid him."

"And if he does?" James asked. "Will you agree to a truce?"

"If he returns all Stephen's lands, I think I will. Robert cannot be blamed for his father's deeds. He did not murder our family; he was only a child at the time. So I took no vow to have vengeance on him. As long as he gives up all claim to Stephen's property and retreats, I can live with letting him be. Godfrey and Geoffrey are dead, and that satisfies me."

James looked at him, wondering why Geoffrey had to die, but not Robert. However, his brother did not volunteer the information; and from the look on his face, James was not about to ask.

Richard rose. "Well, I must speak to St. John and determine our losses. Excuse me, Elizabeth."

After he had left, James turned to Elizabeth. There was a moment's uncomfortable pause between them.

Finally James spoke. "I must apologize, Lady Elizabeth. I have misjudged you. You saved my life back there on the battlements—at no small risk to yourself. I thought you were a conniving Beaufort, out to ruin my brother and myself. I see now that you are just as you presented yourself: an honest woman victimized by Sir Godfrey."

Elizabeth inclined her head. "And I have wronged you, too, James. Many times I feared you and thought you were treacherous. I even—I did not think you would try to rescue Richard. I am sorry."

James laughed shortly and said, "Don't be too sure you wronged me, milady. I am not a good man. In the end, I am loyal to Richard. But more than that I cannot say."

Elizabeth studied him. His face was coolly perfect—nothing showed there to indicate the man beneath. She wondered if anyone, even Richard, really knew him. She realized now that he was trustworthy about anything touching Richard. But she also suspected that she would never really be able to like him.

Richard returned to the fire and sank down on the ground beside Elizabeth. James stretched and declared himself ready for a good night's sleep. When he had gone, Richard put his arm around his wife, and they leaned together in weary contentment.

After a moment, Richard sighed and said, "It is over at last. I have done what I swore to do to avenge my family. I am through with vengeance."

"And will you be able to live happily without it?"

He smiled to himself and said, "Yes, quite happily, I think. I have had enough of war and plotting and running and chasing. I think now that all I really want to do is be at Norcastle with the woman I love, just oversee my lands and rear my children."

Elizabeth said teasingly, "Yes, you seem to have quite a bit of readiness for getting children. Now, as for rearing them, I'm not so sure."

Richard laughed and wrapped his arms around her. "Hush, you saucy wench, or I shall have to discipline you."

SHARON STEPHENS is a pseudonym for bestselling author Candace Camp. Ms. Camp is also a licensed attorney and lives in Temple, Texas, with her husband and child.